**Nora Roberts** is the number one *New York Times* bestseller of more than 200 novels. With over 450 million copies of her books in print, she is indisputably one of the most celebrated and popular writers in the world. She has achieved numerous top five bestsellers in the UK, including number one for *Savour the Moment* and *The Witness*, and is a *Sunday Times* hardback bestseller writing as both Nora Roberts and J. D. Robb.

Become a fan on Facebook at
**www.facebook.com/norarobertsjdrobb**
and be the first to hear all the latest from Piatkus
about Nora Roberts and J. D. Robb.

www.noraroberts.com
www.nora-roberts.co.uk
www.jd-robb.co.uk

# NORA ROBERTS

## *True* BETRAYALS

piatkus

PIATKUS

First published in Great Britain in 2015 by Piatkus

1 3 5 7 9 10 8 6 4 2

First published in the United States by G. P. Putnam and Sons in 1995
Mass-market edition published in the United States by Jove in 1996

A CIP catalogue record for this book
is available from the British Library.

ISBN 978-0-349-40798-2

Printed and bound by CPI Group (UK) Ltd, Croydon, CR0 4YY

Papers used by Piatkus are from well-managed forests
and other responsible sources.

MIX
Paper from
responsible sources
FSC® C104740

Piatkus
An imprint of
Little, Brown Book Group
Carmelite House
50 Victoria Embankment
London EC4Y 0DZ

An Hachette UK Company
www.hachette.co.uk

www.piatkus.co.uk

*To Phyllis Grann and Leslie Gelbman*

# Chapter One

WHEN SHE PULLED THE LETTER FROM HER MAILBOX, KELSEY had no warning it was from a dead woman. The creamy stationery, the neatly handwritten name and address, and the Virginia postmark seemed ordinary enough. So ordinary she had simply stacked it with her other mail on the old Belker table under her living-room window while she slipped out of her shoes.

She went into the kitchen and poured herself a glass of wine. She would sip it slowly, she told herself, before she opened her mail. She didn't need the drink to face the slim letter, or the junk mail, the bills, the cheery postcard from a friend enjoying a quick trip to the Caribbean.

It was the packet from her attorney that had shaken her. The packet she knew contained her divorce decree. The legal paper that would change her from Kelsey Monroe back to Kelsey Byden, from married woman to single, from half of a couple to a divorcée.

It was foolish to think that way, and she knew it. She hadn't been married to Wade in anything but the most technical, legal sense for two years, almost as long as they'd been husband and wife.

But the paper made it all so final, so much more so than the arguments and tears, the separation, the lawyers' fees and legal maneuvers.

Till death do us part, she thought grimly, and sipped some wine. What a crock. If that were true she'd be dead at twenty-six. And she was alive—alive and well and back in the murky dating pool of singles.

She shuddered at the thought.

She supposed Wade would be out celebrating with his bright and spiffy-looking associate in the advertising agency. The associate he had had an affair with, the liaison that he told his stunned and furious wife had nothing to do with her or with their marriage.

Funny, Kelsey hadn't thought of it that way. Maybe she didn't feel she'd had to die, or kill Wade, in order to part, but she'd taken the rest of her marriage vows seriously. And forsaking all others had been at the top of the list.

No, she felt the perky and petite Lari with the aerobically sculpted body and cheerleader smile had had everything to do with her.

No second chances had been given. His slip, as Wade had termed it, was never to be repeated. She had moved out of their lovely town house in Georgetown on the spot, leaving behind everything they had accumulated during the marriage.

It had been humiliating to run home to her father and step-mother, but there were degrees of pride. Just as there were degrees of love. And her love had snapped off like a light the instant she'd found Wade cozied up in the Atlanta hotel suite with Lari.

Surprise, she thought with a sneer. Well, there'd been three very surprised people when she'd walked into that suite with a garment bag and the foolishly romantic intention of spending the weekend leg of Wade's business trip with him.

Perhaps she was rigid, unforgiving, hard-hearted, all the things Wade had accused her of being when she'd refused to budge on her demand for a divorce. But, Kelsey assured herself, she was also right.

She topped off her wine and walked back into the living room of the immaculate Bethesda apartment. There was not a single chair or candlestick in the sun-washed room that had stood in Georgetown. Clean break. That's what she had wanted, that's what she'd gotten. The cool colors and museum prints that surrounded her now were hers exclusively.

Stalling, she switched on the stereo, engaged the CD changer, and filled the room with Beethoven's *Pathétique*. Her taste for the classics had been passed down from her father. It was one of the many things they shared. Indeed, they shared a love of knowledge, and Kelsey knew she'd been in danger of becoming a professional student before she'd taken her first serious job with Monroe Associates.

Even then she'd been compelled to take classes, in subjects ranging from anthropology to zoology. Wade had laughed at her, apparently intrigued and amused by her restless shuffling from course to course and job to job.

She'd resigned from Monroe when she married him. Between her trust fund and Wade's income, she hadn't needed a job. She'd wanted to devote herself to the remodeling and redecorating of the town house they'd bought. She'd loved every hour of stripping paint, sanding floors, hunting in dusty antique shops for just the right piece for just the right spot. Laboring in the tiny courtyard, scrubbing brick, digging weeds, and designing the formal English garden had been pure pleasure. Within a year, the town house had been a showplace, a testament to her taste and her effort and her patience.

Now it was simply an asset that had been assessed and split between them.

She'd gone back to school, that academic haven where the real world could be pushed aside for a few hours every day. Now she worked part-time at the National Gallery, thanks to her art history courses.

She didn't have to work, not for money. The trust fund from her paternal grandfather could keep her comfortable enough so that she could drift from interest to interest as she chose.

So, she was an independent woman. Young, she thought, and, glancing over at the stack of mail, single. Qualified to do a little of everything and a lot of nothing. The one thing she'd thought she'd excelled at, marriage, had been a dismal failure.

She blew out a breath and approached the Belker table. She tapped her fingers against the legal packet, long narrow fingers that had received piano lessons, art lessons, fingers that had learned to type, to cook gourmet meals, to program a computer. A very competent hand that had once worn a wedding ring.

Kelsey passed over the thick envelope, ignoring the little voice that hissed the word *coward* inside her head. Instead she picked up another, one with handwriting oddly like her own. It had the same bold, looping style, neat but a little flashy. Only mildly curious, she tore it open.

*Dear Kelsey: I realize you might be surprised to hear from me.*

She read on, the vague interest in her eyes turning to shock, the shock to disbelief. Then the disbelief turned into something almost like fear.

It was an invitation from a dead woman. A dead woman who happened to be her mother.


IN TIMES OF CRISIS, KELSEY HAD always, for as long as she could remember, turned to one person. Her love for and trust in her father had been the one constant in her restless nature. He was always there for her, not so much a port in a storm, but a hand to hold until the storm was over.

Her earliest memories were of him, his handsome, serious face, his gentle hands, his quiet, infinitely patient voice. She remembered him tying bows in her long straight hair, brushing the pale blond tresses while Bach or Mozart sang from the stereo. It was he who had kissed her childhood hurts better, who had taught her to read, to ride a bike, who had dried her tears.

She adored him, was almost violently proud of his

4

accomplishments as the chairman of the English department at Georgetown University.

She hadn't been jealous when he'd married again. At eighteen she'd been delighted that he'd finally found someone to love and share his life with. Kelsey had made room in her heart and home for Candace, and had been secretly proud of her maturity and altruism in accepting a stepmother and teenage stepbrother.

Perhaps it had been easy because she knew deep in her heart that nothing and no one could alter the bond between *herself* and her father.

Nothing and no one, she thought now, but the mother she'd thought was dead.

The shock of betrayal was warring with a cold, stony rage as she fought her way through rush-hour traffic toward the lush, palatial estates in Potomac, Maryland. She'd rushed out of her apartment without her coat, and had neglected to switch on the heater in her Spitfire, but she didn't feel the chill of the February evening. Temper had whipped color into her face, adding a becoming rosy glow to the porcelain complexion, a snap to lake-gray eyes.

She drummed her fingers against the steering wheel as she waited for a light to change, as she willed it to change so she could hurry, hurry. Her mouth was clamped in a thin line that masked its lush generosity as she fought to keep her mind a blank.

It wouldn't do to think now. No, it wouldn't do to think that her mother was alive, alive and living hardly an hour away in Virginia. It wouldn't do to think about that or Kelsey might have started to scream.

But her hands were beginning to tremble as she cruised down the majestically tree-lined street where she'd spent her childhood, as she pulled into the drive of the three-story brick colonial where she'd grown up.

It looked as peaceful and tidy as a church, its windows gleaming, its white trim pure as an unblemished soul. Puffs of smoke from the evening fire curled from the chimney, and the first shy crocuses poked their delicate leaves up around the old elm in the front yard.

The perfect house in the perfect neighborhood, she'd always thought. Safe, secure, tasteful, only a short drive to the excitement and culture of D.C. and with the well-polished hue of quiet, respectable wealth.

She slammed out of the car, raced to the front door, and shoved it open. She'd never had to knock at this house. Even as she started down the Berber runner in the white-tiled foyer, Candace came out of the sitting room to the right.

She was, as usual, immaculately dressed. The perfect academic wife in conservative blue wool, her mink-colored hair swept back from her lovely, youthful face to reveal simple pearl earrings.

"Kelsey, what a nice surprise. I hope you can stay for dinner. We're entertaining some of the faculty and I can always use—"

"Where is he?" Kelsey interrupted.

Candace blinked, surprised by the tone. She could see now that Kelsey was in one of her snits. The last thing she needed an hour before her house filled up with people was one of her stepdaughter's explosions. Automatically she shifted her stance.

"Is something wrong?"

"Where's Dad?"

"You're upset. Is it Wade again?" Candace dismissed the problem with a wave of her hand. "Kelsey, divorce isn't pleasant, but it isn't the end of the world, either. Come in and sit down."

"I don't want to sit, Candace. I want to talk to my father." Her hands clenched at her sides. "Now, are you going to tell me where he is, or do I have to look for him?"

"Hey, sis." Channing strode down the stairs. He had his mother's strong good looks and a thirst for adventure that had, according to his mother, come from nowhere. Though he'd been fourteen when Candace married Philip Byden, Channing's innate good humor had made the transition seamless. "What's up?"

Kelsey deliberately took a deep breath to keep from shouting. "Where's Dad, Channing?"

"The Prof's in his study, buried in that paper he's been writing."

Channing's brows lifted. He, too, recognized the signs of a rage in the making—the spark in the eye, the flush on the cheeks. There were times he would put himself out to bank that fire. And times he would indulge himself and fan it.

"Hey, Kels, you're not going to hang around with these bookworms tonight, are you? Why don't you and I skip out, hit a few clubs?"

She shook her head and tore down the hall toward her father's study.

"Kelsey." Candace's voice, sharp, annoyed, trailed after her. "Must you be so volatile?"

Yes, Kelsey thought as she yanked open the door of her father's favorite sanctuary. *Yes*.

She slammed the door at her back, saying nothing for a moment as the words were boiling up much too hot and much too fast in her throat. Philip sat at his beloved oak desk, nearly hidden behind a stack of books and files. He held a pen in his bony hand. He'd always maintained that the best writing came from the intimacy of *writing*, and stubbornly refused to compose his papers on a word processor.

His eyes behind the silver-framed glasses had the owlish look they took on when he amputated himself from the reality of what was around him. They cleared slowly, and he smiled at his daughter. The desk light gleamed on his close-cropped pewter hair.

"There's my girl. Just in time to read over this draft of my thesis on Yeats. I'm afraid I might have gotten long-winded again."

He looked so normal, was all she could think. So perfectly normal sitting there in his tweed jacket and carefully knotted tie. Handsome, untroubled, surrounded by his books of poetry and genius.

7

And her world, of which he was the core, had just shattered.

"She's alive," Kelsey blurted out. "She's alive and you've lied to me all my life."

He went very pale, and his eyes shifted from hers. Only for an instant, barely a heartbeat, but she'd seen the fear and the shock in them.

"What are you talking about, Kelsey?" But he knew, he knew and had to use all of his self-control to keep the plea out of his voice.

"Don't lie to me now." She sprang toward his desk. "Don't lie to me! She's alive. My mother's alive, and you knew it. You knew it every time you told me she was dead."

Panic sliced through Philip, keen as a scalpel. "Where did you get an idea like that?"

"From her." She plunged her hand into her purse and dragged out the letter. "From my mother. Are you going to tell me the truth now?"

"May I see it?"

Kelsey tilted her head, stared down at him. It was a look that could pick clean down to the bone. "Is my mother dead?"

He wavered, holding the lie as close to his heart as he held his daughter. But he knew, as much as he wished it could be otherwise, if he kept one, he would lose the other.

"No. May I see the letter?"

"Just like that." The tears she'd been fighting swam dangerously close to the surface. "Just a no? After all this time, all the lies?"

Only one lie, he thought, and not nearly enough time. "I'll do my best to explain it all to you, Kelsey. But I'd like to see the letter."

Without a word she handed it to him. Then, because she couldn't bear to watch him, she turned away to face the tall, narrow window where she could see evening closing in on the last bloom of twilight.

The paper shook so in Philip's hand that he was forced to set the sheet on the desk in front of him. The handwriting was unmistakable. Dreaded. He read it carefully, word by word.

Dear Kelsey:

I realize you might be surprised to hear from me. It seemed unwise, or at least unfair, to contact you before. Though a phone call might have been more personal, I felt you would need time. And a letter gives you more of a choice on your options.

They will have told you I died when you were very young. In some ways, it was true, and I agreed with the decision to spare you. Over twenty years have passed, and you're no longer a child. You have, I believe, the right to know that your mother is alive. You will, perhaps, not welcome the news. However, I made the decision to contact you, and won't regret it.

If you want to see me, or simply have questions that demand answers, you'd be welcome. My home is Three Willows Farm, outside of Bluemont, Virginia. The invitation is an open one. If you decide to accept it, I would be pleased to have you stay as long as it suited you. If you don't contact me, I'll understand that you don't wish to pursue the relationship. I hope the curiosity that pushed you as a child will tempt you to at least speak with me.

Yours,
Naomi Chadwick

Naomi. Philip closed his eyes. Good God, Naomi.

Nearly twenty-three years had passed since he'd seen her, but he remembered everything about her with utter clarity. The scent she'd worn that reminded him of dark, mossy glades, the quick infectious laugh that never failed to turn heads, the silvery blond hair that flowed like rain down her back, the sooty eyes and willowy body.

So clear were his memories that when Philip opened his eyes again he thought he saw her. His heart took one hard, violent leap into his throat that was part fear, part long-suppressed desire.

But it was Kelsey, her back stiff, facing away from him.

How could he have ever forgotten Naomi, he asked himself, when he had only to look at their daughter to see her?

Philip rose and poured a scotch from a crystal decanter. It was kept there for visitors. He rarely touched anything stronger than a short snifter of blackberry brandy. But he needed something with bite now, something to still the trembling of his hands.

"What do you plan to do?" he asked Kelsey.

"I haven't decided." She kept her back to him. "A great deal of it depends on what you tell me."

Philip wished he could go to her, touch her shoulders. But she wouldn't welcome him now. He wished he could sit, bury his face in his hands. But that would be weak, and useless.

More, much more, he wished he could go back twenty-three years and do something, anything, to stop fate from running recklessly over his life.

But that was impossible.

"It isn't a simple matter, Kelsey."

"Lies are usually complicated."

She turned then, and his fingers clutched reflexively on the lead crystal. She looked so much like Naomi, the bright hair carelessly tumbled, the eyes dark, the skin over those long, delicate facial bones flushed luminously with passion. Some women looked their best when their emotions were at a dangerous peak.

So it had been with Naomi. So it was with her daughter.

"That's what you've done all these years, isn't it?" Kelsey continued. "You've lied to me. Grandmother lied. She lied."

Kelsey gestured toward the desk where the letter lay. "If that letter hadn't come, you would've continued to lie to me."

"Yes, as long as I continued to think it was best for you."

"Best for me? How could it be best for me to believe my mother was dead? How can a lie ever be best for anyone?"

"You've always been so sure of right and wrong, Kelsey. It's an admirable quality." He paused, drank. "And a terrifying one. Even

10

as a child, your ethics were unwavering. So difficult for mere mortals to measure up."

Her eyes kindled. It was close, much too close to what Wade had accused her of. "So, it's my fault."

"No. No." He closed his eyes and rubbed absently at a point in the center of his forehead. "None of it was your fault, and all of it was because of you."

"Philip." After a quick knock, Candace opened the study door. "The Dorsets are here."

He forced a weary smile onto his face. "Entertain them, dear. I need a few moments with Kelsey."

Candace flashed a look at her stepdaughter. Disapproval mixed with resignation. "All right, but don't be long. Dinner's set for seven. Kelsey, shall I set another place?"

"No, Candace, thank you. I'm not staying."

"All right, then, but don't keep your father long." She eased the door shut.

Kelsey drew a breath, stiffened her spine. "Does she know?"

"Yes. I had to tell her before we were married."

"'Had to tell her,'" Kelsey repeated. "But not me."

"It wasn't a decision that I made lightly. That any of us made lightly. Naomi, your grandmother, and I all believed it was in your best interest. You were only three, Kelsey. Hardly more than a baby."

"I've been an adult for some time, Dad. I've been married, divorced."

"You have no idea how quickly the years go." He sat again, cradling the glass. He'd convinced himself that this moment would never come. That his life was too staid, too stable to ever take this spinning dip on the roller coaster again. But Naomi, he thought, had never settled for staid.

Neither had Kelsey. And now it was time for truth.

"I've explained to you that your mother was one of my students. She was beautiful, young, vibrant. I've never understood why she was attracted to me. It happened quite quickly, really. We were married within six months after we met. Not nearly long enough for either of us to understand how truly opposite we were in nature. We lived in Georgetown. We'd both come from what we could call privileged backgrounds, but she had a freedom I could never emulate. A wildness, a lust for people, for things, for places. And, of course, her horses."

He drank again, to ease some of the pain of remembering. "I think it was the horses more than anything else that first came between us. After you were born, she wanted desperately to move back to the farm in Virginia. She wanted you to be raised there. My ambitions and hopes for the future were here. I was working on my doctorate, and even then I had my eye set on becoming the English department chairman at Georgetown. For a while we compromised, and I spent what weekends I could spare in Virginia. It wasn't enough. It's simplest to say we grew apart."

Safer to say it, he thought, staring into his scotch. And certainly less painful. "We decided to divorce. She wanted you in Virginia with her. I wanted you in Georgetown with me. I neither understood nor cared for the racing crowd she ran with, the gamblers, the jockeys. We fought, bitterly. Then we hired lawyers."

"A custody suit?" Stunned, Kelsey gaped at her father. "You fought over custody?"

"It was an ugly business, unbelievably vile. How two people who had loved each other, had created a child together, could become such mortal enemies is a pathetic commentary on human nature." He looked up again, finally, and faced her. "I'm not proud of it, Kelsey, but I believed in my heart that you belonged with me. She was already seeing other men. It was rumored that one of them had ties to organized crime. A woman like Naomi would always attract men. It was as though she was flaunting them, the parties, her lifestyle, daring me and the world to condemn her for doing as she pleased."

"So you won," Kelsey said quietly. "You won the suit, and me, then decided to tell me she'd died." She turned away again, facing the window that was dark now. In it she could see the ghost of herself. "People divorced in the seventies. Children coped. There should have been visitation. I should have been allowed to see her."

"She didn't want you to see her. Neither did I."

"Why? Because she ran off with one of her men?"

"No." Philip set the glass aside, carefully, on a thin silver coaster. "Because she killed one of them. Because she spent ten years in prison for murder."

Kelsey turned slowly, so slowly because the air was suddenly thick. "Murder. You're telling me that my mother is a murderess?"

"I'd hoped never to tell you." He rose then, sure he could hear his own bones creak in the absolute silence. "You were with me. I thank God you were with me rather than on the farm the night it happened. She shot her lover, a man named Alec Bradley. They were in her bedroom. There was an argument and she took a gun from the drawer of the bedside table and killed him. She was twenty-six, the same age as you are now. They found her guilty of murder in the second degree. The last time I saw her, she was in prison. She told me she would rather you believe her dead. If I agreed, she swore she wouldn't contact you. And she kept her word, until now."

"I can't understand any of this." Reeling, Kelsey pressed her hands over her eyes.

"I would have spared you." Gently Philip took her wrists, lowering her hands so he could see her face. "If protecting you was wrong, then I'll tell you I was wrong, but without apology. I loved you, Kelsey. You were my entire life. Don't hate me for this."

"No, I don't hate you." In an old habit, she laid her head on his shoulder, resting it there while ideas and images spun in her brain. "I need to think. It all seems so impossible. I don't even remember her, Dad."

"You were too young," he murmured, rocked by relief. "I can tell you that you look like her. It's almost uncanny how much. And that she was a vibrant and fascinating woman, whatever her flaws."

A crime of violence being one of them, Kelsey thought. "There are so many questions, but I can't seem to latch on to one."

"Why don't you stay here tonight? As soon as I can get away, we'll talk again."

It was tempting to give in, to close herself into the safe familiarity of her old room, to let her father soothe away the hurts and the doubts, as he always did.

"No, I need to go home." She drew away before she could weaken. "I should be alone for a while. And Candace is already annoyed with me for keeping you from your guests."

"She'll understand."

"Of course she will. You'd better get along. I think I'll go out the back. I'd just as soon not run into anyone right now."

The passionate flush had died away, he noted, leaving her skin pale and fragile. "Kelsey, I wish you'd stay."

"I'm all right, really. All I need to do is absorb it. We'll talk later. Go see to your guests, and we'll talk more about this later." She kissed him, as much a sign of forgiveness as to hurry him along. Once she was alone, she walked behind the desk and stared at the letter.

After a moment, she folded it and slipped it back into her purse.

It had been a hell of a day, she decided. She'd lost a husband, and gained a mother.

# Chapter two

SOMETIMES IT WAS BEST TO FOLLOW YOUR IMPULSES. PERHAPS not best, Kelsey corrected as she drove west along Route 7 through the rolling Virginia hills. But it was certainly satisfying.

Speaking to her father again might have been wiser. Taking time to think things through. But it was much more satisfying to simply hop into the car and head to Three Willows Farm and confront the woman who'd played dead for two decades.

Her mother, Kelsey thought. The murderess.

To distract herself from that image, Kelsey turned up the radio so that Rachmaninoff soared through the half-open window. It was a beautiful day for a drive. That's what she'd told herself when she'd hurried out of her lonely apartment that morning. She hadn't admitted her destination then, even though she'd checked the map to find the best route to Bluemont.

No one knew she was coming. No one knew where she'd gone.

There was freedom in that. She pressed down on the gas and reveled in the speed, the whip of the chilly air through the windows, the power of the music. She could go anywhere, do anything. There was no one to answer to, no one to question. It was she who had all the questions now.

Maybe she'd dressed a bit more carefully than a casual drive in the country warranted. That was pride. The peach tone of the silk jacket and slacks was a good color for her, the breezy lines flattering to her slim frame.

After all, any woman who was about to meet her mother for the first time as an adult would want to look her best. She'd fixed her hair into a neat and intricate braid, and spent more time than usual on her makeup and accessories.

All the preparations had eased her nerves.

But she was beginning to feel them again as she approached Bluemont.

She could still change her mind, Kelsey told herself as she stopped the car in front of a small general store. Asking for directions to Three Willows didn't mean she had to follow them. She could, if she wanted, simply turn the car around and head back to Maryland.

Or she could just drive on. Through Virginia, into the Carolinas. She could turn west, or east toward the shore. One of her favorite indulgences was hopping in her car and driving wherever the whim took her. She'd spent an impulsive weekend at a lovely little bed-and-breakfast on the Eastern Shore after she'd left Wade.

She could go there again, she mused. A call in to work, a stop at a mall along the way for a change of clothes, and she'd be set.

It wasn't running away. It was simply leaving.

Why should it feel so much like running away?

The little store was so crammed with shelves and dairy cases and walls of tools that three customers made a crowd. The old man behind the counter had an ashtray full of butts at his elbow, a head as bald and shiny as a new dime, and a fresh cigarette dangling from the corner of his mouth. He squinted at Kelsey through a cloud of smoke.

"I wonder if you could tell me how to get to Three Willows Farm."

He stared at her another minute, his smoke-reddened eyes narrowing with speculation. "You'd be looking for Miss Naomi?"

Kelsey borrowed a look from her grandmother, one designed to put the questioner firmly in his place. "I'm looking for Three Willows Farm. I believe it's in this area."

"Oh yeah, it is." He grinned at her, and somehow the cigarette defied gravity and stuck in place. "Here's what you do. You go on down the road a piece. Say 'bout two miles. There's a fence there, a white one. You're gonna wanna make a left on Chadwick Road, and head on down another five miles or so. Go on past Longshot. Got a big wrought-iron fence with the name on it, so's you can't miss it. Next turn you come to's got two stone posts with rearing horses on 'em. That's Three Willows."

"Thank you."

He sucked in smoke, blew it out. "Your name wouldn't be Chadwick, would it?"

"No, it wouldn't." Kelsey went out, letting the door swing shut behind her. She felt the old man's eyes on her even as she pulled the car back onto the road.

Understandable, she supposed. It was a small town and she was a stranger. Still, she hadn't liked the way he'd stared.

She found the white fence and made the left out of town. The houses were farther apart now as the land took over, rolling and sweeping with the hills that were still caught between the haze of winter and the greening of spring. Horses grazed, manes ruffling in the breeze. Mares, their coats still thick with winter, cropped while their young gamboled nearby on spindly, toothpick legs. Here and there a field was plowed for spring planting, squares of rich brown bisecting the green.

She slowed the car at Longshot. It wasn't a road, as she'd assumed, but a farm. The curvy wrought-iron gate boasted the name, and through it she could see the long sweep of a macadam lane leading up to a cedar and stone house on the crest of a hill. Attractive, she mused. Commanding. Its many levels and terraces would afford breathtaking views from every inch.

The lane was lined with elms that looked much older and much more traditional than the house itself, which was almost arrogantly modern, yet it perched on the hill with a territorial pride.

Kelsey sat there for some time. Not that she was terribly interested in the architecture or the scenery, as compelling as it was. She knew if she continued down this road, she wouldn't turn back.

Longshot, she decided, was the point of no return. It seemed ironically appropriate. Closing her eyes, she willed her system to level. This was something she should do coolly, pragmatically. This wasn't a reunion where she would launch herself weeping into the arms of her long-lost mother.

They were strangers who needed to decide if they would remain so. No, she corrected. *She* would decide if they would remain so. She was here for answers, not love. Not even reasons.

And she wouldn't get them, Kelsey reminded herself, if she didn't continue on and ask the questions.

She'd never been a coward. She could add that to her list of vanities, Kelsey told herself as she put the car in gear again.

But her hands were cold as she gripped the wheel, as she turned between the two stone posts with their rearing horses, as she drove up the gravel lane toward her mother's house.

In the summer, the house would have been shielded by the three graceful willows for which it had been named. Now, the bowed branches were just touched with the tender green of approaching spring. Through their spindly fans she could see the white Doric columns rising up from a wide covered porch, the fluid curves of the three-story plantation-style house. Feminine, she thought, almost regal, and like the era it celebrated, gracious and stately.

There were gardens she imagined would explode with color in

a matter of weeks. She could easily picture the scene heightened by the hum of bees and the chirp of birdsong, perhaps the dreamy scent of wisteria or lilac.

Instinctively her gaze lifted to the upper windows. Which room? she wondered. Which room had been the scene of murder?

A shiver walked down her spine as she stopped the car. Though her intention had been to go straight up to the front door and knock, she found herself wandering to the side of the house where a stone patio spilled out of tall French doors.

She could see some of the outbuildings from there. Tidy sheds, a barn that looked nearly as stately as the house itself. Farther out, where the hills curved up, she could see horses cropping and the faint glitter of sun striking water.

All at once another scene flipped over the vision. The bees were humming, the birds singing. The sun was hot and bright and she could smell roses, so strong and sweet. Someone was laughing and lifting her up, and up, until she felt the good strong security of a horse beneath her.

With a little cry of alarm, Kelsey pressed a hand to her lips. She didn't remember this place. She didn't. It was her imagination taking over, that was all. Imagination and nerves.

But she could swear she heard that laughter, the wild, free seduction of it.

She wrapped her arms around her body for warmth and took a step in retreat. She needed her coat, she told herself. She just needed to get her coat out of the car. Then the man and woman swung around the side of the house, arm in arm.

They were so beautiful, staggeringly so in that flash of sunlight, that for a moment Kelsey thought she was imagining them as well.

The man was tall, an inch or more over six feet with that fluid grace certain men are born with. His dark hair was windblown, curled carelessly over the collar of a faded chambray shirt. She saw his eyes, deeply, vividly blue in a face of angles and shadows, widen briefly in what might have been mild surprise.

"Naomi." His voice had the faintest of drawls, not slow so much as rich, like a fine, aged bourbon. "You have company."

Nothing her father had told her had prepared her. It was like looking in a mirror at some future time. A mirror polished to a high sheen so that it dazzled the eyes. Kelsey might have been looking at herself. For one mad moment, she was afraid she was.

"Well." Naomi's hand clamped hard on Gabe's arm. It was a reaction she wasn't aware of, and one she couldn't have prevented. "I didn't think I would hear from you so soon, much less see you." She'd learned years before that tears were useless, so her eyes remained dry as she studied *her daughter*. "We were about to have some tea. Why don't we go inside?"

"I'll take a rain check," Gabe began, but Naomi clung to his arm as if he were a shield, or a savior.

"That's not necessary." Kelsey heard her own voice, as from a distance. "I can't stay long."

"Come inside, then. We won't waste what time you have."

Naomi led the way through the terrace doors into a sitting room as lovely and polished as its mistress. There was a low, sedate fire in the hearth to ward off the late-winter chill.

"Please sit down, be comfortable. It'll only take me a moment to see about the tea." Naomi shot one quick glance at Gabe, and fled.

He was a man accustomed to difficult situations. He sat, drew out a cigar, and flashed Kelsey a smile fashioned to charm. "Naomi's a bit flustered."

Kelsey lifted a brow. The woman had seemed as composed as an ice sculpture. "Is she?"

"Understandable, I'd say. You gave her a shock. Took me back a step myself." He lighted the cigar and wondered if the raw nerves so readable in Kelsey's eyes would allow her to sit. "I'm Gabe Slater, a neighbor. And you're Kelsey."

"How would you know?"

Queen to peasant, he thought. It was a tone that would

normally challenge a man, certainly a man like Gabriel Slater. But he let it pass.

"I know Naomi has a daughter named Kelsey whom she hasn't seen in some time. And you're a little young to be her twin sister." He stretched out his legs and crossed them at his booted ankles. They both knew he'd yet to take his eyes off her. And he knew he didn't intend to.

"You'd pull off the dignified act better if you sat down and pretended to relax."

"I'd rather stand." She moved to the fire and hoped it would warm her.

Gabe merely shrugged and settled back. It was nothing to him, after all. Unless she took a few potshots at Naomi. Not that Naomi couldn't handle herself. He'd never known a woman more capable or, in his mind, more resilient. Nonetheless, he was too fond of her to let anyone, even her daughter, hurt her.

Neither did it concern him that Kelsey had obviously decided to ignore him. He took a lazy drag on his cigar and enjoyed the view. Stiff shoulders and a rigid spine didn't spoil it, he mused. It was a nice contrast to the long, fluid limbs and fancy hair.

He wondered how easily she spooked, and if she'd be around long enough for him to test her himself.

"Tea will be right in." Steadier, Naomi came back into the room. Her gaze locked on her daughter, and her smile was practiced. "This must be horribly awkward for you, Kelsey."

"It isn't every day my mother comes back from the grave. Was it necessary for me to think you were dead?"

"It seemed so, at the time. I was in a position where my own survival was a priority." She sat, looking tailored and unruffled in her dun-colored riding habit. "I didn't want you visiting me in prison. And if I had, your father would never have agreed to it. So, I was to be out of your life for ten to fifteen years."

Her smile shifted a few degrees, going brittle. "How would the parents of your friends have reacted when you told them your mother was doing time for murder? I doubt you'd have been a popular little girl. Or a happy one."

Naomi broke off, looking toward the hallway as a middle-aged woman in a gray uniform and white apron wheeled in a tea tray. "Here's Gertie. You remember Kelsey, don't you, Gertie?"

"Yes, ma'am." The woman's eyes teared up. "You were just a baby last time. You'd come begging for cookies."

Kelsey said nothing, could say nothing to the damp-eyed stranger. Naomi put a hand over Gertie's and squeezed gently. "You'll have to bake some the next time Kelsey visits. Thank you, Gertie. I'll pour."

"Yes, ma'am." Sniffling, she started out, but turned when she came to the doorway. "She looks just like you, Miss Naomi. Just like you."

"Yes," Naomi said softly, looking at her daughter, "she does."

"I don't remember her." Kelsey's voice was defiant as she took two strides toward her mother. "I don't remember you."

"I didn't think you would. Would you like sugar, lemon?"

"Is this supposed to be civilized?" Kelsey demanded. "Mother and daughter reunite over high tea. Do you expect me to just sit here, sipping oolong?"

"Actually, I think it's Earl Grey, and to tell you the truth, Kelsey, I don't know what I expect. Anger certainly. You deserve to be angry. Accusations, demands, resentments." With hands that were surprisingly steady, Naomi passed Gabe a cup. "To be honest, I doubt there's anything you could say or do that wouldn't be justified."

"Why did you write me?"

Taking a moment to organize her thoughts, Naomi poured another cup. "A lot of reasons, some selfish, some not. I'd hoped you'd be curious enough to want to meet me. You were always a curious child, and I know that at this point in your life you're at loose ends."

"How do you know anything about my life?"

Naomi's gaze lifted, as unreadable as the smoke wafting up the flue. "You thought I was dead, Kelsey. I knew you were very much alive. I kept track of you. Even in prison I was able to do that."

Fury had Kelsey stepping forward, fighting the urge to hurl the tea tray and all the delicate china. It would be satisfying, oh so satisfying. But it would also make her look like a fool. Only that kept her from striking out.

Sipping tea, Gabe watched her struggle for control. Highstrung, he decided. Impassioned. But smart enough to hold her ground. She might, he thought, be more like her mother than either of them knew.

"You spied on me." Kelsey bit off the words. "You hired, what, detectives?"

"Nothing quite so melodramatic as that. My father kept track of you while he could."

"Your father." Kelsey sat down. "My grandfather."

"Yes, he died five years ago. Your grandmother died the year after you were born, and I was an only child. You're spared a flood of aunts and uncles and cousins. Whatever questions you have, I'll answer, but I'd appreciate it if you'd give us both a little time before you make up your mind about me."

There was only one she could think of, one that had continued to hammer at the back of her mind. So she asked it, quickly, before she could draw away from it.

"Did you kill that man? Did you kill Alec Bradley?"

Naomi paused, then lifted her cup to her lips. Over the rim, her eyes stayed steady on Kelsey's. She set the cup down again without a rattle.

"Yes," she said simply. "I killed him."


"I'm sorry, Gabe." Naomi stood at the window, watching her daughter drive away. "It was really unforgivable of me to put you in that position."

"I met your daughter, that's all."

On a weak laugh, Naomi squeezed her eyes shut. "Always the master of understatement, Gabe." She turned then, standing in the strong light. It didn't bother her that the sun would highlight the fine lines around her eyes, show her age. She'd spent too long away from it. Too long away. "I was afraid. When I saw her, so much came flooding back. Some expected, some not expected. I couldn't deal with it alone."

He rose and went to her, laying his hands on her shoulders to soothe the strong, tensed muscles. "If a man isn't happy to help a beautiful woman, he might as well be dead."

"You're a good friend." She lifted a hand to his, squeezed. "One of the very few I can drop all pretenses with." Her lips curved again. "Maybe it's because we've both done time."

A quick smile lifted the corners of his mouth. "Nothing like prison life to pack down common ground."

"Nothing like prison life. Of course, a youthful run-in over a poker game doesn't quite come up to murder two, but—"

"There you go, one-upping me again."

She laughed. "We Chadwicks are so competitive." She moved away from him, shifting a vase of early daffodils an inch to the right on a table. "What did you think of her, Gabe?"

"She's beautiful. The image of you."

"I thought I was prepared for that. My father had told me. And the photographs. But to look at her and see myself, it still staggered me. I remember the child, remember the child so well. Now, seeing her grown up . . ." Impatient with herself, she shook her head. The years passed. She knew that better than anyone. "But beyond that." She glanced over her shoulder. "What did you think of her?"

He wasn't sure he could, or would, explain precisely what he'd thought. He, too, had been staggered, and he was a man rarely surprised. Beautiful women had walked in and out of his life, or he in and out of theirs. He appreciated them, admired them, desired them. But his first glimpse of Kelsey Byden had all but stopped his heart.

He would dissect that interesting little fact later, but for now Naomi was waiting. And he knew his answer mattered.

"She was running on nerves and temper. She doesn't quite have your control."

"I hope she never needs it," Naomi murmured.

"She was angry, but smart enough, and curious enough, to hold on to her temper until she gauged the lay of the land. If she were a horse, I'd have to say I need to see her paces before I could judge if she has heart, endurance, or grace. But blood tells, Naomi. Your daughter has style."

"She loved me." Her voice shook, but she didn't notice. Nor did she notice the first tear that spilled over and trailed down her cheek. "It's difficult to explain to someone who's had no children what it's like to be the recipient of that kind of total, uncompromising love. Kelsey felt that for me, and for her father. It was Philip and I who lacked. We didn't love enough to keep that unit whole. And so I lost her."

Naomi brushed at the tear, caught it on her fingertip. She studied it as if it were some exotic specimen just discovered. She hadn't cried since she buried her father. Hadn't seen the point.

"I'll never be loved that way again." She flicked the tear away and forgot it. "I don't think I understood that until today."

"You're rushing your fences, Naomi. That's not like you. You had all of fifteen minutes with her today."

"Did you see her face when I told her I killed Alec?" There was a smile on her lips as she turned back to Gabe, but it was hard, brittle as glass. "I've seen it in dozens of others. Civilized horror. Decent people don't kill."

"People, decent or otherwise, do what they need to do to survive." He had reason to know.

"She won't think so. She might have my looks, Gabe, but she'd have her father's mores. Christ, they don't come any more decent than Dr. Philip Byden."

"Or more foolish, since he let you go."

She laughed again, easier this time, and kissed him firmly on the mouth. "Where were you twenty-five years ago?" She shook her head, nearly sighed. "Playing with your Crayolas."

"I don't recall ever playing with them. Betting with them, maybe. Speaking of bets, I've got a hundred that says my colt will outrun yours at the Derby in May."

Her brow rose. "And the odds?"

"Even."

"You're on. Why don't you come down and take a look at my prize yearling before you leave? In a couple of years she'll leave anything you put against her in the dust."

"What did you name her?"

Her eyes glinted as she opened the terrace doors. "Naomi's Honor."

SHE'D BEEN SO COOL, KELSEY thought as she unlocked her apartment door. So cold. Naomi had admitted to murder as casually as another woman might admit to dyeing her hair.

What kind of a woman was she?

How could she have served tea and made conversation? So polite, so controlled, so horribly detached. Leaning against the door, Kelsey rubbed at the headache storming behind her temples. It was all like some insane dream—the big, beautiful house, the placid setting, the woman with her face, the dynamic man.

Naomi's newest lover? Did they sleep in the same room where a man had died? He'd looked capable of it, she thought. He'd looked capable of anything.

With a shudder, Kelsey pushed away from the door and began to pace.

Why had Naomi written the letter? she wondered. There'd been no emotional storm, no fatted calf, no desperate apologies for the lost years. Only a polite invitation to tea.

And the calm, unhesitating admission of guilt.

So, Naomi Chadwick wasn't a hypocrite, Kelsey thought wryly. Just a criminal.

When the phone rang she glanced over and saw that her message machine was blinking. Kelsey turned away and ignored both. She had two hours before her shift at the museum, and no need, no desire, to speak with anyone before then.

All she had to do now was convince herself that her mother's reappearance didn't have to change her life. She could go on just as she had before—her job, her classes, her friends.

She dropped down on the sofa. Who was she trying to fool? Her job was no more than a hobby, her classes a habit, and her friends . . . Most of them had been shared with Wade, and therefore, in the odd by-product of divorce, they had divvied up sides or simply faded into the background so as not to be touched by the trauma.

Her life was a mess.

She ignored the knock at the door.

"Kelsey." Another quick, impatient rap. "Open the door or I'll have the apartment manager open it for me."

Resigned, Kelsey rose and obeyed. "Grandmother."

After lifting her cheek for the expected kiss, Milicent Byden strode into the apartment. She was, as always, flawlessly dressed and coiffed. Her hair was tinted a glossy auburn and swept back from a polished face that could, at a glance, pass for sixty rather than eighty. She kept her figure trim with unsentimental diet and exercise. Her size-six Chanel suit was a pale blue. She tugged off matching kid gloves and set them down on an occasional table, then laid her mink over a chair.

"You disappoint me. Sulking in your room like a child." Her almond-colored eyes scraped over her granddaughter as she sat, crossing her legs. "Your father's desperately worried about you. Both he and I have called you at least half a dozen times today."

"I've been out. And Dad has no reason to be worried."

"No?" Milicent tapped a lacquered fingernail against the arm of the chair. "You burst in on him last night with the news that that woman has contacted you, then you dash off and refuse to answer your phone."

"That woman is my mother, and you and he knew she was alive. It caused an emotional scene, Grandmother, which I'm aware you might consider to be in poor taste, but that I felt was very justified."

"Don't take that tone with me." Milicent leaned forward. "Your father has done everything to protect you, to give you a decent upbringing and a stable home. And you attack him for it."

"Attack him?" Kelsey threw up her hands, knowing such an outward display would count against her. "I confronted him. I demanded answers. I demanded the truth."

"And now that you have it, are you satisfied?" Milicent inclined her head. "You would have been better off, all of us would have been better off, if she had stayed dead to you. But she was always selfish, always more concerned with herself than anyone else."

For reasons Kelsey could never have explained, she picked up the spear of battle. "And did you always hate her?"

"I always recognized her for what she was. Philip was blinded by her looks, by what he saw as vivacity and verve. And he paid for his mistake."

"And I look like her," Kelsey said softly, "which explains why you've always looked at me as though I might commit some horrible crime at any moment—or at least an unforgivable breach of etiquette."

Milicent sighed and sat back. She wouldn't deny it, saw no reason why she should. "I was concerned, naturally, about how much of her was in you. You're a Byden, Kelsey, and for the most part you've been a credit to the family. Every mistake I've watched you make has her stamp on it."

"I prefer to think I've made my own mistakes."

"Such as this divorce," Milicent said wearily. "Wade comes from a good family. His maternal grandfather is a senator. His father

28

owns one of the most prestigious and well-respected advertising agencies in the east."

"And Wade is an adulterer."

On a little sound of impatience, Milicent waved a hand. The diamond wedding ring on her widow's hand glinted like ice. "You would blame him, rather than yourself or the woman who seduced him."

Almost amused, Kelsey smiled. "That's right. I would blame him. The divorce is final, Grandmother, as of yesterday. You're wasting your time there."

"And you have the dubious honor of being the second Byden in family history to divorce. In your father's case, it was unavoidable. You, however, have done what you've made a habit of doing all your life: reacting impulsively. But that's another issue. I want to know what you intend to do about the letter."

"Don't you think that's between me and my mother?"

"This is a family matter, Kelsey. Your father and I are your family." She tapped her finger again, carefully selecting both words and tone. "Philip is my only child. His happiness and well-being have always been primary in my life. You are his only child." With genuine affection, she reached up and took Kelsey's hand. "I want only the best for you."

There was no arguing with that. However much her grandmother's code of behavior grated, Kelsey knew she was loved. "I know. I don't want to fight with you, Grandmother."

"Nor I with you." Pleased, she patted Kelsey's hand. "You've been a good daughter, Kelsey. No one who knows you and Philip would doubt your devotion. I know you'd do nothing to hurt him. I think it would be best if you gave me the letter, let me handle this business for you. You've no need to contact her, or put yourself through this turmoil."

"I've already contacted her. I went to see her this morning."

"You ..." Milicent's hand jerked, then settled. "You saw her. You went to her without discussing it first?"

"I'm twenty-six years old, Grandmother. Naomi Chadwick is my mother, and I don't have to discuss meeting her with anyone. I'm sorry if it upsets you, but I did what I had to do."

"What you wanted to do," Milicent corrected. "Without thought for the consequences."

"As you like, but they're my consequences. I'd think you and Dad would have to agree it's a normal reaction on my part. It may be difficult for you, but I can't imagine why it would make you so angry."

"I'm not angry." Though she was. Furious. "I'm concerned. I don't want some foolish emotional reaction to influence you. You don't know her, Kelsey. You have no idea how clever or how vindictive she is."

"I know she wanted custody of me."

"She wanted to hurt your father because he'd begun to see through her. You were the tool. She drank, and she had men, and she flaunted her flaws because she was so sure she would always win. And she ended by killing a man." Milicent drew a deep breath. Even the thought of Naomi burned at her heart. "I suppose she tried to convince you it was self-defense. That she was protecting her honor. Her *honor*."

Unable to sit any longer, Milicent rose. "Oh, she was clever, and she was beautiful. If the evidence against her hadn't been so damning she might have convinced a jury to absolve her. But when a woman entertains a man in her bedroom in the middle of the night in nothing more than a silk robe, it's difficult to cry rape."

"Rape," Kelsey repeated, but the word was only a shocked whisper and Milicent didn't hear.

"Some believed her, of course. Some will always believe that kind of woman." Eyes hard, she snatched her gloves from the table and began to tap them against her palm. "But in the end, they convicted her. She was out of Philip's life, and yours. Until now. Will you be so stubborn, so selfish as to let her back in? To cause your father this kind of grief?"

30

"This isn't a choice between him or her, Grandmother."

"That's exactly what it is."

"For you, not for me. Do you know, before you came here, I wasn't sure I would see her again. Now I know I will. Because she didn't defend herself to me. She didn't ask me to choose. I'm going to see her again and decide for myself."

"No matter whom it hurts?"

"As far as I can see, I'm the only one who's risking anything."

"You're wrong, Kelsey, and it's a dangerous mistake. She corrupts." Stiffly, Milicent smoothed on her gloves, finger by finger. "If you insist on pursuing this relationship, she'll do whatever she can to destroy the bond between you and your father."

"No one could do that."

Milicent lifted her gaze, and it was sharp as steel. "You don't know Naomi Chadwick."

# Chapter Three

No, Kelsey didn't know Naomi Chadwick. But she would.

Kelsey's years of higher education hadn't been wasted. If there was one thing she knew how to do well, it was how to research a subject. Any subject. Naomi was no exception.

For the next two weeks, she spent most of her free time poring over microfilm at the public library. Her first stop was the society page, where she read the announcement of the engagement of Naomi Anne Chadwick, twenty-one, daughter of Matthew and Louise Chadwick of Three Willows Farm, Bluemont, Virginia, to Professor Philip James Byden, thirty-four, son of Andrew and Milicent Byden, Georgetown.

A June wedding was planned.

Kelsey found the wedding announcement. It was a shock to see her father looking so young, so carelessly happy, his fingers entwined at his heart with Naomi's. He'd worn a rosebud boutonniere. Kelsey wondered if it had been white, or perhaps a sunny yellow.

Beside him, Naomi glowed. The grainy newsprint couldn't diminish the luster. Her face was impossibly young, heart-breakingly beautiful, her lips curved, her eyes bright, as if on the verge of a laugh.

They looked as though they could face anything together.

It shouldn't hurt. Kelsey told herself it was foolish to be hurt by a divorce that had happened without her knowledge. But these two young, vital people had created her. Now they were no more to each other than painful memories.

She made hard copies of what she wanted, made notes on the rest, as she would for any report. With feelings of amusement and bafflement, she found her own birth announcement.

There was little after that, an occasional squib about attendance at a ball or charity function. It seemed her parents had lived a quiet life, out of the Washington glitter for the short term of their marriage.

Then there was the custody suit, a terse little article that had merited space in *The Washington Post*, she imagined, due to her paternal grandfather's position as undersecretary of the Treasury. She read the names—her own, Naomi's, her father's—with a sense of detachment. The *Post* hadn't wasted much of its dignity on a domestic squabble.

She found a few articles on Three Willows and racing. One mentioned the tragedy of a promising colt who had broken down at a race and was shot. It merited a single picture, of Naomi's beautiful, tear-streaked face.

Then there was murder.

Such matters rated more space, a few prominent headlines.

### LOVERS' QUARREL ENDS IN TRAGEDY
### PASTORAL VIRGINIA SCENE OF VIOLENT DEATH

Her mother was described as the estranged wife of a Georgetown English professor and the daughter of a prominent Thoroughbred breeder. The victim was somewhat flippantly referred to as a playboy with ties to the racing world.

33

The story was straightforward enough. Alec Bradley had been shot and killed in a bedroom at Three Willows Farm. The weapon belonged to Naomi Chadwick Byden, who had notified the police. She and Bradley had been alone in the house at the time of the shooting. Police were investigating.

The Virginia papers were a bit more informative. Naomi never denied firing the fatal shot. She claimed, through her attorney, that Bradley had attacked her and she had resorted to the weapon in self-defense.

The facts were reported that Naomi and Bradley had a friendly relationship, and had been seeing each other socially for weeks. And, of course, that Naomi was in the midst of a messy custody suit over her three-year-old daughter.

A week after the murder, there were more headlines:

## VIRGINIA WOMAN ARRESTED FOR MURDER
### *New Evidence Derails Claim of Self-Defense*

And damning evidence it was. Kelsey's blood chilled as she read of the photograph taken by a detective hired by her father's lawyers to obtain ammunition for the custody battle. Rather than an illicit affair, the detective had recorded murder.

He'd testified at the trial as well. Stubbornly moving from page to page, she read on. About witnesses who agreed, under oath, that Naomi and Bradley behaved, in public, as intimate friends. That Naomi was an expert marksman. That she enjoyed parties, champagne, the attention of men. That she and Bradley had quarreled the evening of his death over his flirtation with another woman.

Then Charles Rooney had taken the stand and told his story. He'd taken dozens of photographs of Naomi, at the track, at the farm, at various social events. He was a licensed private investigator in the state of Virginia, and his surveillance reports were carefully documented.

They formed a picture of a reckless, beautiful woman who craved excitement, who was eager to break the bonds of an inhibiting marriage to an older man. And one who, on the night of the murder, invited the victim into her home, where she was alone and dressed only in a negligee.

Rooney was unable to swear to what was said between the two, but his photographs and his observations said a great deal. The couple had embraced, brandy was poured. Then, they appeared to argue and Naomi had stormed upstairs. Bradley had followed.

Eager to fulfill his duties, Rooney had climbed a handy tree and aimed his telephoto lens at the bedroom window. The argument had continued there, becoming more heated. Naomi had slapped Bradley's face, but when he'd turned to go, she'd pulled a gun out of the nightstand drawer. The camera had captured the shock on his face, and the fury on Naomi's as she fired.

Kelsey stared at the photo for a long time, and at the headline above it that shouted GUILTY! Carefully, she made more copies, then shut off the machine and gathered her files and notes. Before logic could interfere with emotion, she found a pay phone and dialed.

"Three Willows."

"Naomi Chadwick, please."

"May I ask who's calling?"

"This is Kelsey Byden."

There was a small, strangled sound quickly muffled. "Miss Naomi's down at the stables. I'll buzz her."

Moments later an extension was picked up. Kelsey heard Naomi's voice, cool as sherbet over the line. "Hello, Kelsey. It's good to hear from you."

"I'd like to talk to you again."

"Of course. Whenever you like."

"Now. It'll take me an hour to get there. And I'd prefer that we be alone this time."

"Fine. I'll be here."

Naomi hung up and wiped her damp hands on her jeans. "My daughter's coming, Moses."

"So I gathered." Moses Whitetree, Naomi's trainer, trusted employee, and longtime lover, continued to study his breeding reports. He was half Jew, half Choctaw, and had never taken the mix for granted. He wore his hair in a long graying braid down his back. There was the glint of a silver Star of David around his neck.

Whatever there was to know about horses, he knew. And he preferred them, with few exceptions, to people.

"She'll have questions."

"Yes."

"How do I answer them?"

He didn't glance up, didn't need to. He knew every nuance of Naomi's face. "You could try the truth."

"A lot of good the truth's done me."

"She's your blood."

It was always so simple for Moses, Naomi thought impatiently. "She's a grown woman. I hope she's her own woman. She won't accept me simply because we share blood, Moses. I'd be disappointed if she did."

He set his paperwork aside and rose. He wasn't a big man, only a few pounds and a few inches over his onetime dream of being a jockey. In his worn-down boots he was eye level with Naomi. "You want her to love you, to accept you, but you want her to do it on your terms. You've always wanted too much, Naomi."

With tenderness she touched a hand to his wind-bitten cheek. It was impossible to stay irritated with him. He was the man who had waited for her, who never questioned her, who had always loved her.

"So you've always told me. I didn't know I would need her so much until I saw her again, Moses. I didn't know it would matter as much as it does."

"And you wish it didn't."

"Oh, I wish it didn't."

That he understood. He'd spent most of his life wishing he didn't love Naomi. "My people have a saying."

"Which people?"

He smiled. They both knew he made up half of his sayings and twisted the other half to suit his purposes. "Only the foolish waste their wishes. Let her see what you are. It'll be enough."

"Moses." A groom looked into the office, then tipped his hat toward Naomi. "Miss. I don't like the way Serenity's favoring her near foreleg. Got some swelling, too."

"She ran well this morning." Moses's brow puckered. He'd been up before dawn to watch the early workouts. "Let's take a look."

Moses kept his office in a small area at the front of the stables. It was cramped and often smelled of horse urine, but he preferred it to the airy space his predecessor had used in a whitewashed building near the west paddock.

Moses often said the earthy smell of horses was French perfume to him and he didn't want any fancy digs away from the action.

In truth, the stables were nearly as sparkling as any luxury hotel, and usually busier. The concrete slope between the lines of stalls was scrubbed and spotless. The individual stalls were marked with an enameled plaque with the name of each horse scrolled in gold. It was an affectation of Naomi's father's that she'd continued when she'd taken over running the farm.

There were scents of horses, of liniment, of hay and grain and leather—a potpourri Naomi had missed sorely during her years in prison and one she never failed to appreciate.

It was, to her, the scent of freedom.

As Moses passed, horses stuck their heads out of stalls. He, too, had a scent, one they recognized. His boots might have clattered quickly along the slope, but there was always time for a quick stroke, a murmured word.

Stable hands continued their work. Perhaps pitchforks or currycombs moved with more enthusiasm now that the man was in view.

"I was going to take her out to pasture when I saw how she favored the leg." The groom paused beside Serenity's box stall. "Noticed the swelling and thought you'd want to take a look for yourself."

Moses merely grunted, passing his hands over the glossy chestnut coat. He studied the filly's eyes, smelled her breath, murmuring to her as he worked his way down from cheek to chest to leg.

There was swelling just above the fetlock, and some heat. As he applied some slight pressure, the filly jerked back and blew a warning. "Looks like she's knocked into something."

"Reno was riding her this morning." Naomi remembered that the jockey had made a special trip to the farm for the workout. "See if he's still here."

"Yes'm." The groom scurried off.

"She had a beautiful run this morning." Eyes narrowed, Naomi crouched beside Moses and examined the lame leg herself, gently lifting it forward and back to check for shoulder strain. "Looks like an overreach," she muttered. There was discoloration, a sign of blood clotting under the skin. The bone was probably bruised, she thought. If they were lucky, there'd be no fracture. "She was due in Saratoga next week."

"She might still make it." But he didn't think so, not on that leg. "We can get the swelling down. Better call the vet, though. An X-ray wouldn't hurt."

"I'll take care of it. And I'll talk to Reno." She straightened, hooking an arm around the mare's neck. They were an investment, a business, but that didn't negate her love for them. "She's got the heart of a champion, Moses. I don't want to hear that she can't race again."

LESS THAN AN HOUR LATER, Naomi watched grimly as the filly's injury was treated. Already a stream of cold water had been applied directly to the wound. Now Moses himself was massaging the

38

bruise with a mixture of vinegar and cool water. Her vet stood in the stall and prepared a syringe.

"How long before she can start training again, Matt?"

"A month. Six weeks would be better." He glanced toward Naomi. Matt Gunner had a long, pleasant face, kind eyes. "The bone's bruised, Naomi, and there's some tissue damage, but there's no fracture. You keep her stabled, keep up the massage, some light exercise, and she'll do."

"We were going at a fast pace," Reno put in. The jockey stood just outside the box, watching the procedure. He'd changed from his morning workout into one of the smart tailored suits he preferred. But he was a racetracker. There was nothing of more concern to him, or the others, than a Thoroughbred's delicate legs. "I didn't notice any change of gait."

"Neither did I," Naomi added. "Reno says she didn't stumble. I was watching the run this morning and I would have noticed if she had. This filly has a quiet temperament. She's not one to kick in her stall."

"Well, she took a hard knock," Matt said. "If your groom hadn't been alert, it would have been a great deal worse. This'll ease the pain. There you go, girl. Easy now." He slid the needle under Serenity's flesh just above the wound. She rolled her eyes, snorted, but didn't struggle. "She's strong and she's healthy," Matt said. "She'll run again. Moses, there's nothing I can tell you about treating that leg that you don't already know. You give me a call if it heats up. Otherwise . . ." He trailed off, staring over Naomi's shoulder.

"Excuse me." Kelsey stood back, clutching her purse and her file. "I'm sorry to interrupt. I was told up at the house I'd find you here."

"Oh." Distracted, Naomi dragged a hand through her hair. "I lost track of time. We've had a small crisis here. Matt, this is my daughter, Kelsey. Kelsey Byden, Matt Gunner, my vet."

Matt reached out, the syringe still in his hand. He drew it back, flushed. "Sorry. Hello."

39

Nerves aside, she had to smile. "Nice to meet you."

"And Moses Whitetree," Naomi continued. "My trainer."

Moses continued to massage the mare's leg and merely nodded.

"Reno Sanchez, one of the best jockeys on the circuit."

"*The* best," he said with a wink. "Nice to meet you."

"And you," Kelsey said automatically. "You're busy here. I can wait."

"No, there's nothing more I can do. Thanks for coming so quickly, Matt. Sorry I interrupted your day, Reno."

"Hey, no problem. I've got plenty of time before the first post." He looked at Kelsey again with undisguised admiration. "You'll have to come to the track, see me ride."

"I'm sure I'd enjoy it."

"Moses, I'll be back to check on her myself again later. Why don't we go up to the house?" Naomi gestured, careful, very careful not to make contact, then led the way out the rear of the building.

"You have a sick horse?"

"Injured, I'm afraid. We'll have to scratch her from her races for the next several weeks."

"That's a shame."

Kelsey glanced toward a paddock where a yearling was being put through his paces on a longe line. Another, with a rider up, was being led by a handler toward the walking ring. A groom was giving a glossy chestnut a bath, spraying streams of water over the gelding with a hose. Other horses were simply being walked in wide, repetitive circles.

"Busy place," Kelsey murmured, aware that eyes had turned her way.

"Oh, most of the work gets done in the morning, but it'll be busy again when the track closes this afternoon."

"You're racing today?"

"There's always a race," Naomi said absently. "But right now we've still got mares dropping foals, so what doesn't get done in the morning happens in the middle of the night." She smiled a little. "They always seem to have them in the middle of the night."

"I guess I didn't realize you had such a large operation."

"In the last ten years we've become one of the top Thoroughbred farms in the country. We've had a horse do no less than show in the last three Derbies. Won the St. Leger and Belmont. Took the Breeders' Cup two years running. One of our mares took a gold in the last Olympics." Naomi cut herself off with a laugh. "Don't get me started. I'm worse than a grandmother with a wallet full of snapshots."

"It's all right. I'm interested." More, Kelsey mused, than she'd realized. "Actually, I took riding lessons when I was a girl. I guess most of us go through a horse-crazy stage. Dad hated it, but ..." She trailed off, suddenly understanding why he'd been so unhappy when she'd developed the traditional girlhood obsession with horses.

"Of course he did," Naomi said with a thin smile. "It's perfectly understandable. But you had your lessons anyway?"

"Yes, I hounded him for them." She stopped, and looked straight into her mother's eyes. She could see the small, subtle signs of aging that she'd been too nervous to notice at their first meeting. Fine lines fanning out from the eyes. Others, either from temper or worry, gently scoring the high, creamy forehead. "It must have hurt him to see me, simply to see me day after day."

"I don't think so. However Philip came to feel about me, he adored you." She looked away then because it was easier to stare at the hills. A horse whinnied, high and bright, a sound sweeter to Naomi than any aria. "I haven't asked you about him. How is he?"

"He's well. He's the chairman of the English department at Georgetown now. Has been for seven years."

"He's a brilliant man. And a good one."

"But not good enough for you."

Naomi lifted a brow. "Darling Kelsey, I was never good enough for him. Ask anyone." Naomi tossed her hair back and continued to walk. "I'm told he married again."

41

"Yes, when I was eighteen. They're very happy together. I have a stepbrother, Channing."

"And you're fond of them, your family."

"Very."

Naomi crossed the same patio, used the same terrace doors as she had the first time. "What can I get you? Coffee, tea? Some wine, perhaps?"

"It isn't necessary."

"I hope you'll indulge Gertie. She made cookies when she heard you were coming. I know you don't remember, but you meant a great deal to her."

Trapped, Kelsey thought, by manners and compassion. "Tea and cookies then. Thanks."

"I'll tell her. Please sit down."

She didn't sit. It seemed only fair that she take a closer look at her mother's things. At first glance the room was quietly elegant, a world apart from the bustle and manure-coated boots of the stable area. The low fire burned sedately, rose-colored drapes were pulled back to welcome the sun. That sun shone on a dozen or so lovely crystal horses in clear and jewel hues. The Oriental rug on the polished chestnut floor picked up the colors of the drapes and the creamy tones of the sofa.

Nothing ostentatious, nothing jarring. Until you looked again. The walls were covered in watered silk, the same cool ivory as the upholstery. But the paintings, large and abstract, were explosions of bold and restless color. Violent works, Kelsey thought, sated with passion and anger. And signed, she saw with a jolt, with a bloodred N C.

Naomi's work? she wondered. No one had mentioned that her mother painted. No amateurish works these, Kelsey decided, but skilled and capable and disturbing.

They should have unbalanced the steady dignity of the room, she thought as she turned away. Yet they humanized it.

There were other telling touches throughout the room. A statue of a woman, her alabaster face carved in unfathomable grief, a glass heart in pale green with a jagged crack down the center, a small bowl filled with colored stones.

"Those were yours."

Guiltily, Kelsey dropped a pebble back into the bowl and turned. Gertie had wheeled in the tea tray and stood, beaming at her. "I'm sorry?"

"You always liked pretty rocks. I kept them for you when you . . ." Her smile wobbled. "When you went away."

"Oh." How was she supposed to answer that? "You've worked here a long time, then."

"I've been at Three Willows since I was a girl. My mother kept house for Mr. Chadwick, then I took over when she retired. Moved to Florida. Chocolate chip was always your favorite."

The woman looked as though she could devour Kelsey whole. The desperate yearning in her eyes was difficult to face, the desperate joy beneath that, worse. "They still are," Kelsey managed.

"You come sit and help yourself. Miss Naomi got a phone call, but she'll be right along." All but humming with happiness, Gertie poured tea, arranged cookies on a plate. "I always knew you'd come back. Always knew it. Miss Naomi didn't think so. She fretted about it all the time. But I says to her, 'She's your girl, isn't she? She'll come back to see her mama all right.' And here you are."

"Yes." Kelsey made herself sit and accept the tea. "Here I am."

"And all grown up." Unable to help herself, Gertie stroked a hand over Kelsey's hair. "A grown-up woman now." Her lined face crumpled as she let her hand fall. Turning quickly, she hurried from the room.

"I'm sorry," Naomi said when she came in moments later. "This is an emotional time for Gertie. It must make you uncomfortable."

"It's all right." Kelsey sipped her tea. Oolong this time, she noted with a tiny smile. Understanding, Naomi laughed.

"Just my subtle sense of humor." She poured herself a cup, then sat. "I wasn't sure you'd come back."

43

"Neither was I. I'm not sure I would have, at least so soon, if Grandmother hadn't all but forbade me to."

"Ah, Milicent." Trying to relax, Naomi stretched out her long legs. "She always detested me. Well," she said, and shrugged, "it was mutual. Tell me, have you been able to satisfy her high standards?"

"Not quite." Kelsey's smile came and went. It felt disloyal to discuss her grandmother.

"Family honor," Naomi said, nodding. "You're absolutely right. I shouldn't goad you into criticizing Milicent. Besides, I'm not the one who should be asking the questions."

"How can this be so easy for you?" Kelsey set down her cup with a snap of china against china. "How can you sit there so calmly?"

"I learned a great deal about taking what comes when I was in prison. You have the reins here, Kelsey. I've had a lot of time to think this through, and I had to promise myself before I contacted you that I would accept whatever happened."

"Why did you wait so long? You've been out of prison for . . ."

"Twelve years, eight months, ten days. Ex-cons are more obsessive than ex-smokers, and I'm both." She smiled again. "But that doesn't answer your question. I considered contacting you the day I got out. I even went to your school. Every day for a week I sat in my car across the street and watched you in the little playground. Watched you and the other girls watching the boys and pretending not to. Once I even got out of my car and started across the street. And I wondered if you'd smell prison on me. I could still smell it on myself."

Naomi moved her shoulders, chose a cookie. "So, I got back in my car and drove away. You were happy, you were secure, you didn't know I existed. Then my father became ill. The years passed, Kelsey. Every time I thought about picking up the phone or writing a letter or just walking back into your life, it seemed wrong."

"Why now?"

"Because it seemed right. You're not so happy, not so secure, and I thought it was time you knew I existed. Your marriage is over, you're at a crossroads. Perhaps you don't think I can understand how you feel, but I do."

"You know about Wade."

"Yes. And your job, your academic career. You're fortunate you inherited your father's brain. I was always a lousy student. If you don't want the cookies, stick a few in your purse, will you? Gertie will never know the difference."

With a sigh, Kelsey picked one up and took a bite. "I don't know how to feel about all of this. I don't know how to feel about you."

"Reality is rarely like those big, emotional reunions on *Oprah*," Naomi commented. "Long-lost mother reunited with daughter. All is forgiven. I'm not asking for all to be forgiven, Kelsey. I'm hoping you'll give me a chance."

Kelsey reached for the file she'd set beside her on the sofa. "I've done some research."

The hell, Naomi decided, and reached for another cookie. "I thought you might. Newspaper articles on the trial?"

"Among other things."

"I can arrange for you to have a transcript."

Kelsey's fingers faltered on the file. "A transcript?"

"I'd want one if I were in your place. It's public record, Kelsey. If I had something to hide, I couldn't."

"When I came here before, I asked if you were guilty and you said yes."

"You asked if I'd killed Alec, and I said yes."

"Why didn't you tell me you'd claimed self-defense?"

"What difference does it make? I was convicted. I paid my debt to society, and I am, according to the system, rehabilitated."

"Was it a lie, then? Was it a legal maneuver when you said you'd shot him to protect yourself from rape?"

"The jury thought so."

45

"I'm asking you," Kelsey shot back, firing up. "A simple yes or no."

"Taking a life isn't simple, whatever the circumstances."

"And what were they? You let him into your house, into your bedroom."

"I let him into my house," Naomi said evenly. "He came into my bedroom."

"He was your lover."

"No, he was not." Hands icily calm, Naomi poured more tea. "He might have been eventually. But I hadn't slept with him." Her gaze met her daughter's. "The jury didn't believe that, either. I was attracted to him. I thought he was a charming fool, harmless and amusing."

"You fought with him over another woman."

"I'm territorial," Naomi said blithely. "He was supposed to be madly in love with me—which meant I was allowed to flirt and he wasn't. And because he was beginning to bore and annoy me, I decided to break off the relationship. Alec didn't want it to be broken. So we had a scene, in public. Then another one later, in private. He was furious, called me a few names, tried to make his case with some rough handling. I didn't care for it and ordered him to leave."

Though she fought to keep it calm, her voice shook as the night flooded back. "Instead, he followed me upstairs and called me several more names, and got quite a bit rougher. Apparently he decided he would show me what I'd been missing by forcing me into bed. I was angry, and I was afraid. We struggled, and I realized he would do exactly what he'd threatened to do. I broke away, got my gun. And I shot him."

Without a word, Kelsey flipped open the file and took out the copy of the newspaper photo. When Naomi took it only a quick spasm at the side of her mouth betrayed any emotion.

"Not terribly flattering to either of us, is it? But then, we didn't know we had an audience."

46

"He isn't touching you. He has his hands up."

"Yes. I guess you had to be there." She handed the photo back. "I'm not asking you to believe me, Kelsey. Why should you? Whatever the circumstances, I'm not blameless. But I've paid. Society has given me another chance. That's all I'm asking you to do."

"Why did you let me think you were dead? Why did you allow that?"

"Because I felt I was. Part of me was. And whatever my crimes, I loved you. I didn't want you to grow up knowing I was in a cage. I couldn't have survived those ten years thinking of that. And I needed to survive."

There were other questions, dozens of them swirling around in Kelsey's head like bees. But she didn't think she could bear to hear the answers. "I don't know you," she said at last. "I don't know if I'll ever feel anything for you."

"Your father would have instilled a sense of duty in you. Certainly Milicent would have. I'm going to use it and ask you to come here, to stay here for a few weeks. A month."

Kelsey was completely taken aback for a few moments. "You want me to live here?" she finally managed to say.

"An extended visit. A few weeks of your life, Kelsey, for the lifetime I lost." She didn't want to beg. God, she didn't want to beg, but she would if there was no other choice. "It's selfish of me, and not terribly fair, but I want the chance."

"It's too much to ask."

"Yes, it is. But I'm asking anyway. I'm your mother. You can't avoid that. You can choose to avoid me if that's what you want, but I'll still be your mother. We'll have time to see if there's anything between us. If not, you'll walk away. I'm betting you won't walk away." Naomi leaned forward. "What are you made of, Kelsey? Is there enough Chadwick in there for you to accept a dare?"

Kelsey angled her chin. It was a risk. Perhaps she'd needed it to be put that way rather than as a request. "I won't promise a month.

But I'll come." She was surprised to see Naomi's lips tremble once before they curved into that cool, steady smile.

"Good. If I can't enchant you, Three Willows should. We'll have to see how much you picked up in those riding lessons."

"I don't get thrown easily."

"Neither do I."

# Chapter Four

Dinner with the family was a civilized affair. Excellent food was served with dignity—like any last meal, Kelsey thought as she spooned up her leek soup. She didn't want to think of the evening in her father's house as an obligation, or worse, as a trial, but she knew it was both.

Philip made casual conversation, but his smile was strained. Since Kelsey had told him of her upcoming visit to Three Willows, he'd been able to think of little else but the past. It seemed disloyal somehow to Candace that his mind should be so full of his first wife, his nights restless and disturbed by memories of her. No matter how often he told himself it was illogical, foolish, even indulgent, he couldn't quite chase away the fear that he was losing the child he'd fought so hard to keep.

A woman now. He had only to look at her to be reminded of that. Yet he had only to close his eyes to remember the girl. And the guilt.

Milicent waited until the roast chicken was served. Normally, she disliked discussing unpleasant matters over a meal. But, as she saw it, she'd been given no choice.

"You leave tomorrow, I'm told."

"Yes." Kelsey took a sip from her water glass. Watched the thin lemon slice dip and float. "First thing in the morning."

"And your job?"

"I've resigned." Kelsey lifted a brow in challenge and acknowledgment. "It was little more than volunteer work. I may look for something at the Smithsonian when I get back."

"It may be difficult to get anything with your record of coming and going."

"It may."

"The Historical Society's always looking for an extra pair of hands," Candace put in. "I'm sure I could put in a word for you."

"Thank you, Candace." Always the peacemaker, Kelsey thought. "I'll think about it."

"Maybe you'll catch racing fever." Channing winked at Kelsey. "Buy yourself some stud and make the circuit."

"That would hardly be acceptable, or wise." Milicent dabbed a napkin at her lips. "Such things may seem romantic and exciting at your age, Channing, but Kelsey's old enough to know better."

"It sounds like a great deal to me, hanging out at the stables, placing a few bets at the track." He shrugged, making quick work of his dinner. "I wouldn't mind spending a few weeks playing in the country."

"You could visit me. It'd be fun."

"Is that all you can think of?" Incensed, Milicent set her fork down with a clatter. "Fun? Have you no idea what this is doing to your father?"

"Mother—"

But Milicent overrode Philip's objection with an impatient wave of her hand. "After all the pain and unhappiness we went through, to have that woman simply snap her fingers to make Kelsey come running. It's appalling."

"She didn't snap her fingers." Under the table, Kelsey balled her

50

hands into fists. It would be much too easy to create a scene, she told herself. "She asked, I agreed. I'm sorry if this hurts you, Dad."

"My concern's for you, Kelsey."

"I wonder . . ." Candace spoke up, hoping to ward Milicent off and salvage some of the evening. "Is it really necessary for you to stay there? It's only an hour or so away, after all. You could move more slowly, go out on a weekend now and then." She glanced toward Philip to gauge his reaction, then smiled bolsteringly at Kelsey. "It seems more sensible."

"If she was sensible, she would never have gone out there."

Kelsey bit back a sigh at her grandmother's comment and sat back. "It's not as if I've signed a contract. I can leave at any time. I want to go." This she addressed to her father. "I want to find out who she is."

"Sounds natural to me," Channing said over a bite of chicken. "If I'd found out I had a long-lost mother who'd done time, that's what I'd do. Did you ask her what it was like inside? I'm a sucker for those women-in-prison movies."

"Channing." Candace's voice was a horrified whisper. "Must you be so crude?"

"Just curious." He speared a perfectly boiled new potato. "Bet the food sucked."

Delighted with him, Kelsey let out a laugh. "I'll be sure to ask her. God, are Channing and I the only ones around here who don't see this as some drawing-room melodrama? You should be relieved I'm not running traumatized to some therapist or washing my shock away with cheap wine. I'm the one who has to make the adjustments here, and I'm doing the best I can."

"You're thinking only of yourself," Milicent said between stiffened lips.

"Yes, I am. I'm thinking of myself." Enough was enough, Kelsey decided, and she pushed back from the table. "It might interest you to know that she had nothing but good things to say about you," she told her father. "There's no insidious plot to turn me against

51

you. And nothing could." She walked to him, bending down to kiss his cheek. "Thanks for dinner, Candace. I really have to get home and finish packing. Channing, if you have a free weekend, give me a call. Good night, Grandmother."

She hurried out. The moment she shut the door behind her, she took a deep gulp of air. It tasted like freedom, she thought. She intended to enjoy it.

IN THE MORNING, GERTIE MET Kelsey at the door. "You're here." The woman snatched Kelsey's suitcases before Kelsey could object. "Miss Naomi's down to the stables. We didn't know what time you'd come, so she told me to call her when you got here."

"No, don't bother her. I'm sure she's busy. Let me take those. They're heavy."

"I'm strong as an ox." Gertie backed up, still beaming. "I'll show you up to your room. You just bring yourself, that's all."

She might have been small and thin, but Gertie strode effortlessly up the stairs, chattering. "We got everything ready. It's good to be busy again. Miss Naomi, she doesn't take any care at all. Hardly needs me around."

"I'm sure that's not true."

"Oh, for company, she does. But she eats like a bird and does for herself mostly before I can do for her." Gertie led the way down a wide hall, carpeted in faded cabbage roses. "Sometimes she has people over, but not like there once was. Used to be there was always people and parties."

She stepped across a threshold and set both cases on an elegant four-poster bed.

The room streamed with light from a double window seat that faced the hills, the long slim windows overlooking the gardens. Deep colors and floral accents gave the room an elegant, European feel.

"It's lovely." Kelsey stepped to a cherry vanity table where tulips speared up out of fluted crystal. "Like sleeping in a garden."

"It was your room before. 'Course it was done up different then, all pink and white—like a candy cane." Gertie gnawed at her lip when she saw the surprise in Kelsey's eyes. "Miss Naomi said if you didn't like it, you could take the room across the hall."

"This is fine." She waited for a moment, wondering if she'd be bombarded with some sensory memory. But all she felt was curiosity.

"Your bathroom's through here." Anxious to please, Gertie opened a door. "You just ask if you need any more towels. Or anything, anything at all. I'll go call Miss Naomi."

"No, don't." On impulse Kelsey turned away from the suitcases. "I'll go on down. I can unpack later."

"I'll do that for you. Don't you worry about that. You go on down and have a nice visit, then you can have lunch. You want to button that jacket. The air's chilly."

Kelsey fought back a smile. "All right. I'll be back for lunch."

"Make your mama come. She needs to eat."

"I'll tell her." Kelsey left Gertie happily opening the suitcases. It was tempting to do a quick turn around the house, to poke into rooms and explore hallways. But it could wait. The day might have held the chill of the dying winter, but it was gloriously sunny. And, Kelsey hoped as she went out, promising.

She wasn't going to start the visit by chasing at shadows. It would have to be done, of course. Still, it seemed harmless to enjoy one uncomplicated day in the country, with the smells of hardy spring blooms and new grass in the air, the panorama of hills and horses and sky. She could look on it, at least for now, as a short vacation. Until she'd literally packed her bags, she hadn't realized just how much she'd needed to get away from the confinement of her apartment, the fill-in job, the tedious routine of learning to be single again.

And here, she thought as she caught the first poignant smell of

53

horse, was something else to be learned, after all. She knew nothing about the racing world, nothing of the people and little of the animals that composed it.

So, she would study and find out. It seemed to follow that the more she discovered, the better she would understand her mother.

As before, there was activity at the stables, horses being walked or washed, men and women carrying tack, hauling wheelbarrows. Kelsey tolerated the sidelong glances and outright stares and walked inside.

A groom was bandaging a mare's legs in the first box. Kelsey hesitated when he cut his eyes up to hers. His eyes were shadowed under the bill of his cap, and his face was incredibly old, cracked like neglected leather left in the sun.

"Excuse me, I'm looking for Ms. Chadwick."

"Grew up, did ya?" The man shifted a tobacco plug into the pocket of his cheek. "Heard you was coming. There now, sweet thing, hold your water."

It took Kelsey a moment to realize the last comment was addressed to the mare and not to her. "Is something wrong with her?" Kelsey asked. "The horse?"

"Just a little sprain. Old she is, but still likes to run. You remember the days, don't you, girl? Won her first race and her last, and a goodly number between. Twenty-five she is. Was a spry young filly when you last saw her." His grin, mostly toothless, flashed. "Don't remember, I expect, her nor me. I'm Boggs. Put you up on your first pony. Forget how to ride, have you?"

"No. I can ride." Kelsey reached out a hand to stroke the old mare's cheek. "What's her name?"

"Queen Vanity Fair. I just call her Queenie."

The mare whickered, her soft brown eyes looking deeply into Kelsey's. "She's too old to race now," Kelsey murmured.

"Or to breed. Queenie's in retirement, but she gets to thinking she's still a girl and kicks up her heels. If I was to bring a saddle in here, her ears would perk right up."

"She can still be ridden, then?"

"With the right rider. Your ma's in the breeding shed, out the back, to your left. Big doings today."

"Oh. Thank you . . ."

"Boggs. Welcome home." He turned back, running his gnarled, callused hands as gently as silk over the mare's legs. "Best to wear boots around here next time."

"Yes." Nonplussed, Kelsey looked down at her soft Italian flats. "You're right."

She walked through the stables, pausing with a quick look over her shoulder before stopping by Serenity's box. She was rewarded by a welcoming snort and nuzzle.

Outside, she didn't require Boggs's directions. There was enough activity around the outbuilding to the left to have drawn her in any case.

She recognized Gabe, and was torn for a moment as to who looked more magnificent, he or the rearing chestnut stallion he was fighting to control. He stood at the horse's head, boots planted, muscles straining, the reins shortened while the stallion quivered and called.

His own hair flying in the breeze, Gabe tossed back his head and laughed. "Anxious, are you? Don't blame you a bit. Nothing like having a beautiful female ready for sex to get the blood moving. Hello, Kelsey." He continued to control the stallion without looking around. He'd known she was there. He almost believed he'd smelled her, as the stallion scented the mare. "You're just in time for the main event. Aren't skittish, are you?"

"No, I'm not."

"Good. Naomi's inside with the mare. Longshot and Three Willows are about to breed a champion."

Kelsey skimmed her gaze over the horse. Handlers were positioned around him, helping Gabe to keep the stud from charging the shed. Magnificent he was, his coat already gleaming like flame from sweat, his eyes fierce, his muscles bunched.

"You're going to turn him loose on some poor, unsuspecting mare?"

Gabe grinned. "Believe me, she'll be grateful."

"She'll be terrified," Kelsey disagreed, and strode into the shed. She saw her mother and Moses calming the mare, who looked to be every bit as eager to get on with things as the stallion. She, too, was a chestnut, as regal as her intended mate. Even though she was hobbled, protected at the neck by a thick jacket of leather and canvas, she looked proud and valiant.

"Kelsey." Covered with grime and sweat, Naomi wiped a hand over her brow. "Gertie was supposed to let me know when you got here."

"I told her not to bother. I'm in the way?"

"No . . ." Naomi looked doubtfully at Moses. "But things are about to get a little frantic. And graphic."

"I know a little about sex," Kelsey said dryly.

"Stay here," Moses added, "and you'll learn more. She's ready," he said to one of the handlers.

"Keep back out of the way," Naomi warned her daughter. "This isn't as simple as an hour in the local motel."

She could smell the sex. Even as Gabe and his handlers brought the stallion in, the air in the shed thickened with it. Sharp, edgy, elemental. The mare called out, in protest or welcome, and the stallion answered with a sound that caused something to tighten in Kelsey's stomach.

Orders were given; movements were quick. In a powerful lunge, the stallion reared up and mounted the mare. Wide-eyed, Kelsey stared as Moses stepped in and assisted in the most technical aspect of the coupling. Then her breath caught as she saw why the mare wore the leather neck cover. Surely the stallion would have bitten through her flesh without it. He plunged wildly, his need frantic and somehow human.

He covered her, commanding, demanding. She accepted, her eyes rolling in what Kelsey thought must surely be pleasure.

Hardly realizing it, she moved closer, fascinated by the passionate frenzy of mating. Her own heart was pounding, her blood hot. The quick, sharp pang of arousal staggered her.

She found herself looking at Gabe. Sweat was running down his face. His muscles strained against his shirt. And his eyes were on hers. It was shocking to see her own primitive and unexpected reaction mirrored there. Staggering to have the vision flash through her mind of being taken as the mare was being taken, fiercely, violently, heedlessly.

He smiled, a slow movement of lips that was both arrogant and charming. Smiled, she thought, as if he knew exactly what she was thinking. As if he'd intended her to think it.

"Incredible, isn't it?" Naomi stepped back beside her. It was the third mare they'd bred that morning and her body was aching with the effort. "Hundreds of pounds lost in the most basic of needs."

"Does it—" Kelsey cleared her throat. "Does it hurt her?"

"I doubt she notices if it does." Out of her back pocket Naomi took a plain blue bandanna to mop her damp throat. "Some stallions breed very kind, like a shy or longtime lover." She grinned wryly at the panting horses. "There's not a shy bone in that one's body. He's a beast. And what woman doesn't want a beast now and again?" She glanced at Moses.

The intellect, Kelsey thought as her pulse danced. It would be better, or at least more comfortable, to explore the logistics. "How do you choose which stallion for what mare?"

"Bloodlines, dispositions, tendencies, even color. We make up genetic charts. Then you cross your fingers. Christ, I know it's a cliché, but I could use a cigarette. Let's get some air. They're nearly done here."

Naomi pulled a stick of gum out of her pocket as she stepped outside. "Want some?"

"No, thanks."

"It's a poor substitute for tobacco." She sighed a little as she folded the stick in her mouth. "But most substitutes are poor in any case." Tilting her head, she studied her daughter more thoroughly. "You look tired, Kelsey. Restless night?"

"Somewhat."

Naomi sighed again. Her daughter had once been so open with her, a chatterbox of news and questions. Those days, like so many others, were over. "You can tell me if you'd rather I leave it alone, but I'd like to ask if Philip is against this visit."

"I think it's more accurate to say he's hurt by my decision to accept your invitation."

"I see." Naomi looked down at the ground, and nodded once. "I'd tell you I'd talk to him myself, try to reassure him, but I think it would only make matters worse."

"It would."

"All right, then. He'll be uneasy for a few weeks." Her eyes were hard when she looked up again. Dammit, she deserved this—one short month out of so many years. "He'll survive. I can't be dead just because so many people would prefer it." She glanced over as Gabe led the sweaty stallion out of the shed. Her smile bloomed, softening her face again. "So, do you think we have a merger?"

"If not, it's not for lack of trying." He slapped the stallion's neck before giving the reins to a handler. "The first of many, I hope. Well, Kelsey, you've had an interesting initiation into life on a horse farm. If you stick around till after the first of next year, you'll see the results of today's tryst."

"That's a very understated description for what went on in there. She didn't appear to have much choice in the matter."

"Neither did he." Grinning, Gabe took out a cigar. "That kind of primitive attraction doesn't allow for choice. Moses will let me know if we need a repeat performance," he said to Naomi, "but I've got a hunch we won't."

"I'd ask for odds, but I prefer to go with your hunch on this one. Excuse me just a minute. I want to check on the mare."

Kelsey looked over to where the stallion was being cooled down.

"Shouldn't you be over there, exchanging lies and letting him puff on that cigar?"

"I gave up lying about my sex life in high school. Do I make you nervous, Kelsey, or is it just the atmosphere?"

"Neither." He made her something, all right, she thought. But that was her problem. "So you own the neighboring farm, then? Longshot?"

"That's right."

"I admired your house from the road. It's quite a bit less traditional than the others in the area."

"So am I. The very dignified Cape Cod that stood on the hill when the farm passed into my hands didn't suit me. So I tore it down." He blew out a stream of smoke. "You'll have to come over, have a tour."

"I'd like that, but I think I'll concentrate on touring Three Willows first."

"You won't find a better operation on the East Coast. Unless it's mine." The snort from behind him made him turn, then grin at Moses. "Of course, I'd have the best in the country if I could lure Whitetree away. Double what she pays you, Moses."

"Keep your money, boy. Buy yourself another fancy suit." Moses handed the mare to a stableboy for a rubdown. "Owners like you—flash in the pan."

"That's what you said five years ago."

"That's what I say now. Give me a cigar."

"You're a hard man, Whitetree." Gabe obliged him.

"Yep." Moses stuck the cigar in his pocket for later. "Your groom with the broken nose? There was gin on his breath."

Gabe's easy smile faded, his eyes narrowed. "I'll take care of it."

"Tell your trainer to take care of it," Moses shot back. "It's his job."

"My horses," Gabe corrected. "Excuse me." He turned on his heel and headed for the trailer where the stallion was being loaded.

"He'll never learn, that one," Moses muttered.

59

"There's no chain of command as far as Gabe is concerned." Watching Gabe confront the groom, Naomi shook her head. "You should have told his trainer, Moses."

"And Jamison shouldn't need me to tell him what goes on under his nose."

"Ah." Kelsey held up a hand. "Would you mind telling me what's going on?"

"Gabe's firing one of his grooms," Naomi told her.

"Just like that?"

"You don't drink when you're working." Moses hissed a breath out of his teeth as the groom's enraged voice carried to them. "Owners should stay out of shedrow business."

"Why?" Kelsey asked.

"Because they're owners." With a shake of his head, Moses strode off toward the stables.

"Never a dull moment." Naomi touched Kelsey's arm. "Why don't we . . . shit."

"What?" Kelsey looked over in time to see the groom swing at Gabe. And to see Gabe evade, once, twice, fluid as a shadow.

Gabe didn't strike back, though the instinct was there, the back alley that always lurked under the civilized man he'd made himself. The groom was pitiful, he thought, and half his size. And the worst of it was that it had taken Moses to point out that he'd had a drunk handling his horse.

"Go back and get your gear, Lipsky," Gabe repeated, icily calm as the groom stood with cocked fists. "You're through at Longshot."

"Who are you to tell me I'm through?" Lipsky ran a hand over his mouth. He wasn't drunk, not yet. He'd had only enough of the gin in his flask to make him feel tall. And mean. "I know more about horses than you ever will. You lucked your way into the big time, Slater. Lucked and cheated and everybody knows it. Just like everybody knows your old man's a drunken loser."

The heat that flashed into Gabe's eyes had the handlers easing

60

back. In tacit agreement they silently formed a ring. It was, they believed, nearly showtime.

"Know my father, do you, Lipsky? I'm not surprised. You're welcome to look him up, have a few drinks. But in the meantime, pick up your gear and the pay that's coming to you. You're fired."

"Jamison hired me. I've been at Cunningham Farm for ten years, and I'll be there after you've gone back to your roulette wheels and blackjack tables."

Over Lipsky's head Gabe saw two of the handlers exchange glances. So, he thought, those were the cards he was dealt. He'd play them out later, but now he had to finish this hand.

"There is no Cunningham Farm, and no place for you at Longshot. Jamison might have hired you, Lipsky, but I write your checks. I don't write checks for drunks. If I see you near any of my horses, I can promise you, it won't be Jamison who deals with you."

He turned, his gaze cutting straight to Kelsey. She stood, like the handlers, watching the show. She had a moment to think she'd prefer that the calm disdain in Gabe's eyes wasn't directed at her before she caught the glint of sun on steel.

The warning strangled in her throat, but Gabe was already whipping back to face the knife. The first lunge sliced almost delicately down his arm rather than plunging into his back. The sight and smell of blood had the handlers shifting quickly from their mildly interested attitudes.

"Keep back," Gabe ordered, ignoring the pain in his arm. His mistake, he thought, was in not judging correctly how far the drink would push. "You want to take me on, Lipsky?" His body was coiled now, ready. When you couldn't walk away from a fight, you dove in and played the odds. "Well, you'll need that knife. So come on."

The blade trembled in Lipsky's hand. For a moment, he couldn't remember how it had gotten there. The hilt had seemed to leap into his hand. But it was there now, and so was first blood. Pride stirred by gin wouldn't allow him to back off.

He crouched, feinted, and began to circle.

"We have to do something." The horror in Kelsey's throat tasted like rusted copper. "Call the police."

"No, not the police." Pale as wax, Naomi clenched her hands at her sides. "Not the police."

"Something. Good God." She watched the blade gleam and lunge, slipping by inches from Gabe's body. No one moved but the two in the center of the circle, then the stallion began to kick in his trailer, excited anew by the scent of blood and violence.

Before she could think, Kelsey grabbed a pitchfork leaning against the side of the shed. She didn't want to dwell on what the tines would do to flesh, so she hefted it and began running forward, only to stumble to a halt when the knife flashed again. It arched up, flying free, as Lipsky hit the ground.

She hadn't seen the blow. Gabe hadn't appeared to move at all. But now he was standing over the groom, his eyes cold, his face as calm as carved stone.

"Let Jamison know where you end up. He'll send your gear and your money." In an effortless move he hauled Lipsky up by the scruff of the neck. The stink of gin and blood curdled in his stomach, sour memories. "Don't let me catch you around here again or I might forget I'm a gentleman now, and break you in half."

He tossed the limp groom down again, and turned to his men. "Let him off on the road. He can ride his thumb out of here."

"Yes, sir, Mr. Slater." They scrambled, as impressed as boys at a school-yard brawl, dragging Lipsky up and carrying him to the truck.

"Sorry, Naomi." In a careless gesture, Gabe raked the hair out of his eyes. "I should have waited to fire him until we were back at Longshot."

She was trembling, and hated it. "Then I would have missed the performance." Forcing a smile on her face, she moved closer. Blood was dripping down his arm. "Come on up to the house. We'll clean that arm."

"That's my cue to say it's just a scratch." He glanced down at it, grateful it wasn't much more than that, no matter how nastily it throbbed. "But I'd be a fool to turn down nursing by beautiful women." He looked at Kelsey then.

She still held the pitchfork, her knuckles white as bone on the handle. Valiant color rode high on her cheeks and shock glazed her eyes.

"I think you can put that down now." He took it from her, gently. "But I appreciate the thought."

Her knees began to shake, so she locked them stiff. "You're just going to let him go?"

"What else?"

"People are usually arrested for attempted murder." She looked back at her mother, saw the wry smile curve Naomi's lips. "Is this how things are handled around here?"

"You'll have to ask Moses," Naomi replied. "He does the firing at Three Willows." Taking the bandanna out of her pocket, she stanched the blood on Gabe's arm. "Sorry I don't have a petticoat to tear up for you."

"So am I."

"Hold it there, press hard," she instructed him. "Let's go up to the house and get it bandaged."

They started off, Gabe keeping his pace slow until Kelsey caught up. He turned his face to hers, and grinned. "Welcome home, Kelsey."

# Chapter Five

KELSEY LEFT THE FIRST AID TO HER MOTHER, AND THE bustling and clucking to Gertie. She would have voted for a trip to the emergency room, but no one seemed particularly interested in her opinion.

Knife wounds, it seemed, were to be taken philosophically and mopped up in the kitchen.

Once Gabe's arm was cleaned, medicated, and bandaged, bowls of chicken soup and hot biscuits were served. Talk was of horses, of bloodlines and races, of times and tracks. Since it wasn't a world Kelsey understood, she was free to observe and speculate.

She had yet to determine Naomi's relationship with Gabriel Slater. It appeared intimate, easy. It was he who rose to refill coffee cups, not his hostess. They touched each other often, casually. A hand over a hand, fingertips against an arm.

She told herself it didn't matter what they were to each other. After all, her mother and father had been divorced for more than twenty years. Naomi was free to pursue any relationship she chose.

And yet it bothered her on some elemental level.

Certainly they suited each other. Beyond the easy flow between them, over and above their interest in horses that consumed them both, there was a strain of violence in each. Controlled, on ice. But as she knew with her mother, and as she'd seen for herself with Gabe, deadly.

"Kelsey might enjoy a trip to the track for some morning work-outs," Gabe put in. He was enjoying his coffee, enjoying watching Kelsey. He could almost see the thoughts circling around in her head.

"The track?" She was interested, despite having her private musing interrupted. "I thought you worked the horses out here."

"We do both," Naomi told her. "Using the track gives a horse a feel for it."

"And the handicappers a chance to gauge their bets," Gabe put in. "The track draws an interesting and eclectic group, particularly in those dawn hours long before post time."

"Dawn's no exaggeration." Naomi smiled at her daughter. "You might not like to start your day quite so early."

"Actually, I'd like to see how it's done."

"Tomorrow?" The lift of Gabe's brow was a subtle challenge.

"Fine."

"We'll meet you there." Naomi glanced at her watch. "I've got to get down to the stables. The farrier's due." As she rose she pressed a hand to Gabe's shoulder. "Finish your coffee. Kelsey, you'll keep Gabe company, won't you? He'll tell you what to expect in the morning." She grabbed a denim jacket and hurried out.

"She doesn't stay in one place very long," Kelsey murmured.

"First part of the year is the busiest in the business." Gabe leaned back, the coffee cup in his hand. "So, should I tell you what to expect?"

"I'd rather be surprised."

"Then tell me something. Would you have used that pitchfork?"

She considered, letting the question hang. "I guess neither of us will know the answer to that."

"I'd lay odds you would have. A hell of a picture you made, darling. More than worth a prick on the arm to see it."

"You're going to have a scar, Slater. You're lucky it was your arm and not your pretty face."

"He was aiming for my back," Gabe reminded her. "I didn't thank you for the warning."

"I didn't give you one."

"Sure you did. Your face was as good as a shout." He slipped a hand into his pocket and pulled out a worn deck of cards. Casually he began a riffling shuffle. "Do you play poker?"

Confused, she scowled at him. "I don't as a rule, but I know the game."

"If you take it up, never bluff. You'd lose more than your shirt."

"Have you? Lost more than your shirt?"

"More times than I care to remember." Out of habit, he began to deal two hands of stud, faces up. "Would you bet on your queen?"

Kelsey moved her shoulders. "I suppose."

He flipped up the next cards. "After a while, if you're smart, you don't risk what you can't afford to lose. I've got plenty of shirts. Your queen's still high."

"So it is." For some absurd reason, she was enjoying the game. On the third card, her spade queen still reigned. And on the fourth. "Still mine. Is it the betting or the horses that interests you?"

"I've got more than one interest."

"Including Naomi?"

"Including Naomi." He turned over the last card, smiled easily. "A pair of fives," he mused. "Looks like they usurp your queen."

Her mouth moved into what was very close to a pout. "It's a shame to lose to such pathetic cards."

"No cards are pathetic if they win." He took her hand, amused when the fingers went rigid. "An old southern tradition. Ma'am." He brought her hand to his lips, watching her. "I owe you for Lipsky. Payment's your choice."

It had been a long time since she'd felt this quickening in the blood. Since it couldn't be ignored, it would have to be fought. "Don't you think it's in questionable taste for you to make a move on me in the kitchen?"

Christ, he loved the way she could come up with those prim little phrases and deliver them in that husky voice. "Darling, this isn't even close to a move." Keeping her hand firmly in his, he turned it palm up. "Lady hands," he murmured. "Teacup hands. I've always had a real weakness for long narrow hands with soft skin."

He pressed his lips to the center, lingering while her pulse bumped like a hammer under his thumb. "That," he said, curling her fingers closed as if to ensure she kept the imprint of his lips there, "was a move. As far as taste goes, yours suits me. You'll probably want to keep that in mind."

He released her hand, scooped up his cards, and rose. "I'll see you in the morning. Unless you're having second thoughts."

Dignity, she reminded herself, was as important as pride. "I'm not having any thoughts at all, Slater, that involve you."

"Sure you are." He leaned down until they were face-to-face. "I warned you not to bluff, Kelsey. You lose."

He left her steaming over cold coffee. It was a damn shame, he thought, that he couldn't indulge himself in a few afternoon fantasies. But he had work to do.


As soon as he returned to Longshot, Gabe sought out Jamison. The trainer had been Cunningham's man, but when Gabe took over the farm, it hadn't taken much to induce Jamison to stay.

His loyalties had always been more with the horses than with the owner.

He was a big-bellied man who liked his food and his beer. Though he'd trained generations of horses that had finished in the money, no one but his staunchest friends would have considered him in Moses Whitetree's league.

He'd come from the county of Kerry as a babe in his mother's arms. His earliest memories were of the shedrow, the smell of the horses his father had groomed.

Jamison had lived his entire life in the shadow of the Thoroughbred. Now, at sixty-two, he sometimes dreamed of owning his own small farm and one champion, just one to carry him comfortably into retirement.

"Well, Gabe." He set aside his condition book and rose as Gabe walked in. "I shipped Honest Abe to Santa Anita, and Reliance to Pimlico. Missed the first post." He smiled wanly. "But I heard you'd had a spot of trouble and thought you'd want to see me before I headed to the track."

"How many times have you caught Lipsky drinking on the job?"

No prevaricating or how was your day with the likes of Gabriel Slater, Jamison thought. He'd known the boy for some twenty years, and had yet to fully understand him. "Twice before. I gave him a warning and told him he'd be cut loose if it happened again. He's a good hand. A weakness for gin, it's true, but he's worked on this farm for a decade." He glanced at the bandage on Gabe's arm and sighed. "I swear on my mother's heart I'd no notion the man would try to stick you."

"Drunks are unreliable, Jamie. You know my feelings about that."

"I do indeed." Jamison folded his hands over his belly. He should be at the track, not here, smoothing feathers. "And maybe I understand why you've no tolerance for that particular weakness. Still, the lads are my province, aren't they? And I followed my own judgment."

"Your judgment was faulty."

"It was."

"A hand drinks on the job, from you down to the lowest stableboy, he's gone. No more warnings, Jamie. No exceptions."

Irritation might have flickered in his eyes, but Jamison nodded. "You're holding the bat, Gabe."

68

Satisfied, Gabe picked up the condition book himself, skimming pages. "I'll be spending more time around the barn and the backstretch," he said. "I don't want you to feel I'm breathing down your neck."

"It's your barn," Jamie returned, his voice stiffening. "Your backstretch."

"Yes, it is. And it was very clear to me today that the men don't consider me an integral part of this operation. That's my fault." He set the book down again. "The first couple of years after the farm changed hands I was involved with building the house and shoehorning my way into the tight little club of owners. Since then I've let most of the day-to-day business stay in your hands and played owner. Now I'm going to get down to work. You're my trainer, Jamie, and as far as the horses go, I'll accept what advice you give me. But I'm back in the game now. I don't intend to lose."

It would pass, Jamison decided. Owners rarely concerned themselves with the real work for long. All they wanted was their spot in the paddock and the purse. "You know your way around a shedrow as well as anyone."

"It's been a long time since I picked up a pitchfork." Gabe smiled as the image of Kelsey brandishing one like a spear flashed into his mind. He looked at the big-faced clock Jamison had nailed to the wall of his office. "We can make it to Pimlico by three. Who'd you send with the filly?"

"Carstairs. Torky's up on her, Lynette's groom."

"Let's go see what kind of team they make."


SINCE SHE WAS LEFT TO HER own devices, Kelsey changed her shoes for boots and headed out. She didn't go toward the stables, aware that she would just be in the way, or stared at as if she were an oddity. Instead she walked toward the soft roll of hills where the horses were at grass.

The quiet, the undeniable peace, were a welcome change from

the frantic morning. Even so, she had to fight a restlessness that urged her to keep walking, keep moving, until she found what was over the next rise.

How could she have walked here as a child and remember nothing? It frustrated her to think that the first three years of her life were a virtual blank. It wouldn't matter in most cases, but her destiny had been skewed in those early years. She wanted them back, wanted to decide for herself what was right, what was wrong.

She stopped by a tidy white fence, leaning on it while a trio of mares began an impromptu race, their babies skipping after them. Another mother stood patiently, cropping grass while her foal suckled.

It was almost too perfect, Kelsey thought. A postcard that was just slightly too clear, too bright for reality. Yet she found herself smiling at the foal, admiring the impossibly delicate legs, the tilt of the somehow elegant head. What would he do, she wondered, if she climbed the fence and tried to pet him?

"Spectacular, aren't they?" Naomi joined her at the fence. The breeze ruffled the hair she'd cut to chin length for convenience more than fashion. "I never get tired of watching them. Spring after spring, year after year. It's soothing, the routine of it. And exciting, the possibility of it."

"They're beautiful. Sedate somehow. It's hard to imagine them streaking down a racetrack."

"They're athletes, bred for speed. You'll see that for yourself tomorrow." Naomi tossed back her hair, then impatient with it, pulled a soft cap out of her jacket pocket and put it on. "The one there, nursing? He's five days old."

"Five?" Surprised, Kelsey turned back, studying the mother and her baby more closely. The foal was sleek and healthy and appeared wise to the ways of the paddock. "That doesn't seem possible."

"They grow quickly. In three years he'll be prime. It starts here, or more accurately in the breeding shed, then goes to that final blur of color at the wire. He'll be fifteen, sixteen hands, perhaps twelve hundred pounds, and he'll race the oval with a man on his back. It's a beautiful thing to watch."

"But not easy," Kelsey commented. "It can't be easy to take something so delicate and turn it into a competitor."

"No." Naomi smiled then. Her daughter already understood. That, she supposed, was in the blood. "It's work and dedication and quite often disappointment. But it's worth it. Every time." She angled her hat so the brim shaded her eyes. "I'm sorry I left you so long. The farrier likes to talk. He was a friend of my father's. He does the work for me here rather than at the track because of old ties."

"It's all right. I don't expect you to entertain me."

"What do you expect?"

"Nothing. Yet."

Naomi looked back at the nursing mare, wishing it could be that easy to bond with her own child. "Are you still angry about this morning?"

"Angry's the wrong word." Kelsey turned away from the fence so she could study her mother's profile. "Baffled is better. Everyone just stood there."

"You didn't." With a grin, Naomi shook her head. "I thought you were going to run that drunken fool through. I envy you that, Kelsey, that knee-jerk reaction that comes from a lack of fear, or a surplus of honor. I froze. I have too much fear and not nearly enough honor left. A lifetime ago, I wouldn't have hesitated either."

She braced herself and shifted to face her daughter. "You're wondering why the police weren't called. Gabe did that for me. He may or may not have handled it differently on his own place. But here ... well, he would have known I'd be reluctant to talk to the police again. Ever again."

"It's none of my business."

Naomi closed her eyes. The simple fact they both had to face was that it was all Kelsey's business now. "I wasn't afraid when they came to arrest me. I was so arrogantly sure that they would end up looking

71

like fools, and I a heroine. I wasn't afraid when I sat in the interrogation room with its long mirror, gray walls, the hard chair designed to make you squirm." She opened her eyes again. "I didn't squirm. Not at first. I was a Chadwick. But the fear creeps up on you, inch by crafty inch. You can beat it back. Not away, but back. Before I left that horrible room with the mirror and the gray walls, I was afraid."

She took a steadying breath, reminded herself she was free of that. Free of it, but for the memories. "Through the trial, the headlines, the stares, I was afraid. But I didn't want to show it. I hated the idea of everyone knowing I was terrified. Then they tell you to stand up, so the jury of your peers can deliver the verdict. Your verdict. You can't beat it back then. It has a choke hold on you and you can't breathe. You might stand there, pretending to be calm, pretending to be confident because you know they're watching you. Every eye is on you. But inside, you're jelly. When they say 'guilty,' it's almost anticlimactic."

She drew another deep breath. "So you see, I'm very reluctant to talk to the police again." She said nothing for a moment, expected no response. "Do you know, we used to come here when you were little? I'd sit you up on the fence. You always loved visiting the foals."

"I'm sorry." And she was, suddenly, deeply sorry. "I don't remember."

"It doesn't matter. See the one there sunning himself? The black? He's a champion. I knew it when he was born. He might prove himself to be one of the best to come out of Three Willows."

Kelsey studied the foal more closely. He was charming, certainly, but she didn't see anything to separate him from the other young in the pasture. "How can you tell?"

"It's in the eyes. Mine and his. We just know."

She leaned on the fence, looking out over the fields with her daughter. And was, for a moment, nearly content.

*

Late that night when the house was quiet and the wind tapped seductively at the windows, Naomi curled her body to Moses. She liked it best when he came to her bed. It had more of a sense of permanence than when she crept up to his rooms above the trainer's shed.

Not that she didn't enjoy the thrill of doing just that. The first time, their first time, she'd walked into his room, surprising him as he sat in his underwear nursing a beer and poring over paperwork.

He'd been a tough seduction, she recalled, stroking a hand along the firm skin of his chest. But his eyes had given him away. He'd wanted her, just as he'd always wanted her. It had just taken her sixteen years to realize she wanted him, too.

"I love you, Moses."

It always jolted him to hear her say it. He supposed it always would. He laid his hand over hers, over his heart. "I love you, Naomi. How else could you have talked me into coming up here with your daughter down the hall?"

She laughed, shifting her head so that she could nibble on his neck. "Kelsey's an adult. I doubt she'd be traumatized even if she knew I had you in bed." She rolled over, straddling him. "And I do have you, Moses."

"It's hard to argue with that since all the blood just drained from my head and into my lap." In an old habit he skimmed his hands up her slim torso to cup her breasts. "You get more beautiful every day, Naomi. Every year."

"That's because your eyes get older."

"Not when they look at you."

Her heart simply melted. "Christ, you destroy me when you get sentimental. I look at Kelsey and see how much I've changed. It's wonderful to see her, to have her close even for a little while." She laughed, shaking her hair back. "And I'm still vain enough to look away from her and into the mirror and see every goddamned line."

"I'm crazy about every goddamned line."

"Being beautiful used to be so important to me. It was like a mission—no, like a duty. Then for so many years it didn't mean anything. Until you." She smiled, bending down to brush his lips with hers. "And now you tell me you like wrinkles."

Moses cupped a hand behind her head, drawing her more firmly to him. As she flowed into the kiss, he shifted her, raising her hips, lowering them so that he slid deep into her. He watched her arch back, thrilling to her quick, throaty moan. He set the rhythm slow, holding her to his pace, drawing the pleasure out for both of them.

FROM THE HALLWAY OUTSIDE her room, Kelsey heard the muffled sounds of lovemaking, the creak of the old mattress, the breathy moans and murmurs. She stood, the cup of tea she'd gone down to brew in one hand, a book in the other, flustered into immobility.

Not once had she ever heard her father and Candace in the night. She assumed they were both too restrained and polite to make noisy love. There was certainly nothing restrained or polite about the sounds only partially smothered by the closed door down the hall.

Nor, she reminded herself, was it polite to stand out here listening. She fumbled with the knob, spilling tea in her rush to get inside.

Her mother, she thought, barraged by dozens of conflicting emotions. And Gabe Slater, she assumed. The emotions his presence behind that door conjured up were best not explored.

The moment she had her own door safely closed, she leaned back against it. Part of her wanted to laugh at the absurdity of it. A grown woman shocked because another grown woman, who happened to be her mother, had an active sex life.

But she wasn't very amused at the moment, at the situation or her own reaction to it. No longer wanting either, she set the tea and book aside. The dark, still sleeping garden beneath her window was silvered with moonlight. Romantic, she thought, laying her brow against the glass. Mysterious. As so much of Three Willows was.

She didn't want romance. She didn't want mystery. At least, she didn't want to want them. She was here because it was important to learn about the half of her parentage that had been taken away from her.

Turning from the window she went back to bed. But she didn't sleep until long after she heard the door down the hall open and close, and the sound of quiet footsteps moving past her room toward the stairs.

# Chapter Six

THE TRACK, AT DAWN. IT WAS A DIFFERENT WORLD FROM THE one Kelsey had expected. Racing to her meant more than speed. It meant gambling and gamblers, fat cigars and bad suits, the smell of stale beer and losers' sweat.

The drunken groom Gabe had fired the day before fit her image of the world she'd imagined much more cozily than the tranquil, somehow mystical reality of the dawn horse.

The track was cloaked in mist when she arrived with Naomi. The horses had left even earlier, to be off-loaded, saddled, and prepped for their workouts. It was quiet, almost serene. Voices were muffled by the fog, and people moved in and out of the trailing mist like ghosts. Men leaned against the sagging rail around the oval, sipping from steaming paper cups.

"They're clockers," Naomi told her. "Speedboys. Some work for the track or *Daily Racing Form*. They'll be here for hours, timing the horses, handicapping them." She smiled. "Chasing speed. I guess that's what we all do. I thought you'd like to see it from this angle first."

"It's ... well, it's beautiful, isn't it? The fog, the trees slipping through it, the all-but-empty grandstands. It's not what I pictured." She turned to the woman beside her, the slim, lovely blonde in denim jacket and jeans. "Nothing seems to be."

"Most people see only one aspect of racing. Two minutes around the oval, over and done in a flash. Thrilling, certainly. Sometimes terrifying. Triumphant or tragic. Often a man or woman is judged the same way. By one aspect, or one act." There was no bitterness in her voice now, but simple acceptance. "I'll take you around to the shedrow. That's where the real action is."

And the real characters, Kelsey discovered. Aging jockeys who'd failed at the post or put on weight hustled for the forty dollars they'd earn per ride as exercise boys. Others, hardly more than children, with an eager look in the eye, loitered, hoping for their chance. Horses were discussed, strategies outlined. A groom in a tweed hat gently walked a crippled horse, singing to it in a soothing monotone.

There was no particular excitement, or anticipation. Just routine, one she realized went on day after day while most people slept or nodded over their first cup of coffee.

She spotted a man in a pale blue suit and shiny boots in earnest conversation with a placid-eyed man in a tattered cardigan. Now and again the man in the suit would punctuate his words with a jab of a pudgy finger. A flashy diamond ring in the shape of a horseshoe winked with every move.

"Bill Cunningham," Naomi said, noting who had captured Kelsey's attention.

"Cunningham?" Kelsey frowned, and flipped through her memory. "Isn't that the name I heard that groom Gabe fired yesterday mention?"

"Longshot used to be Cunningham Farm. Bill inherited it, oh, about twenty-five years ago, I guess." The disdain in her voice leaked through. "He was doing a first-class job of running it into the ground when he lost it to Gabe. Now he has an interest in several horses, owns one or two mediocre ones outright. He lives in

Maryland. The trainer's Carmine, works for Bill and several other owners. Right now Carmine's listening to Bill's instructions, his pontificating, and he's agreeing with everything. Then Carmine will do as he pleases because he knows Bill's an ass. Oops." She let out a sigh. "He spotted us. I'll apologize ahead of time."

"Naomi." In a strutting stride that showed off his boots, Cunningham closed in on them. His eyes glittered like polished marbles as he took Naomi's hands. "A beautiful sight on a gloomy morning."

"Bill." The years had given Naomi a high tolerance for fools, and she offered her cheek. "We don't often see you at workouts."

"Got me a new horse. Claiming race at Hialeah. She took the win as the rider pleased. I was just telling Carmine how she should be worked today. Don't want her rated."

"Of course not," Naomi said sweetly. "Bill, this is my daughter, Kelsey."

"Daughter?" He puffed out his cheeks in feigned surprise. Like everyone else in the area, he already knew about Kelsey. "You must mean sister. Glad to meet you, dearie." He slapped a hand to Kelsey's and pumped vigorously. "Going to follow in your ma's bootsteps, are you?"

"I'm just here to watch."

"Well, there's plenty to see. We'll have her hooked by dusk," he added with a wink to Naomi. "You check with me before you make any bets this afternoon, honey. I'll show you how it's done."

"Thank you."

"Nothing's too good for Naomi's little girl. You know, if I hadn't shied at the gate, I might be your papa. You take care now."

"In a pig's eye," Naomi muttered under her breath as Bill strutted away to harass his trainer. "He likes to think we were an item when the closest we came was me not quite avoiding one sloppy kiss."

"I appreciate your taste. What the hell was he saying about his horse?"

"Oh." Naomi set her hands on her hips and enjoyed a good laugh. "Bill likes to toss the lingo around, thinks it fools people into believing he knows something. Let's see . . . in plain English. He picked up the filly in a claiming race, meaning the owners had put it up for sale. The horse won easily, and Bill met the asking price. He feels the horse shouldn't be rated, or slowed, during the workout." She frowned at his back. "He's the type who pays a jockey extra for every hit of the stick. If a horse isn't whipped over the finish line, Bill feels cheated."

"I'm surprised you were so polite."

"It doesn't cost me anything." She shrugged. "And I know what it is to be an outcast. Come on, Moses should have a rider up by now."

They moved through the paddock area where exercise boys were being given a leg up onto their mounts. With little between them, Kelsey noted. The saddle was so tiny, hardly more than a slip of leather. The boys, as they were called regardless of sex, stood in the high stirrups while mounted trainers walked beside or behind them toward the track.

"That's one of ours." Naomi pointed to a trotting bay. "Virginia's Pride. If you can't resist betting today, you might want to put a couple of dollars on him. He's an amazing athlete, and he likes this particular track."

"Do you bet?"

"Mmmm." Naomi's eyes were on Moses, who rode a half-length behind the bay. "I've always hated to refuse a gamble. Let's watch him run."

There were other horses on the track. The mist was lifting now, and they cut through it like bullets through mesh, exploding through it, shredding it. Kelsey's breath caught at the sight of it, the sounds of it. Huge bodies on thin legs, spewing up dirt, necks straining forward with their tiny riders bent low. Her heartbeat picked up the pulse of the muffled thunder of hooves.

"There." Excitement lifted her voice as she pointed. "That's your horse."

"Yes, that's ours. The track's fast today, but I imagine Moses told the boy to keep him just under two minutes."

"How would the rider know?"

"He has a clock in his head." Gabe's voice came from behind her. Though Kelsey started, she didn't take her eyes off the horse rocketing around the track. "He looks good, Naomi."

"He'll look even better by Derby time." Her eyes narrowed. "That one's yours, isn't he?"

"Double or Nothing." Gabe leaned on the rail as his horse sped past. "He'll look better by May, too."

Kelsey didn't see how. Both horses looked magnificent now, eating up the track, tossing pieces of it toward the sky. They were airborne, those terrifyingly delicate legs lifting off the earth like wings.

She could have stayed there for hours, watching horse after horse, lap after lap. True, it took only a minute or two, and the clockers stood with their stopwatches, the trainers with theirs, but it was timeless to her. Like a lovely animated painting in a worn frame.

"Picked your favorite yet?" Gabe asked her.

"No." She didn't look at him, didn't want him or the memory of what she'd heard in the night to spoil the mood. "I'm not much of a gambler."

"Then I don't suppose you'd like to bet that you'll hit the windows before the afternoon's over."

She shrugged, then found she couldn't resist. "Bill Cunningham offered to give me some tips."

"Cunningham?" Gabe let out a roar of laughter. "Then I hope you've got deep pockets, darling." He leaned against the fence. He considered taking out a cigar, but decided it would spoil his enjoyment of Kelsey's scent. Soft and subtle it was, the kind that crept into a man's senses and lingered long after the woman had slipped away.

"Morning's the best time," Naomi murmured, shading her eyes

as the sun broke through the thinning mist and dazzled. "Clean slate."

"Possibilities." Gabe looked down at Kelsey. "It's all about possibilities."

Later, they walked back to the shedrow. Horses steamed in the cool air as they were unsaddled and walked. Legs were checked for strains, sprains, and bruises. A roan's hooves were oiled. A groom posed another, crouching down, searching for injury. A farrier with leather apron and battered toolbox hammered a shoe.

"Like a painting, isn't it?" Gabe asked, as if he'd plucked the image from Kelsey's brain.

"Yes, it is."

"Everything you see here would have been true a hundred years ago, five hundred. Thoroughbreds' legs can go anytime, so we obsess about them. Look there. Where's the trainer looking?"

She turned to watch a horse being led in, the trainer behind. "At the horse's feet."

"And he'll keep his eyes there." He nodded in another direction. "They were probably around a thousand years ago."

A man in a racing cap dogged Moses at the heels. He was talking fast, puffing to keep up. "Who is he?"

"Jockey agent. They hustle from barn to barn trying to convince everyone they represent the next Willie Shoemaker." Casually, he tucked Naomi's hair behind her ear. "Can I get you some coffee?"

"I'd love some. Kelsey?"

"Sure. Thanks. Is it all right if I get a closer look at your horse while he's being walked?"

"Go ahead."

Naomi settled down on an upturned bucket. The morning's work was nearly done. And the waiting would start. She'd gotten very good at waiting. There was a pleasure in it now, watching her daughter circle with the hot walker. Asking questions, Naomi imagined. The child had always been full of questions. But never aloof, as she was now.

For a moment that morning, as they stood in the mist watching the first horses round the practice track, she'd felt something relax between them. Then the stiffness had come back. Subtle, but then there were so many subtleties to her daughter. So many contrasts.

Kelsey laughed. It was the first time Naomi had heard the sound, easy, without reservations.

"She's enjoying herself," Gabe commented as he passed Naomi a cup of coffee.

"I know. It's good to see it. I'm sitting here telling myself that it won't always be so awkward between us." She eased her dry throat with the hot, sweetened coffee. "I just want to touch her. To hold her, just once. And I can't. She might let me, out of pity. That would be worse than rejection."

"She's here." Gently he ran a hand down her hair, over her shoulder. "She doesn't strike me as the type to be here if she didn't want to be."

"I don't expect her to love me again. But I do want her to let me love her." She reached for the hand on her shoulder, covered it with her own.

Kelsey tried to ignore the intimacy of the pose when she walked back to them. It was their business, she reminded herself. She kept a smile on her face and reached out for the coffee Gabe offered. "Thanks. I've just been given the winner in every race today. I should leave here, I'm told, flush."

"Jimmy's always got a tip," Naomi said. "And they're right as often as they're wrong."

"Oh, but these are sure things." Kelsey grinned as she lifted her cup. "He swore he'd never give Miss Naomi's daughter anything but a cinch tip. I'm supposed to bet on Necromancer in the first because the field's slow and he's generous and should win laughing." She arched a brow. "Did I get that right?"

"No one would guess it's your first day," Gabe said soberly.

"Oh, I'm a quick study." She glanced around. The pace was definitely slowing down, she noted. "What happens now?"

"We wait." Naomi rose, stretched. "Come on. I'll buy us some doughnuts to go with this coffee."


WAITING, IT SEEMED, WAS A way of life around the track. By ten the workday was over for the horses not scheduled to race. Trailers pulled in and pulled out. The track was groomed.

By noon, the grandstands began to fill. The glassed-in restaurant behind them served lunch, catering to those who preferred their racing experience away from the noise and smells of the masses.

In the shedrow, horses were prepped once again. Swollen legs were iced down in buckets. According to personal strategy, some were kept on edge, others soothed like babies. Jockeys donned their silks.

Now the anticipation was there. The excitement that had been missing from the mist-coated morning. Horses pranced, fidgeted, athletes eager to run. Some calmed when their jockeys were tossed onto their backs; others pawed and quivered.

From the paddock area they walked toward the track, single file, some led by grooms, some unaccompanied.

Now the grandstands buzzed, newcomers sprinkled among regulars. All of them hoping today would be their day. The post parade, the foundation of the dozens of racing rituals, began with the horses stepping onto the track. At the bugler's call they circled it, in order of post position. Those eager to bet studied racing forms, horses, jockeys, hoping to pick a winner.

If a horse was sweating, he might be nervous. Advantage or disadvantage? Each player had his own opinion. Bandaged forelegs. Could be trouble. Ah, that one hauling at his bit. Might be bad-tempered today. Or he might be fast.

That one *looks* like a winner.

At the finish line, barely five minutes after it had begun, the parade dissolved like colorful confetti tossed in the air.

It didn't matter to Kelsey. There was too much to see. Odd, the track wasn't really flat at all. It was wide, textured with furrows and air pockets, a circular mile of speed and dreams.

She could all but smell the dreams as she stood at the rail. From the jockeys, from the grandstands. Some were fresh and floral, others stale, powdered dry with dust. And she understood, standing there, what a powerful drug it was to want to win.

"I think I'll take that first tip."

Naomi laughed. She had been expecting it. "Take her up, will you, Gabe? Nobody should face their first window alone."

"I'm sure I can handle it," Kelsey said when Gabe took her hand.

"Everybody thinks that." He wound his way up, inside, where lines were already forming at the windows. "Let me give you a quick lesson on playing the horses. Have you figured out how much cash you'd play?"

She frowned, annoyed. "About a hundred."

"Double it. Whatever you figure you'll play, double it. Then consider it gone. Now, you've got your racing form."

"Yeah, I got it." She didn't understand it, but she had it.

"Normally, you'd need about four hours in a quiet place to study it, reviewing the races in order, eliminating horses, ranking others. Best to whittle it down to two or three. No binoculars, huh?"

"No, I didn't think—"

"Never mind, you can borrow mine." He eased her into a line, draped an arm companionably over her shoulder. He didn't smile. He wanted to, but he didn't. She was listening to him as a prized student would to a veteran teacher. "Now you want to forget betting the doubles or the exactas, any of the combinations. And you want to bet to win."

"Of course I do."

"That's right, aggressive betting—it's its own reward. Betting to show is for wimps." He had the satisfaction of seeing the man in the line beside him wince and curl his shoulders. "Did you check the odds board?"

"No," she said, feeling like a fool.

"Your horse is at four to one. That's fine. Betting favorites is for cowards. Too bad you told me you weren't much of a gambler or I wouldn't have let you eat or drink before betting."

"What?"

"Never eat or drink before you pick a winner, Kelsey."

Her eyes narrowed. "You're making this up."

"Nope. It's all gospel." Now he grinned. "And it's all bullshit. Bet to play because it's fun. Close your eyes and pick a number. Horses are athletes, not machines. You can't figure them."

"Thanks a lot." Amused now, she stepped up to the window. "Ten dollars on Necromancer." She shot a look at Gabe. "To win."

With his arm still around her shoulder, Gabe reached for his wallet. "Fifty on number three. To win."

Clutching her own ticket, she frowned. "Who's number three?"

"Couldn't say." He slipped the ticket into his pocket.

"You just bet a number, just a number?"

"A hunch. Want to make a side bet on who comes in first? Your tip or my hunch?"

"Another ten," she shot back.

"And you said you weren't much of a gambler."

He got her back to the rail just as the horses entered the starting gate. Foolish it might have been, but her heart was thudding, her palms damp. At the clang of the bell she strained forward, dazzled by the blur of color.

No misty workout now, but a crowd of muscled bodies fighting for position, their riders a burr on their backs. In seconds they reached full stride, with front-runners hugging the rail. The sound was overwhelming, thunder in front, roaring in back. Then they were at the turn.

"Number three's got it," Gabe said in her ear.

Kelsey shook him off. "They've barely started."

She could hear jockeys screaming, threats or encouragement, while their whips flashed. Down the stretch, the wire in sight, and Kelsey had forgotten the bet entirely. Every emotion was caught up

85

in the race itself, the showmanship of it, the drama of speed. She saw a horse coming from behind, straining, digging in. Hardly aware of the decision, she began to root for him, thrilled by that flash of courage and heart.

He nipped the leader on the outside and took the wire by half a length.

"Oh, did you see him!" She threw her head back and laughed. "He was beautiful."

Gabe hadn't seen the finish, but he'd seen her. The polite mask had melted away with excitement, revealing the passion and energy of the woman beneath. He wanted that woman more than he'd ever wanted a winning hand.

Lips pursed, Naomi considered the look in Gabe's eyes. That was something she'd have to think about. "Your horse finished fifth," she told Kelsey.

"It doesn't matter." Kelsey drew a deep breath. She could still smell the glamour. "It was worth it. Did you see how he came up like that? It was almost out of nowhere."

"Number three," Gabe said, and waited until her eyes met his. "My hunch paid off."

"That was number three?" She turned toward the winner's circle, torn between annoyance at losing to him, and her enjoyment of watching the horse win. "This must be your lucky day."

"You could be right."

"So." She slid her eyes up to his and smiled. "Who do you like in the next race?"

SOMETIME DURING THE afternoon she devoured a hot dog and washed it down with a watered-down soft drink. She felt a surprising stab of pride, very personal, when Virginia's Pride dominated his field. It was so obvious, she thought, even to her untrained eye, that there wasn't another horse in the race to compare with him.

Another, less identifiable emotion pricked her when Gabe's horse crossed the wire first.

As dusk fell, the grandstands were littered with losing tickets, cigarette butts, and shattered hopes.

"Can I interest you two ladies in some dinner?"

"Oh." Distracted, Naomi buttoned up her jacket. She was already looking for Moses. "I'm going to be at least another hour here. Why don't you take Kelsey?"

Instinctively, Kelsey sidestepped. "I don't mind waiting for you."

"No, go ahead. Have fun. I'll see you at home in a couple of hours."

"Really, I—" But Naomi was already hurrying away. "I appreciate the offer, Gabe, but—"

"You're too well mannered to refuse." He took her arm.

"No, I'm not."

"Then you're too hungry. A single hot dog doesn't fuel all that energy. And I can help you count your winnings."

"I don't think that's going to strain anyone's math." In any case, she was hungry. She let him guide her through the parking lot to a bottle-green Jaguar. "Nice car."

"She's fast."

He was right. Kelsey leaned back and enjoyed the ride through the pearling twilight. She'd always liked to drive fast, top down, radio blasting. Wade had lectured her countless times as he'd stuck to the heart of the speed limit. Sensible, she thought now. Responsible.

But he'd never understood that now and again she had to cut loose, do something, anything, full out. He'd preached moderation, and she had agreed—except when she couldn't. An impulsive spending spree, a speeding ticket, a last-minute urge to fly to the Bahamas. Those quicksilver changes in her had been the cause of most of their domestic quarrels.

Small stuff, she'd always thought. Incorrectly, she realized now. What had her impulsive surprise visit to Atlanta gotten her?

Freedom, she reminded herself, and determinedly closed the book on it.

When she began to pay attention to the scenery again, she realized they were nearly at Bluemont. "I thought we were going to have dinner."

"We are. Do you like seafood?"

"Yes. Is there a restaurant out here?"

"One or two. But we're eating in. I called home earlier. How does grilled swordfish strike you?"

"That's fine." She straightened in her seat, listening to the alarm bells in her head. "How did you know I'd be coming to dinner?"

"I had a hunch." He cruised down the road, zipped through the iron gates and up the drive. "You can take a look at the house before we eat."

His gardener had been busy. Beds had been tidied for spring so perennials could flaunt their new growth. A few brave daffodils had already bloomed, their bright yellow heads nodding charmingly.

Funny, she'd never have picked Gabe as the daffodil type.

The front door was flanked by beveled glass panels etched in geometric designs. With the light inside glowing through them, they glinted like diamonds. She remembered now that his jockeys' silks had resembled diamonds as well. A dramatic red and white.

"How did you pick your colors, the silks?"

"A straight flush, diamonds, eight through king." He opened the door. "A hand of cards. I drew the ten and jack against the odds. People will tell you that's how I came into this place. Winning a hand of cards."

"Did you?"

"More or less."

She stepped inside into a tiled atrium, all open space, dizzying ceilings with arched skylights. The copper rail that circled the second floor followed a gently curving staircase. Huge terra-cotta pots hung suspended, spilling out greenery.

"Quite an entrance," she managed.

"I don't like to be closed in. I'll get you a drink."

"All right." She followed him through a wide arch into a living area. This too opened into another room through archways. Glass doors invited the night inside; lamps, already lit, softened it.

There was a fire crackling in a hearth of river stone. A table was set in front of it. For two, she noted. A white cloth, candles. Champagne chilled in a bucket beside it.

"Did you also have a hunch that Naomi wouldn't be joining us?"

"She usually goes into conference with Moses after a day at the track." He opened the bottle with a quick, celebrational *pop*. "Do you want to look around, or would you rather have dinner right away?"

"I'll look around, since I'm here." She accepted the glass, noting there was no matching flute by the second plate. "You're not celebrating?"

"Sure I am. I don't drink. Why don't we start upstairs and work down?"

He led her out, up the curving stairs. She counted four bed-rooms before they climbed a short flight into the master suite. This was a split-level affair, the bedroom three tiled steps above the sitting area. A stone fireplace would warm the foot of the lake-sized platform bed, and the skylight would invite a restless sleeper to watch the moon.

Like the rest of the house, it was a mix of the classic and the modern. A Chippendale table held an abstract bronze-and-copper sculpture. A Persian carpet glowed on the floor beneath a free-form coffee table of polished teak.

Meissen vases beside modern art. The art, the painting, drew her. Even from across the room, Kelsey recognized it as a work by the same artist who had done those in her mother's home.

So much passion, she thought as she studied the frenetic brush-strokes, the violent juxtaposition of primary colors. "Not a very restful piece for a bedroom."

"It seemed to belong here."

"N. C.," she murmured. "Did Naomi paint this?"

"Yes. Didn't you know she painted?"

"No, no one mentioned it. She's very talented. I know several art dealers who would be begging at her door."

"She wouldn't thank you for it. Her art's personal."

"All art's personal." She turned away from it. "Has she always painted?"

"No. You should ask her about it sometime. She'll tell you whatever you want to know."

"I'll have to decide what that is first." Sipping her champagne, she wandered the room. "I don't know what that dignified Cape Cod looked like, but I doubt it could have measured up to this." More at ease, she turned back. "Did you horrify the neighborhood by having it razed?"

"Appalled everyone within twenty miles."

"And enjoyed every minute of it."

"Damn right. What's the use of having a reputation if you can't live up to it?"

"And what is your reputation?"

"Slippery, darling, very slippery. Anyone would tell you that being alone with me in my bedroom's the first step to perdition."

"It's a long way from the first step to the last fall."

"Not as far as you might think."

With a shrug, she tossed back the rest of her drink. "Tell me about the card game."

"Over dinner." He held out a hand. "I'm a sucker for atmosphere, and a lot closer to that last fall than most."

Intrigued, she put her hand in his. "That doesn't sound very slippery to me, Slater."

"I'm just getting started."

Downstairs he refilled her glass. Some invisible servant had already set two silver-domed plates on the table, lit the candles, and switched on music. They sat down to Gershwin.

"The card game?"

"All right. How much do you know about poker?"

"I know what beats what. I think." She took a bite of the delicately grilled fish and closed her eyes. "This definitely beats the track cooking all to hell."

"I'll tell the cook you said so. Anyway, about five years ago I was in a game, a marathon. Big stakes, heavy hitters."

"Around here?"

"Not around here, here. In the dignified Cape Cod."

She narrowed her eyes. "Isn't gambling illegal in this state?"

"Call a cop. Do you want to hear this or not?"

"I do. So you were in a big, illegal poker game. Then what?"

"Cunningham was having a run of bad luck. Not just during the game, but for several months. His horses were breaking down. He hadn't had any finish in the money for more than a year. He had a pile of outstanding debts. He figured, like most do when they're on a downswing, that all he needed was one big score."

"Hence the poker game."

"Exactly. I had interest in a horse, and he'd been running well. So I was"—he smiled devilishly—"flush. I wanted a farm like this, always had. I went into the game thinking that if I didn't lose my stake I might finesse enough for another horse. Work my way up."

"Sounds sensible, in a skewed sort of way." Reckless was how it sounded, she thought. Admirably reckless. "Obviously you won more than a horse."

"I couldn't lose. It was one of those sweet moments when everything falls in your lap. If he had three of a kind, I had a full house. He had a straight, I had a flush. His trouble really started when he couldn't let it go. He was down about sixty, sixty-five."

"Hundred?"

Charmed, he took her hand, kissed it lavishly. "Thousand, darling. And he didn't have it to lose. Not cash, anyway. So he upped the stakes, wouldn't take no for an answer."

"And, of course, you tried your best to bring him to his senses."

"I told him he was making a mistake. He said he wasn't." Gabe moved his shoulders. "Who am I to argue? There were only four of us left by then. We'd been at it for about fifteen hours. This was going to be the last hand. Five thousand to open, no limit on raises."

"That was twenty thousand before you even got started?"

"And over a hundred and fifty by the time it got down to me and Cunningham."

Her fork stopped halfway to her mouth. "A hundred and fifty thousand dollars on one hand?"

"He thought he had a winner, kept bumping the pot. I had the last raise, bumped it another fifty myself. I thought it might put him out of his misery. But he matched it."

She lifted her glass and sipped slowly to wet her dry throat. She felt she could almost be there, sweaty-palmed and dry-mouthed with a small fortune riding on the turn of a card.

"That's a quarter of a million dollars."

He grinned. "You are a quick study. I felt sorry for him, but I'm not going to say I didn't relish the moment when I laid down that straight flush to his three kings. He didn't have the cash." Gabe tipped more champagne into her glass. "He barely had the assets. So we made a deal. You could say Cunningham bet the farm and lost it."

"You just kicked him out?"

Gabe inclined his head, studied her. "What would you have done?"

"I don't know," she said after a moment. "But I don't think I could have thrown the man out of his own house."

"Even after he'd gambled with money he didn't have?"

"Even then."

"So, you're a soft touch. We made a deal," Gabe said again, "that satisfied both of us. And, because I played against the odds, I got something I'd wanted my whole life."

"That's quite a story. I guess you met the unlucky Bill Cunningham at the track."

"No, at least not initially. I used to work for him."

"Here?" She set down her fork. "You used to work here?"

"I walked hots, shoveled manure, polished tack. For three years I was one of Cunningham's boys. He had a fine line back then. Of course, he never gave a good goddamn about the horses. They were just money to him. He cared a lot less about the people who took care of them. Our rooms were like little cells, cramped, dingy. He didn't believe in putting any of his capital into unnecessary improvements."

"I don't think it bothered you at all to take his house."

"I didn't lose any sleep over it. When I left here, I did some time at Three Willows. Now, that's a farm. Chadwick had the touch. So does your mother. When I left—I was about seventeen then—I figured I'd come back one day, money dripping out of my pockets, and buy myself one place or the other."

"And you did."

"In a manner of speaking."

"What did you do while you were away?"

"That's another story."

"Fair enough." Relaxed with food and wine, she propped her chin on her fist. "I bet you hated that Cape Cod."

"Every fucking inch of it."

Laughing, she leaned back again and picked up her glass. "I think I'm starting to like you. I hope you didn't make all that up."

"I didn't have to. Want dessert?"

"I can't." With a little moan, she pushed away from the table to wander the room. "When I first saw this house, I thought it looked arrogant and territorial. I think I was right." She closed her eyes for a moment. "My point of no return."

"What?"

"Nothing." She shook her head and walked closer to the windows. "It must be quite a feeling to look out any window and see so much of your own."

"What do you see out of yours?"

93

"A restaurant, a small shopping center with a terrible little boutique and a wonderful bakery. It's practically next door to the Metro and I thought I wanted convenience."

He put his hands on her shoulders, then turned her so that they were face-to-face. "But you don't."

"No." The quick tremble caught her by surprise when he skimmed his hand up the side of her neck.

"What then?"

"I haven't decided."

He framed her face, letting his fingers dip into her hair. "I have."

His mouth lowered to hers, soft at first, testing, hardly more than a nibble that gave them both the choice to step back. But she didn't, not with his taste still vibrating on her lips and the low, drugging ache of unexpected need churning.

She didn't step back, but forward, her arms winding recklessly around his neck, her mouth melding hotly with his.

So much to feel. She'd forgotten there was so much to feel. Or perhaps she'd never known. There was nothing civilized or tentative about this embrace. It was groping and wild, an explosion of sensation that mocked the gentle candlelight and soft music.

She stripped his mind clean. There was nothing left for him but naked sensation, the smell of her, the taste, which mixed together like some exotic drug. The feel of her straining against him, the sound of his quickened breathing as she dragged him greedily closer. The need for her, sharp and edgy as a knife, peeled away the layers of manners, behavior, and ethics he'd carefully crafted, and bared the reckless man beneath.

He needed to touch her. His hands streaked down, over, in a desperate race to possess. She arched under them, eager for more. Hurry, she wanted to beg him to hurry, not to let her think, not to let her reason.

Then he ran a hand over her face, combing her hair behind her ear. The image of him performing that same careless gesture for her mother only hours before flashed into her mind.

The horror, and the shame, were like two vicious, heavy blows. She shoved away, fighting for air. "Don't." She stumbled back when he reached for her. "Don't touch me." She could still taste him. Still want him. "How could you do this? How could I do this?"

"I want you." He had to fight every instinct in his body to keep from lunging forward and taking what had nearly been his. "You want me."

Because it was true, urgently true, she had no choice but to strike back. "I'm not a mare to be hobbled and serviced. And I didn't come here tonight so you could find out if the daughter takes after the mother."

To restrain them, Gabe stuck his hands in his pockets. "Clarify."

"I'm not excusing myself, but at least I have the decency to stop this before it goes any further. You have no decency at all." She shoved her tumbled hair back. Fury, fueled by an acid guilt, turned her voice into a whip. "Is this all just another game to you, Slater? Lure the daughter, wine and dine her, charm her into bed and see if she's as good as the mother? Did you place bets, calculate the odds?"

He took a moment before he answered. When he did, neither his face nor his voice revealed any of the clawing anger. "You think I'm sleeping with Naomi?"

"I know you are."

"I'm flattered."

"You're—What kind of a man are you?"

"You have no idea, Kelsey. None at all. I doubt very much you've come across my kind in that nice, comfortable little world of yours." He stepped forward, curling his hand around the back of her neck. It was a small, nasty way of paying her back. But he was feeling small, and he was feeling nasty.

However stiff she held her spine, her body began to tremble. "Take your hands off me."

"You like my hands on you," he said softly. "Right now you're afraid, excited, but afraid, and wondering what you would do if I

95

dragged you upstairs. Hell, why go to all that trouble when there's a floor right here?" His voice was smooth and cool as cream, but there was a light in his eyes, a dangerous burn. "What would you do, Kelsey, if I took you right here, right now?"

Fear clawed up her throat, shredding her voice. "I said take your hands off me."

He could read the terror on her face. It was clear as a scream even when he released her and stepped back. It didn't quite fade, nor did the feelings of disgust that simmered inside him.

"I'll apologize for that. Only for that." He studied her for a moment. The color he'd deliberately frightened out of her cheeks was coming back. "You're quick to judge, Kelsey. Since you've made up your mind, we won't waste time discussing fact or fantasy. I'll take you home."

# Chapter Seven

NAOMI WAS TYING THE BELT OF HER ROBE WHEN SHE HEARD the front door slam. Surprised by the angry sound, she hesitated before going out into the hall. Was it her place, she wondered, to question Kelsey after an evening out? She had no precedent. If she'd lived through those teenage years with Kelsey, through the late-night talks, the arguments and worries, through the triumphs and tragedies of adolescence, she'd know.

But she had no guideposts, only instincts. The sound of Kelsey's feet rushing up the stairs decided her.

She opened her own door, certain she could keep the whole experience very casual. No prying, just a quick how was your evening. One look at Kelsey's face erased all intentions.

"What happened?" Before either of them could think, she moved forward to take Kelsey's arms. "Are you all right?"

Still revving on temper, Kelsey went instantly on the attack. "How can you associate with him, much less . . . God, you all but asked me to spend the evening with him."

"Gabe?" Naomi's fingers tightened. She trusted Gabe implicitly, without question. But a small female dread curled in her gut. "What did he do?"

"He kissed me," Kelsey shot back. Her color flared at the ridiculously lame understatement of what had happened between them.

"Kissed you," Naomi repeated, while relief and amusement twined through her. "And that's it?"

"Don't you care?" Frustrated, Kelsey jerked back. "I'm telling you he kissed me. I kissed him back. We were groping at each other. And it wouldn't have stopped if I hadn't remembered."

Out of your depth, Naomi, she thought. If they couldn't deal as mother to daughter, perhaps they could begin as woman to woman. "Come in and sit down."

"I don't want to sit." But Kelsey followed Naomi into the bedroom.

"I do." Rearranging her thoughts, Naomi settled on the padded stool of her vanity table. "Kelsey, I know you might still be raw from your divorce. But you are divorced, and free to develop other relationships."

Kelsey stopped her restless pacing and gaped. "*I'm* free? This isn't about me. It's about you."

"Me?"

"What's wrong with you?" Now there was insult added to temper, insult that the woman who shared her blood could be so shallow. "Don't you have any pride?"

"Actually," Naomi said slowly, "I've often been told I have too much. But I don't see how that applies at the moment."

"I'm telling you that your lover wanted to sleep with me, and it doesn't apply?"

Naomi's mouth worked silently before she could get it around the words. "My lover?"

"God knows how you can let him touch you," Kelsey barreled on. "You've known him for years and you must see what he is. Oh, he's attractive, and he may be charming on the surface. But he has no scruples, no honor, no loyalties."

Naomi's eyes flashed, her jaw stiffened. "Who are you talking about?"

"Slater." On the edge, it was all Kelsey could do to keep from screaming. "Gabriel Slater. How many lovers do you have?"

"Just one." Naomi folded her hands and drew a deep breath. "And you think it's Gabe." After a moment's consideration, she began to smile. Then, to Kelsey's astonishment, she began to laugh. "I'm sorry. I'm sorry. I'm sure this isn't funny to you." Helpless, she pressed a hand to her stomach. "But it's wonderful, really. I'm so flattered."

Kelsey spoke through gritted teeth. "He said the same thing."

"Did he?" Chuckling, Naomi wiped a tear from her eye. "You mean you actually asked him if he was sleeping with me? God, Kelsey, he's in his thirties. I'm nearly fifty."

"What difference does that make?"

She couldn't stop it. Naomi's smile spread like a sunbeam. "Now I'm really flattered. Do you actually believe a gorgeous—God knows he's gorgeous—hot-blooded man like Gabe would be romantically interested in me?"

She studied Naomi as dispassionately as her mood allowed, taking in the classic features, the slim, elegant body in the simple white robe. "I didn't say anything about romance," Kelsey said flatly.

"Oh." Naomi nodded, struggling to compose herself. "Well, now. So you assume that Gabe and I are, what, engaged in a hot, sexual affair?" She pursed her lips. "I'm feeling younger all the time."

"Before you bother to deny it, I'll say two things." Head high, Kelsey looked down at her mother. "First, it's none of my business who you sleep with. You can have twenty lovers and it's none of my concern. Second, I heard you last night. In here, with him."

"Oh." Naomi blew out air. "That is awkward."

"Awkward?" The word all but exploded out of her mouth. "This is *awkward*?"

Realizing she was going to have to be very clear and precise, Naomi lifted a hand. "Let's handle your statements in order. First, despite what you think or have been told, I've never been promiscuous. You may not choose to believe me, but your father was my first lover. There was no one else until two years after I got out of prison. He's been my only lover since." She stood so they were eye to eye.

"If that's true, it's even worse. How can you not care that he would cheat on you this way?"

"No man would cheat on me more than once," Naomi said in a tone Kelsey not only believed, but understood. "It wasn't Gabe you heard in here with me last night, Kelsey. It was Moses."

She couldn't speak. It was impossible to ignore the truth when it was slapped so neatly across her face. Silently she sank to the bench herself. "Moses. Your trainer."

"Yes, Moses. My trainer. My friend, and my lover."

"But Gabe—he's always touching you."

"To risk a cliché, we're very good friends. Gabe is, excepting Moses, my closest friend. I'm sorry you misunderstood."

"Jesus." Kelsey squeezed her eyes shut as everything she'd said rushed back to humiliate her. "Oh, Jesus, no wonder he was so angry. The things I said."

Risking rejection, Naomi brushed a hand over Kelsey's hair. "I don't suppose you bothered to ask him?"

"No." Her own words came back to her, stinging like bullets. "No, I was so sure, and I was so ashamed that he'd made me forget myself, even for just a minute. I've never—with Wade it was always—It doesn't matter," she said quickly. "The point is, I jumped in with both feet and said some filthy things to him."

"You were in a difficult position. I'll call him and explain."

"No, I'll go over in the morning and apologize face-to-face."

"Hateful, isn't it? Apologizing?"

"Almost as bad as being wrong." It was always a chore to swallow pride. "I'm sorry."

"There's no need where I'm concerned. You've walked into a world filled with strangers, Kelsey. You trusted your instincts. Whatever you did tonight, you did because you have a strong moral code, a finely developed sense of right and wrong."

"You're making excuses for me."

"I'm your mother," Naomi said quietly. "Maybe we'll both get used to that in time. Go get some sleep. And if you don't want to face the lion in his den alone tomorrow, I'll go with you."

BUT SHE WENT ALONE. IT WAS a matter of self-respect. At first she thought she'd drive over, but that would be so quick. Despite lying restless most of the night, she had yet to come up with the exact words or tone she wanted to use.

She decided to ask for a mount, and clear both head and nerves with a ride from farm to farm.

She found Moses rubbing liniment over the throat of a roan gelding. Foolishly she found herself hesitating. How did she approach him now that she knew he was Naomi's lover?

For the moment she just stood back and watched him. His hands were gentle, darkly tanned, wide at the palm. At his wrist he wore a bracelet of hammered copper. There was nearly as much gray as black in his braid. He had a distinctive face, though no one would have called it handsome, with its prominent nose and weather-scored skin. His body was tough and wiry, with little of the lithe muscular grace of Gabe's.

"Hard to figure, isn't it?" There was a touch of amusement in Moses's voice. He didn't have to turn for Kelsey to deduce it would be reflected in his eyes. "A beautiful woman like her. Rich. Classy. And a half-breed runt like me." He set the liniment aside and reached for a bowl of watery gruel. "Can't blame you for being surprised. Surprises me all the time."

"I'm sorry?"

"Naomi figured she should let me know she told you about us."

Wincing, Kelsey rubbed a hand over her face. How much more embarrassing could it possibly get? "Mr. Whitetree."

"Moses, let's make it Moses, considering the situation. Come on, boy." Murmuring, he urged the gruel on the gelding. "Try a little now. Just a little at a time. I fell in love with her when I first came to work here as a groom. She'd have been about eighteen then. I'd never seen anything like her in all my life. Not that I expected her to look at me twice. Why should she?"

Kelsey watched him nurse the horse, saw the kindness, the strength, the simple sturdiness. "I think I can see why." Making the gesture, she stepped into the box until they were shoulder to shoulder. "What's wrong with him?"

"King Cole here's got laryngitis."

"Laryngitis? Horses get laryngitis? How can you tell?"

"See here?" Taking her hand, Moses guided it over the throat. "You can feel it's swollen."

"Yes, poor thing." She made soothing noises as she rubbed gently. "Is it serious?"

"Can be. If it's severe, the air passage gets blocked and he can choke."

"You mean die?" Alarmed, she pressed her cheek to the gelding's. "But it's just a sore throat."

"In you. In him it's different. But he's coming along, aren't you, fella? He can't take food yet, but gruel or some linseed tea."

Tea for a horse, Kelsey thought. "Shouldn't the vet see him?"

"Not unless it worsens. We keep him warm, use eucalyptus inhalations, smear camphor on his tongue three, four times a day. He's not coughing anymore, and that's a good sign."

"How much of the doctoring do you do yourself?"

"We only call Matt in when we can't handle it."

"I thought a trainer trained."

"A trainer does everything. Sometimes it seems the horses are the least of it. You spend a day with me sometime, you'll see."

"I'd like that."

It had been an offhand remark, nothing he'd expected her to pick up on. Thoughtful, he eyed her. "I start before dawn."

"I know. And you probably don't want me tagging along. But I was wondering if there was something I could do while I'm here. Muck out stables or clean tack. I wouldn't expect to be trusted with the horses, but I hate doing nothing."

Her mother's daughter, Moses mused. Well, they'd see. "There's always something to do around here. When do you want to start?"

"This afternoon, maybe tomorrow. There's something I have to do this morning." Her mood shifted downward at the thought. "I'd rather shovel manure than do it, but it can't be avoided."

"Come down when you're ready, then."

"I appreciate it. I wonder, is there a riding horse I could borrow this morning? I do know how to ride."

"You're Naomi's daughter. That means you know how to ride and you don't have to ask for permission to take a horse."

"I'd rather ask."

"We'll saddle up Justice, then," he decided. "He'd suit you."


THE ROAN GELDING LIKED TO run. He'd been retired for three years, but he had never accepted his lowered status as a riding mount. He was often used to pony a contender onto the track for the post parade, and though he preferred to run, he performed his duties with dignity.

He'd never been a champion, as Moses explained to Kelsey. But neither had he been common, and he had finished steadily in the money throughout his career.

She didn't care if he'd lost every race, not when he took her flying over the hills, his body running like an oiled engine beneath hers.

He responded eagerly to the slightest pressure of her knees, moving from churning trot to fluid gallop, as happy as she to have the morning and the rising fields stretched out before them.

This was a pleasure she realized she'd denied herself for too long. And one she wouldn't deny herself again, no matter how her muscles might ache later. Even when she left Three Willows, she'd find a way to indulge herself in this one delight.

Maybe she'd give up her apartment entirely, move out of town. There was no reason she couldn't buy a small place of her own, and a horse. She might have to have it stabled, of course, but that could be arranged. If she absorbed enough from Moses, she could even work at a stable.

She gulped in the cool wine of early spring, the smell of grass and young growing things. Why in the world did she ever think she had to stay in an office or gallery hour after hour when she could be outside, doing something for the sheer joy of it?

She shook back her hair and laughed as they sailed over a narrow creek and thundered up a rise.

Then she reined in, spotting the spread of buildings below.

Longshot. Leaning forward, she patted Justice's neck and studied the scene. The ride had done her a great deal of good, but it hadn't solved the essential problem. She still hadn't a clue how to approach Gabe.

"So, we'll play it by ear," she muttered, and clucked Justice into a dignified trot.

Gabe saw her come down the rise. He stayed where he was, by the fence watching a yearling respond to the longe. He wasn't any more calm than he'd been the evening before. Nor, he realized as she rode closer, so slim and straight and golden on the majestic Thoroughbred, did he want her any less.

He took another drag on his cigar, expelled smoke lazily. And waited.

As she dismounted and walked the gelding toward Gabe, Kelsey supposed she had been more miserable. But past miseries never seem as huge as current ones.

"You ride well," he commented. "An old trooper like this takes a steady hand."

"I usually have one. If you have a few minutes, I'd like to talk to you."

"Go ahead."

Why should he make it easy? she asked herself, and swallowed another lump of pride. "Privately. Please."

"Fine." He took the reins and signaled a groom. "Cool him off, Kip."

"Yes, sir."

Kelsey lengthened her stride to keep up as Gabe turned away from the stables. "You have a nice operation here. It all looks very similar to Three Willows."

"Want to talk shop?"

"No." She let the attempt at small talk wither and die. "I realize you're busy. I'll try not to take up much of your time." Then she closed her mouth and said nothing more until he slid open a glass door at the rear of the house.

It opened into the tropics. Lushly blooming plants tumbled from pots and basked in the sunlight that streamed through the glass roof. A tiled pool glinted in the center, oval-shaped and invitingly blue.

"It's beautiful." She trailed a finger over a flashy red hibiscus. "I guess we didn't get this far last night."

"Continuing the tour didn't seem appropriate." He sat on a striped lounge chair and stretched out his legs. "This is private."

She watched the smoke curl from the tip of his cigar toward the gently rotating fans suspended from the ceiling. "I came to apologize." Nothing, absolutely nothing tasted less palatable.

He merely arched a brow. "For?"

"My behavior last evening."

As if considering, he tapped out his cigar in a silver bucket of sand. "You demonstrated varied behavior last evening. Can you be more specific?"

She rose, helplessly, to the bait. "You're hateful, Slater. Cold, arrogant, and hateful."

"That's quite an apology, Kelsey."

"I did apologize. I came over here choking on it, but I apologized. You don't even have the decency to accept it."

"As you pointed out last night, I'm lacking in decency." Lazily, he crossed his ankles. "I'm to assume from this sudden turnabout that you confronted Naomi and she set you straight."

Her only defense was to angle her chin. "You could have denied it."

"Would you have believed me?"

"No." Infuriated all over again, she whirled away from him. "But you could have denied it. You have to be able to see what it felt like to believe what I believed and to find myself . . ."

"What?"

"Crawling all over you." She all but spat the words as she spun around. "I won't deny it. I jumped right into your arms. I didn't think—couldn't think. I'm not proud of it, but I won't pretend it was one-sided. I have needs, too, and urges, and—dammit, I'm not cold!"

He wasn't sure which surprised him most, the sudden vehemence of her last statement or the tears glittering in her eyes. "I'm the last one you'd have to convince of that. Why in hell would you have to convince yourself?"

Appalled, she fought back the tears. "That's not the point," she said. "The point is I made an enormous mistake. I said things to you that you didn't deserve and that I regret." She dragged both hands through her hair, then let them fall. "God, Gabe, I thought you'd been in her room the night before. I'd heard . . ."

"Moses?" he finished.

She shut her eyes, sighed. "The fool's always the last to know. I thought it was you. And the idea that you'd go from her to me— that I'd let you . . ." She trailed off again. "I'm sorry."

She looked so lovely, the sun gilding her hair, regret darkening her eyes. He nearly sighed himself. "You know, I really wanted to

106

stay pissed off at you. I figured it was going to be easy and, Christ knows, safer." He pushed out of the chair. "You look tired, Kelsey."

"I had a lousy night."

"Me too." He reached up to touch her cheek, but she stepped back.

"Don't. Okay? I feel like an idiot saying it. More than an idiot knowing it, but I'm in a vulnerable state right now. And you seem to set me off."

He bit back a groan. "I appreciate you sharing that with me, darling. It's sure to help me sleep at night. 'Don't touch me, Gabe, I might start crawling all over you again.'"

She had to smile. "Something like that. Why don't we start this whole business from the top?" She offered a hand. "Friends?"

He looked down at her hand, then back into her eyes. "I don't think so." Watching her, he edged closer.

"Listen ..." She could already feel the heat, moving up from her toes. "I don't want to get involved. It's lousy timing for me." Cautious, she took a step back.

"Too bad. I'm real pleased with the timing myself."

"I'm telling you—" She stepped back again, met empty air. Kelsey caught the grin in his eyes seconds before she hit the water. It was pleasantly cool, but no less of a shock. She surfaced, dragging wet hair out of her eyes. "You bastard."

"I didn't push you. Thought about it, but didn't." Helpfully, he offered a hand to haul her out.

Her eyes lit. She grasped it, tugged. She might as well have pulled at a redwood.

"Don't bluff, Kelsey." He simply released her hand and sent her under again. This time she took it philosophically and dragged herself over the side. Sat.

"Nice pool."

"I like it." He sat cross-legged beside her. "Come back sometime, take a real swim."

"I might just do that."

"It's almost better in the winter. You can feel smug watching the snow fall outside."

"I bet." Idly, she wrung out her hair, then flicked water in his face. "Gotcha."

He merely took her hand, pressed the wet palm to his lips, and watched her eyes go smoky. "Gotcha," he echoed.

She scrambled up while her heart flailed around in her chest. "I've got to get back."

"You're wet."

"It's warm enough out." She resisted, barely, the urge to retreat again when he unfolded his legs and rose. "A textbook spring day."

He wondered if she had any idea how desirable she was, flustered with nerves. "I'll drive you back."

"No, really. I want to ride. I'd almost forgotten how much I enjoy it. I want to take advantage of it while I'm here, and—" She pressed a hand to her jittery stomach. "Oh, God, I've got to stay away from you."

"Not a chance." He hooked a finger in the waistband of her jeans and jerked her an inch closer. "I want you, Kelsey. Sooner or later I'm going to have you."

She forced a breath in and out. "Maybe."

He grinned. "Place your bets." And released her. "I'll get you a jacket down at the stables."


SHE GOT OUT FAST. TEN MINUTES later she was galloping back toward Three Willows. Gabe waited until she'd disappeared over the first rise before he turned away.

"Fine-looking filly, that."

The voice was like a twisting knife in his side. A sneak attack, impossible to defend against. But he didn't startle easily. Gabe's face was a neutral mask as he looked at his father.

Not much change, he noted. Rich Slater still had style. Maybe it leaned toward snake-oil salesman, but it was style nonetheless.

He was a big man, broad through the shoulders, long through the arms. His natty gabardine suit was just a little snug around the chest. His shoes shone like mirrors, and his hair, glossily black, was trimmed under a snappy gray fedora.

He'd always been striking, and had used his looks—the stunning blue eyes, the quick smile—to charm the unwary. Nearly six years had passed since Gabe had seen him, but he knew what signs to look for.

The lines etched deep that no amount of pampering or praying could smooth out. The broken capillaries, the over-bright sparkle in the eye. Rich Slater was exactly as he'd been six years earlier and for most of his life. Drunk.

"What the fuck do you want?"

"Now, is that any way to greet your old man?" Rich laughed heartily and, as if Gabe had tossed out the red carpet, wrapped his arms around his son. There was the unmistakable scent of whiskey under the peppermint on his breath.

It was a combination that had always turned Gabe's stomach.

"I asked what you wanted."

"Just came by to see how you were doing, son." He slapped Gabe on the back before he leaned away. He didn't sway, didn't totter. Rich Slater could hold his drink, he liked to say.

Until the second bottle. And there was always a second bottle.

"You've done it this time, Gabe. Hit the jackpot. No more shooting craps in alleys for you, hey, son?"

Gabe took Rich by the arm and pulled him aside. "How much?"

Though his eyes flashed once, he feigned hurt. "Now, Gabe, can't a father come visit his own flesh and blood without you thinking I'm after a handout? I'm doing fine, I'll have you know. Built me up a stake out West. Been playing the horses, just like you." He laughed again, all the while judging and calculating the worth around him. "But I wouldn't like settling down your way. You know me, boy, got to keep footloose."

He took out a cigarette, snapped a gold-plated lighter he'd had monogrammed at the mall. "So, who was the sexy blonde? Always had an eye for the ladies." He winked. "And they always had an eye for you. Just like your old man."

Even the thought of it had Gabe's blood boiling. "How much do you want this time?"

"Now, I told you, not a dime." Not a dime, Rich thought as he looked toward the near paddock where the yearling was still being worked. A man could make a splash with a couple of horses like that. A real splash. No, he didn't want a dime. He wanted a great deal more.

"Fine horse, that. I recollect how you used to pay more attention to the horses at the track than the game."

And whenever he had, Gabe remembered, he'd been treated to the back of his father's big hand. "I don't have time to discuss my horses with you. I have work to do."

"When a man makes a score like you've done here, he doesn't need to work." Or to sweat, Rich thought bitterly. Or to hustle for petty cash. "But I'm not going to hold you up, no indeed. Thing is, I'm planning on being in the area awhile, looking up some old friends." He smiled as he blew out smoke. "Since I'm going to be in the neighborhood I wouldn't say no to spending a few days in that fancy house of yours. Have a nice visit."

"I don't want you in my house. I don't want you on my land."

Rich's easy smile dimmed. "Too good for me now, are you? Is that it? Got yourself all dolled up now and don't want to be reminded where you come from. You're an alley cat, Gabe." He jabbed a finger into his son's chest. "You always will be. Don't matter if you live in a fine house and fuck fancy women. You're still a stray. You forget who put a roof over your head, food in your belly."

"I haven't forgotten sleeping in doorways or going hungry because you'd gotten drunk and lost every penny my mother had slaved for." He didn't want to remember. He hated that the

110

memories dogged him like his own shadow. "I haven't forgotten sneaking out of some stinking room in the middle of the night because we didn't have the rent money. There's a lot I haven't forgotten. She died in a charity ward, coughing up blood. I haven't forgotten that."

"I did my best by your mother."

"Your best sucked. Now, how much is it going to cost me to make you disappear?"

"I need a place to stay." His nerves were taking over, bringing a whine to his voice. Unable to help himself, he reached for the flask in his back pocket. "Just for a few days."

"Not here. Nothing about you is going to touch this place."

"Christ Almighty." He took a long drink, then another. "I'll tell you straight; I've got some trouble. A little misunderstanding about a game in Chicago. I was working it with this other guy, and he got sloppy."

"You got caught cheating and now somebody's looking to blow off your kneecaps."

"You're a cold-blooded son of a bitch." The flask was from the second bottle. Rich was working through it quickly. "You owe me, and don't you forget it. I just need to lay low for a few weeks, till it cools off."

"Not here."

"You're just going to kick me out, let them kill me?"

"Oh, yeah." Gabe studied his father with a humorless smile. "But I'll give you an even chance. Five thousand ought to help you go to ground and keep you there."

Rich looked around the farm, the well-tended buildings, the glossy horses. He was never too drunk not to calculate his take. "It isn't enough."

"It'll have to be. Keep away from the house, and my horses. I'll go write you a check."

Rich tipped up the flask again while Gabe strode away. It wasn't enough, he thought as the whiskey turned to bitterness in his blood. The boy had hit the big time and all he wanted was a piece of the action.

And he'd get it, Rich promised himself. He'd given the boy a chance. Now they'd play out the game another way.

# Chapter Eight

IT WAS FOOLISH TO BE NERVOUS. YET PHILIP CONTINUED TO check his watch between sips of white wine. Kelsey wasn't late. He was early.

It was even more foolish to think she might have changed in some way during the two weeks she'd been gone. That she might look at him differently somehow. Or find him lacking—as he'd found himself lacking when he'd watched the woman he'd once loved taken away to prison.

There was nothing he could have done. And no matter how many times he'd told himself that, the words rang hollow. The guilt had eaten at him for years, soothed only by the care and love he'd given his daughter.

Yet even now, two decades later, he could see Naomi's face as it had looked the last time he'd seen her.

It was a six-hour drive from Washington to Alderson, West Virginia. Six hours to travel from the tidy, civilized world of university life to the gray and bitter reality of a federal facility. Both were regimented, both cloistered for their own purposes. But one was fueled by hope and energy, the other by despair and anger.

No matter how he'd prepared himself, it had been a shock to see Naomi, vivid, arrogantly alive Naomi, behind the security screen. The months between her arrest and her sentencing had taken their toll. Her body had lost its subtle feminine roundness, so she'd appeared angular and bony in the shapeless prison uniform. Everything had been gray—her clothes, her eyes, her face. It had taken every ounce of will inside him to meet her silent, steady gaze.

"Naomi." He felt foolish in his suit and tie, his starched collar. "I was surprised you wanted to see me."

"Needed to. You learn quickly in here that what you want is rarely a consideration." She was three weeks into her sentence, and for the sake of her sanity had already stopped crossing off days on her mental calendar. "I appreciate your coming, Philip. I realize you must be dealing with a lot of backlash right now. I hope it won't affect your position at the university."

"No." He said it flatly. "I assume your attorneys will appeal."

"I'm not hopeful." She folded her hands, linking her fingers tight to keep them from moving. Hope was another weight on her sanity that she'd coldly dispatched. "I asked you to come here, Philip, because of Kelsey."

He said nothing, couldn't. One of his deepest fears was that she would ask him to arrange for Kelsey to visit, to bring his child into this place.

She had a right. He knew in his heart she had a right to see her child. And he knew in his heart he would fight her to the last breath to keep Kelsey away from the horror of it.

"How is she?"

"She's fine. She's spending a day or two at my mother's so I could . . . make the trip."

"I'm sure Milicent's delighted to have her." The sarcasm whipped back into her voice. The ache crept back into her heart. Determined to finish what she'd begun, Naomi banished both. "I assume you haven't explained to her, as yet, where I am."

"No. It seems . . . No. She believes you're visiting someone far away for a while."

"Well." A ghost of a smile flitted around her mouth. "I am far away, aren't I?"

"Naomi, she's only a child." However unfair, he would use her love for Kelsey. "I haven't found the right way to tell her. I hope, in time, to—"

"I'm not blaming you," Naomi interrupted. She leaned closer, the shadows under her eyes mocking him. "I'm not blaming you," she repeated. "For any of this. What happened to us, Philip? I can't see where it all started to go wrong. I've tried. I think if I could pinpoint one thing, one time, one event, it would be so much easier to accept everything that happened after. But I can't." She squeezed her eyes shut, waiting until she was sure she could speak without a tremor in her voice. "I can't see what went wrong, but I can see so many things that went right. Kelsey. Especially Kelsey. I think of her all the time."

Pity, the overwhelming weight of it, smothered him. "She asks about you."

Naomi looked away then, around the drab visiting room. Someone nearby was weeping. But tears were as much a part of this place as the air. She studied the walls, the guards, the locks. Especially the locks.

"I don't want her to know I'm here."

It wasn't what he'd expected from her. Off balance, he fumbled between gratitude and protest. "Naomi—"

"I've thought this through very carefully, Philip. I have plenty of time to think now. I don't want her to know they took away everything and put me in a cage." She drew a deep steadying breath. "It won't take long for the scandal to die down. I've been out of your circle for nearly a year as it is. Memories are short. By the time she goes to school, I doubt there'll be much more than a murmur, if that, about what happened in Virginia."

"That may be, but it hardly deals with now. I can't just tell her you've disappeared, Naomi, and expect her to accept it. She loves you."

"Tell her I'm dead."

"My God, Naomi, I can't do that!"

"You can." Suddenly intense, she pressed a hand to the security screen. "For her sake, you can. Listen to me. Do you want her to visualize her mother in a place like this? Locked up for murder?"

"Of course I don't want it. She can't be expected to understand, much less cope with it, at her age. But—"

"But," Naomi agreed. Her eyes were alive again, passionate, burning. "In a few years she'll understand, and she'll have to live with it. If I can do anything for her, Philip, I can spare her from that. Think," she insisted. "Think. She could be eighteen by the time I get out. All her life she'll have pictured me here. Would she feel obligated to come here herself to see me? I don't want her here." The tears came then, breaking through the dam of self-control. "I can't bear it, even the thought of her coming here, seeing me like this. What would it do to her? How would it damage her? I tell you, I won't take that chance. Let me protect her from this, Philip. Dear God, let me do this one last thing for her."

He reached out so that their fingertips met through the iron mesh. "I can't stand to see you in here."

"Could any of us bear to see her sit where you are?"

No, he couldn't. "But to tell her you're dead. We can't predict what that would do to her. Or how any of us would live with the lie."

"Not so big a lie." She drew her fingers back, stemmed the tears. "Part of me is dead. The rest wants to survive. Quite desperately wants to survive. I don't think I could if she knew. She'll be hurt, Philip. She'll grieve, but you'll be there for her. In a few years she'll barely remember me. Then she won't remember me at all."

116

"Can you live with that?"

"I'll have to. I won't contact her or interfere in any way. I won't ask you to visit me here again, nor will I see you if you come. I'll be dead to her, and to you." She braced herself. Their time was almost up. "I know how much you love her, and the kind of man you are. You'll give her a good life, a happy one. Don't scar it by making her face this. Please, promise me."

"And when you're released?"

"We'll deal with that when it happens. Ten to fifteen years, Philip. It's a long time."

"Yes." It made his stomach knot to imagine it. What, he thought, would it do to a child? "All right, Naomi. For Kelsey's sake."

"Thank you." She rose then, fighting nausea. "Good-bye, Philip."

"Naomi—"

But she walked straight to the guard, through the door that clanged shut behind her. She hadn't looked back.

"DAD?" KELSEY PUT HER HAND on Philip's shoulder and gave it a little shake. "What century are you in?"

Flustered, he rose. "Kelsey. I didn't see you come in."

"You wouldn't have seen a fleet of Mack trucks come in." She kissed him, drew back, then with a laugh kissed him again. "It's good to see you."

"Let me look at you." Did she seem happier? he wondered. More settled? The thought caused a quick, ungenerous tug-of-war inside him.

"I can't have changed that much in two weeks."

"Just tell me if you feel as good as you look."

"I feel great." She slipped into a chair and waited for him to settle across from her. "The country air, I suppose, someone else's cooking, and manual labor."

"Labor? You're working on the farm?"

"Only in the most menial of capacities." She smiled up at the waitress. "A glass of champagne."

"Nothing else for me, thank you." Philip looked back at his daughter. "Are you celebrating?"

"Pride took his race at Santa Anita today." Kelsey was still flushed with pleasure at the win. "I muck out his stall when he's at Three Willows, so I feel some part of responsibility for the victory. In May Virginia's Pride is going to take the Derby." She winked. "That's a sure thing."

Philip sipped his wine, hoping it would open his throat. "I didn't realize you'd become so involved . . . with the horses."

"They're wonderful." She took the glass the waitress set in front of her, lifted it in a toast. "To Pride, the most gorgeous male I've ever seen. On four legs, anyway." She let the bubbles explode on her tongue. "So, tell me, how is everyone? I thought Candace would be with you."

"I suppose she understood that I wanted you to myself for a couple of hours. She sends her love, of course. And Channing. He has a new girl."

"Of course he does. What happened to the philosophy major?"

"He claimed she talked him to death. He met this one at a party. She designs jewelry and wears black sweaters. She's a vegetarian."

"That ought to last about five minutes. Charming can't go much longer than that without a burger."

"Candace is certainly counting on that. She finds Victoria—that's her name—unsettling."

"Well." Kelsey opened her menu and skimmed. "She wouldn't find anyone settling right now where Channing's concerned. He's still her baby."

"The most difficult thing any parent ever does is to let go. That's why most of us just don't." He covered her hand with his. "I've missed you."

"I haven't really gone anywhere. I wish you wouldn't worry so much."

"Old habit. Kelsey"—he tightened his grip on her hand—"I asked you to have dinner with me for a couple of reasons. I'm not sure you won't find one of them unpleasant, but I felt you'd prefer to hear it from me."

She stiffened. "You said everyone was all right."

"Yes. It's about Wade, Kelsey. He's announced his engagement." He felt her hand go limp. "Apparently it's to be a small wedding, in a month or two."

"I see." Odd, she thought, that there should still be so much emotion to swirl and collide inside her. "Well, that was quick work." She hissed out a breath, annoyed by the edginess of her own tone. "Stupid of me to resent it, even for a minute."

"Human, I'd say. However long you were separated, the divorce is barely final."

"That was just a paper. I know that. The marriage ended in Atlanta, more than two years ago." She picked up her glass, considered the wine bubbling inside. "I was going to be civilized and wish him the best. Nope." She drank deeply. "I hope she makes his life hell. Now, I think I'll try the blackened redfish. I feel like something with a little bite to it."

"Are you going to be all right?"

"I'm going to be fine. I am fine." She closed her menu. After they'd given their order, she found herself smiling at her father. "Were you afraid I'd throw a tantrum?"

"I thought you might need a shoulder to cry on."

"I can always use your shoulder, Dad, but I'm finished crying over what's done. Maybe working, really working for a living's changing my outlook."

"You've been working for years, Kelsey, since you graduated from high school."

"I've been playing at jobs for years. None of them mattered to me."

"And this does? Mucking out stalls matters to you?"

The snap in his voice warned her. She chose her words carefully. "I suppose I feel a part of a system there. It's not simply one race or one horse. There's a continuity, and everyone has a part in it. Some of it's tedious, some of it's rushed, and it's all repetitive. But every morning it's new. I can't explain it."

And he would never understand it. All he knew at that moment was that she sounded so much like Naomi. "I'm sure it's exciting for you. Different."

"It is. But it's also soothing. And demanding." Might as well get it done, she told herself, and she continued quickly. "I'm thinking of giving up my apartment."

"Giving it up? And what? Moving permanently to Three Willows?"

"Not necessarily." Why did it have to hurt him? she wondered, then sighed. Why had it hurt her to hear Wade was about to remarry? "That hasn't been discussed. But I've been giving some thought to moving out to the country. I like seeing trees out of my window, Dad. Seeing land instead of the next building. And I enjoy very much what I'm doing now. I'd like to keep doing it, see if I'm good at it."

"Naomi's influencing you. Kelsey, you can't let these kinds of impulses seduce you into rushing from one way of life to another. You can't possibly understand the world you're toying with after so short a time."

"No, I can't claim to understand it fully. But I want to." She held back as their salads were served. "And I want to understand her. You can't expect me to walk away from her until I do."

"I'm not asking you to walk away, but I am asking you not to leap in without considering all the consequences. There's more than the romance of a horse at dawn, or that last gallop over the finish line. There's ruthlessness, cruelty, ugliness. Violence."

"And it's as much a part of who I am as the smell of books in the university library."

120

"Why, it's Kelsey, isn't it? Naomi's lovely daughter." Bill Cunningham sauntered over, a drink from the lounge in one hand, his diamond horseshoe winking on the other. "No mistaking that face."

Perfect timing, she thought, and forced a smile. "Hello, Bill. Dad, this is Bill Cunningham, an associate of Naomi's. Bill, my father, Philip Byden."

"Why, I'll be goddamned. It's been years." Bill stuck out a hand. "Don't believe I've seen you since the day you snatched Naomi out from under my nose. Teacher, aren't you?"

"Yes." With the coolness he reserved for careless students, Philip nodded. "I'm a professor at Georgetown University."

"Big time." Bill grinned, laying a hand on Kelsey's shoulder for a quick, intimate squeeze. "You got yourself a real beauty here, Phil. It's a pure pleasure seeing her around the track. Heard your mama's top three-year-old outdistanced the field at Santa Anita today."

"Yes, we're very pleased."

"Things are going to shake down different in Kentucky. Don't let her talk you into laying your paycheck on Three Willows' colt, Phil. I've got me the winner. You give your mama a kiss for me, honey. I've got to get back to the bar. Little meeting."

As he walked away, Kelsey picked up her salad fork and began to eat with every appearance of interest.

"That's the kind of person you want to associate with?"

"Dad, you sound like Grandmother. 'Standards, Kelsey. Never lower your standards.'" But Philip didn't smile. "Dad, the man's an idiot. Very similar to the pompous, blustering idiots I've run into at the university, in advertising, at galleries. You can't escape them."

"I remember him," Philip said stiffly. "There were rumors that he bribed jockeys to lose, or to deliberately force another horse into the rail."

She frowned, and shoved the salad aside. "So add sleazy to

pompous and blustering. He's still an idiot, and not someone I intend to cultivate a friendship with."

"He runs in the same circle as your mother."

"Parallel lanes, perhaps. There's a great deal I don't know about her, or trust about her, at this point. But I do know that Three Willows is more than a farm to her, the horses more than business assets. It's her life."

"It always was."

"I'm sorry." Kelsey reached out helplessly to take his hands. "I'm sorry that she hurt you. I'm sorry that what I'm doing now has brought all that hurt back. I'm asking you to trust me to look at the whole, to make my own choices. I need a goal in my life, Dad. I may have found it."

He was afraid she had, and that when she reached it he would no longer recognize her. "Just promise me you'll take more time, Kelsey. Don't commit to anything, or to anyone, without more time."

"All right." She hesitated. "You haven't asked about her."

"I was working up to it," Philip admitted. "I wanted your impressions."

"She seems very young. She has this incredible well of energy. I've seen her start at dawn and keep going until after dark."

"Naomi loved to socialize."

"I'm speaking of work," Kelsey corrected. "She never socializes. At least she hasn't since I've been there. To tell you the truth, with all the work, I don't see how anyone would have the strength left to party. She's usually in bed before ten." No point, she thought, in mentioning that Naomi wasn't always sleeping alone. "She's very controlled, very contained."

"Naomi? Controlled? Contained?"

"Yes." She paused, waiting while their entrées were served. "I take it she wasn't always, but that's exactly how I'd describe her now."

"How do you feel about her?"

"I don't know. I'm grateful she isn't forcing the issue."

"You surprise me. Patience was never part of her makeup."

"I suppose people can change. I may not understand her, but I do admire her. She knows what she wants and she works for it."

"And what does she want?"

"I'm not sure," Kelsey murmured. "But *she* is."

FROM THE SHADOWS OF THE BAR, Cunningham watched Kelsey and her father talk over their meal. A pretty picture, he thought. All dignity and class. He rattled the ice in his bourbon.

"Quite a looker," Rich Slater said from beside him. "Something familiar about her." He laughed, carefully pacing himself with his own drink. It wouldn't do to muddle his thinking just now. "I guess there's something familiar about all beautiful young women after a man passes a certain age."

"Naomi Chadwick's daughter. Spitting image of her."

"Naomi Chadwick." Rich's eyes gleamed, with pleasure and with bitter memory. He was here, after all, to dredge up memories. And to profit by them. "There's a filly a man doesn't forget. My son's neighbor now. Small world." He enjoyed another swallow of whiskey. Quality stuff—since Cunningham was buying. "You know, I think I saw her around the boy's place a couple of weeks ago. He'd have his eye on her if I know Gabe."

"He's been cozy with the mother. Guess it follows he'd be cozy with the daughter." And Gabe Slater wouldn't have had the chance to be cozy with either, Cunningham thought now, if it hadn't been for a hand of cards. Things would be different.

Things were going to be different.

"If he plays his cards right," Cunningham continued, picking at his own scab, "he could erase the border between the farms."

Rich eyed Kelsey with more interest. So, his son was making time with the ice bitch's daughter. That would be something he could use. "Now, wouldn't that be something? That kind of merger would make them the top outfit in the state, I'd say."

"It might." Cunningham lifted one finger, signaling another round. "Wouldn't care for it myself. I'd just as soon see that connection shaken a bit." He reached into the nut bowl, popped three into his mouth. Casual, he told himself. Keep it casual. It wouldn't do for Rich Slater to know just how much he was banking on the deal. "Now, this business we're talking about. It might just accomplish that in the long term."

Calculating, Rich admired the diamond ring on Cunningham's finger. "And would that extra benefit be worth an appropriate bonus?"

"It would."

"Well now, we'll just see what we can do about that." He shot Kelsey another look. "We'll just see what we can do. I'm going to need those traveling expenses, Billy boy."

Reaching inside his jacket, Cunningham took out an envelope. He slipped it into Rich's eager hands under the bar. The unsettling sense of déjà vu had him glancing over his shoulder. "Count it later."

"No need, no need at all. You and me go back a ways, Billy. I trust you." Once the envelope was safely tucked away, he lifted his glass again. "And may I say it's a pleasure doing business with you again. Here's to old times."


BY NOON THE NEXT DAY, Kelsey was concentrating on her lesson on the longe line. The five-year-old mare on the other end was patient, and knew a great deal more about the process than she did.

It wasn't the horse being trained, but Kelsey.

"Bring her to a trot, change her direction," Moses demanded. The girl had potential, he'd decided. She wanted to learn, therefore she would. "She'll do anything you want. You get a yearling in there, he won't be so accommodating."

"Then give me a yearling," she called back, and flipped her whip. "I can handle it."

"Keep dreaming." But perhaps in a few weeks he'd assign her one. If she was still around. She had good hands, he mused, a good voice, quick reflexes.

"How long has she been at it?" Naomi asked.

"About thirty minutes."

Naomi rested a boot on the lowest fence rail. "Both Kelsey and the mare still look fresh."

"They've both got stamina."

"I appreciate your taking the time to teach her, Moses."

"It's no hardship. Except I think she's got her eye on my job."

She laughed, then saw he wasn't quite joking. "Do you really think she's that interested in training?"

"Every time I spend an hour with her I feel like a sponge that's been wrung dry. The girl never quits asking questions. I made the mistake of giving her one of my breeding books a few days ago. When she came back with it she all but gave me a goddamned quiz. Pumped me about blood factors, dominant and codominant alleles."

"Did you pass?"

"Just. I used to watch you do this." Grinning, he tugged on his earlobe. "Ah, the fantasies. A man without fantasies is a man without a soul. I had a hell of a soul where you were concerned."

"You still do. I'll prove it to you later. Here comes Matt."

"I didn't know you'd sent for the vet."

"I didn't." Naomi ran her tongue around her teeth. "He said he was in the neighborhood and thought he'd stop in to check out that case of sore shins."

Moses glanced back at Kelsey. Ah, the fantasies, he thought again. "Yeah. Right."

Smothering a laugh, Naomi welcomed the vet. "Well, Matt, what's the verdict?"

"She's doing fine. A blister's not necessary."

"Nice of you to take the time to stop by," Moses commented.

"I was over at Longshot. One of his colts was injured."

"Serious?" Naomi asked.

"Could have been. A puncture. It was small, easily overlooked. There was a lot of infection." He kept his eyes on Kelsey as he spoke, admiring. "I had to lance it. Too bad. Jamison said the horse was supposed to ship off to Hialeah tomorrow."

"Three Aces?" Instantly sympathetic, Naomi laid a hand on Matt's arm. "Gabe was going down with him. That horse has been running like a dream."

"They'll both be staying home for now."

"I'll give Gabe a call later. Try to cheer him up."

"He could use it." Matt switched his attention back to Kelsey. "Everyone seems healthy around here." When Kelsey acknowledged him with a quick wave, he grinned. "She looks like she's been doing that all her life."

When Moses took pity on him and signaled Kelsey to stop, she walked the horse over to the fence. "She's so sweet-natured." She rubbed her cheek against the mare's. "I wish you'd give me a brat, Moses, so I could feel I was accomplishing something."

"All journeys begin with one step. We'll see how many more you take before you trip."

"He's always boosting my confidence." She tipped back the cotton cap she wore. "Well, Matt, is this a professional or a social visit?"

"A mix. I had to stop in at Longshot."

"Oh?" As casually as possible, Kelsey led the mare out of the paddock. "Problem?"

"An injury." He repeated his explanation.

"But Three Aces looked wonderful the last time I saw him run. When did it happen?"

"From the look of it, three or four days ago."

"He ran at Charles Town three days ago. Won by a full length." Frowning, she stroked the mare. "A puncture?"

"About the size of a sixpenny nail, just above the fetlock."

"How does that happen?"

"Could have happened in transport, some sharp edge. That's likely. Unlikely it was deliberate."

"You mean that someone might have injured the colt so he couldn't run, or worse."

"Unlikely," Matt repeated. "It wasn't that serious."

"How do you treat it?"

She listened carefully as he spoke of lancing and antiseptics, the difference between punctures and tears.

"See what I mean?" Moses muttered to Naomi. "She'll be cramming veterinary books next." His eyes narrowed as he looked toward the stables. "Expecting anyone?"

"No." Naomi pursed her lips and studied the young man approaching. Lean, narrow-shouldered, pretty face. Levi's and a sweatshirt. Ordinary enough, she mused. But the boots gave him away. They would have cost a cool three hundred.

"Anyone know the cowboy?"

"Hmm?" Curious, Kelsey turned, then let out a shout of pleasure. "Channing!" She raced forward, cracking Matt's heart when she threw her arms around the young man. "What are you doing here?"

"Thought I'd check the place out before I head down to Lauderdale. Spring break."

"Haven't you outgrown that yet?"

"Outgrown girls in bikinis? I don't think so. Man, look at you. You look like an ad for country living." He slung an arm around her shoulders and glanced at the trio by the fence. "Don't tell me that's your mother."

"That's Naomi. Come on, I'll introduce you." She kept her arm around his waist. "Channing, this is Naomi Chadwick, Moses Whitetree, and Matt Gunner. Channing Osborne, my stepbrother."

"Welcome to Three Willows." Naomi extended a hand, amused and charmed when Channing brought it to his lips. "Kelsey's told me about you."

"Only the good parts, I hope. You've got a great place here."

"Thanks. We'll give you a tour. I hope you can stay awhile."

"I'm loose." Unable to resist, he reached over the fence to stroke a hand down the mare's nose. "Just heading down to Florida for a week or so."

"To ogle coeds," Kelsey put in. "Channing's in pre-med, so he calls it anatomy lessons."

He grinned and reached up to scratch the mare's ears. "Hey, youth is fleeting. Ask anyone. Am I breaking something up?"

"Not at all," Naomi assured him. "You're just in time for lunch. Matt, you'll join us, won't you?"

"Wish I could. I've got to get over to the Bartlett farm. One of their foals is colicky."

"Hey, you're a vet?" Channing perked up. "I always thought it would be cool to treat animals. They don't complain as much as people, right?" he added quickly when Kelsey shot him a surprised look.

"There's that. But people don't generally bite and kick. I'll take a rain check, Naomi, thanks. Kelsey, good to see you again. Nice to meet you."

"I'll walk you up. Kelsey, bring Channing along when you're ready."

"If I know you, you're ready now. Want to take that tour after you eat?"

"Sounds good to me."

"I didn't know you were interested in animal medicine."

He shrugged, embarrassed. "Just in passing. It's a kid thing."

They began to walk slowly. "I remember you wanting to save birds when they bashed into the picture window. And that old fleabag mutt you brought home one time, with the limp?"

"Yeah." He smiled, but the humor didn't reach his eyes. "Mom put the skids on that. Off to the pound. I guess he walked the last mile on three legs."

"I'd forgotten that." She laid her head against his shoulder.

128

"She was afraid he'd turn. He must have been a hundred years old."

"He wasn't a pureblood," Channing corrected, then shrugged. "No big deal. She could never handle animals around the house with her allergies. Besides, like I said, it was a kid thing."

Why hadn't she ever heard that resigned tone in his voice before? she wondered. Maybe she hadn't listened to it. "Do you want to be a doctor, Channing?"

"Family tradition," he said easily. "I never thought about being anything else. Oh, except for an astronaut when I was six. Osborne men are surgeons, and that's that."

"Candace would never push you into doing something if she knew your heart wasn't in it."

With a half laugh Channing stopped and looked at her. "Kels, you were eighteen when they got married, and you had one foot out the door. Mom runs things. She does it subtly and she does it well. But me and the Prof, we pretty much do what we're told."

"You're angry with her over something. What is it?"

"Hell, she yanked the allowance from my trust fund because I balked at taking a full course load this summer. I wanted to work, you know. Get a taste of the real world. I had a construction gig lined up. You know, so I could wear a hard hat and make rude kissy noises at the secretaries who walked by at lunchtime. I just wanted a couple of months away from the books."

"That sounds reasonable enough. Maybe if I talk to her for you …?"

"No, she's not too happy with you at the moment, either. This business," he said, gesturing to encompass the farm. "She sees it as a strain on the Prof. The Magnificent Milicent is feeding that little neurosis."

Kelsey blew out a breath. "So, we're in the same boat. Listen, are you really set on Lauderdale and bikinis?"

"If you're about to suggest that I go home, kiss and make up—"

"No. I was going to suggest that you spend spring break here. I don't think Naomi would object if you hung out with me and the horses."

"Playing big sister?"

"Yeah, got a problem with it?"

"No." He leaned down and kissed her forehead. "Thanks, Kels."

# Chapter Nine

THE GROOM'S NAME WAS MICK. HE'D BEEN BORN AND BRED in Virginia and liked to boast that he'd forgotten more about horses than most people ever learned. It might have been true. Certainly throughout his fifty-odd years as a racetracker he'd tried every aspect of the game. In the early years he'd risen from stableboy to exercise boy. He often boasted of how he'd gotten up on horses for Mr. Cunningham during the man's heyday.

Before he'd hit twenty, he'd still been small and light enough to jockey. Though he'd never moved from apprentice to journeyman, he'd worn the silks. He didn't like people to forget it.

For a short unmemorable time, he'd bluffed his way into the trainer's position at a small farm in Florida. He'd even owned a gelding for a year—or at least fifteen percent of one. Maybe the horse had never lived up to his potential, proving himself to be nothing more than a Morning Glory who worked out fast and raced slow. But Mick had been an owner, and that was the important thing.

He'd come back to Cunningham's when he'd heard the farm had changed hands. His position as groom satisfied him, particularly since Gabriel Slater had the look of a winner. And always had, in Mick's memory.

He enjoyed the fact that the younger hands often deferred to him. They might have called him Peacock behind his back because he always sported a bright blue cap and tended to strut. But it was done with affection.

His thin, lined face was known at every track from Santa Anita to Pimlico. That was just the way Mick wanted it.

"Track's slow," Boggs commented, and meticulously rolled a cigarette.

Mick nodded. The hard morning rain had tapered off to an incessant drizzle, and that was fine. Slater's Double or Nothing shone on a muddy track.

It was the slow time between workout and post. Mick sat under an overhang watching the rain drip from the eaves and thinking about the ten dollars burning a hole in his pocket. He figured to put it on Double's nose and watch it grow.

He pulled out a crumpled pack of Marlboros to join Boggs in a smoke.

It was quiet. The jockeys would be in their quarters, or taking a steam to sweat off one more pound before post time. The trainers would be poring over the books, and the owners huddled inside, enjoying the dry warmth and coffee. There was little activity around the shedrow, but it would liven up again soon.

"Funny seeing Miss Naomi's girl around," Mick said conversationally. "She rode over to Longshot a couple of weeks ago, rode off again soaking wet."

Boggs nodded, blew out smoke. "Heard."

"She was up on that roan gelding of yours. Handled him fine."

"Rides like her mother. Makes a picture."

They sat, two lifelong bachelors, and smoked in silence.

A full five minutes passed before Mick spoke again. "Somebody else came by the barn that day."

"Yeah?" Boggs wouldn't ask who. It wasn't the way they communicated.

"Haven't seen him around for a while, but I recognized him, all right." He tossed the minute stub of his cigarette into a puddle and watched it sizzle out. "Forgot his connection with the man till I seen them together. Hit me then, all right. I remember when Mr. Slater was working as a stableboy for Mr. Cunningham."

"Yep. About fifteen years ago. Came over to Three Willows after. Stayed a time."

"Year or two. Hard worker, didn't chew your ear off. Still doesn't say nothing 'less it's supposed to be said. Always was a loner." He chuckled a bit. "Never did think I'd be working for him."

"Made something of himself."

"That he did. Lots wouldn't think he coulda done it, the way he used to hang around and hustle up card games. Just another track rat, they'd figure. But I knew different."

"Always liked the boy myself." Boggs rubbed at a bruise on his forearm where a yearling had nipped him. "Had a look about him. Still does."

"Yeah. I was there the day Lipsky tried to stick him. Didn't say no more than he had to then, either."

Boggs spat on the wet ground, more an assessment of Lipsky than out of necessity. "Man's got no business being drunk and handling a stud."

"That's the truth." Mick fell silent again, thought idly about lighting up another smoke. "Mr. Slater, he's got no use for drunks. I forgot how his father used to slide into the bottle till I saw him 'round the barn that day."

"Rich Slater?" Boggs's interest perked up. "He came around Longshot?"

"That's what I'm telling you. The day Miss Naomi's girl rode off wet. Had himself all polished up like a Bible salesman." To better enjoy the relay of information, Mick decided to indulge in that second smoke. "They talked for a little bit. Couldn't hear what Mr.

Slater had to say. No reading that boy's face either. Gambler's eyes he's got." He chuffed out smoke, then inhaled deeply, secure in his old friend's interest. "You could hear the old man, though, a-laughing and a-jawing about how he was in the money and he'd just come by to see how his boy was doing."

"Come by to soak him, more likely."

"Gotta figure it. Didn't like the way he was looking 'round the place, like he was adding up figures on a computer. Polly had a yearling on the longe. Inside Straight, Mr. Slater named him. That Polly's got fine hands, she does."

"She does," Boggs agreed, seeing nothing odd about Mick's circuitous story. He nodded a greeting to one of the track grooms as the man passed. "A good yearling manager. Might be Moses is grooming Miss Kelsey for that at Three Willows. Old Chip's talking about retiring again."

"Always is. Just blowing smoke. So"—Mick rounded back to his point "Mr. Slater, he goes on up to the house. Old Rich, he hangs around, sipping outta his flask. Silver one, shiny. He corners Jamison for a while. Pumping him, I figure. Then Mr. Slater, he comes back, gives the old man a check, and boots him out. Subtlelike, but he gave him the boot for all that."

"Never had much use for Rich Slater."

"Me neither. Some say the apple it don't fall far from the tree. But with these two I figure it took a long roll. He's got class, Mr. Slater does. And he listens when you tell him something. Asks me the other day what I might think about that puncture in Three Aces' foreleg."

"That's a good horse."

"He is that. So I tell Mr. Slater it don't look like no accident to me. He just looks, and he thanks me, real polite-like." He rose, bones creaking. "I'm gonna take me a look at Double."

"I think I'll get me some coffee."

They parted, Mick wandering into the gloom of the stables. The rain drummed on the roof, muffling the sounds of horses shifting in their boxes. Another groom was adjusting a blanket on a filly. Mick stopped a moment, studying the lines.

A little wide-fronted, he decided. The filly would probably paddle. No problem like that with Double. He was an even sixteen hands high, pure black with well-sloped shoulders and a short, strong body that had plenty of heart room.

Most of all, Double had courage.

Mick sauntered back toward the box. He liked to give Double a little pep talk before a race. And to look into the colt's eyes and see if it was a day to put a bet down.

"Well now, boy, we called out some rain just for you." Mick opened the box door, and scowled. "What the hell you doing in here, Lipsky? You got no business around Mr. Slater's horse."

Lipsky remained crouched, and eyed Mick as he ran a hand up and down Double's leg. "Just taking a look. Thought I might lay down a bet."

"You go ahead and do that, but you clear out."

"I'm going. I'm going." Lipsky angled his body away, but Mick's eyes were keen.

"What the hell you doing with that?" In one fierce move, Mick clamped a hand on Lipsky's arm. The knife glinted, thin-bladed and bright in the dim light. "You bastard. Going to cut him, were you?"

"I wasn't going to hurt him." Wary, Lipsky shifted his eyes over the door of the box. There wasn't much time. "I was just going to fix it so he wouldn't race today." Or ever, he thought, once he'd severed a tendon. "Slater's got it coming."

"You got what you had coming," Mick corrected. "And nobody messes with my horses. You lowlife, you did Three Aces, too."

"Don't know what you're talking about. Look, it was a bad idea. No harm done, though. You can see for yourself I never touched him."

"I'll take a look, all right. Now we'll go see what Mr. Slater wants done about this."

Lipsky jerked back, furious that the scrawny old man had such an iron grip. "You ain't turning me in."

"The hell I ain't. I'm turning you in, and you put a mark on this colt, I'll spit on your grave if Mr. Slater decides to kill you."

"I ain't touched his fucking horse." Desperate, Lipsky struck out. As the two men began to grapple, Double danced nervously to the side.

The knife sliced through the air, and deflected by Mick's forearm, the point nipped across the colt's flank. Shocked by the pain, Double reared. Mick cursed and drew in the breath to shout. Then there was no air at all as the blade plunged in, just above his belt.

"Jesus." As stunned as his opponent, Lipsky yanked the blade free and stared at the spreading blood. "Jesus Christ, Mick. I didn't mean to stick you."

"Bastard," Mick managed. He stumbled forward just as the colt, aroused and terrified by the scent of blood, reared. A hoof caught Mick at the base of the skull. After one bright flash of pain, he felt nothing, even when he fell face forward and the colt's thrashing hooves trampled him.

Panic nearly had Lipsky racing from the box, but he held on, cowering in the corner. It wasn't his fault, he told himself. Hell, he wasn't no murderer. He'd never have pulled a knife on Old Mick, especially seeing as he was stone-cold sober. If Mick had just listened, it wouldn't have happened. Wiping his fist across his sweaty mouth, he backed toward the door. He eased the bloody knife into his boot before slipping silently out of the box. Back hunched, he hurried out into the rain.

He needed a drink.


"THIS IS GREAT." CHANNING stood in the wet grandstands, eating a hot dog. "I mean," he said through a mouthful, "who'd have thought there was so much to it? It's been like watching rehearsals for some hot Broadway play."

Charmed by him, Naomi smiled. If she could have hand-picked a sibling for her daughter, it would have been Channing Osborne. "I'm sorry we couldn't provide better weather."

"Hey, it just adds to the drama. Horses thundering through the rain, colors flying, mud spewing." He grinned and washed down the hot dog with Coke. "I can't wait."

"Well, it won't be long now," Kelsey assured him. "In fact, they must be about ready to prep the horses for the post parade. You want to go take a look?"

"Sure. It's really nice of you to let me hang out, Naomi."

"I'm just glad you chose us over sun, sand, and bikinis."

"This is better." In a gesture she found charming, he offered her his arm. "When I get back next week, I can brag to all my sun-burned, hungover pals how I juggled two gorgeous women."

"What about the vegetarian?" Kelsey asked him.

"Who, Victoria?" His grin was quick and careless. "She dumped me when she realized I was an unconvertible carnivore."

"Very shortsighted of her," Naomi decided.

"That's what I said. I'm a prize, right, Kels?" He glanced down at his stepsister and saw that her attention was focused elsewhere. Well, well, he thought, studying Gabe. He hadn't seen that look in Kelsey's eyes for a long, long time. "Somebody you know?"

"Hmmm? Oh." Distracted, she reached up to adjust the brim of her cap. "Just a neighbor."

Gabe broke off his conversation with Jamison and turned to watch them approach. Damn, the woman looked good wet. He shifted his gaze from her to the man with his arm around her shoulder.

Too young to be competition, he decided. He doubted if the guy was old enough to buy beer. But there was a territorial sense in the drape of the arm and a look in the eyes that was a combination of curiosity and warning.

The stepbrother, Gabe concluded, and he stepped forward to meet them.

137

"Haven't you dried off yet?" he said to Kelsey, and watched the vague annoyance flit over her face.

"It's a new day, Slater. This is Channing Osborne, Gabriel Slater."

"It's nice you could pay your sister a visit."

"I thought so."

It amused Gabe that Channing increased his grip several unnecessary degrees for the handshake. "How's the mare, Naomi? I've been meaning to come by and take a look myself."

"She's definitely in foal. And healthy. I heard about Three Aces when Matt stopped by yesterday. Is he healing well?"

Gabe's thoughts darkened, but his eyes remained placid. "Yeah. He'll be back in top form in a few weeks."

"You've got Double or Nothing running today, don't you?"

Gabe looked back at Kelsey. Because he wanted to touch her, and to irritate her, he skimmed a knuckle down her cheek. "Keeping track of the competition, darling?"

"You could say that. Your colt's running head to head with ours."

"Want another side bet? You still owe me ten."

"Fine. In the spirit of things, we'll say . . . double or nothing."

"You're on. Want to take a look at the winner?"

"I've already seen Virginia's Pride, thanks."

He grinned, took her hand. "Come on."

As he tugged her away, Channing frowned. "Has that been going on long?"

"I'm beginning to think so." Looking after them, Naomi rubbed her wet nose. "Does it worry you?"

"She took the whole divorce thing hard. I don't want somebody taking advantage of that. How much do you know about him?"

"Quite a bit, really." Naomi sighed. "I'll fill you in later. Now I suppose we'll go with them so you can stop worrying."

"Good idea." He glanced down at her as they walked into the barn. "You're okay, Naomi."

Pleased, she took his hand. "So are you, Channing."

*

"You know I want to whip your butt out on the track, Slater, but I am sorry about Three Aces. I don't suppose there's anything I can do, but . . ."

"Fallen for them, haven't you?"

Kelsey tipped up her brim to get a better look at him. "For who?"

"The horses."

She shrugged and continued to walk toward the rear of the stables. "So what if I have?"

"It looks good on you, the way it softens you up." Deliberately he slowed her down. He wanted another moment before they reached the box. "When are you coming back?"

She didn't pretend to misunderstand him, but she did choose to evade. "I've been busy. Moses gives us a lot to do."

"Would you rather I came to you?"

"No." Edgy, she glanced over her shoulder. Naomi and Channing were only a few paces behind. "No," she repeated. "And this isn't the time to discuss it."

"Do you think your brother would go for my throat if I scooped you up and kissed you right here?"

"Certainly not." Dignity was failing her. "But I might."

"You're tempting me, Kelsey." Instead, he brought her hand to his lips. "Tonight," he murmured. "I want to see you tonight."

"I've got company, Gabe. Channing's visiting."

"Tonight," Gabe repeated. "You come to me, or I come to you. Your choice." He stopped at the box, keeping her hand in his. "Hello, boy. Ready to . . ." He trailed off as he spotted the line of blood, still red and fresh against the black coat. "Goddammit."

He yanked open the door and had hardly taken a step inside before he saw the body crumpled in the bedding.

"Stay back." Without looking, he flung out an arm to block Kelsey.

"What happened to him? The poor thing's bleeding." Focused on the colt, she pressed forward. When Gabe was forced to snatch at the halter to keep the horse from rearing, she saw the form sprawled in the bloody hay. "Oh, God. Oh, my God, Gabe."

"Hold him!" Snapping out the order, Gabe wrapped Kelsey's limp fingers around the halter.

"What is it?" Alarmed by the pallor of Kelsey's cheeks, Naomi surged forward. The breath hissed between her teeth. "I'll call an ambulance." She pressed her hand over Kelsey's. "Can you handle this?"

Kelsey blinked, nodded, then cleared her throat. "Yes, yes, I'm all right." But she was squeamish enough to keep her back to what lay in the corner of the box.

"Oh, man." Channing swallowed hard, then put himself between Kelsey and Gabe, who crouched over the body. "I'm only pre-med," he said quietly, and squatted down. "But maybe . . ."

It took only one close look to realize that he could have been as skilled and experienced a surgeon as his father had been, and he would still have been helpless.

There was blood everywhere, pools of it coagulating in the stained hay. The gouge in the back of the skull had welled with it. A bright blue cap, now streaked with red, lay partially under the bedding.

"That horse must have gone crazy," Channing said grimly. "Kelsey, get out of here. Get away from him."

"No, I've got him." Fighting to keep her breath even, she stroked the colt's neck. "He's shaking. He's terrified."

"Dammit. He just killed this guy!"

"No, he didn't." Gabe's voice was low and hard. He'd gently rolled Mick over. The groom's pulled-up shirt exposed a vicious stab wound in the abdomen. "But somebody did."

LATER, KELSEY STOOD SHIVERING in the drizzle trying to pretend she was drinking the coffee Channing had pressed on her.

"You should get away from here," he said again. "Let me take you home, or at least inside the clubhouse."

"No, I'm all right. I need to wait. That poor man." She looked away, out into the shedrow. It didn't seem energetic or glamorous now. It was simply muddy, dreary. People were gathered in tight little groups, eyeing the barn, waiting. "Gabe's been in there a long time with the police."

"He can handle himself." He glanced over to where Naomi sat on a barrel, under an overhang. "Maybe you should go over with your mother. She looks really spooked."

Kelsey stared at the entrance to the barn. She wanted to be in there, to hear what was being said, to know what was being done. "Gabe and I found him," she murmured. "I feel like I should help."

"Then go help Naomi."

Kelsey let out a long breath. "All right. You're right." But it was hard to walk over, to face that blank look in Naomi's eyes. "Here." She held out her untouched coffee. "Brandy'd be better, but I don't have any handy."

"Thanks." Naomi accepted the cup and forced herself to sip. It had nothing to do with her, she reminded herself again. The police wouldn't come, they wouldn't take her away this time. "Poor Mick."

"Did you know him very well?"

"He's been around a long time." She sipped again. No, it didn't have that slapping warmth of brandy, but it helped. "He and Boggs played gin rummy once a week, gossiping like little old ladies. I guess Mick knew as much about my horses as he knew about Gabe's. He was loyal." She drew in a shaky breath. "And he was harmless. I don't know who could have done this to him."

"The police will find out." After a moment's hesitation she laid a hand on Naomi's shoulder. "Do you want me to take you home?"

"No." Naomi reached up, covered her daughter's hand with hers. They both realized it was the first time they'd touched without reservation. "I'm sorry, Kelsey. This is a horrible experience for you."

"For all of us."

"I would have spared you from it." She looked up, her eyes meeting Kelsey's. "I'm not much good under these circumstances."

"Then I'll have to be." Kelsey turned her hand so that their fingers meshed. Naomi's were stiff with cold. "You're going home," she said firmly. "The police may want to talk to me, so Channing will take you."

"I don't want to leave you here alone."

"I'm not alone. Gabe's here, and Moses. Boggs." She glanced over to where the old man stood alone in the rain, grieving. "It's pointless for you to stay when you're so upset. You go home, take a hot bath, and lie down. I'll come up as soon as I get back." She softened her tone, leaned closer. "And I don't want Channing here. He'd feel as if he was doing some manly act if he took you away."

"That was a nice touch." Hating herself for the weakness, Naomi rose. "All right, I'll go. My being around a crime scene only causes more speculation in any case, but please, don't stay any longer than you have to."

"I won't. Don't worry."

Alone, Kelsey settled down on the barrel her mother had vacated and prepared to wait.

It didn't take long.

A uniformed officer stepped outside, scanned the groups of people, and focused in on her. "Miss Byden? Kelsey Byden?"

"Yes."

"The lieutenant would like to speak with you. Inside."

"All right." She ignored the speculative looks and slid off the barrel.

Inside, the routine of death was already under way. The last police photos had been taken, the yellow tape cordoning off the far end of the barn was in place.

Gabe's eyes blazed once when he spotted her. "I told you there was no need for her to be here."

"You both found the body, Mr. Slater." Lieutenant Rossi stepped over the tape and nodded to Kelsey. He was a twenty-year veteran of the force with a craggy, handsome face and sharp cop's eyes. His hair, dark and thick and streaked with dignified gray, was only one of his many vanities. His body was a temple, fueled with vitamins, health juices, and a stringent low-fat diet, and honed by exercise.

He might spend most of his time behind a desk with a phone at his ear, but it didn't mean he had to go to seed.

He loved his work, and thrived on procedure. And he hated murder.

"Ms. Byden, I appreciate your waiting."

"I want to cooperate."

"Good. You could start by telling me exactly what happened this morning. You were here since dawn."

"That's right." She told him everything, from unloading the horses through the morning workouts. "We stayed down at the track awhile. It was my stepbrother's first trip, and we decided that he might like to watch the horses being prepped for post time."

"And that would have been about what time?"

"Close to noon. Things are quiet between about ten and noon. We walked up here from the track and ran into Gabe. He was in the shedrow, talking to his trainer."

She glanced over Rossi's shoulder to look for him, and saw with dull horror the shiny plastic bag being carried out on a stretcher.

Cursing under his breath Gabe ducked beneath the tape and blocked her view. "This doesn't have to be done now. And certainly not here."

"No, it's all right." Gamely, Kelsey swallowed her nausea. "I'd rather get it over with."

"I appreciate that. So, you ran into Mr. Slater just outside here?"

"Yes. We talked for a few minutes, ragged each other because we had a horse running in the same race. I came in with Gabe to look at his colt. My mother and stepbrother were a little behind us."

"Your mother?"

"Yes. It was actually her horse that was to run against Gabe's. She owns Three Willows. Naomi Chadwick."

143

"Chadwick." It rang a distant bell. Rossi jotted it down. "So the four of you came in."

"Yes, but they were behind us a bit. They didn't get to the box until after—after we did. I guess Gabe and I saw the wound on the colt's left flank at the same time. He went in, and stopped, tried to block me. But I was worried about the colt, so I followed behind him. I saw the blood, and the body in the corner. I held the horse's head because he was starting to rear, and Channing and Naomi came up. She went right away to call an ambulance and Channing went into the box, thinking, I suppose, that he might be able to help. I thought—I suppose we *all* thought for a moment—that the horse had done it. Until Gabe turned the body over, and we saw ..." She would never forget what she'd seen. "We saw he hadn't. Gabe told Channing to call the police."

"And there was no one around the stall when you and Mr. Slater came in."

"No. I didn't see anyone. Some of the grooms were inside, of course. But it was still a little early for prepping."

"Did you know the deceased, Ms. Byden?"

"No. But I've only been at Three Willows for a few weeks."

"You don't live there?"

"No, I live in Maryland. I'm just spending a month or so there."

"I'll need your permanent address for the record, then." When she gave it to him, he slipped his pad back into his pocket. "I appreciate your time, Ms. Byden. I'd like to talk to your mother and your stepbrother now."

"I had Channing take her home. She was very upset." In an unconscious move, Kelsey shifted her stance, placing her feet a bit wider, straightening her shoulders. "In any case, they were both with me all morning. Neither of them could have seen anything I didn't."

"You'd be surprised what one person sees that another doesn't. Thank you." He dismissed her by turning back to Gabe. "My information is that a man named Boggs might have been the last person to see the victim alive. Does he also work for you?"

"He works for Three Willows."

"He's outside," Kelsey informed Rossi. "I'll tell him to come in." She hurried out, eager to be away from the flat-voiced questions and shrewd eyes. Boggs was where she'd seen him last, simply standing in the rain. "There's a Lieutenant Rossi who wants to speak to you." She took his hands, vainly trying to warm them between hers. "I'm so sorry, Boggs."

"We was just talking. Just sitting over there and talking. We had a card game on for tonight." Tears streamed down his face along with the rain. "Who'da done that to him, Miss Kelsey? Who'da done Old Mick that way?"

"I don't know, Boggs. Come on, I'll go in with you." She slipped her arm around him and guided him back toward the barn.

"He don't have no family, Miss Kelsey. A sister, but he hadn't seen her in more'n twenty years. I've got to take care of things for him, see that he gets buried proper."

"I'll take care of it, Boggs." Gabe stepped outside, intercepting them before they entered. "You tell me what you want him to have, and we'll arrange it."

Boggs nodded. It was only right. "He thought high of you, Mr. Slater."

"I thought high of him. Come and see me as soon as you're able. We'll set everything up."

"He'da appreciated it." Head bowed, Boggs walked inside.

"The lieutenant says you're free to go." Gabe took Kelsey's arm and steered her away. "I'll take you home."

"I should wait for Boggs. He shouldn't be alone now."

"Moses will see to him. I want you out of here, Kelsey. Away from it."

"I can't be. I'm as close to it as you are."

"You're wrong." He half dragged her across the muddy shedrow. "The box is mine. The colt is mine. And, dammit, Mick was mine."

"Slow down!" She dug in her heels and managed to grab him by the jacket. He might have shown little more than a flare or two of emotion inside the barn, but he was on slow burn now and ready for flash point. No cool gambler's eyes now, she thought. They were hot and lethal.

"You're getting out of here now. And you're staying out of it."

She could have argued. She certainly could have struggled against the grip he had on her arm. But she waited until they'd reached his car.

Then she simply turned and wrapped her arms around him. "Don't do this to yourself," she murmured.

He held himself rigid, prepared to jerk away and shove her into the car. "Do what?"

"Don't blame yourself, Gabe."

"Who else?" But his body relaxed, and curled itself to hers. He pressed his face into the cool, damp comfort of her hair. "Jesus, Kelsey, who else am I going to blame? He was trying to protect my horse."

"You can't know that."

"I feel it." He drew her away. His eyes were calmer now, but whatever was going on just behind that deep, cool blue had Kelsey trembling. "And I'm going to find whoever did this to him. Whatever it takes."

"The police—"

"Work their way. I work mine."

# Chapter Ten

DEATH COULDN'T INTERFERE WITH THE ROUTINE OF A thoroughbred farm. Not the death of a horse, or a man. Dawn still signaled workouts. There were races to be run, legs to be wrapped, coats to be quartered and strapped. Talk around the paddocks or shedrow at sunrise might have been of murder and Old Mick, but the pace didn't flag. It couldn't.

There was a foal with a case of eczema, a yearling filly who still refused a rider, and a colt competing in a maiden race. Grieving and gossip had to be accomplished while filling feed tubs and walking hots.

"Maybe you want to see to strapping Pride now that he's been cooled, Miss Kelsey." Though his eyes were shadowed, his face drawn, Boggs was up and about his duties. He offered Kelsey the reins. "He always seems happier when you do it."

"All right, Boggs." Her hand covered his gnarled one. "Is there anything I can do for you?"

His eyes drifted past her as they focused on something private. "Ain't nothing to do, Miss Kelsey. Just don't seem right, that's all. Don't seem right."

She simply couldn't turn away. "Would you mind coming with me? I'm still a little nervous about grooming the next Derby winner."

They both knew it was an excuse, but Boggs nodded and trudged along beside her. It was raining again, the same slow, incessant drizzle that had marred the previous afternoon. Though it was closing in on ten A.M., the mist hung stubbornly. Inside the barn, stableboys were busy mucking out, so the air was perfumed with the smells of manure, hay, and mud.

At Queenie's box, Kelsey paused and handed the colt's reins back to Boggs. "This'll only take a minute."

She took a carrot out of her back pocket, offering it to the mare while she nuzzled the soft ears. "There you go, old lady. You didn't think I'd forget, did you?" The mare nibbled the carrot, then Kelsey's shoulder, curving her neck in response to the caress. Though she was aware of Boggs's interest, Kelsey completed what had become a daily routine with a kiss on Queenie's cheek.

"I know, I've already taken plenty of ribbing about female equiphilia." After a last pat, Kelsey turned back to Boggs and the colt. "And maybe I'm hooked, but I've caught more than one male groom cozying up to a horse."

"Your granddaddy loved that mare." Boggs led Pride to his box where Kelsey had already cleaned out the soiled night bedding and replaced it with clean wheat straw for day. "He'd sneak her sugar cubes every afternoon. We all pretended not to notice."

"What was he like, Boggs?"

"He was a good man, fair. He had a quick temper in him and could crack like lightning." As he spoke, his eyes scanned the box, noting that Kelsey had seen to the colt's fresh water and hay net. His job usually, but he was sharing it with her, as he shared the colt. "Wouldn't tolerate laziness, no sir, but if you did your work you got paid well and on time. Known him to sit up all night with a sick horse and to fire a man on the spot for a shoddy grooming."

Kelsey crouched down, running her hands down Pride's legs to check for swellings or injuries. Boggs had already washed the leg wraps and hung them with the clothespins he kept clipped to his pant leg.

"Sounds as though he was a hard man to work for." Satisfied, she rubbed the light dampness of rain from the colt with straw.

"Not if you did what you was hired to do." He watched as she took the dandy brush from Pride's grooming kit. "You've got the touch, Miss Kelsey," he said after a moment.

"I feel as though I've been doing this all my life." She soothed the colt with murmurs and strokes as he shifted and shied. His temperament, like most aristocrats, was high-strung. "He's a little restless this morning."

"Sharp's what he is. His mind's already at the starting gate."

Kelsey continued to remove mud from the colt's saddle area, belly, and fetlocks. "I'm told he ran well yesterday." She set the dandy brush aside and took up a hoof pick. "I guess it seems cold, thinking about races and times after yesterday."

"Can't be no other way."

"You were friends with him a long time."

"About forty years." Boggs took out a tin of tobacco and helped himself to a pinch. "He was already an old hand when I come along."

"I've never lost anyone close to me." Kelsey thought of Naomi, but it was impossible to remember whatever grief she'd felt at three. "I don't want to say I can imagine what you must be feeling, but I know if you want some time off, Naomi would give it to you."

"No place else I'd rather be than here. That policeman, he had a look about him. He'll find who done that to Mick."

Kelsey dampened a sponge and wiped the colt's eyes, outward from the corners. She enjoyed the way he looked at her while she tended to him, the recognition and the trust they'd begun to build between them. "Lieutenant Rossi. I didn't like him. I don't know why."

"Well, there's cold blood in there. But cold blood means he'll think, and keep thinking step by step till it's done."

Kelsey set the sponge aside and picked up the body brush and currycomb. She remembered the light in Gabe's eyes. There had been a need for revenge there, she decided. And she understood the sentiment too well. "Will that be enough for you, Boggs?"

"It'll have to be."

"There you are." Channing leaned against the box door. He watched her a moment, the steady hands, the new muscles working in her shoulders. "You look just like you know what you're doing."

"I do know what I'm doing." And the fact never failed to delight her. "Missed you at breakfast."

"Overslept." His grin was more charming than sheepish. "My body clock's not used to eating at five A.M. Listen, Matt dropped by. I'm going to go hang out with him on a couple of house calls. Barn calls. Whatever."

"Have fun."

He hesitated. "You're okay, right?"

"Sure, I'm okay."

"I'll be back in a couple of hours. Oh, and Moses said if I found you, he wants you back on the longe line."

"Slave driver," she muttered. "As soon as I'm finished here."

SHE HAD NO TIME TO BROOD. A thorough strapping of a horse took an experienced groom an hour, and Kelsey about a quarter hour longer. Then it was time for the midday feeding, oats, bran, and nuts that needed to be mixed, measured, weighed. She added a tablespoon of salt, Pride's vitamin supplement, and electrolytes. Because he tended to be a finicky eater, she treated him to a helping of molasses to sweeten the feed.

Later, she would bring him an apple. Not just to spoil him, she thought. Moses had explained that horses required succulents added to their feed. Pride preferred apples to carrots. He had a taste for the tart Granny Smith variety.

"Now you're set," she murmured when he settled into his midday meal. "And you eat it all, hear?"

He munched, eyeing her.

"We've got a lot riding on you, sweetheart. And I think you'd like standing in the winner's circle with a blanket of red roses."

He snorted, what Kelsey took as the equine equivalent of a shrug. She chuckled, giving him one last caress. "You can't fool me, boy. You want it as much as we do."

Rolling her shoulders, she left the barn to face the rest of the day's work.

She doubted that Moses had anything sadistic in mind when he whipped her through the morning, but the result was the same. By three, her still-developing muscles were sore, she was covered with mud, and her system was sending out urgent signals for fuel.

After thoroughly scraping her boots, she went into the house through the kitchen and headed straight for the refrigerator. With a little cry of pleasure, she pounced on a platter of fried chicken.

She had her mouth full of drumstick when Gertie came in. "Miss Kelsey!" Outraged by the sight of her little girl leaning against the counter in filthy jeans, Gertie bustled to a cupboard for a plate. "That's no way to eat."

"It's working for me," Kelsey said with her mouth full. "This is great, the best chicken I've had in my entire life." She swallowed. "This is my second piece."

"Sit down at the table. I'll fix you a proper lunch."

"No, really." Sometimes manners simply didn't apply. Kelsey bit in again. "I'm too dirty to sit anywhere, and too hungry to clean up first. Gertie, I've taken three cooking courses, one of them at the Cordon Bleu, and I could never make chicken like this."

Flushing delightedly, Gertie waved a hand. "Sure you could. It was my mama's recipe. I'll walk you through it sometime."

"Well, you outdo the Colonel all to hell." At Gertie's blank look, Kelsey laughed. "Kentucky Fried. Gertie, I could compose a sonnet to this drumstick."

"Go on. You're teasing me." Red as a beet now, Gertie poured Kelsey a glass of milk. "Just like that brother of yours. Why, you'd think the boy hadn't eaten a home-cooked meal in his life."

"He's been in here charming you out of house and home, hasn't he?"

"I like to see a boy with a healthy appetite."

"He's got that." And so, Kelsey thought, did she, as she debated whether or not to eat one more piece. "Is Naomi around?"

"Had to go out."

"Mmm." So, Kelsey thought, it was just the two of them. Perhaps it was time she took advantage of the opportunity and asked Gertie some questions. "I've wondered, Gertie, about that night. Alec Bradley."

Gertie's face sobered. "That's done and gone."

"You weren't home," Kelsey prodded gently.

"No." Gertie picked up a dishcloth and began polishing the already spotless range. "And I've cursed myself every day for it. There we were, my mama and me, at the movies and eating pizza pie while Miss Naomi was all alone with that man."

"You didn't like him."

"Hmmph." She sniffed and slapped her rag on the stove. "Slick he was. Slick like you'd slide right off if you was to put a hand on him. Miss Naomi had no business with the likes of him."

"Why do you suppose she . . . went around with him?"

"Had her reasons, I suppose. She's got a stubborn streak does Miss Naomi. And I expect she was feeling stubborn about your daddy. Then she was feeling low about losing a horse at the track.

He went down and they had to shoot him. She took that hard. That'd be about the time she was seeing that man."

Gertie's derision was plain. She refused, had always refused, to call Alec Bradley by name.

"He was handsome. But handsome is as handsome does, I say. I tell you what the crime was, Miss Kelsey. The crime was putting that sweet girl in jail for doing what she had to do."

"She was protecting herself."

"She said she was, so she was," Gertie said flatly. "Miss Naomi wouldn't lie. If I'd been home that night, or her daddy, it wouldn't have happened. That man would never have laid a hand on her. And she wouldn't have needed the gun."

Gertie sighed, took the rag to the sink and rinsed it out thoroughly. "Used to make me nervous, knowing she had that gun in her drawer. But I'm glad she had it that night. A man's got no right to force a woman. No right."

"No," Kelsey agreed. "No right at all."

"She still keeps it there."

"What?" Uneasy, Kelsey set down the half-eaten chicken leg. "Naomi still has the gun upstairs?"

"Not the same one, I expect. But one like it. It was her daddy's. Law says she can't own a gun now, but she keeps it just the same. Says it reminds her. I say what does she need to be reminded of such a time for? But she says some things you don't want to ever forget."

"No, I suppose she's right," Kelsey said slowly. But she wasn't certain she would sleep more peacefully knowing it.

"Maybe it's not my place to say it, but I'll say it anyway." Gertie sniffled once, then snatched a tissue to blow her nose. "You were the sun and the moon to her, Miss Kelsey. You coming back here like this, it's made up for a lot. There's no getting back what was lost, no taking back what was done, but old wounds can still be healed. That's what you're doing."

Was it? Kelsey wondered. She was still far from sure of her own motivations, her own feelings. "She's lucky to have you, Gertie," she murmured. "Lucky to have someone who thinks of her first, and last." Wanting to clear the tears from Gertie's eyes, she lightened her voice. "And very lucky to have someone who can cook like you."

"Oh, go on." Gertie waved a hand, then dashed it over her eyes. "Plain food, that's what I do. And you haven't finished that last piece you took. You need more meat on your bones."

Kelsey shook her head just as the chimes sounded from the front door. "No, Gertie, I'll get the door. Otherwise I'll eat this, platter and all."

She took the milk with her, guzzling as she went. She passed a mirror and rolled her eyes. Dirt streaked her cheeks. The cap she'd tossed aside in the mudroom hadn't prevented her hair from becoming hopelessly tangled. She hoped, as she wiped at the mud with the sleeve of her manure-stained shirt, that the visitor was horse-related.

Far from it.

"Grandmother!" Kelsey's shock mixed with chagrin as Milicent winced at her appearance. "What a surprise."

"What, in the name of God, have you been doing?"

"Working." Kelsey saw the spotless Lincoln outside, the driver stoically behind the wheel. "Out for a drive?"

"I've come to speak with you." Head erect, Milicent crossed the threshold with the same unbending dignity that Kelsey imagined French aristocrats had possessed when approaching the guillotine. "I felt this was much too important to discuss over the phone. Believe me, I do not enter this house lightly, or with any pleasure."

"I believe you. Come in, please, and sit down." At least Naomi was out of the house on some errand. Kelsey could thank fate for that. "Can I offer you something? Coffee, tea?"

"I want nothing from this house." Milicent sat, her starched linen suit barely creasing with the movement. She refused to satisfy petty curiosity by studying the room and focused instead on her granddaughter. "Is this how you spend your time? You're as grimy as a field hand."

"I've just come in. You might have noticed, it's raining."

"Don't take that tone with me. This is inexcusable, Kelsey, that you would waste your talents and your upbringing. Worse still, that you would send this family into a tailspin while you play out this little drama."

"Grandmother, we've been through all this." Kelsey set the milk aside and moved over to stir up the fire. Whether it was the rain or the visit, the room was suddenly chilled. "I'm well aware of your feelings, and your opinions. I can't believe you came all this way just to reprise them for me."

"You and I have rarely been sympathetic to each other's wishes, Kelsey."

"No." Thoughtfully, Kelsey replaced the poker and turned back. "I suppose we haven't."

"But in this, I can't believe you would go against me. Your name was in the paper this morning. Your name, in connection with a murder at a racetrack."

News travels, Kelsey mused. She'd been up and at the barn before the first paper delivery. "I didn't realize that. If I had, I certainly would have called Dad to reassure him. I was there, Grandmother. The man who was killed was a groom at the neighboring farm. My part in the investigation is very incidental."

"That you were there at all is the entire point, Kelsey, at a race-track, associating with the sort of people they attract."

Kelsey tilted her head. "They attract me."

"Now you're being childish." Milicent's lips compressed. "I expect more of you. I expect you to think of the family."

"What does that poor man being killed yesterday have to do with the family?"

"Your name was linked with Naomi's. And her name in

155

connection with a murder brings up old scandals. I shouldn't have to spell all this out for a woman of your intelligence, Kelsey. Do you want your father to suffer for this?"

"Of course not! And why should he? Why would he? Grandmother, an old man was brutally murdered. By sheer coincidence I happened to find him. Naturally, I had to give a statement to the police, but it ends there. I didn't even know him. And as far as Dad goes, he's completely removed from this."

"Stains are never completely removed. This world, Kelsey, is not ours. You were warned what to expect, what kind of people you would mingle with. Now the worst has happened. And because your father is too softhearted to take a stand, it's up to me. I'm going to insist that you pack your things and come home with me today."

"How little things change." Naomi stood in the doorway, pale as marble. Her slate-gray suit only accented the delicate fragility of her frame. But fragility can be deceptive. When she stepped forward, she was as elegant and as powerful as one of her prized fillies. "I believe I overheard you say something quite similar to Philip once."

Milicent's face went still and hard. "I came to speak with my grandchild. I have no desire to speak to you."

"You're in my home now, Milicent." Naomi set her purse aside, and with seamless poise chose a chair. "You're certainly free to say whatever you like to Kelsey, but you won't run me off. Those days are over."

"Prison taught you little, I see."

"Oh, you can't begin to know all it taught me." Her blood was cold now, without sentiment. That pleased her. She'd never been sure how she would react if she confronted Milicent again.

"You're the same as you ever were. Calculating, sly, unprincipled. Now you'd use Philip's daughter to satisfy your own ends."

"Kelsey is her own woman. You don't know her well if you believe she can be used."

"No, I can't." Kelsey stepped between them, not to block the venom, but to speak her mind. "And don't talk around me, either of you. I'm not a pawn in anyone's game. I came here because I wanted to, and I'll stay until I decide to leave. You can't order me to pack, Grandmother, as though I were a child, or a servant."

Color leaped into Milicent's cheeks and rode high. "I can insist that you do what's right for the family."

"You can ask me to consider what's right. And I will."

"You've pushed yourself on her." Milicent rose, her eyes boring into Naomi. "Using sentiment and sympathy to draw her to you. Have you told her about the men, Naomi, the drinking, the total disregard for your marriage, your husband and child? Have you told her that you set out to ruin a man, to destroy my son, but only succeeded in ruining yourself?"

"That's enough." Kelsey stepped back, hardly realizing the gesture put her squarely in Naomi's corner. "Whatever questions I have, whatever answers I'm given, don't involve you. I'll make my own judgments, Grandmother."

Milicent fought to keep her breathing even. Her heart was thumping dangerously fast. She, too, would make her own judgments. "If you stay here, you'll force me to take steps. I'll have no choice but to alter my will, and to use the power I have to revoke your grandfather's trust."

It was sorrow rather than shock that settled in Kelsey's eyes. "Oh, Grandmother, do you think the money matters so much? Do you think so little of me?"

"Consider the consequences, Kelsey." She picked up her bag, certain the threat would bring the girl quickly to heel.

"Hey, Kels, you'll never guess what I . . ." Channing came to an almost comical halt two strides in front of Milicent. "Grandmother!"

157

Enraged, Milicent whirled on Naomi. "So, you'd have him as well? Philip's daughter, and now the son he considers his own."

"Grandmother, I'm just—"

"Quiet!" Milicent snapped at him. "You paid once, Naomi. And I swear to God you'll pay again."

After she swept out, Channing hunched his shoulders. "Ah, bad scene, huh?"

"And one of the more colorful ones." Drained, Kelsey rubbed her hands over her face. "Channing, you did call Candace and tell her you were here, didn't you?"

"I called her." He stuck his hands in his pockets, then drew them out again. "I just told her I was okay and settled in. I didn't mention where I was settled. I thought I'd avoid the complications." He blew out a breath as Kelsey continued to stare at him. "I guess I'd better let her know before it gets any stickier."

Kelsey shook her head as he clattered up the stairs. "Channing's prone to leaving out vital pieces of information." She glanced back at her mother. "Want a drink?"

Naomi managed a smile and eased her shoulders back against the cushion. "Why not? Two fingers of whiskey ought to take out some of the sting."

"We'll try it." Kelsey walked to the sideboard and poured. "I'm sorry for that."

"So am I. Kelsey, the money might not be important to you, but it's your heritage. I don't want to be responsible for your losing it."

Absently Kelsey ran a fingertip over one of Naomi's crystal horses, following the flow of glass from withers to tail. "I have no idea if she can block my trust fund. And if she can, well, I haven't exactly been squandering the interest to date." With a shrug, she handed Naomi a glass. "I don't particularly want to lose it, either, but I'll be damned if she'll rein me in with dollar signs. Cheers." She rapped her glass against Naomi's.

"Cheers?" With a shake of her head, Naomi began to laugh.

Letting her eyes close, she ordered her body to relax. "Oh, Christ, what a day."

She'd spent the last two hours with her lawyers, working out the details on how to align her own wishes with the ones her father had outlined before his death. Now, she thought, if Milicent made good on her threats to cut Kelsey off, she'd have to make further adjustments.

She opened her eyes again and tossed back the first swallow. "I was awfully proud of you, the way you stood up for yourself."

"Same goes. When I saw you in the doorway, I thought, Jesus, she's like a lightning bolt, frozen. Cold, sharp, and deadly."

"She's always affected me that way. Not that everything she said was completely off the mark. I've made mistakes, Kelsey, very bad mistakes."

Kelsey turned the glass in her hand, around and around. "Did you love Dad when you married him?"

"Yes, oh yes." For a moment, Naomi's eyes softened. "He was so shy and smart. And sexy."

Kelsey choked on a laugh. "Dad? Sexy?"

"Those tweed jackets. That dreamy, poetic look in his eyes, that calm, patient voice reciting Byron. That unflagging kindness. I adored him."

"When did you stop?"

"It wasn't a matter of stopping." Naomi set her half-finished whiskey aside. "I wasn't so patient, or so kind. And the dreams we had were different ones. When things began to go wrong, I wasn't smart enough to compromise. To bend. It was one of my mistakes. I thought I could hold him by proving I didn't need him. I opened the distance, raced away from him. And I lost. I lost Philip, I lost you, I lost my freedom. A very high price for pride."

She grimaced as the doorbell rang again. "It looks like the day isn't over yet."

"I'll get it." For the second time that afternoon, the visitor was unwelcome. "Lieutenant Rossi."

"Ms. Byden, sorry to disturb you. I have a few follow-up questions for you and your mother."

"We're in the sitting room. Is there any progress, Lieutenant?" she asked, as she led the way.

"We're investigating."

Trained eyes took in the sedate comfort of the room, as well as the two glasses of whiskey, the half-full glass of milk. Naomi rose as he entered. As a man, he appreciated her grace. As a cop, he admired her control.

"Lieutenant Rossi." Though her skin had gone cold, she offered a hand. "Won't you sit down? Would you care for some coffee?"

"I appreciate the offer, Ms. Chadwick, but I've had my quota for the day. I just have a few more questions."

"Of course." They always had a few more questions. She sat again, keeping her spine erect. "What can I help you with?"

"You were fairly well acquainted with the victim."

"I knew Mick." Keep the answers short, Naomi reminded herself. Say nothing more than necessary.

"He was employed at Longshot for the last five years, approximately."

"I believe that's correct."

"He also worked for the previous owner, Cunningham?"

"On and off."

"Off," Rossi continued, "when he was fired, about seven years ago."

"Bill Cunningham let Mick go, as I recall, because he felt Mick was too old. At the time, my trainer offered Mick a position here, but he decided to leave the area."

"The information I have is that he worked the tracks in Florida during that two-year period."

"I believe so."

"Would you know if he had any enemies?"

"Mick?" She dropped her guard for a moment, the question was so absurd. "Everyone loved Old Mick. He was an institution, a kind of monument to the best in racing. Hardworking, tough-minded, bighearted. No one disliked him."

"But someone killed him." Rossi waited a beat, fascinated by the way Naomi drew herself in. "The horse was injured. Mick Gordon was assigned to that horse as groom. My report is that there was a long, shallow slice on the left flank, approximately twelve inches in length." He took out his book as if checking facts. "Preliminary reports indicate that this wound was caused by the same weapon used against the victim."

"Obviously someone was trying to hurt the colt, and Mick tried to stop him," Kelsey put in. "Moses told me that colt's very level-headed. He'd never have trampled Mick if he hadn't been hurt or frightened."

"That may be." Rossi had to wait for the autopsy report before he could be sure if the knife had killed Mick Gordon, or the horse had. Murder or attempted murder, he intended to close the case. "Mr. Slater's colt was competing with yours that day, Ms. Chadwick."

"Yes, or he would have been if it hadn't been necessary to scratch him."

"And your horse won, didn't he?"

She kept her eyes level, steady. "By a neck, as we say. He paid three to five."

"You and Mr. Slater have a history of competition. Particularly in the last year between these two horses. He's edged you out of the top spot several times."

"Double or Nothing is an admirable colt. A champion. So is my Virginia's Pride. They're incredibly well matched."

"I don't know much about racing myself." He smiled placidly. "But, from an amateur's standpoint, it seems it would be to your benefit to"—he tipped his flattened hand back and forth—"shift the odds."

"That's an uncalled-for accusation, Lieutenant." In automatic support, Kelsey dropped a hand on her mother's shoulder. "Absolutely uncalled-for."

"It's not an accusation, Ms. Byden. It's an observation. Horses are sometimes deliberately injured, drugged, even killed to up another's chances, aren't they, Ms. Chadwick?"

"Unscrupulous and criminal behavior happens in all walks of life." She fought against trembling. Cops' eyes could detect even the slightest fear. "Those of us in racing prefer to say it happens much more often in the show ring than at the track."

"Three Willows doesn't need to resort to tactics like that," Kelsey said, furious. "And I've told you that my mother was with me all morning. Dozens of people saw us."

"They did," Rossi agreed. "As a veteran of the racing world, Ms. Chadwick, wouldn't you agree that an owner, or a trainer, interested in improving his chances, would hire someone to do the job rather than risk harming a horse himself?"

"Yes, I would."

"You don't have to answer questions like this." The outrage of it seared Kelsey's throat.

"I'm sure your mother is well aware of her rights," Rossi said coolly. "And the procedure of a murder investigation."

"I'm perfectly aware of both, Lieutenant. And equally aware that those rights don't always protect the innocent." Her lips curved humorlessly. "Certainly not the half-innocent. I could remind you that my colt wasn't the only other contender in that race, and that not once in the fifty years that Three Willows has been in operation have we been cited for any infraction. But I'm sure you know that. Just as I know an ex-convict always carries a cloud of suspicion. Is there anything else I can tell you?"

"Not for the moment." A hell of a woman, he thought, and tucked away his pad. He was going to have to schedule extra time to study her file a little more closely. "I appreciate the time. One thing, Ms. Byden. You did say you met Mr. Slater outside the barn yesterday, before the two of you went in to look over the horse."

"Yes, he was talking to his trainer."

"Thank you. I'll see myself out."

"That was outrageous!" Kelsey exploded the moment the door closed. "How could you just sit there and take it? He all but accused you of paying for murder."

"I expected it. And he won't be the only one to consider the possibility. After all, I'm once guilty."

"Don't be so calm, dammit!"

"I'm not. The pretense is all I've got." Weary, she rose. She needed a quiet room, a bottle of aspirin, and the coward's escape of sleep. But she paused, took a chance by framing Kelsey's face in her hands. "You're not even considering it a possibility, are you? That I might have had a hand in this."

"No." There was no hesitation.

"Then I'm wrong," Naomi murmured. "It seems I have a great deal more than pretense. Go for a ride, Kelsey. Work off some of that anger."

SHE WENT FOR A RIDE, BUT HER temper continued to rage. She headed for Longshot with a dual purpose. Handing over Justice's reins to a willing groom, she strode from barn to house.

Too stirred up to think of the propriety of knocking on the front door, she went in through the pool house, moving from spring to high summer, then up a short flight of stairs into the steady warmth of a casually furnished great room.

She realized then, because she hadn't a clue which direction to take, that she was trespassing. Upbringing warred with instinct until she turned left and headed down a corridor. So, she thought, she'd work her way to the front door, go outside, and knock. Unless, of course, she found Gabe in the meantime.

It wasn't his voice she heard, not immediately. It was Boggs's, his grainy tones coming through an open door.

"He wouldn't want no fancy service, Mr. Slater. None of that flowers and organ music stuff. Once when we were sitting around, he told me how he thought he'd want to be cremated, and maybe his ashes could be spread over the practice track here. So's he'd always be a part of the place. Sounds kinda funny, I guess."

"If that's what he wanted, that's what we'll do."

"That's good, then. I've got some money set aside. I don't know what it costs to do things that way, but—"

"Let me do this for him, Boggs," Gabe interrupted. "I'm not sure I'd be sitting here today if it hadn't been for Mick. I'd appreciate it if you'd let me take care of him."

"I know it ain't the money, Mr. Slater. Maybe it's not my place to say, but he was real proud of you. Told me he knew the first time he saw you hustling to walk hots at the track that you'd amount to something. I sure am going to miss him."

"So am I."

"Well, I better get back." He stepped out of the doorway, flushed a bit when he saw Kelsey. "Miss," he muttered, tipping his cap and hurrying off.

Ashamed at having so blatantly eavesdropped on a private conversation, she stepped into the doorway to apologize.

He sat at a beautiful old desk, the arched window behind him letting in the watery sunlight. Wherever there wasn't glass welcoming the light, there were books. The two-level library was stunning, and unmistakably masculine.

The man who owned it had his head in his hands.

Embarrassment melted into compassion. She stepped forward, murmuring his name. Her arms were around him before he lifted his head. "I didn't know you were so close to him. I'm sorry. I'm so sorry."

He hadn't felt grief, not in years. Not since his mother. It surprised him how deep it could cut. "He was good to me. I must have been about fourteen the first time he grabbed me by the scruff of the neck. He took an interest in me—I don't know why—and talked Jamie into hiring me. And he made sure I learned. Goddammit, Kelsey, he was seventy. He should have died in bed."

"I know." She drew away. "Gabe, Rossi was just at the house."

"Busy man." Gabe dragged his hands through his disheveled hair. "He left here less than an hour ago."

"I think he's got some idea that Naomi's involved." When Gabe said nothing, she moistened her lips. "I need to know if you think so."

Composed again, he studied her. "No, I don't. And neither, I see, do you. Rossi has a couple of ideas. The other is that I arranged the business myself." He waited a beat. "Double or Nothing's heavily insured."

"You'd shoot yourself in the foot first." She let out a sigh. "That was the other reason I came over. I could tell when he was questioning me that he was toying with the idea. I guess I came over to warn you."

"I appreciate it." He rotated his shoulders once to ease the lingering tension. Kelsey, standing there in splattered work clothes, compassion in her eyes, took care of the rest. "You look good, darling."

"Yeah, mud's becoming."

"On you." He took her hand, played with her fingers. "Why don't you sit on my lap awhile?"

Amused, she tilted her head. "Is that the setup, or the punch line, Slater?"

In answer he tugged, cradling her when she tumbled. "Yeah." He inhaled deeply, nuzzling her hair. It smelled of rain, and of spring. "This is exactly what I needed. Sit still, Kelsey. You'll cause a lot more trouble by wriggling around. Believe me."

"I'm not a lap sitter."

"So learn." Testing, he grazed his teeth over her earlobe, pleased with her quick shudder. "You only came over to tell me about Rossi?"

"That's right."

165

This time he exhaled deeply. "Okay. But I'm going to have to find a way to make you pick up the pace here. I'm starting to suffer."

"I think you're tougher than that." She rested her head in the curve of his shoulder. It was entirely too comfortable, entirely too tempting. "I'm not playing games."

"That's too bad. I usually win."

# Chapter Eleven

"Sure you don't want a blindfold?" Kelsey tucked an arm around Channing's waist. "A last cigarette?"

He tipped down his red-framed Oakley sunglasses. "You're a riot, Kels."

"No, really, I feel like I'm sending you off to the firing squad alone."

"I can handle Mom." He unstrapped his helmet from the back of his Harley. "And the Prof's no problem."

"And Grandmother?"

With a grimace, he slipped on the helmet. "Hey, I've been dodging those bullets for years. As long as my brilliant mind keeps me in the top fifteen percent of my class, they can't hassle me much."

"The trusty shield of a four-point-oh." She'd used it herself. "What about this summer?"

"Mom's just going to have to accept that there's more to my life than hitting the books."

"My brother." Grinning, she tapped her fingers on the side of his helmet. "The hard hat."

"Actually, Naomi offered me a job here this summer."

"Here?"

"Channing Osborne, stableboy. I like it. I like her." In a lithe move, he straddled the bike. "You know, I stopped by here to be sure you were all right. I had this image planted of some hard-faced, hard-living bitch with a drink in one hand and a forty-five in the other."

"Sowed," Kelsey said dryly, "by the Magnificent Milicent."

"With a few seeds tossed out by Mom. They're as solidly aligned against you being here as they were *for* you marrying Wade the Weenie."

He glanced back toward the house. It made a lovely picture with the willows greening, the daffodils and hyacinths spearing up in their Easter-egg hues of yellow and blue and pink.

"She's not anything like she's painted, is she?"

"It doesn't seem so," Kelsey murmured. "I'm glad you came, Channing. I'm glad you got to meet her."

"Hey, it was the most interesting spring break I've ever had." He leaned forward to kiss her good-bye. "And I'll be back. See you in a couple of months."

"I—" She wanted to tell him she couldn't guarantee she'd be here, but he'd kicked the engine to life. With a final salute, he roared off down the drive.

Lost in her own thoughts, she walked back to the house. Had she decided to stay? Kelsey asked herself. The month Naomi had asked of her was almost up. Yet neither of them had mentioned plans to leave.

And what was waiting for her back in Maryland, in that tidy Bethesda apartment? Job hunting, solitary meals, and the occasional lunch with a friend who would sympathize over the divorce, then mention a cousin office pal old friend who just happened to be single.

The idea was more than depressing.

Here, she had work and a world she already loved, a lifestyle that suited her nature, people who accepted her for what she could do.

And there was Gabe.

She wasn't quite sure what was going on there, but it would be a great deal more difficult, and certainly inconvenient, to try to figure it out if she moved away.

It would be dishonest to say he didn't fascinate her. His moods, impossible to read one minute, bold as a banner headline the next. She appreciated his humor, the easy charm, the equally easy arrogance.

He'd moved her in so many ways. The way he'd grieved for Old Mick, standing solemnly in the soft dawn light while Boggs had ridden slowly around the practice track, spreading the old man's ashes. He'd held her hand, she remembered, trusting her to understand the ritual.

That kind of loyalty and love couldn't be learned.

Yet he could be hard, ruthless enough to gamble and win a small fortune. Even that intrigued, and the underlying recklessness that had pushed him to raze another man's house and build his own.

Then, of course, there was that basic animal attraction, the kind she'd never felt before for any man. Even her husband.

"Kelsey?" Naomi paused at the foot of the stairs. The girl looked so solemn, she thought. "Missing Channing already?"

"No, I was thinking of . . ." She trailed off, blew her breeze-tousled hair out of her eyes. "Nothing really." Realigning her thoughts, she studied Naomi. Slim, strong, self-contained. "It was nice of you to offer him a job this summer."

"Not that nice. He has a strong back, willing hands, and I enjoy having him around. The house has been empty a long time."

"I think he wants to be a vet."

"So he told me."

"He told you." With a baffled laugh, Kelsey shook her head. "He's never mentioned it to me. Not once. I've always thought he was revved to be a surgeon, like his father."

"Sometimes it's easier to tell those secret hopes to someone who isn't so close. He loves you. Admires you. Could be he's afraid you'd be disappointed in him."

"I couldn't be." Her breath came out in an impatient gush. "Candace has been talking for years about him carrying on the Osborne tradition. I just assumed he wanted it too. Why do people try to shoehorn their children into slots?"

"Family honor. A terrifying obligation."

She opened her mouth, closed it again. Family honor. Hadn't that been why she'd married Wade? How many times had she been told how perfect he was for her, until she'd believed it.

Good family, good prospects, excellent social standing. It had been her duty, after all, to marry well, and to marry properly.

God, had she loved him at all?

"And when you can't hold up that obligation," Kelsey said slowly, "it's the worst kind of failure. I don't want that for Channing."

"He'll do what's right for himself. You did."

"Eventually."

"You can talk about eventually when you're my age. Kelsey . . ." She wasn't quite sure of her approach. Casual, she decided, was probably best. "I'm going down to Hialeah. I want to watch Virginia's Pride run. And I want to stick close to him after what happened at Charles Town."

"Oh." So, she wasn't to have the last week after all. "That makes sense. When are you leaving?"

"In the morning. I thought you might like to go with me."

"To Florida?"

"Well, it's not spring break, but it should be quite a spectacle."

As cautious as Naomi, she nodded. "I'd like to see it."

"Good. How would you feel about taking the rest of the day off?"

Kelsey's brows lifted. She hadn't seen Naomi take more than an hour off in over three weeks. "For?"

"What else?" Naomi's laugh was quick, bright, and young. "Shopping. What's the fun of taking a trip if you can't splurge on some new clothes first?"

Kelsey's grin flashed. "I'll get my purse."

IN A DINGY HOTEL ROOM OFF Route 15, Lipsky gulped down warm Gilbey's gin. The ice machine a few feet outside his door was on the fritz. Not that he cared. Warm or chilled, the liquor went down the same.

"I tell you, sooner or later they're going to come looking for me."

"You're probably right. You got sloppy." Rich straightened his bolo tie. "Neatness counts, friend."

"I was just going to take care of the horse." With his free hand, Lipsky reached for the cigarette smoldering in a chipped glass ashtray crammed with butts. "Just enough so he couldn't race, that's all."

"But that wasn't your job," Rich reminded him with an affable grin. "Eyes and ears open, remember? Just eyes and ears until I told you different."

"You didn't bitch when I fixed his other colt." Resentment gleamed in Lipsky's red-rimmed eyes. "You gave me another hundred for it."

"You were tidy, Fred. I did tell you, I believe, not to take chances. But"—he spread his arms wide—"that's behind us now. And Gabe's favorite colt won't be wearing a saddle for another week or so." It fit nicely into the master plan, the damaged horses, even the murder. Such things stirred gossip and excited the press. Feeling generous, Rich reached into his pocket. He carried his lucky money clip, the oversize silver dollar sign he'd picked up in Houston. There was nothing he liked better than to have it straining with bills.

Normally, he would load it with singles, putting a fifty or, if he was lucky, a C-note on the outside. He was really in the groove now, he thought. The money clip was fat with hundreds. He peeled one off and laid it on the table.

Lipsky stared at it with a mixture of hunger and guilt. "I wouldn't have hurt the Peacock. Nobody coulda paid me to hurt Old Mick."

"An unfortunate accident." In sympathy, Rich patted a hand on his shoulder.

Lipsky gulped more gin. "I never killed nobody. Maybe I cut a few, when they deserved it. But I never killed nobody before." He could still see Mick's face, the shock, the pain, the way his eyes had rolled back right before the horse reared and felled him.

And he could see the blood pumping and pooling, Mick's trademark blue cap going red with it . . .

He snatched the bottle and poured another shot. "He shouldn't have poked his nose in."

"An excellent rationalization." Rich poured a glass for himself. He hated to see a man drinking alone, even a revolting specimen like Lipsky. But he kept his cigarettes and his monogrammed lighter tucked away. "Now it's time to consider the next move."

"The cops are going to come looking for me. Plenty of people saw me around the track that day, at the shedrow."

"You were hustling rides," Rich reminded him. "Perfectly permissible. You're a familiar face at the track, Fred. Otherwise, the guards would have blocked you from entering the barn."

"Yeah, and sooner or later somebody's going to remember that I did. Then they'll notice I ain't been back." He tamped out his cigarette, spilling ash and old butts over the rickety table. "Then they'll remember I carry a blade."

"Your deductive powers are admirable. My advice is to run, lose yourself in Florida, California, Kentucky. Maybe Mexico. They've got tracks south of the border."

"I ain't living in no foreign country. I'm an American."

"Ah, patriotism." Rich toasted with his glass of gin. "You're a resourceful man, Fred. Otherwise I wouldn't have put you on the payroll. But I'm afraid we'll have to sever our relationship, under the circumstances."

"It's going to take more than a hundred."

Rich's smile never wavered, but his eyes turned gelid. "Now, Fred, you wouldn't put the arm on me, would you?"

Desperation was leaking sweat down Lipsky's back. He could smell himself. "I can't take the rap for this alone. If I'm going to run, I need money. Fuck, Rich, I was working for you. You got a part in this."

"Is that the way you see it?"

"The way I see it, I need ten thousand. To hide, and to keep my mouth shut about you if I don't hide good enough. It ain't too much to ask, Rich."

Rich sighed. He'd been afraid it would come to this. "I understand your position, Fred. I truly do. Listen, let me make a phone call, see what I can come up with." He bolstered his smile with another pat on Lipsky's shoulder. "Give me a little privacy, huh?"

"Yeah, okay. I gotta piss anyhow." He rose and staggered into the bathroom.

Rich didn't pick up the phone. Instead, he took a small vial out of his inside coat pocket. It really was a shame, but he couldn't afford to call Lipsky's bluff. Even if he paid, odds were the man would sing like a bird the minute the cops nailed him. And they'd nail him, Rich thought, as he tapped the liquid into Lipsky's gin.

"Come on back, Fred. We got it all taken care of." He was beaming when Lipsky reeled back into the room. "I'll have the money for you tomorrow."

Relief and liquor had Lipsky tumbling into his chair. "No shit, Rich?"

"Hey, we go back a ways, don't we? Rollers like us, we take care of each other." He lifted his glass. "Here's to old friends."

"Yeah." Eyes tearing in gratitude, Lipsky brought his glass to his lips. "I knew I could count on you."

"Yeah." Rich's smile hardened as he watched Lipsky literally drink himself to death. "You can count on me, Fred."

PALM TREES AND STRIPED awnings, brilliant sunshine and trailing bougainvillea. Men in white suits and women in sundresses. The ambience added to the glamour of the track. But Hialeah Park was still about racing.

At the Gulfstream receiving barn, horses arched their necks, pranced, sniffed the air, athletes psyching themselves up for competition. Many of the sights and sounds were the same as Charles Town; vendors still hawked *Daily Racing Form*, handicappers still hovered, working the odds. But the weather itself, the sheer glory of it, drew a different breed from the chilly spring in Virginia.

Kelsey amused herself watching a woman teetering on ice-pick heels leading a filly around the walking ring. Her shoulder-length rhinestone earrings flashed.

"Nobody could call a horse a dumb animal looking at that."

Kelsey glanced up at Gabe. "Meaning?"

"What do you see when you look at her face?"

"The horse or the woman?"

"The horse."

Obliging, Kelsey looked back at the filly, plodding, head down behind the giggling woman. "Embarrassment."

"You got it. That's Cunningham's latest acquisition."

"The horse or the woman?"

"Both."

She let loose a laugh, and realized how glad she was she'd come. Maybe it was the quick peek at summer, or the simple pleasure of discovering herself a part of a close-knit group. But she was glad.

"I heard you'd be here, but I didn't see you at morning workout."

"I just got in an hour ago," he told her. "What do you think of Miami?"

"Well, some of the grooms were grumbling this morning about losing sleep—gunshots outside their quarters—and I cruised the beach yesterday and it hit me that I must be an adult: I had no desire to strap on Rollerblades. Other than that"—she drew in a deep breath—"I love it. It's a beautiful park."

"The bottom line. Racetrackers don't have much use for the outside world anyway."

"I wouldn't go that far."

"You're not a racetracker." He looked down at her. "At least not yet."

She frowned, unsure if she'd been complimented or insulted. Rather than pursue it, she watched the losers returning from the first race. The winners, she knew, would be taken to the "spit box" so that samples of urine and saliva could be tested for drugs.

But it was the losers she thought about now, her heart aching a little to see them limping in, their flanks sweaty, faces dirty. If a filly could feel embarrassed by being led around in public by a tarted-up Barbie doll, she wondered how deeply these suffered the pangs of failure.

"Sad, isn't it?" she murmured. "Like watching soldiers struggling back from the front. All that color and show, and in just a couple of minutes, it's done."

"It's a hell of a couple of minutes. Too bad you missed the Florida Derby. Now, that's a show. Acrobats, a camel race."

"Camels? Really?"

"Never bet on one."

They walked past the tack rooms around the backstretch. It was nearly time for the second race, and Pride was in the third. She wanted to see Reno before Moses gave him that leg up. It had become her personal superstition to add her last wish for good luck before he walked his horse from the paddock.

"Not going to head for the windows?" Gabe asked her.

"Nope. I've picked my horses. Pride in the third and Three Aces in the fifth." She stopped to buy a lukewarm Pepsi from an ancient black man. "I've got my own system now."

Gabe accepted the can, took a swallow, and handed it back to her. "And what is that?"

"Sentiment. I just bet my heart."

"It's a lot to lose."

She shrugged. "Gambling's no fun without the risk."

"Damn right. Come here." They were nearly at Pride's saddling stall and there was plenty of traffic.

"Cut it out, Slater." But he'd already caught the ponytail she'd looped through the back of her cap.

"I'm just going to kiss you. The risk's on both sides."

She thought she heard some of the grooms hooting with laughter before her mind went blank. She'd wondered if that first, that only, intellect-sapping kiss had been a fluke. A coincidence. A one-time trip.

Apparently not.

There was something about his mouth. She opened hers to it eagerly, swamped in the taste, the texture, the heat. It moved against hers, clever and tormentingly slow, as if there was all the time in the world to sample. On a moan of agreement, she plunged her hands into his hair, holding on until the sounds of the track were no more than misty white noise.

I want. It was all he could think. He'd spent so much of his life wanting—decent food, a clean bed, the simple peace of living without fear. As he'd grown, those wants had grown with him. He'd wanted women and power and the money that would ensure both.

But he'd never craved anything, certainly not anyone, as he craved now. One woman. One night. He'd have gambled everything he had for the chance of it.

"How much longer?" he murmured against her lips.

"I don't know." She struggled to catch her breath. "I don't know you."

"Sure you do."

176

"I didn't know you existed a couple of months ago." She drew away, surprised her legs didn't fold under her. "I'm not—" She straightened her cap with a shaky hand as applause rang out behind them. "We need to talk about this later. Without an audience."

"Well." He skimmed a fingertip over her jaw. "I accomplished something, anyway. The word's already going out that you're off limits."

"That I'm—" She set her teeth. "Is that what that was for? Some sort of macho claim staking?"

"No. It was for me, darling. But it worked. See you around."

She kicked the soda can she'd dropped when he'd kissed her. "Idiot," she muttered. Fighting for dignity, she turned and nearly ran into Naomi.

"It's odd," Naomi began while Kelsey struggled for words. "Watching that. If you'll pardon the analogy, I often have the same sensation when I see one of my horses led to the track. It's like watching your child get on the school bus, or recite in a class play. You suddenly realize that they're not just your child anymore, and that there's so much you don't know about them."

"He just did it to annoy me."

Though her heart was still swelling, Naomi smiled. "Oh, I don't think so." She took a chance and lifted a hand to Kelsey's cheek. "Confused?"

"Yes."

But not ready to talk about it. "Would you like me to speak with Gabe? He won't appreciate it, but he's fond enough of me to put up with the intrusion."

"No. I'll handle it." She glanced around. There were still a number of grinning faces pointed her way. "Don't we have a race coming up?" she snapped. "You're not being paid to gawk."

As Kelsey stalked over to the saddling stall, Naomi let out a grin of her own.

*

177

ON THE TRACK, PRIDE RAN LIKE a dream, bursting through the gate with a fierce look in his eyes and Reno driving him on. At the first turn, he was fighting for position, but after that it was over. Down the backstretch there were three lengths of daylight between him and the closest contender.

"Looks like a rich man's horse," she heard someone comment behind her.

Yes, she thought, he did. But money had nothing to do with it.

Gabe joined her at the fifth race, as cool and casual as if they'd recently shared a sandwich rather than a torrid, public embrace. "Reno ran a smart race."

"He and Pride make a good team." She shot Gabe a look. "The best team on the circuit."

"We'll see," he murmured. "Keep your eye on Cunningham's Big Sheba. Tell me what you see."

Frowning, Kelsey watched the horses being loaded in the gate. The big bay filly was fractious, nervous. She took a swipe, a bad-tempered kick, at a groom and sent him sprawling.

"She's wound up. That's not unusual." She shifted her gaze to Three Aces. He was giving his own handlers a fight. "Your colt's feeling frisky himself."

"Just watch."

The bell sounded. Horses charged. Cunningham's filly took the lead, her long legs extended, digging up dirt. Kelsey narrowed her eyes behind the binoculars. Big Sheba was sweating heavily by the first turn.

"She's fast. Why is he pushing her so hard?" She winced as the jockey used the bat, quick and often.

"He's doing what he's been told."

At the halfway mark she began to flag, just a fraction, but enough for the field to close. Kelsey felt her eyes begin to tear. Big Sheba had gallantry, but she didn't have wind. And they were hurting her.

On the backstretch she fell a half-length behind Gabe's colt,

178

then a length. Sheer heart kept her in the place position by a nose when they crossed the wire.

"That's inexcusable." Furious, she whirled on Gabe. "There have to be rules."

"We've got plenty of them. None say you can't push a horse past its limits. Rumor is she's got lung trouble. So the idiot has his jockey run her full out at seven furlongs. He wants the fucking Derby so much he'll kill her to have a shot at it."

"I thought he was just a fool."

"He's a fool, all right. An ambitious one. He wants that first jewel."

"Don't we all?"

"Yeah. The difference is just how far we'll go to get it."

He left her to head down to the winner's circle. Kelsey turned her back on the track. Suddenly it had lost a great deal of its glamour.

# Chapter Twelve

Jack Moser ran a clean place. Maybe some of his clientele rented a room by the hour, but that was none of his nevermind. Jack figured what went on behind closed doors went on behind closed doors at the Ritz Hotel just as it did at his place.

Only they paid more for it.

He didn't have bugs, wouldn't tolerate carryings-on after the decent hour of midnight, and paid extra so his guests could have cable.

At twenty-nine dollars a pop for a single, it wasn't a bad deal.

Children under eighteen stayed for free.

He gave his guests the amenity of a sliver-sized bar of Ivory soap along with the bath-mat-size towels, and for their convenience, he had a deal going with the nearby diner to deliver meals after six A.M. and before ten P.M.

Maybe he slipped some of the cash under the table and didn't push for ID, but that was his business.

The sheets were laundered, the bathrooms disinfected, and there was a good sturdy lock on each and every door.

He liked the summers best, when vacationing families heading north or south spotted his blinking vacancy sign. Mostly they just tumbled out of their aging station wagons and into bed. Didn't have to worry about them spraying beer on the walls or tearing up the sheets.

He'd been watching people come and go for twelve years and figured he knew a thing or two about them. He knew when a couple rented a room to cheat on a spouse, when a woman was hiding out from the guy who was as likely to put his fist in her eye as look at her. He recognized the losers, the drifters, the runners.

He'd pegged room 22 as a runner.

None of my nevermind, Jack told himself as he hooked the passkey from the peg-board. The guy had paid cash for three nights in advance. So what if he'd had the smell of fear around him, or if he'd had a way of looking over his shoulder as if he was expecting somebody to shove a knife in his back?

He'd paid his eighty-seven bucks plus tax and hadn't made a peep since.

Which was the problem. Room 22's time was up, and according to skinny-butted Dottie, the housekeeper, his lock was still bolted and the DO NOT DISTURB sign was out. Just the way it had been for three days.

Well, he was going to have to be disturbed, Jack thought as he strode across the parking lot to the line of identical gray doors and shaded windows. Room 22 could come up with another day's rent, or get his butt moving.

Jack Moser didn't extend credit.

He knocked first, sharp, authoritative. Nobody but Jack knew the secret pleasure it gave him to hustle along a deadbeat. "Manager," he said crisply, and caught Dottie poking her head out of 27 where her cart was parked, to give him the eye.

"Probably dead drunk," she called out.

Jack sighed, and straightened his sloped shoulders. "Just do your job, Dottie. I'll handle this." He knocked again, missing the face

181

she made at him. "Manager," he repeated, then slipped his key into the lock.

The smell hit him first, gagging him. His first thought was that 22 had ordered something from the diner that had disagreed with him, violently. His second was that it would take a frigging case of Lysol to cover the stench.

Then he had no thought at all. He saw what sat slumped at the tiny, scarred table, eyes staring, body bloated. Whoever had checked into 22 had metamorphosed in three days into a thing as horrible as anything Jack had ever seen on a late-night horror movie.

He staggered back, overwhelmed by the sight and the odor. A strangled cry caught in his throat, and he threw up on his shoes. It didn't stop him from running. He continued to run even after Dottie hurried into room 22 and began to scream.

THE BODY HAD ALREADY BEEN bagged by the time Rossi pulled up at the motel. It had been through sheer doggedness and a touch of luck that he was there at all. His ears didn't perk up at every suspicious or unattended death that came into Homicide. But the name Fred Lipsky had rung a bell. It was a name on his list, one he'd been unable to check out.

Now, it seemed, he had his chance.

The medical examiner, Dr. Agnes Lorenzo, was packing up. Rossi nodded to the small, athletic woman with graying hair and puppy-dog eyes. "Lorenzo."

"Rossi. I thought this was Newman's case."

"It ties into one of mine. What have we got?" He hooked his badge to his pocket and moved through the uniformed men stationed at the open door.

The body was already zipped, ready for transfer to the morgue. The air still smelled ripe, but it wasn't a smell that affected him much anymore. He scanned the room, taking in the unmade bed, the bag of clothes tossed in the corner, the dust left over from the forensics team. A bottle of gin, three-quarters empty, a single glass, and an ashtray full of Lucky Strike butts.

"Don't ask me for cause of death, Rossi," Dr. Lorenzo began. "I can tell you it occurred forty-eight to sixty hours ago. No wounds, no sign of a struggle."

"Cause of death?"

She'd known he would ask, and smiled thinly. "His heart stopped, Rossi. They all do."

He ignored the jibe and formed a picture. A man drinking alone. Angry? Guilty? Afraid? Why did a man rent a cheap room to drink in when he already had a cheap room thirty miles away?

And if Lipsky had been running, it meant he had something to hide.

Since he'd taken her sarcasm well, Dr. Lorenzo decided to give him a break. "He had about three hundred in his wallet, and an expired credit card. There was a copy of *Daily Racing Form* in his bag, four days old, and a knife in his left boot."

Rossi sprang to attention like a setter on point. "What kind of knife?"

"Six inches long, thin blade, smooth edge."

Rossi's cop's heart began to swell. Forensics would have the knife, and if there was any trace of blood, man or horse, they'd find it. "Who found him?"

"Manager. Name's Moser. He might still be in the office over there, with his head between his knees."

"Not everyone's as tough as you, Lorenzo."

"You're telling me." She stepped outside again, sorry the spring air was marred by the whoosh of traffic on Route 15. She'd left a body on the slab, and now she had another to add to her backlog. Every day, she thought, was a picnic.

"I'll need a copy of the autopsy report."

"Two days."

"Twenty-four hours, Lorenzo. Be a pal."

"We're nobody's pals, Rossi." She turned away and got into her car.

"Hey." He grabbed her door before she could close it. He'd known Agnes Lorenzo for three years. She didn't have many buttons that could be pushed, but he'd uncovered a few. "You know that stiff you did last week? Gordon. Mick Gordon. Old man, gut-knifed."

She pulled out a cigarette, a habit she no longer bothered to feel guilty about. "The one who got his skull cracked and most of his internal organs smashed for good measure? Yeah, I remember."

"I think this stiff's the one who did him."

She blew out smoke. She hadn't gotten a close look at the knife. There had been no need for her to examine it. But she remembered the wound. She had dozens of wounds filed in her head, never to be forgotten.

She nodded. "The weapon could be right. Okay, Rossi, I'll burn the midnight oil for you, but I can't promise all the tests will be done."

"Thanks." He closed her door, forgot her, and zeroed in on the office and Jack Moser.

GABE LEARNED ABOUT LIPSKY ten minutes after he returned from Florida. The press had found a gold mine in Dottie, the housekeeper.

The news that Lipsky had died in a motel room spread from barn to track, from groom to exercise boy. Gabe's twice-weekly housekeeper brought him the news, and the paper, before he'd done more than tossed his bags on his bed.

Fury flared, like a gasoline-soaked match. He was working on banking it when Rossi tracked him down.

"Nice to see you again, Mr. Slater."

"Lieutenant." Gabe offered the paper he'd brought down with

him, then sat in the sun-drenched living room. "Odds are you're here to tell me about this."

"You win." Rossi set the paper aside and made himself comfortable. "Fred Lipsky worked for you up until a few weeks ago."

"Up until I fired him, which I'm sure you know. He was drunk."

"And objected to the termination."

"That's right. He pulled a knife, I knocked him down, and I thought, mistakenly, that that was the end of it." His face still sternly controlled, he edged forward. "If I'd had any suspicion that he would have used that knife on one of my men, or one of my horses, he wouldn't have walked away."

"You don't want to make statements like that to a cop, Mr. Slater. It hasn't leaked to the press yet, but the knife in Lipsky's possession at the time of his death was the weapon that killed Mick Gordon. As yet, no one can definitely place Lipsky at the scene at the time of the murder. But we have a weapon and we have motive—revenge."

"Case closed?" Gabe finished.

"I like them neat before I close them. This one isn't neat. How well did you know Lipsky?"

"Not well. He came with the farm."

The statement made Rossi smile. "An interesting way of putting it."

"When I took over here, I kept on anyone who wanted to stay. It wasn't their fault Cunningham played lousy poker."

Intrigued, Rossi tapped his pencil against his pad. "That's a true story, then. Sounded made up. No point in mentioning a deal like that would be on the shady side of the law?"

"No point at all," Gabe agreed.

"I'll talk to your trainer again, and the men. I'm interested to know if anyone who did know him thinks he was suicidal."

"You want me to think Lipsky killed himself?" The rage began to work in him again, gnawing away. "Why? Out of guilt?

Remorse? That's shit, Lieutenant. He was as likely to stick a gun in his mouth or put a rope around his neck as he was to dance on Broadway."

"You said you didn't know him well, Mr. Slater."

"Not him, but I know the type." He'd been raised by Lipsky's type. "They blame everyone else, never themselves. And they don't take that last dive because they're always figuring the angles. They drink and they cheat and they talk a big game. But they don't kill themselves."

"An interesting theory." And one Rossi subscribed to himself. "Lipsky didn't eat a gun or string himself up. He drank a nasty cocktail of gin and what I'm told is called acepromazine. Are you familiar with it?"

Gabe's voice was carefully blank. "It's used to relax horses. It's a tranquilizer."

"Yeah, so I'm told. Funny, I thought when a horse broke his leg, you put a gun behind his ear."

"The noise annoys the customers," Gabe said dryly. "And every break isn't terminal. There's a lot that can be done so that a horse doesn't have to be put down. Quite often he can race again, or breed. When there's nothing else to be done, a vet gives the horse an injection. There's not supposed to be any pain. I've always wondered how the hell anyone knows that."

"You won't be able to check with Lipsky. Do you keep any of that stuff around here?"

"It's administered by a vet, as I said. Nobody puts a horse down on a whim, Lieutenant."

"I'm sure you're right. It would be a hell of an investment to lose."

"Yeah." Gabe's voice was cool. "Have you ever seen it happen?"

"No."

"The horse stumbles on the track, falls. The jockey's off him like a flash, panicked, fighting it back. Everything gets quiet and grooms race out from everywhere. It doesn't have to be their horse.

186

It's everybody's horse. Then you call the vet, and when there's no choice, when it can't be put off, the vet finishes him—behind a screen, for privacy."

"Have you ever lost one that way?"

"Once, about a year ago during a morning workout. That's a more dangerous time than a race. The rider's relaxed. Everybody is." He could still remember it, the helplessness, the impotent anger.

"This was a pretty filly. The Queen of Diamonds, I called her. The groom in charge of her cried like a baby when it was over. That was Mick." Gabe resisted the urge to ball his hands into fists. "So if you're telling me that somebody finished off Lipsky the way you finish off a terminal horse, I have to say they sent him off in better style than he deserved."

"Do you hold a grudge, Mr. Slater?"

"Yes, Lieutenant, I do." Gabe's eyes were steady and shielded. "You want to ask me if I killed Lipsky, I have to say no. I'm not sure what the answer would be if I'd known what you've told me today, and if I had found him first."

"You know something, Mr. Slater, I like you."

"Is that so?"

"It is." Rossi offered one of his rare smiles, an expression that never sat quite comfortably on his face. "Some people dance all around questions, some fumble, some sweat. But not you." Rossi picked a mote of lint from the leg of his trousers. "You hated the son of a bitch, and might have killed him if you'd had the chance. And you're not afraid to say so. Thing is, not only do I like you, I believe you." He rose. "Now, it could be you're bluffing me through this, and I'll find out if you paid a quick visit to that motel. But I always circle around, so that doesn't worry me." He took another long, careful study. "But I don't think so. Lipsky would've gotten one peep at you through the judas hole and barricaded himself in for the duration. Do you mind if I go down and talk to your men now?"

"No, I don't mind." Gabe stayed where he was; Rossi knew the way. He closed his eyes and concentrated on relaxing one vertebra at a time.

HE GAVE ROSSI AN HOUR BEFORE he went down to the barn himself. The atmosphere was charged with the combination of excitement and dread that blooms around death. Men stopped their gossiping and instantly looked busy when Gabe appeared.

He found Jamison in conference with Matt over the injured colt.

"The inflammation's down," Matt was saying. "It's healing well. Go to changing the dressing once a day, using the same antiseptic."

"He's going to scar."

Matt nodded, eyeing the long healing slice along the flank. "More than likely."

"Goddamned shame." Jamison picked up the syringe to bathe the wound. "Prime-looking horse like this."

"It'll add to his prestige," Gabe commented, moving up to take the colt's halter himself. He ran his knuckles down Double's cheek, as a man might caress a woman. The colt responded by butting his hand, playful as a puppy. "Battle scars," he murmured. "It won't affect his time, or his ambition. How soon can we put a rider up on him?"

"Don't be in a hurry." Matt jerked aside as the colt swung his head and aimed for his shoulder, no longer a puppy but nine hundred pounds of temperament. The teeth missed by an inch or so. "This one's always testing me. Like to take a chunk out of me, would you, fella?" He gave the colt a good-natured slap on the neck when he was sure Gabe had tightened his grip. "He'll run in Kentucky for you, Gabe. If I was a betting man, I'd put money on him myself."

Gabe accepted Matt's diagnosis, then turned to his trainer. "Jamie?"

"I've been laying out a new training schedule for him. It'll either work, or it won't."

"That'll have to do, then. Did Rossi talk to you?"

Jamison's eyes turned grim as he completed the new dressing. "Yeah. He was down here, asking his questions. Got everybody all stirred up. Peterson figures it was a mob hit. Kip thinks it was a woman. Lynette didn't take to that and took some skin off his nose. They've been arguing over it, with the boys taking sides."

"Nobody thinks it was suicide?"

Jamison shot Gabe a look and stepped out of the box. "Nobody that knew him."

"He could have gotten his hands on some acepromazine," Matt reminded Jamison. "He'd have known what it would do. Surely he had to know the authorities would catch up with him eventually."

"A man like Lipsky could have lost himself at a hundred tracks." Jamison looked back at the colt. He was dressing the wound himself, as penance for his part in it. "I should have fired him months ago. Everything might've been different then." And Mick might have been alive.

"That part's done," Gabe said. "But it's not over. Whoever gave Lipsky that last drink is part of it."

"I'll tell you what I told Rossi." Matt scratched his chin as they headed outside. "It had to be someone who knows horses, and who had access to veterinary supplies." He smiled wanly. "Which doesn't narrow it down too much."

"It includes all of us." Gabe watched Matt's jaw go slack. "And several hundred others. Thanks for stopping by."

Matt swallowed nervously. "No problem. I'll check on the colt in a couple of days. I, um, think I'll drop by Three Willows."

"Oh." Eyeing Matt, Gabe took out a cigar and lit it casually. "Is there a problem over there?"

"No, no. I just . . . Well."

Gabe's smile came easily. Most of the tension drained away. "She's a pleasure to look at, isn't she?"

Matt flushed, a curse of pale skin. "It isn't a hardship. Channing told me he thinks she might stay around awhile." He'd done his best to pump Channing for details, but the young man was either very discreet or very dense when it came to his stepsister.

"Oh, I think she'll stay awhile." Gabe was going to make certain of that. "And you look all you want." He swung an arm over Matt's shoulder as he walked Matt to his truck. "A saint couldn't blame you for it. But watch where you touch, Doc."

As Matt fumbled for a response, Gabe opened the truck door for him. "Mine," he said simply.

"You—" He broke off, flushed crimson. "I didn't realize. Kelsey never . . . I never—"

"If I thought you had, I'd have to hurt you." Gabe's smile was friendly, even sympathetic, but the warning was clear. "Give Kelsey my best when you see her."

"Sure." Scurrying to leave, Matt scrambled into the truck. "But you know, maybe I should just get back. I've got a pile of paperwork."

"Then I'll let you get to it." Gabe stepped back, grinning as he watched the truck zip up the long lane.

"You scared the boy white." Jamison thumbed out one of his favored cherry Life Savers.

"Just saving him some trouble down the road."

"That may be." Studying the last of Matt's dust, Jamison let the cool, slick flavor dissolve on his tongue. "Does she know you've put your brand on her?"

Gabe chuffed out smoke, remembering, with fondness, her reaction to his very deliberate public kiss. "She's a bright woman."

"Bright women are the ones who give a man the most trouble."

"I haven't had any trouble in a long time." And he hadn't known just how much he'd wanted some. "I might just drive over myself, and see if I can stir some up." The distraction

190

would do him good, he decided, and he turned to look at his trainer.

He'd been focused on the colt in the barn, and on Matt. Now he could see the lines of weariness, the shadowed eyes. "You look beat, Jamie."

He'd been sleeping poorly, and he'd found it harder yet to choke down a decent meal since Mick's murder.

"I've got a lot on my mind."

"One thing you can get off of it is any responsibility for what happened to Mick." When Jamison merely looked away, Gabe tossed down his cigar and ground it out. The expression in Jamison's eyes only churned up his own feelings of guilt. "Okay, you used poor judgment in keeping him on. I used it in firing him in front of the men. You want to consider that the trigger, fine. But it wasn't the finger that pulled it."

"I see him—Mick—every time I close my eyes." Jamison's voice was low, strained. "The way he must have looked when Lipsky and the colt got done with him. It should never have happened, Gabe." He let out a sigh. There was no answer for that. He knew there was none. "The Derby's in three and a half weeks. That colt's got to be ready, and it's my job to make him so. But I look at him, and I think how proud Mick was to be grooming him."

Saying nothing, Gabe looked out over the hills. His hills. The Derby was more than a race. More even than a goal. It was the Holy Grail he'd been chasing all of his life.

Now, after a lifetime of struggle, and five years of concentrated effort, it was nearly within reach. Maybe it would be empty when he finally grasped it, but he had to know.

"The colt's got to run, Jamie. If you can't work with him, I'll pass him to Duke." Duke Boyd, the assistant trainer, was competent. They both knew it. But he didn't have that extra flair Jamison had been born with. "One way or another, he'll be ready for Churchill Downs."

191

"I'll do my job," Jamison said, and rubbed his tired eyes.

"I need your heart in it."

Jamison dropped his hands. "You'll have it, goddammit. And my soul as well."

He turned away and stalked back to the barn.


KELSEY KNEW SHE WASN'T supposed to fall in love with the horse. But intellect had nothing to do with it. She was as fascinated with the new wobbly-legged foal as she was with the older colts—and had been kicked only once in return for her affection.

Perhaps because she'd taken that philosophically, and had hauled herself up and brushed herself off, Moses began to increase her training.

He liked her style, the way she responded to the horses. And what was more important, he liked the way they responded to her.

Still, he was pleased when he saw she was as much nerves as eagerness when he took her to the yearling stable. He'd consulted with the yearling manager, and between them, they'd culled out this particular filly, a bold little chestnut, weighing in at a trim seven hundred and fifty pounds.

The light was gold, almost liquid with dawn. It poured onto the filly's coat, inflamed it. Eyes dazzled, Kelsey stood just inside the box. She was sure she'd never seen anything quite so beautiful in her life.

"She's got spirit," Moses said as he worked with a handler to calm her as she was saddled. "And she's got heart. That's why Naomi called her Honor. Naomi's Honor."

As if responding to her name, the filly butted Moses, hard. The vibration sang up his shoulder. He gave a firm jerk on the short-ened reins, and continued.

"You'll be the first weight she's had on her back. Now, don't go thinking she's sweet and eager to please. She's used to having her freedom. We can't know what to expect. She's a lot stronger than you." He glanced back at Kelsey, as if dismissing her slight frame in the padded jacket and hat. "So you have to be smarter." He stroked a hand over the yearling, neck to withers. "And kinder."

That was why he'd chosen Kelsey. No one could work successfully with yearlings without kindness.

The stall was quiet. Moses spoke so softly they might have been in church. He clucked to the yearling, then to Kelsey, signaling her to move in and make her connection.

Her heart was thudding, so loud and hard in her throat she was sure it would spook the yearling. But her hands were gentle, her movements slow. She spoke barely above a whisper, watching Honor's ears prick to the sound of her voice.

"You're so pretty. So pretty, Honor. I can't wait to ride you. We're going to be friends, you and I."

The yearling snorted, reserving judgment. Her ears laid back when Moses slipped the bridle over her head.

"Easy now," Kelsey murmured. "Nobody's going to hurt you. Before long, you'll be a queen around here. I bet that feels strange, doesn't it?" She continued to soothe while Moses tightened the saddle. "You should try panty hose. I'll lay odds they're more uncomfortable than this little saddle."

The light changed subtly, warmed.

"I'm going to give you a leg up," Moses told her. "Remember what I said to do?"

"Yes." She had to take a deep, clearing breath. "I don't sit in the saddle yet. The bellying comes first."

"That's right. Remember, it's an announcement. You're telling her this is what she's here for. Slow now. And remember where the door is if you need to get out quick."

The idea of that had Kelsey taking one more breath before she put her knee, and her welfare, in Moses's hands.

The yearling shied, surprised, annoyed as Kelsey draped herself over the saddle. Kelsey felt the agitated movement under her and refused to think about being sprawled over several hundred pounds of irritated horse. She followed Moses's instructions and her own instincts, easing herself up and around, shifting her weight to saddle and stirrups.

Honor danced, kicking out with a hind leg, trying to shift to get a good clean shot at Moses. Instinctively, Kelsey leaned forward, spoke softly, firmly in the yearling's ear.

"Stop that. You don't want everyone to think you're common."

It wasn't magic. The voice and the tone didn't immediately calm her. But after a few more arrogant maneuvers, the yearling settled.

"She likes me," Kelsey announced.

"She's thinking about how to shake you off her back."

"No." Kelsey grinned down at Moses. "She likes me."

"We'll see." He made Kelsey sit until he was satisfied. "All right. Let's get to work."

This, as Moses explained, was kindergarten. Kelsey would simply sit in the saddle while the handler walked Honor on the yearling track, the high walls preventing both of them from being distracted from the job at hand.

Once the yearling had become accustomed to a rider's weight, she would be turned loose by the handler. And Kelsey would guide her.

They'd learn together.

"How did she do?" Naomi asked when she joined him.

"Like you'd expect. She's got plenty of Chadwick in her." Moses put a hand over hers, squeezed briefly in one of his rare displays of public affection. "I thought you'd come down and watch for yourself."

"I was too nervous." She watched Kelsey control the yearling with a light tug on the reins. "She's been here a month, Moses. She hasn't said anything about leaving." Naomi hooked her thumbs in her front pockets. "With everything that's happened in the past couple of weeks, I keep waiting for her to pack up and go."

"You're not looking close enough, Naomi." He smiled a little when Kelsey forgot the training and leaned forward to press her face into the yearling's mane. "She's not going anywhere."

At Moses's signal, Kelsey straightened, then walked the yearling sedately over. "She's gorgeous, isn't she?"

"Yes." The pride that welled up in Naomi was almost frightening. She lifted a hand to stroke the yearling, and let her fingertips brush against Kelsey's. "You look wonderful together."

"I feel wonderful." After Moses had fed Honor a carrot as a reward, Kelsey held out a hand. "Don't I deserve one?"

"I guess you do, at that."

She accepted one and bit in. "Now that I've stopped being terrified, I can enjoy it." After patting Honor on the neck, she tried not to gloat. "Can I work her tomorrow, Moses?"

"And the day after," he said. "She's your responsibility now."

"Really?" She wanted to leap off and kiss him, but settled for beaming at him. "I won't let you down."

"You do, and I'll dock your pay."

Now she grinned. "I'm not getting paid."

"You've been on the payroll for two weeks." He had the satisfaction of seeing her jaw drop. "You get your first check on Friday."

"But it isn't necessary. I'm just—"

"You do the work, you get the pay." He said it firmly. He was, after all, in charge of this particular matter. "Of course, you're starting at the bottom. That's about where you started, isn't it, Naomi?"

"Rock bottom," she replied with a grimace. "My father insisted I earn every penny of my salary, paltry as it was. The idea was, when it all came to be mine, I'd appreciate it more. He was right."

Kelsey considered. It was probably best, more of a business arrangement. "How paltry?"

195

"You should probably clear about two hundred a week," Moses told her.

She lifted a brow. "When do I get a raise?"

With a laugh, Naomi stepped closer. "He'd have appreciated you." Gently, she skimmed her fingertips over the yearling's throat. "She likes you."

Kelsey sent Moses a smug smile. "That's what I said."

"I missed twenty-three birthdays." Naomi's tone shifted Kelsey's attention back. And now her eyes were wary. "Twenty-three Christmases. A lot to make up for." Steadying herself, she looked up and met her daughter's eyes. "I'd like to start, if you'll let me. Will you take her?"

"Take her?" Staggered, Kelsey stared. "Honor? You want to give her to me?"

"I'd like you to accept her. No strings. I realize it might be a bit awkward to keep a horse in an apartment"—she struggled to keep her voice light—"but she can stay here as long as you like. Moses can work with her, if that's what you want. But she'd be yours, if you'll take her."

Swamped with emotion, Kelsey dismounted, slowly. Her palms grew damp on the reins, and she felt the warm breath of the yearling across the nape of her neck.

"I'd love to take her. Thank you."

"You're welcome. I have to get back. I have a lunch meeting."

Kelsey took a step forward, then stopped, suddenly pushing the reins into Moses's hand. She had to dash to catch up with Naomi's long strides. She laid a tentative hand on Naomi's shoulder, and did what came more simply, more naturally than she'd imagined. She kissed her.

"Thank you," she said again, but the rest of the words slid down her throat when Naomi embraced her, held her hard.

And where, Kelsey thought as she felt the urgency, the need pulse from her mother, had this passion come from? How could it have been there all along and never showed?

"I'm sorry," Naomi murmured, and stepped back quickly. "I'll have the ownership papers drawn up right away. I'm late," she managed, and hurried away.

Conflicting emotions battered her. Kelsey stood helplessly, wishing she understood herself, much less the woman who'd given birth to her.

"I don't know what to do."

"You're doing fine." Moses handed her back the reins. "Now go groom your horse."

# Chapter Thirteen

DAYS PASSED QUICKLY. KELSEY HAD A HORSE OF HER OWN, an intriguing romance with a fascinating and frustrating man, and a fresh curiosity about the mother she was beginning to love.

She hadn't expected to love Naomi. To wonder about her, certainly. Perhaps to come to respect her. But it was impossible to live in such close proximity with a woman of Naomi's breed and not have emotions become tangled.

There wasn't much time to dwell on it. As the Bluegrass Stakes approached, the gateway for the all-important Derby, both Three Willows and Longshot were hives of activity.

Kelsey wasn't ready to admit it, but she was already visualizing Honor covered in a blanket of red roses a couple of Derbies down the road.

Today, she was taking an important step toward that goal.

A starting gate was set up outside the practice oval at Three Willows. Though there was no longer any bite of winter, the air was still cool. Kelsey tugged nervously at her jacket, hoping she wasn't transmitting any of her tension to Honor.

A Thoroughbred was born to run, she reminded herself. This

was just a lesson in format. No amount of champion blood could carry a horse over the finish line if it didn't learn how to go through a steel cage and come out running.

"Heard you think you've got a contender here." Gabe sauntered over and rubbed a hand over the yearling's nose. Honor laid her ears back and eyed Gabe, then, approving of scent and touch, perked them up again and sidled closer.

"I know I've got one." Kelsey put a proprietary hand on Honor's halter. "I haven't seen you around in a couple of days."

"Miss me?"

"Not particularly." Kelsey could be grateful she hadn't fallen into that humiliating habit of waiting by the phone. Yet. "We're all pretty busy these days."

"We've got Double back in full training."

She dropped all pretense and caught his hand. "Oh, that's wonderful! I'm so glad."

He pleased himself by taking a nip at her knuckles. "Remember you said that after he wins the Derby."

"My money's on Pride." And so was her heart. "Though I might set some aside for Double to place."

"We're sending him out to Keeneland for a race. Jamie wants him to have a solid test before the Bluegrass Stakes."

"Are you going?" she said casually.

"I'm going everywhere the colt goes, including the winner's circle at Churchill Downs." He stroked a hand down her hair, in much the same way he had caressed the horse. "Want to keep me company?"

She turned to check the cinches on Honor's saddle. "I'm planning on joining Naomi in the winner's circle."

He gave her hair a sharp tug. "To Keeneland, darling. A couple of days, more or less alone." He moved closer. She carried the scent of horses about her now, twined with her own fragrance of citrus and spring. "I wonder how many times I can make love with you on one quick out-of-town trip."

199

The muscles in her thighs turned to warm wax. "Is there a record?"

"There would be." Eyes on hers, he leaned down and caught her bottom lip between his teeth. "You have"—he nipped once, and watched her pupils widen—"the most incredible mouth."

"Leave the girl alone." Trying to look annoyed, Moses gave Gabe a hefty shove on the arm. "You going to fraternize with the competition, Kelsey, or are you going to do your job?"

She picked up her hat and lifted her chin. "I can do both." She turned toward her horse, and Moses obliged her with a leg up.

"Cocky," he muttered at her.

"Confident," she corrected. And anything but, she walked Honor toward the steel cage.

The gate doors were open, to ease the yearling into the notion of moving through the confining tunnel. Honor swung her head once and tried to veer off. Testing, Kelsey knew, the balance of power.

"Oh no, you don't," she muttered. "I'm still in charge here. You don't want to embarrass us both in front of company, do you?" A touch of the knees, a firm hold on the reins, and Kelsey pressed her on, bringing Honor to a full halt when they were closed in by the gate.

"It's not so bad, is it?" she murmured. "And you hardly have to spend any time in here at all. What really counts is once you're through." Slowly, they walked out the other side, circled, and repeated the process.

"She's got good hands," Moses commented.

"She looks more like Naomi than ever on the back of a horse." Gabe tucked his hands in his pockets. There might have been a better way to spend the morning than watching Kelsey guide the flashy yearling through the lesson. But he couldn't think of one. "How's it going between them?"

"Slow, steady. It's not a flashy sprint, but I'd say they passed the first turn when Naomi gave her that yearling."

"She has high hopes for that horse."

"She's got higher hopes for the girl." Gauging the tin... angled himself to face Gabe. "I know she's got a father, t... here. So I'm taking it on myself to tell you to mind y... Kelsey isn't one of the disposable types, and it would upset ... if you hurt her girl."

Gabe's face closed up. When he spoke there was none of the resentment he felt, none of the temper, only mild curiosity in his voice. "And you're assuming I will."

Moses plucked a cigar from Gabe's pocket and stuck it in his own. "Don't pull that inscrutable shit on me. My tribe held the trophy for inscrutable while your ancestors were still huddled in caves eating their meat raw. And I'm not assuming anything. The two of you look good together." He shifted his eyes to check on Kelsey's progress. "Just make sure you think it through. You don't know if a roll in the hay's going to hurt anybody until you're picking the straw out of your hair."

Gabe's lips quivered into a smile. "Which tribe did that one come from? The inscrutable one or the lost one?"

"Just don't push her over the wire too fast. She's got heart." Irritated with himself, Moses trudged across the grass to fine-tune Kelsey's work.

Yes, she had heart, Gabe agreed, studying her as she listened intently to the trainer's advice. And blue blood.

There were plenty who knew him who would say he had no heart at all. And no one would mistake his blood for blue. It hadn't stopped him before. He didn't intend to let it stop him now.

There were any number of women who were willing to overlook those particular flaws in his breeding. Many who had. More, he thought coolly, who would shrug aside a drunk, abusive father, a short stint in a cell, and a lingering taste for playing against the odds.

But he didn't want any number of women, he decided while Kelsey guided her mount into the gate and steadied her in the confining tunnel. He wanted this woman.

...e waited, taking out a pair of sunglasses as the sun grew stronger. The morning was slipping away, and he needed to get back to his own operation. But he drew on his store of patience, staying on the sidelines until Kelsey dismounted.

"She did well," Kelsey said, pressing a kiss to the yearling's cheek before offering her a carrot. "She wasn't afraid at all."

"I want to see you tonight."

"What?" She turned her head, her cheek still brushing Honor's glossy hide.

"I'd like to take you out tonight. Dinner, a movie, a drive. Your choice. A date," he continued when she only studied him with eyes that grew more speculative. "I realize I've neglected that particular ritual with you."

"A date?" She rolled the idea around. "Such as you pick me up, we go somewhere and do some planned activity, then you bring me home and walk me to the door?"

"That's more or less what I had in mind."

"Well, it would be different." She cocked her head, considering. "I have to be up at five, so we'll need to make it an early evening. I wouldn't mind seeing a movie, say a seven o'clock show. Maybe a pizza after."

Now it was his turn to consider. It wasn't the sort of evening he'd expected her to choose. Maybe it was about time they learned about each other. "An early movie and a pizza. I'll pick you up around six." He tipped up her chin, kissed her almost absently.

"Hey, Slater," she called after him. "Do I get to pick the movie?"

He kept walking but glanced over his shoulder. "No subtitles."

"On a first date?" She laughed at him. "What kind of woman do you think I am?"

"Mine," he shot back, and she stopped laughing.


THERE WAS NOTHING ROMANTIC about a pizzeria crowded with teenagers. Which had been precisely Kelsey's point. Keep it casual, she'd decided. Avoid a situation where things could become too intense and try to find out what made Gabriel Slater tick.

"This is perfect." She settled into the booth with paper place mats of Italy printed in red and green. "I'd almost forgotten there was life beyond racing horses."

"It happens to all of us." Amused at finding himself dining with a woman in a place that sported pictures of grinning pizzas and calzones on the wall, he stretched out his legs. "You've taken to it quickly, and in a big way."

"A talent of mine. Or a flaw, depending on your point of view. Why do anything if you don't do it full out?" She relaxed and propped her feet on his bench. "That way you either reap the glory, or you crash and burn."

"Is that what you're after, Kelsey? Glory?"

She smiled. "I always get glory and satisfaction confused." She glanced up at the waitress, back at Gabe. "Your pick. I'll eat anything."

"I won't. Bring us a small—"

"*Large*," Kelsey corrected him.

"Large," he said with a nod. "Pepperoni and mushrooms, a couple of Pepsis."

"Very conservative," Kelsey noted when the waitress walked off.

"I like to know what I'm eating." It came, he supposed, from a lifetime of scrambling for scraps. "Speaking of which, wasn't it you who ate about two gallons of popcorn less than an hour ago?"

Still smiling, she toyed with the simple gold chain around her neck. "Movie popcorn doesn't count. It's simply part of the experience, like the music score."

"Was there a music score? Hard to tell."

"So I'm shallow," she said with a shrug. "I like action films. I actually wrote a script once, for this course I was taking. Lots of good battling evil in car chases and gunfire."

"What did you do with it?"

Absently she tapped her foot in rhythm with the Guns N' Roses number blaring from the jukebox. "I got an *A*, then I put it away. I decided against sending it off because if anyone actually bought it, they'd start changing everything and it wouldn't be mine anymore." The waitress served their drinks in big red plastic cups. "Besides, I didn't want to be a writer."

"What, then?"

"Lots of different things." She moved her shoulders, then leaned forward for her cup. "It always depended on my mood. And the courses I was taking." Her smile was quick and slightly off center. "I'm very big on taking courses. If you want to know a little about anything, from computer science to interior design, I'm your girl."

"Makes sense. You grew up with a college professor." He lifted his cup. "Knowledge is sacred."

"That's part of it, I suppose. But mostly I figured if I tried enough things, sooner or later I'd hit on the right thing."

"And have you?"

"Yes." She sighed. "My family would be quick to point out that I've said that before. But this is different. I've said that before, too," she murmured. "But it is. Nothing I've done has ever felt as right as this, as natural. As real. God knows I've never worked as hard in my life."

To remind herself, she glanced down at her hands. They were toughening up, she thought. She liked to believe she was toughening up with them.

"What about you? Have you hit on the right thing?"

He kept his eyes on hers. For an instant she thought she saw secrets behind them, and hungers that had nothing to do with the scents of garlic and melted cheese.

"It's possible."

"Do you always look at a woman so that she thinks you could start nibbling away at her, from the toes up?"

His lips curved, slow, easy, but his eyes didn't change. "No one's ever asked." He laid a hand on her ankle, which rested on the seat beside him, and began to caress it. "But now that you mention it, it might be an interesting way to end the evening."

The waitress plopped down their pizza, along with a couple of white plastic plates. "Enjoy your meal," she said automatically, and hurried off to fill her next order.

"I love the atmosphere here." Cautious, Kelsey put her feet on the floor and sat up. "But I got off the track. I was asking about your farm. Have you found what you wanted there?"

He used a plastic knife to separate some slices, then slid one onto her plate, one onto his. "It suits me."

"Why?"

"You know, darling, you might have made a mistake giving up writing. At least journalism."

"You can't have the answers without asking the questions." She took her first bite, stinging with red-pepper flakes, stringy with cheese, and sighed with approval. "At least with some people. Don't you like questions, Slater?"

He avoided that one and skipped back to the one before. "It suits me because it's mine."

"It's that simple?"

"No, it's that complicated. You don't want to spoil the evening with a rundown of my life story, Kelsey. Bad for the appetite."

"I have a strong stomach." She licked sauce from her thumb. "You know mine, Gabe. At least several of the highs and lows. There's no moving to the next stage for me without some understanding of who I'm moving with." She continued to eat while he frowned at her. "That's not an ultimatum, or a guarantee. It's just a fact. I'm attracted to you, and I like being with you. But I don't know you."

If she did, he knew there was a good chance her other feelings would dim considerably. Long odds. Well, he'd played them before. When the prize was rich enough. "Let me tell you something about yourself first. The only child of a devoted daddy. Well connected, sheltered. Spoiled."

The last rankled a little, but she wouldn't deny it. "All right. It's true I got almost everything I wanted when I was growing up. Emotionally. Materialistically. I suppose a lot of it was to make up for the lack of having a mother. But I didn't notice the lack."

"A big house in the suburbs," he went on. "Good schools. Summer camp, three squares, and ballet lessons."

If he was trying to annoy her, he was succeeding. Coolly, she chose another slice. "You forgot piano, swimming, and equestrian."

"It's all part of the whole. Proms, the college of your choice, and a big splashy wedding to top it off."

"Don't forget the long, tedious divorce. What's your point, Slater?"

"You haven't got a clue where I came from, Kelsey. I'll tell you and you still won't understand it."

But he would tell her, he decided. And see how the cards fell.

"Maybe I'd go to bed at night not quite hungry. There might have been enough money for food that time, or I'd managed to steal or beg enough. Kids make good panhandlers, good thieves," he added, watching her eyes. "Adults feel sorry for them, or over-look them."

"A lot of people are put in the position where they have to ask for money," she said carefully. "It's nothing to be ashamed of."

"That's because you've never had to ask. Or take." He rattled the ice in his cup, then set it down. "At night I'd probably be listening, or trying not to listen, to the fighting going on in the next room. Or my mother crying. Or the neighbor earning an hour's pay with some faceless john. If I was lucky, I'd wake up in the same bed I went to sleep in. If I wasn't, my mother would come in in the middle of the night, and we'd sneak out before we were tossed out because my father had lost the rent money again."

She saw the picture he was painting for her, and it was dark with harsh edges. "Where did you grow up?"

"Nowhere. It might have been in Chicago, or Reno, or Miami.

206

In the winter we stuck to the south, because the weather's better and the tracks run longer. It might have been anywhere. Places all look the same if you're broke and running. Of course, the old man would say we were just moving on. That he was working on a big score. My mother scrubbed toilets so we didn't starve, and he took most of her pay and blew it on the horses, or the cards, or how far a fucking grasshopper would jump. It didn't matter what the bet was as long as he could flash a few bills and play the big shot."

He spoke without passion, the bitterness barely a flicker in his eyes. "He liked to cheat. Mostly he was good at it, but if he wasn't, my mother scraped enough together to keep him from getting his arms broken. She loved him." And that was the most bitter of all the pills he had had to swallow. "Lots of women loved Rich Slater."

He continued to eat, as if to prove to himself it didn't matter anymore. "He liked to hurt them. Some women keep coming back for another fist in the face. They wear their black eyes and split lips like badges. My mother was one of those. If I tried to stop him, he'd just beat the hell out of both of us. She never thanked me for it, used to tell me I just didn't understand. She was right," he added. "I never understood it."

"There must have been somewhere you could have gone. A shelter. Social services. The police."

He simply looked at her, the flawless complexion, the breeding that went down to the bone. "Some people get swept into dirty corners, Kelsey. That's the way the system works."

"No, it doesn't have to. It shouldn't."

"You've got to look for help, expect it to be there, have the nerve to ask for it. My mother didn't do any of that. She kept her eyes down, expected nothing, asked for nothing."

It was Kelsey's eyes that held him now, the horror and the pity that darkened them.

"But you were only a child. Someone should have ... done something."

"I wouldn't have thanked them for it. I grew up being taught to spit if I saw a cop, to think of social workers as interfering paper pushers whose job it was to keep you from doing what you wanted. So I avoided them. Sometimes I went to school, sometimes I didn't. Christ knows he didn't care, and my mother didn't have the energy left to reel me in. So I did pretty much as I pleased. The old man liked me to hang out with him, sometimes to shill, or to drum up a game of my own. And if I was there I could make sure some money was left once he got too drunk to care."

"You must have thought of running away, of getting away from him."

"Sure, I thought about it. But I figured if I stayed, I could keep him from beating her to death. And I did, for what good it did any of us. My mother died in a charity ward. Pneumonia. I gave it six months, squirreling away the money I made hustling games or jobs at the track. Then I took off. I was thirteen."

And tall for his age, he remembered. Canny. Already old.

"The old man caught up with me a few times. The problem was I had a taste for the horses, so I usually ended up at a track. So did he. He'd knock me around, shake me down. I could usually buy him off."

"Buy him off?"

"If I'd been having a run of luck, I'd have money. A couple of hundred would send him off to a game of his own, or the nearest bar." Of course, Gabe thought, the price had gone up since then. "Every time I cut loose, I'd start over—with one thing in mind. One day I'd have my own. He wouldn't touch me. Nobody would. You're not eating."

"I'm sorry." She reached out and caught his hand firmly in hers. "I'm really sorry, Gabe."

It wasn't pity he was looking for. He realized now that he'd wanted her to be horrified, wanted her to look at him and cringe back. He'd have an excuse then, wouldn't he, to step away from her and stop the headlong race to a future he couldn't see.

"I spent some time in jail over a poker game I wasn't quick enough to spot as a sting." He waited for her to comment on that, but she said nothing. "I was a small fish, but I got reeled in with the big ones. When I got out, I was smarter. I worked some short cons, but I was more into gambling than the grift. Working at stables was a good way to earn a stake. And I liked the horses. I stayed clean because I didn't like prison. I didn't drink because every time I started to I smelled my old man. And I got lucky."

Finished, he sat back and lit a cigar. "Understand better now?"

Did he really think she couldn't see the anger, the scarred-over hurt? People might pass by their table and see a man chatting over a meal, enjoying the company. But if they looked into his eyes, really looked, how could they miss that cold, steely rage? Determined, she put her hand back on his.

"Maybe I can't understand the way you mean. But I think I know it was a nightmare to live with an alcoholic who—"

"He's not an alcoholic," Gabe cut in, his tone frigid. "There's a difference between an alcoholic and a drunk, Kelsey. No twelve-step program is going to change the fact that he's a drunk, a mean one, who likes to beat up on women, or anyone weaker than he is. And it wasn't a nightmare. It was life. My life."

She withdrew her hand. "You'd rather I didn't understand."

He turned his cigar, stared at the tip. He hadn't realized that simple, unquestioning sympathy would bring so many memories, and the feelings that went with them, swirling to the surface. "You're right. I'd rather you look at me and take what you see. Or leave it."

"We're both a product of our upbringing, Gabe. One way or another. I'm not going to care about someone because of what they seem to be. Not again. And if you want me, you're going to have to accept that I care."

He tapped out his cigar. "That definitely sounds like an ulti-matum."

"It is." She shoved her plate aside and picked up her jacket. "It's a long drive home. We'd better get started."

SHE WOULD THINK A GREAT deal about the little boy who had hustled and conned his way through childhood. A child who had gone to bed at night listening to whores and drunks instead of lullabies.

How much of the boy remained with the man, she didn't know. More, she thought, than Gabe believed. More, she was certain, than anyone would ever be allowed to see.

He had, quite simply, refashioned himself. The smooth, easy manners, the stunning house on the hill, his stable of champions. How many of the upper crust of the racing circle knew his back-alley upbringing? If they did, was it considered some amusing eccentricity?

Whatever Gabe wanted to the contrary, she was beginning to understand him. And whether he could see it or not, she already cared.

IT WAS NEARLY ONE A.M. WHEN Bill Cunningham hurried to answer the banging at his front door. Over his naked paunch he wrapped a Chinese red silk robe. A peek through the window made him glad Marla, his latest honey, was a sound sleeper. He liked to think it was great sex that had her snoring away in his big water bed. But more likely it was the 'ludes she ate like candy.

Whatever the reason, it relieved him that he was alone to greet his late and unwelcome visitor.

"I told you never to come here," Cunningham hissed while smoothing down what was left of his hair. Once the Derby was over, he was going to treat himself to a weave.

"Now, now, Billy boy, nobody saw me." Rich was past the midpoint of a solid drunk. He didn't wobble, didn't so much as slur a word. But it showed in the sun-bright glitter in his eyes. "And if they did, hell—no law against a man visiting an old poker buddy, is there?" He grinned, casting his gaze around the opulent foyer. Old Bill had bounced back pretty well, Rich noted, and figured he could squeeze his pal for a few more bills. "How about a drink?"

"Are you crazy?" Despite the fact that only Marla was in the house, and she was cruising on barbiturates, Cunningham whispered. "Do you know the cops have been here? *Here*," he repeated, as if his overdone home were as sacrosanct as a church. "Asking questions because some big-mouthed groom told them I'd let Lipsky shovel shit for a couple of days."

"Told you that was a mistake. But a little one." He held up two fingers close together, squinted at them. "Where's the bar, Bill? I'm dry as the fucking Sahara."

"I don't want you drinking in my house."

Rich's grin only widened, but his eyes turned hard. "Now, you don't want to talk to a business partner like that, Bill. Especially since I have a new proposition for you."

Cunningham moistened his lips. "We've got our deal."

"Just what I want to talk about. Over a friendly drink."

"All right, all right. But make it quick." He shot a look up the stairs as he walked by them, going into a sunken living room done in golds and royal blue. "And quiet. I've got a woman upstairs."

"You dog." Rich gave him a friendly poke in the ribs. "Don't suppose she's got a friend. I've been dry there awhile, too."

"No. And keep your distance. I don't want her to know about you, or any of this. She's built, but she's not bright."

"Best kind of woman." With an appreciative sigh, Rich dropped down into a wide-backed chair covered in gold velvet. "You sure know how to live, pal. I always said, that Billy boy, he knows how to live."

"Just make sure you don't go around saying it now."

211

Cunningham poured two drinks, both twelve-year-old scotch. It seemed like a waste on Rich, but he needed to impress. Always. "You were supposed to handle Lipsky."

"I did." Pleased with himself, Rich swirled the scotch, sniffed it, then swallowed it. "Classy, don't you think, to put him down like you put down a horse?"

Cunningham's hand shook as he lifted his glass. "I don't want to hear about that. I'm talking about before. Jesus, Rich, nobody was supposed to get killed. Old Mick was like a saint around the track."

"An unforeseen complication," Rich said, getting up to refill his glass. "And Lipsky certainly paid for it. But seeing that he did adds to my overhead, Bill. It's going to cost you another ten thousand."

"Are you nuts?" Cunningham sprang up, spilling some scotch. "You did that on your own, Rich."

"To protect your investment. It would have taken the cops five minutes to have Lipsky pointing the finger at me. It points at me," he said affably, "it points at you. So, another ten, Billy. It's a fair price."

He swallowed hard. The money that had come into his hands for Big Sheba had been a miracle. But the miracle had a price. "You might as well ask for ten million. I'm leveraged to the hilt."

Rich had expected that and was ready to be reasonable. "I can wait until after May, no problem. What's a couple of weeks between friends? Now . . ." He crossed his legs. "I've come up with an idea, Billy. A little variation on our theme that will pay off for both of us. You want to collect at Churchill Downs, and so do I. But I also have a job to do, and a score to settle with that boy of mine."

"I don't give a good goddamn about your family problems, as long as the job gets done." But the idea of paying Gabe back began to creep through him, warming more thoroughly than the scotch. "This business with Lipsky damn near ruined things."

"Not to worry. Not to worry." Lazily, Rich waved his glass. "I've got it covered—with, as I said, a little alteration."

"What kind of alteration?"

"Well now," Rich sighed, sipped. "I'm going to tell you. And I think you're going to appreciate the irony of the deal, Billy boy. I really think you are."

LATER, WHEN CUNNINGHAM crawled back into bed, he was shivering. He wasn't a bloodthirsty man, he assured himself. It wasn't his fault two people were dead. Just the luck of the draw, as Rich had said.

Maybe he was crazy to have tied in with Rich Slater, but he was desperate. And the timing had fallen so perfectly in his lap, he'd considered it a sign. Rich's adjusted plan made a hideous kind of sense.

What choice did he have? Cunningham asked himself. If he lost at Churchill Downs there would be no more Marlas, no more big country house, no more strutting into the paddock.

Big Sheba was, he'd thought, his ace in the hole. He'd sunk his money, every spare dollar and all he could borrow, into that filly. And she had short lungs. He squeezed his eyes shut, cursing himself for gambling on the horse.

He needed the Derby, just the Derby, to recoup. Once that was done, he'd breed her. He could live well on the price of her foals.

It had been done before, he thought, going back over Rich's plan. And he'd slipped through that without much more than a ripple. One race, he thought, just one good race.

Needing warmth, he wrapped himself around Marla until her snoring lulled him to sleep.

# Chapter Fourteen

IT WAS A LONGER DRIVE THAN KELSEY REMEMBERED FROM rural Virginia to suburban Maryland. A long time to think. She didn't doubt she would meet with resistance. And unless things had changed in the last few weeks, formidable resistance. Candace was sure to have contacted Milicent to tell her Kelsey was on her way.

Better to face them all at once, Kelsey decided. To shock them, disappoint them, outrage them. A perfect description, she thought with a wry smile. Candace would be shocked, her father disappointed, and her grandmother outraged.

And she, she hoped, would be happy.

When she pulled up in the drive, her father was working in the flower bed. He wore an old sweater, patched at the elbows, and grimy-kneed chinos to weed the just-budding azaleas.

The surge of love came first as she dashed from her car and across the neatly trimmed lawn to hug him. They stayed, knee to knee, admiring the flourishing shrubs.

"I love this house," she murmured, resting her head on his shoulder. "Just recently I realized how lucky I was to grow up here."

She thought of Gabe and brushed a hand over salmon-colored blooms. "How lucky I was to have you, to have flowers in the yard." She smiled a little. "Ballet lessons."

"You hated ballet lessons after six months," he remembered.

"But I was lucky to have them."

He studied her face, brushed at the hair that tumbled over her shoulders. "Is everything all right, Kelsey?"

"Yes."

"We've been worried about you. This recent violence—"

"I know." She cut him off. "It's horrible, what happened to both of those men. I wish I could tell you it doesn't affect me, but of course it does. But I am all right."

"I like seeing that for myself. Phone calls aren't the same." He gathered his gardening tools in a wire basket. "Well, you're home now. That's what matters. Let's go around through the back or Candace will skin me alive for tracking the floors."

Kelsey slipped an arm around his waist as they walked. "I see Grandmother's car."

"Yes, Candace phoned her when you said you were driving in. They're inside, planning for the spring charity ball at the club." He shot her a sympathetic smile. "I believe finding you a suitable escort is at the top of their list."

She winced automatically, then remembered. "The spring ball. That's in May, isn't it?"

"Yes, the first Saturday."

That was the day when spring came to Kentucky, she thought. The same day every year. Derby day. She supposed missing the ball would be another sin on her part.

"Dad." She waited as he set down his tools in the little mud-room that was as spotless as the rest of the house. "I'm not going to be in town that weekend."

"Not in town?" He moved through to the kitchen to wash his hands. "Kelsey, you haven't missed a spring ball since you were sixteen."

215

"I realize that. I'm sorry, but I have plans." He said nothing, only dried his hands on a towel. The disappointment, she thought, had already begun. "I have plans," she repeated. "I'd better tell all of you about them at once."

"All right, then." Trying not to worry, he went with her to the sitting room.

Candace and Milicent were already there, chatting over tiny, crustless sandwiches and Dresden cups of tea. Jasmine, Kelsey deduced after a discreet sniff of the air. It occurred to her that if she'd been at the barn at this time of day, she might be wolfing down a sloppy cold-cut sub and strong black coffee.

Her tastes, among other things, had changed quickly.

"Kelsey." With a delighted laugh, Candace rose to kiss both of her stepdaughter's cheeks. Kelsey caught the subtle scent of L'Air du Temps that mixed with the tea and her grandmother's signature Chanel.

Drawing-room scents, Kelsey thought; she'd gotten entirely too used to barnyard ones. She embraced Candace with more enthusiasm, almost in apology.

"You look wonderful. New hairdo?"

Instinctively Candace patted her short sable locks. "You don't think it's too ingénue, do you? I swear Princeton can talk me into anything."

"It's perfect," Kelsey assured her, remembering suddenly that she hadn't visited Princeton, or any other hairdresser, for that matter, in weeks. "Hello, Grandmother." The greeting, like the kiss on the cheek, was stiff and dutiful. "You're looking well too."

"You've gained back some weight, I see." Milicent sipped her tea, appraising Kelsey over the rim. "It's flattering. Be careful you don't let it go too far, though. Small bones don't carry weight well."

"Most of it's muscle." Kelsey flexed her biceps just to irritate. "It comes from shoveling manure and hauling hay." Smiling, she turned to a dubious Candace. "I'd love some tea. Don't worry, I washed up after the morning workout."

"Of course, of course. Sit down, dear. Philip, you're not carrying that garden with you?"

"Not a speck." He accepted the tea and a tiny sandwich without complaint. When Channing returned home that evening, Philip knew he'd have company on a refrigerator raid. "The azaleas are early this year. I don't think they've ever looked better."

"You say that every spring." Affectionately, Candace patted his hand. "You know, we're the only house on this block without a gardener, and there isn't a yard that can compete with ours. Not when Philip gets done working his magic."

"A nice hobby," Milicent agreed. "I've always preferred tending my own roses."

She turned her attention to Kelsey. At least, she thought, the girl had had enough sense to dress suitably. She'd been nearly certain Kelsey would flaunt her prickly stubbornness by driving out in muddy boots. But the apricot-toned jacket and slacks were flattering, and tasteful.

"As it happens," she began, "Candace and I were just discussing the floral arrangements for the spring ball. We're on the committee. You have a good eye for such things, Kelsey. We'll delegate you to work with the florist."

"I appreciate the confidence, but I'll have to pass. I'm afraid I won't be here."

"For the ball?" Candace laughed again, poured more tea. "Of course you will, dear. It's expected. I realize you might feel a little awkward, with the divorce finalized, and Wade attending with his fiancée, but you mustn't let it bother you. In fact, Milicent and I were just working on a solution to that problem."

Kelsey started to explain, then stopped. "Oh, were you?"

"Yes, indeed." All enthusiasm, Candace added a lump of sugar to her tea. "It was certainly sweet of Channing to escort you last year, but we hardly want that to become a tradition. In any case, people will talk less if you have a more conventional date." The perfect hostess, she offered around the tray of cucumber sandwiches. "As it happens, June and Roger Miller's son has just moved back to the area. You must remember Parker, Kelsey. He's been practicing oral surgery in New York for the last few years, and has just taken a position with a prestigious practice in D.C." She added with a sly smile, "Parker's never married."

"Yes, I remember him." Excellent family, social status. The right schools, the right profession, the right everything. It wasn't his fault, Kelsey supposed, that she saw him as a Wade Monroe clone.

"I've already spoken with the Millers." Pleased with the maneuver, Milicent sipped the delicately fragrant tea. "Parker will escort you. It's all arranged."

Typical, Kelsey thought, fighting a rising anger. It was all so typical. "I'm sure Mr. and Mrs. Miller are delighted to have Parker back in the area, and you'll have to give him my best. But I won't be here. I'm leaving for Kentucky this week, and won't be back until after the first weekend in May."

"Kentucky?" Milicent snapped her cup down in its saucer. "Why on earth are you going to Kentucky?"

"The Derby. Even in your circles, Grandmother, it's an acceptable event. I imagine it'll be a very hot topic of conversation at the ball after Three Willows' colt wins it." She looked at her father, hoping he would understand. "I'm going to be there when he does."

"This is inexcusable," Milicent shot back. "The Bydens are founding members of that club, back to your great-grandfather. We have always attended the ball."

"Things change." Kelsey fought to keep her tone reasonable rather than hard. "I have a job, a responsibility, and a need. I'm not willing to overlook any of them for a dance at the country club. And, Candace, as much as I appreciate your concern, I don't want an arranged escort. I'm involved with someone."

"Oh." Candace blinked and struggled to look pleased. "Well, of course, dear, that's delightful. You must bring him."

"I don't think so." In sympathy, she squeezed Candace's hand. "I don't think he's the country club type."

"One of your stable hands, I suppose," Milicent said bitterly.

"No." Unable to help herself, Kelsey didn't leave it at that. "He's a gambler."

"You're just like your mother." Spine ramrod stiff, Milicent rose. "I warned you," she said to Philip. "You wouldn't listen to me about Naomi, and you wouldn't listen to me about her daughter. Now we all pay the price."

"Milicent." Standing quickly, Candace hurried out of the room after her mother-in-law.

Kelsey set her tea aside. She'd been sorry almost before the words were out. Not because of Milicent's feelings, but her father's.

"That wasn't very tactful of me," she began.

"Honesty was always more your forte than tact."

His voice was weary and stirred up more guilt.

"You're disappointed. I wish there was a way I could do what I need to do and not disappoint you."

"It's a situation that can't please everyone." He rose, turning his back to her as he walked to the windows. He could see his azaleas, the tight buds just freeing up the inner blossoms. The blossoms wouldn't stay trapped, but would burst through the well-meaning protection and spring defiantly to life.

"You've connected with her," he said softly. "I can't say I didn't expect it. So much about you is the same, so much more than your looks. A part of me, a part I'm ashamed of, wants to tell you that you're making a mistake. That you don't belong there. That part of me doesn't want to see how happy it makes you that you do belong there."

"I feel as though I've found what I'm supposed to do. That I don't need to race around the next corner to see if there's something there more interesting, more important. That's all I was doing with my life. We both know it."

"You were searching, Kelsey. That's nothing to be ashamed of."

"I'm not ashamed of it. But I'm tired of it. I'm good with the horses, with the work, with the people. I can't go back to my apartment, to busywork jobs, to weekends at the club. I feel as if I'm . . ."

"Opening up?" Because it hurt him to look at them now, he turned away from the flowers. "Breaking free?"

"Yes. I didn't know how dissatisfied I was—especially with myself."

"That may be." Candace swept back in. Her jaw was set, her eyes angry. "But you had no reason to be rude. Your father and I, and your grandmother, are only trying to help you through a difficult time."

"I think," Kelsey said slowly, "the problem is that this isn't as difficult for me as you think."

"Then you might think of others. About how Philip feels. About how all of this looks to outsiders."

"Candace," Philip said, "this isn't necessary."

"Isn't it?"

"Maybe you're right, Candace. I'm very much concerned how Dad feels. I'm sorry, but I don't have your sensibility about what outsiders think. I don't want to embarrass you," she continued, "or cause problems between the two of you."

"Yet you encouraged Channing to deceive me and stay at that place."

Boggy ground, Kelsey thought, and cursed Channing for leading her onto it. "I encouraged him to stay, yes."

"Now he has some notion about going back there, working there this summer." Flushed with emotion, Candace gripped the back of a chair. "She might have lured you away, Kelsey, but I won't have her corrupting Channing."

"Good God." At wits' end, Kelsey dragged her hands through her hair. "Where does this come from? You haven't even met the woman, but you've cast her as some B-movie siren who seduces young boys and destroys all she touches. She didn't open her home to Channing to corrupt him or to spite any of you. She did it for me. And she offered him the job because he showed an interest in the farm."

"Well, I won't have it." Candace detested sounding shrewish, resented the fact that Kelsey's stubbornness made her so. "I won't have my son loitering around racetracks and associating with gamblers and a convicted murderer."

Kelsey dropped her hands. "That's certainly between you and Channing."

"Yes, it is. It's quite true I have no right to tell you what to do." Her lips quivered. She'd done her best by Kelsey, her very best to be a friend, a guiding force instead of the textbook stepmother. And now, it seemed, she'd failed. "Even if I did, you'd continue to do as you choose. As you've always done."

Philip stepped forward, as perplexed as he was hurt by the outburst. "Candace, we're losing the perspective here. It's only a club dance."

"I'm sorry, Philip." Her angry embarrassment over the scene with Milicent pushed her forward. Milicent was more than her mother-in-law. She was her friend, and her ally. "I feel I must have my say in this. It's much more than a dance. It's a matter of loyalty, and proper behavior. This situation cannot go on. You've hurt your father enough by choosing Naomi over him."

"Is that what you think I'm doing?" She whirled on her father. "Is that what you think? Can't you believe that I'm capable of caring for both of you? Of learning to accept, and forgive?"

"You've nothing to forgive Philip for," Candace put in staunchly. "He did everything that was right."

"I did what I thought best," he murmured. "This is difficult for me, Kelsey. I can't tell you it isn't. But I still want what's best for you."

"I'm trying to find out what that is. Or, if not what's best, at least what's right. I don't want to hurt you in the process."

"I'm sure you don't," Candace said wearily. She'd never really understood her stepdaughter. Why should that change now? "The problem here, Kelsey, is the same as it's always been. You look straight ahead toward a goal and don't notice the consequences of achieving it. And when you have it, you don't always want it."

The thumbnail analysis stung more than any whip of anger. "Which makes me cold and shallow." Her voice trembled no matter how she fought to control it. "It's not the first time that's been pointed out to me, so it's hard to argue."

"That's not true." Philip took her by the shoulders. "And certainly not what Candace meant. You're strong-minded, Kelsey, and you can be stubborn. Those are virtues as well as flaws."

Candace took a mental step in retreat. She knew from experience her preferences would never hold against a united front. "We're concerned about you, Kelsey. If I criticized too harshly, it's only because of that concern, and the fact that the situation is becoming difficult for everyone. The recent publicity has stirred up old memories. People are beginning to talk, and that puts your father in a delicate position."

"Two men were killed." Steadier, Kelsey stepped back. "I had no control over that, nor do I have any over the gossip it generates."

"Two men were killed," Philip repeated. "Can you expect us not to worry?"

"No. I can only tell you it had nothing to do with me, or Three Willows. Violence happens everywhere. The racing world isn't a hive of vice and debauchery. There's no time or energy for either when you're up at dawn every morning. It's work. Hard work. Some of it tedious, some of it exciting, and all of it, to me, rewarding. There's no partying every night with champagne and mobsters. Hell, most nights we're sound asleep before ten. I've watched foals being born and seen grown men sing a sick horse to sleep at night. It's not a Disney movie, but it's no orgy of sin, either."

Philip said nothing. He knew he'd lost. It might have been Naomi standing there, defending a world he had never understood, and could never belong to.

"I'm sure it has its merits." Candace tried for calm. "I've watched the Kentucky Derby myself on television, and there's no denying the horses are magnificent, the entire event exciting. Why, the Hanahans had an interest in a racehorse a few years ago. You remember, Philip. We're not condemning the entire . . . profession"—she supposed it was called—"we're concerned about your associations. You did say you were involved with a gambler."

Kelsey let out a huff of breath. "I said that to needle Grandmother. What I should have said was that I'm interested in a man who owns a neighboring farm. I'm sorry I caused trouble. Now I'll apologize in advance because I'm about to cause more. I'm not renewing the lease on my apartment. I'm going to stay on at Three Willows, at least for the time being. I may look for a house later in the year, but I'm going to keep working at the farm."

Candace put a hand on Philip's arm, a gesture of support and unity. "No matter what the consequences?"

"I'll do my best to minimize them. I realize you won't want to visit me there, so I'll come to you as often as I can. I'll be out of town for a while, but I'll call." She picked up her purse and twisted the strap in her hands. "I don't want to lose you, either of you."

"You can't. This will always be your home." As Philip gathered his daughter close, Candace said nothing.


It seemed to take longer to drive back. A sobering interlude where Kelsey wavered between tears and anger. Most of the anger died by the time she pulled up at Three Willows. It left too much room for hurt.

She turned from the front door. She didn't want to go inside just yet and face Naomi. Certainly it would be poor form to discuss with her what had been said about her and the world she lived in. Better, Kelsey decided, to get over it first. To just sit with the fading daffodils and blooming dogwoods until the inner storm passed.

She lost her chance for solitude when Gabe stepped onto the patio.

"I've been looking for you."

"Oh. I thought you'd gone."

He joined her on the narrow stone bench that looked out over early pinks and columbine. "I'm not leaving until tonight." He'd wanted to see her again. A simple-enough reason to juggle his plans. Taking her chin in his hand, he had a good look. She'd been crying. Both that and the fact that it unnerved him came as a surprise.

"What's wrong?"

She shook her head, shifted away. "Do you spend much time on self-reflection?"

"Not if I can avoid it."

"It's hard to do that when your faults are held up in front of you like a mirror. You look at them, and you see yourself."

He slipped an arm around her shoulders, and kept his voice light. "Who's been mean to you, baby? I'll go beat him up."

With a half laugh she nuzzled against him, then drew away. "I'm not a nice person, Gabe. And I hardly ever think about trying to be. It used to surprise me when someone would tell me I was spoiled or stubborn or single-minded. And I could say to myself, that's not true. I'm just doing what seems right to me."

Restless, she rose, leaving him on the bench while she took a few steps along the bricked path that wound through the infant flowers. "When Wade said I was cold and self-absorbed, rigid, unforgiving, all those things, I could rationalize that he'd said it to justify his own adultery. I wasn't hot enough in bed, so he found someone who was. I wasn't sympathetic enough, interested enough in his career; someone else was. I refused to overlook the fact that I'd found him cozied up with another woman. If I was too rigid to understand his physical needs, well, that was my problem. I've never had any trouble tossing the baby out with the bathwater. Break a marriage vow? The marriage is over, and that's that. Well, I am rigid."

She spun back, ready to dare him to disagree. "There's right and there's wrong. There's truth and there are lies. There's law and there's crime. Take seat belts."

Cautious, he nodded. "All right. Take seat belts."

"Maybe before it was passed into law I'd forget to use mine. You're busy, you're in a hurry, you're just going down the block. Why bother? But the minute the law was passed, Kelsey straps herself in. Every time, no question."

"And you figure that makes you rigid."

"Before they passed the law it was just as stupid not to use them. The law didn't change the basic common sense. But I could ignore common sense, never the law. Well, speed limits," she admitted. "But whenever I overlooked them, I rationalized it. If I went to Atlanta to try to fix my marriage, if I knew something was wrong with it and I was willing to make the effort to work on it, why wasn't I willing to forgive what I found there? Because he'd made a promise. He'd taken a vow, and he'd broken it. That was enough for me."

Gabe rubbed a hand over his chin. "Do you want me to tell you that you were wrong to dump the bastard, Kelsey? I can't, for two reasons. One, I agree with you, and two, I want you myself. I can say that if it had been you and me, and I'd walked in on you cozied up with another guy, he'd be dead and you'd be sorry. Does that help any?"

She closed her eyes, scrubbed both hands over her face. "How did I get into all of this?"

"My guess is you've had a rough morning. Where've you been?"

"I went to see my father." She wanted to cry again, ridiculously, and turned away until she had the tears fought back. "I wanted to tell him, face-to-face, that I was giving up my apartment and staying on here. At least for now."

"So, he gave you a hard time."

"No, not really. Not him. He's the kindest man in the world. I'm hurting him." She let the tears come now. The hell with them. "I don't want to. I don't want to make him unhappy, but I just can't bend enough, not enough to make it all right for everyone."

He didn't say anything, but simply rose and gathered her close. He never battled words against tears. It was best to let them flow until they ran clean.

"This is stupid." Sniffling, she searched her pocket for a tissue, then took the bandanna Gabe offered. "This whole thing started over a stupid dance, the Derby, and the dentist."

"Why don't we sit down again and you can decode that for me?"

"It's tradition," she said, and plopped down on the bench again. "And living up to family expectations. I'm not going to claim that my childhood was fraught with peril, but there's always been the Byden name to live up to, especially where my grandmother's concerned."

She balled the bandanna in her hand, wished she could ball her anger and resentments with it and heave it away. "She's still miffed at me for divorcing Wade, putting that blot on the family honor. Needless to say, she's furious about my being here." Struggling to lighten her own mood, she forced a smile. "I have been, in the best gothic tradition, cut out of her will."

"Well . . ." He picked up her hand and toyed with her fingers. "You can always move in with me. Be a kept woman. That ought to show her."

"Christ, I'd have my name expunged from the family Bible for that."

When he realized he'd been only half joking, he released her hand. "Can't have that, can we? So, what about the dance, the Derby, and the dentist?"

"Sounds like the title of a very bad play." Trying to relax, she lifted her hair off her neck and shoulders, then let it fall again. "When I went to see Dad, I had the bonus of Grandmother and Candace, my stepmother, eating cucumber sandwiches and planning the floral arrangements for the spring ball at the country club. Which they fully expected me to attend. They'd even arranged for my escort, since I've refused to date since I walked out on Wade. They'd—"

"Hold it." He held up a hand. "For my personal interest, run that last part by me again. About not dating."

"I haven't gone out with anyone in two years. Partly because until the divorce was final, it felt wrong, and partly, mostly because I didn't want to. Sex has never been a driving force in my life."

He picked up her hand again, kissed it. "We can fix that."

"I'm trying to explain." She tugged on her hand, found it firmly caught in his, and gave up. "The dentist, an oral surgeon, is the son of friends who's recently relocated to D.C. He meets all the Byden standards. You, by the way, don't."

"That's the nicest thing you've ever said to me. Let's go back to my place and celebrate."

"You're making me feel better. I wasn't ready to feel better." Smiling, she laid her head against his shoulder. "Anyway, I had to tell them not only that I wasn't interested in Doctor Acceptable, but that I wouldn't make it to the spring ball at all. It's the first Saturday in May."

"The Derby. Now all the pieces fall into place."

"Yes, the Derby. That started a row, a fairly civilized one initially, but Grandmother was getting under my skin. So"—she gazed slyly at him from under her lashes—"I told her I was involved with a gambler, just to piss her off."

"You've got a nasty streak." He caught her face in his hand and kissed her hard before she could decide to evade or not. "I like it."

"They didn't. Grandmother stormed out, my father looked devastated, and Candace was so angry. We've butted heads before, but this time she aimed low. And she hit the mark. The longer I stay here, the more it disturbs the family. And since I'm too rigid to bend, I won't look for a compromise."

"Sometimes there isn't any compromise."

"Nice people find them."

A delicate situation, he thought, studying the young geraniums in the patio pots. A family situation, and he had very little experience with family.

"Did it ever occur to you that your family isn't looking for a compromise either?" He watched as she turned her face slowly to his. "All or nothing. Isn't that basically how they've put it?"

"I . . . hadn't thought of it that way."

"No, because you're so cold, you're so rigid, you're so hard that you've automatically taken all the blame for it. They can toss out the guilt, threaten to disinherit you, tell you how selfish you are, but it's all your fault?"

To her knowledge no one had ever taken her side against the family. Certainly not Wade. It had always been she who'd caused the scenes, ruffled the feathers. Strange that it had never passed through her mind that their side of issues was as unyielding as her own.

"I'm doing what I want, regardless—"

"Regardless of what?" he demanded. Perhaps he'd never had a family to shelter him, but neither had he had one to lock him in with guilt and obligation. "Regardless of the fact that some people have to make adjustments? If you trotted off to your dance with the designated dentist, would it make any difference?"

"No," she said after a long moment. "It would just postpone the next scene."

"Are you staying here to spite them?"

"Of course not." Insulted, she snapped her head back. "Of course not," she said again, this time more subdued. "This must seem awfully foolish to you. All of this chaos over propriety and tradition."

"I just figure you've beaten yourself up long enough over who you are and what you want. Feeling better?"

"Much." She let out a big, cleansing sigh. "I'm glad you were still around, Slater."

"I wanted to see you again before I left." His fingers slid over the nape of her neck, teasing out chills. "You're screwing up my schedule, Kelsey."

"Oh?" She kept her eyes on the hands she'd folded in her lap.

"I'm starting to think about you before my eyes are open in the morning. I figure there are three times when a man's most vulnerable. When he's drunk, when he's lost himself in sex, and at that instant right before he wakes up. I don't drink and I haven't had any interest in sex with another woman since I saw you. But you've caught me in that one instant when the defenses are down."

She'd had men recite poetry to her who hadn't stirred her so deeply. Emotionally, romantically, sexually. She'd lifted her gaze to his as he'd spoken, drawn by that soft, alluring voice. Now she was caught. Now she was defenseless.

"I'm afraid of you." She'd had no idea she'd felt it, much less that she'd been about to say it.

"Good, that makes us even."

He framed her face, slowly combing her hair back with his fingers, drawing out the moment so that they would both remember. Birdsong, spring flowers, the slant of the afternoon sun. Then the jolt of mouth against mouth, the quick leap of a heart, the long, slow moan of mutual pleasure.

"What happens inside me when I do that scares the hell out of me." He rested his brow against hers while the new and almost familiar emotions worked through him. "The fact that as soon as I've done it I want to do it again scares me even more."

229

"Me too. It's probably best you're going away for a few days. There's so much to think about."

"I've about finished thinking, Kelsey."

She nearly had her breath back and nodded. "Me too." With some regret she eased away. "Good luck at Keeneland, and thanks for the shoulder. I needed it. I guess I needed you."

# Chapter Fifteen

NAOMI DIDN'T QUESTION KELSEY'S DECISION TO ACCOMPANY the team to Kentucky. She'd wanted her there, badly, but hadn't allowed herself to take it for granted. Naomi no longer took anything for granted.

The only disagreement between them occurred when Kelsey insisted on paying her own expenses. Naomi simmered over it privately during the packing and preparations, throughout the flight, and while they'd checked into their hotel. It wasn't until she'd asked Kelsey to join her in her suite that the simmering boiled over.

"This is absurd." Agitated, Naomi paced, ignoring the light meal and bottle of wine she'd ordered up to help keep the discussion amiable. "You're here with Three Willows Farm. You'll be helping Boggs with Pride. It's a simple business expense."

"I'm here," Kelsey corrected, "because I want to be here, because I wouldn't miss the Bluegrass Stakes or the Derby for anything in the world. And I'm extra baggage as far as Pride's concerned. Moses and his team don't need me."

"I do," Naomi shot back before she could stop herself. "Do you know what it means to me to have you here? To have you *want* to be here? To know after all this time and all the loss that you'll be standing with me, not just at post time, but through all the wonderful foolishness that goes on before that final two minutes? I'd rather have you here from now until the first Saturday in May than win a dozen Derbies. And you won't even let me settle your hotel bill."

More than a little taken aback, Kelsey stared as her mother stalked around the room. She'd never seen Naomi so overwrought, so brimful of emotion. Finally, here was the woman who had laughed for her wedding photo, who had flirted recklessly with men. Who had killed one.

"It just didn't seem right to me," Kelsey began, but stopped the moment Naomi whirled on her.

"Why isn't it right? Because I wasn't the conventional mother? Because I was in a cell when I should have been teaching you to tie your shoes?"

"That's not what I—"

"I don't expect you to forgive that," Naomi snapped back. "I don't expect you to forget it. You're not required to love me, or even to think of me as your mother. But I thought you were beginning to think of Three Willows as your home."

And how, Kelsey wondered, had she started this whirlwind by simply using her own charge card? "I do," she said carefully, ready to parry the next explosion. "That doesn't mean I want to take advantage of it, or you."

But the explosion didn't come. Naomi sat, deliberately fighting back her anger. "If you don't want to accept the trip from me, I'd like you to accept it from Three Willows. Your association there might very well have cost you at least part of your inheritance. I regret that."

"So, this is a payment on guilt? All right." Kelsey threw up her hands when Naomi's eyes went to smoke. "This is silly. I didn't realize you were so worked up over it. Pay the bill if it's important to you." She tossed back her hair. "You know, I've always wondered where my temper came from. Dad is placid as a lake.

And you, you're so cool, so controlled, so in charge. It's worth losing a fight to have seen that I come by my temperament honestly."

"I'm glad I could solve one of life's little mysteries for you." After a jerky shrug, Naomi plucked a strawberry from the fruit plate she'd ordered. "Win or lose, a fight makes me hungry. Want to eat?"

"Yeah." Kelsey chose a slice of apple. "I want to tell you something," she began in a tone that had Naomi's hand pausing as she poured wine. "I do think of you as my mother. I wouldn't still be here if I didn't."

Naomi leaned forward and kissed Kelsey's cheek; then, steadying her hand, she filled their glasses.

"To the women of Three Willows." She tapped her glass against Kelsey's. "I've waited a long time to drink to that."

THE DAYS BEFORE THE BLUEGRASS Stakes passed in a blur. Kelsey met more people than she could ever remember. She rose each morning at dawn to watch the workouts, worrying, comparing Pride to every other colt and filly who soared through the mist. She haunted the shedrow, studying jockeys, judging trainers, and badgering Boggs for tidbits of news or speculation.

Whenever she could corner him, she harassed Reno, prodding him for his thoughts, grilling him over strategy. She worried over him, over the colt, over the track.

"Hey," he asked her, "who's going to ride that colt, you or me?"

She pouted a bit, rocking back on her heels as the two of them spent a private moment with Pride. "You are. But—"

"But you'd rather have your hands on the reins."

The pout turned into a small smile. "Maybe." She stroked Pride's nose, enjoying its warmth, its softness. "I guess I've got the fever."

"You're burning up with it." Reno hooked his thumbs in the pockets of his navy silk suit. He had a woman waiting for him, and a great deal on his mind.

"That's part of it, isn't it? The nerves, the ambition." She took the apple she'd been saving and held it out to Pride. "The love."

"It gets to you," Reno agreed. It would be of no use telling her that sooner or later other things would interfere with the innocence of it. The numbers, the angles, the odds. She'd find out for herself, he thought, and gave her a friendly pat on the back. "You keep our boy happy, kiddo. And remind him about that Kentucky colt. Keep him on edge."

With a wink, Reno sauntered out of the barn.

"You don't have to worry about that flash in the pan," Kelsey assured Pride. "He can't compare to you."

Pride crunched his apple, obviously in complete agreement.


MIDNIGHT HOUR, A KENTUCKY-BRED colt, was the local favorite. He'd been the surprise winner of the Florida Derby, outdistancing both Pride and Double by a neck. The small, easily spooked roan was getting a lot of national press.

And Kelsey had to admit, this one was a beauty. The classic lines, the unpredictable disposition, the fire in the eyes. The colt used a shadow roll on the track, to prevent him from shying at shadows and things that weren't there. But he could run. She'd seen that for herself.

Bill Cunningham's filly had her supporters as well. One didn't have to admire the man to admire his horse. Sheba had heart and courage and could break through the gate like a tornado. But the sound of her wheezing after a hard workout chilled Kelsey's blood.

There were others who showed heart and grit, not the least of which was Gabe's Double. But Kelsey's money was on Pride. She told herself it wasn't simply loyalty, not even simply love, but the eye she was beginning to develop under Moses's careful tutelage. The colt was one in a million. As she was sure her own Honor was.

The day of the Stakes, she stood beside her mother, eager to have her confidence justified.

"He looked so good this morning."

Kelsey took long, deep breaths. She wanted to enjoy the post parade, the pageantry, the anticipation. But she couldn't stop talking.

"Moses said he had Reno hold him back a little, because he wanted to keep him on edge. The field's hard and fast, just the way he likes it. I heard some of the clockers. The sentiment's riding with Midnight Hour, but the cool heads are split almost even between Pride and Double." She rubbed a hand over her mouth. "Still, Sudden Force might be the missing link. That's the chestnut colt in from Arkansas. He looked ready this morning. And we can't count out Cunningham's filly. She's got such heart."

Amused and impressed, Naomi ran a soothing hand up and down Kelsey's arm. "Just take a deep breath. It'll all be over in a few minutes."

"I just have time to wish my two favorite ladies good luck." Gabe slipped between them, kissed them both. "Looks like we're both seven to five," he commented, studying the odds board. "What do you say the winner buys dinner?"

"And the loser springs for the champagne." Naomi gave him a quick grin. "I've always preferred to have a man buy my drinks."

"Good one," Kelsey murmured. Then, rather than taking a breath, she held it. The horses were being led to the gate.

From the shelter of the stands, Rich watched his son. The boy had always had taste in females. And the devil's own luck with them. Just like his old man, Rich thought, and patted the derrière of the tipsy little blonde he'd picked up the night before.

"Keep your eye on number three," he told her. "I've got me an interest in that horse. A real close interest."

The bell sounded. The horses surged forward and the woman beside him squealed and began to cheer boozily for number three.

Rich narrowed eyes shielded behind mirrored lenses. The local favorite had the lead, with the colt from Arkansas pressing close to the rail. The pack was hardly more than a blur of color and pounding legs, but he never lost sight of number three. Cunningham's filly ran valiantly, clipping the lead down to a neck by the first turn. But already Virginia's Pride was bursting out of the pack, eating up the light, spewing up turf.

Rich nodded slowly, a smile beginning to curve his mouth. Double won the rail and streaked up the inside on the backstretch. Even the thunder of hooves was lost in the wild cheers of the crowd. For an instant, one of those gorgeous photographic moments, three horses were neck and neck, strides almost in unison, silks blazing.

Then Pride drove forward, a nose, a neck, a half-length. They crossed the wire within fractions of a second, Virginia's Pride, Double or Nothing, Big Sheba. Win, place, show.

Rich tossed back his head and laughed. "Honey, I've hit the big time."

She pouted, swirled her beer. "Number three didn't win."

Rich laughed again, fingering the ticket for the thousand dollars he'd put on Pride's nose. "That's what you think, darling. Old Richie's hunches always pay off."

"OH, GOD." KELSEY STILL HAD her hands covering her mouth. Toward the end she'd nearly given in to the urge to place them over her eyes. "He did it! He won!" On a whoop of laughter she tossed her arms around Naomi. "Congratulations! It's just the prelude to the Derby. I can feel it."

"So can I." Naomi squeezed back hard, ignoring the sudden intrusion of cameras and press. "Come with me to the winner's circle. I want you with me."

"You couldn't keep me away." She swung back to Gabe. For someone who'd just lost by half a length, he looked awfully pleased with himself. "Your colt ran a good race."

"He did. Yours ran better." He tugged the braid that rained down her back. "This time. See you at dinner."

THE VICTORY GLOW WASN'T allowed to distract anyone from the job at hand. They'd stay in Kentucky until after the Derby, moving from Keeneland to Churchill Downs.

Dawn still meant workouts, clockers, black coffee, and trainers watching from the backside rail.

Only this was the Derby. Workouts were no longer a private affair. Even as exercise boys roused themselves from bed, reporters were setting up equipment. Television, newspapers, magazines all wanted features; all wanted that definitive interview, that perfect picture.

Kelsey knew what hers would have been.

The soft dawn, that most magical time for horse and horseman, with mist rising, blurring color, muffled sound. And the signature twin spires of the track spearing up through it. Tubs of hot water added steam. Birds sang their morning song.

Spring had come to Louisville, but there was still a vague chill at this hour, bracing, exciting. It touched off more white steam from the flanks and shoulders of horses returning from a gallop. Pampered and pushed, they slipped through the mists as magically as any Pegasus rising from hooves to wings.

But they were athletes. It was easy to forget that these half-ton creatures balanced on breadstick legs had been born to run.

Of the thousands of Thoroughbreds foaled every year, only a few, a special few, would ever walk through the morning fog at this track, on this week. Only one would stand on Saturday with a blooming blanket of red roses over its glistening back.

Grooms carried the tubs and the wrappings, moving through

the thinning swirl among the horses while the sun streamed softly, burning away the dawn, turning dew to diamonds. A cat meowed, boot heels crunched. And then the sound of hooves on dirt, eerily disembodied at first, then growing, swelling as the grayish mists parted like water, a colt swimming through them.

That was her picture, the memory Kelsey would take with her, quiet and comforting amid all the colors and the pageantry.

"What are you doing?"

Kelsey said nothing at first, simply took Gabe's hand in hers. She should have known he would walk into the scene and make himself part of the memory. "Taking a picture. I don't want all this to get lost with the parties and the press and the pressure."

"You're up early for someone who couldn't have gotten to bed before two."

"Who can sleep?"

In answer, Gabe nodded toward a stableboy who was leaning back against the barn wall, dozing. She laughed and took a deep gulp of air, swallowing the scents of horse, liniment, leather, manure.

"It's too new to me. I saw your jockey working Double this morning. They looked good."

"I saw you, leaning on the backstretch rail. You looked good."

"I don't know how you have the energy to flirt with all that's going on. This is like Mardi Gras, a Kiwanian convention, and the Super Bowl rolled into one." She began to walk. "Parades, hot-air balloon races, owners' dinners, trainers' dinners. That steamboat race yesterday. I've never seen anything like it."

"I won five thousand."

She snorted. "Figures. Who was foolish enough to bet against you?"

He grinned. "Moses."

She tugged down the brim of her cap. "Well, with his ten percent of Saturday's purse, he can afford it."

"You're getting cocky, darling."

238

"I've always been cocky. You're going to the museum for the draw, aren't you?"

"Wouldn't miss it." He hadn't missed the drawing of the field in five years. His presence, or lack of it, would make no difference as to which position his colt was assigned, but it was his colt. "There's breakfast in the old paddock before. Hungry?"

Moaning, she pressed a hand to her stomach. "I've done more grazing than a holstein since I got to Louisville. I think I'll skip it. If you . . ." She trailed off, noting his attention had wandered. No, she realized; it was more than that. It had focused, frozen, beamed in like a laser on something back at the shedrow. "Something wrong?"

"No." For an instant he'd thought he'd seen his father. That familiar swagger, the pastel suit so out of place among denim and cotton. But it had been only a glimpse. And surely Rich Slater wouldn't be wandering around the barns at Churchill Downs at an hour past dawn. "No," he said again, and shook off the automatic dread. "If you don't want to eat, come watch me."

He didn't think any more about it. Before the morning was over, Gabe was busy analyzing his colt's number-three position with Jamison and his jockey.


"WE GOT THE RAIL." KELSEY stood with Boggs in the barn, nibbling on one of the apples she had in her pockets while the old groom hooked wraps on a line. "It's a sign from God."

Boggs took one of the clothespins clipped to his pant leg and meticulously hooked a royal blue wrap. "I figure God watches the Derby, like everybody. Probably got His favorite." He ran his fingers over a saddle, well worn, the irons rubbed and polished by his own hand. "I might just put some of these dead presidents I got in my pocket down on that colt."

"I thought you never bet."

"Don't." With the same slow care, he draped a blanket over the line. "Not since April '73."

He shot her a look to see if she realized that was the year her mother had killed Alec Bradley. When there was nothing in her eyes but mild interest, he continued.

"Was at Keeneland, too. Over to Lexington for the Stakes race. Three Willows had a Derby hopeful then, too. Fine colt. I loved that colt more'n I ever loved a woman. Name was Sun Spot. I guess I got me a fever, 'cause I put a month's pay on him. He came out of the gate like a whirlwind, like he could already see the wire. At the first turn, the colt beside him stumbled, bumped him hard. Spot went down. Knew as soon as I saw him go he'd not race again. Shattered his near foreleg. Nothing to do but put him down. Your ma put the gun behind his ear herself. Was her colt, and she cried when she did it, but she did what had to be done." He sighed, gustily. "So I ain't never bet since. Maybe it's bad luck if I do."

She put an arm around Boggs and together they studied the tools of his trade, the drying wrappings, the blinkers, the blankets and cotton padding. "Nothing's going to happen to Pride."

He nodded, taking the apple Kelsey offered him. "It's a mistake to love a horse, Miss Kelsey." He polished the apple on his shirt and handed it back to her. "They break your heart one way or another."

She only smiled, tossed the apple up, caught it. "Is this for me, Boggs, or for Pride?"

His gummy grin split his face. "He does like his apples."

"Then I'd better go give it to him."

When she started out, Boggs shifted, then scratched his throat. "You know, I saw somebody today I ain't seen in a while. Somebody I knew back in that spring of '73."

"Oh?"

Stalling, Boggs took the apple from her and twisted it in his gnarled hands so that it came apart in two neat halves. "Mr. Slater's old man."

"Gabe's father? You saw him here?"

"Thought I did. But my eyes aren't what they were. Funny he'd be here. I recollect he was around the day Spot went down. Kicked

240

up a fuss, too, like as if Miss Naomi had planned to lose the race and the horse that day. 'Course he was drunk. But Rich Slater's persuasive. They checked the horse for drugs."

Kelsey stood, the sun at her back, her face in shadow. "And what did they find?"

"They didn't find nothing in that colt. The Chadwicks run clean. But they found them in the colt that bumped him. Amphetamines."

"Who owned the colt?"

"Cunningham." He spat on the ground. "Funny, isn't it? Fingers pointed at Cunningham at first, but it turned out the jockey'd done it. Benny Morales, damn good rider he was. Left a note that said so before he hung himself in Cunningham's tack room."

"God, that's horrible."

"There's plenty that don't smell so sweet around racehorses, Miss Kelsey. Rich Slater, he had it figured that the Chadwicks bribed Benny to drug his horse, so's even if he won, he'd be disqualified if'n they found out. That's pure shit, of course, but a man like that's got to point the blame at somebody. Thing was, most everybody lost that day. Probably wasn't him I saw, but I figured if it was, you might want to keep your distance."

"I will."


RICH SLATER HAD NO intention of crossing paths with anyone from Three Willows. He was there as a spectator. And although it would certainly have been wiser for him to be well away from Louisville on Saturday, he wanted a front-row seat.

He was on a roll. A wad of bills in his pocket, a willing woman in his bed, and a raucous round of parties at his fingertips. He'd made it, finally, to the big time. And the best part, the sweetest part, was the people who would go down as he went up.

He had to admit, he was brilliant—and he made sure he didn't get drunk enough to share that opinion with anyone but himself.

Not only would he pay off an old debt and slap down his ungrateful son, he would also make a small fortune doing it.

And really, he was doing nothing at all. He'd simply put the right instrument in the right hands.

The Chadwick bitch would pay. Naked, he padded over to the honor bar to raid the stingy bottles of liquor. His companion for Derby week was passed out on the bed, her tight little body sprawled on the tangled sheets. He'd proved his manhood there, he told himself, and toasted the reflection in the mirror.

He still had it.

With the glass in his hand, Rich preened in front of the mirror. His vanity was blind to the loose flesh sagging at his waist. He saw the body of a thirty-year-old, trim and tough. The body he'd passed on to his son, who had blown him off with a five-thousand-dollar check.

Wouldn't let your dad spend a night under your roof? I'll own the fucking roof when I'm done.

He tossed back the whiskey and watched his throat ripple as he swallowed. The boy thought he was better than anybody. Always had. In a couple of days he wouldn't be so high and mighty. In a couple of days, the worm would have turned.

He really had to thank circumstances, past and present, for giving him the opportunity. Cunningham was a bonus, one that had fallen beautifully into his lap. Of course the man was a fool, but fools were the best birds to pluck.

And he was going to be plucking Cunningham for many years to come. A nice steady sideline of blackmail would bring in a nice steady income. But the payoff, oh, the payoff would come just before six P.M. on Saturday. A job, he was sure everyone would agree, well done.

He opened another bottle, poured another drink. He wondered if Naomi Chadwick would remember him. If he walked right up to her, took a handful of that pretty little butt, would she remember him? He was tempted to try it, to walk right up and give her a quick squeeze and a wink.

He didn't like the idea that a woman, any woman, could forget Rich Slater.

He remembered her, all right. He remembered that fancy, spoiled bitch, advertising herself in low-cut dresses or skintight jeans. Strutting around the track like a filly in heat, spreading her legs for any man who could still get a hard-on.

He'd wanted her, bad. Wanted to lift those frilly skirts and dive in. Show her what a real man could do. But when he'd offered, she'd looked at him as though he were something smeared on the bottom of her boot after a walk through the paddock. And she'd laughed at him. Laughed until he'd wanted to smash his fist into that beautiful face.

Maybe he would have, Rich thought, absently pounding one clenched hand into the palm of the other. Maybe he would have if that half-breed Jew hadn't come along.

*"Problem here, Miss Naomi?"*

*"No, Moses, no problem. Just a track rat. How's our boy doing?"*

She'd sashayed off, flicking her tail, to coo over her prize colt. And Rich had had no choice but to go home to the dingy rooms he'd rented and smash his fist into his wife's pale, homely face instead.

Thought she was too good for him. She'd cost him his pride that day, but he'd cost her a great deal more later when he'd fixed the race. That hadn't been his intention, of course. Nobody could have predicted Morales would lose control of his hyped-up horse and knock into hers so hard.

But then again, he thought now. Then again, it had turned out fine. Better than fine, because he'd been smart, he'd been cagey, and he'd used the circumstances against her. He'd paid her back, all right. But he wasn't through.

The ten years she'd spent in prison had been only partial payment. The rest of the debt was coming due Saturday.

*

KELSEY PASSED ON THE Derby day breakfast at the governor's mansion. Not only couldn't she eat, she couldn't bear the idea of being so far away from the track.

Post time for the first race was precisely eleven-thirty. Like the grooms, jockeys, and trainers, Kelsey was there by six. The idea of going back to the hotel at noon for a nap was impossible. Instead, she stayed with Boggs and some of the other crew, nibbling on the fried chicken she'd bought.

"Still here?" Moses dropped down on the ground beside her and poked in the bucket for a thigh.

"Where else?" She was eating from nerves rather than hunger, and washed down the chicken with ginger ale.

"You could sit in your box. It's already a hell of a show. The infield's packed, grandstand's filling up."

"Too nervous. Besides, some reporter will just stick a microphone or a camera in my face."

"You won't avoid them here, either. Your mama's got pull. You could hide out in the Matt Winn Room."

"Uh-uh." Kelsey licked her fingers. "That's for businessmen. Might as well be sitting in a boardroom. That's no place to watch the race. How's Naomi?"

"Wired. You wouldn't know it to look at her, but she's wound tight. Half of that's you being here. She wants you holding that trophy with her."

"We could do it, couldn't we?"

"I'm not going to tempt the gods and say so." He squinted up at the sky. "Good day. Dry, clear. We've got a fast track."

"I was out there earlier while they were prepping it. It's beautiful, all those neat furrows. I was going to watch some of the early races, but it just made me jittery." Because her stomach still had too much room to flutter, she chose another piece of chicken. "Have you seen Gabe?"

"He's sharing the box with Naomi. He'll be back around to harass Jamie and stand in the paddock while his colt's saddled."

244

"Things were so busy yesterday, I barely saw him." And never alone. "I didn't know whether to bring it up, since I have a pretty good idea how he feels, but Boggs mentioned that he thought he saw Gabe's father."

"When?" Moses asked so quickly, Kelsey was flustered.

"Well, uh, Thursday, late morning. He said he wasn't sure. Moses?" She scrambled to her feet because he'd already gotten up and was heading toward the barn.

"The man's trouble," he spat out. "Bad medicine."

"Bad medicine?" She wanted to smile, but she couldn't make her lips obey. "Come on, Moses."

"Some people carry trouble with them, and like to pass it out. Rich Slater's like that." He moved quickly to Pride's box, satisfying himself, then forcing himself to relax. Horses picked up on emotions. He wanted Pride edgy, revved, but not spooked. "If he's around, I don't want him near here."

"The guards won't let anyone in who isn't authorized. Boggs wasn't even certain. Besides, what trouble could he cause?"

"None." Moses stroked the colt's nose, murmured to him softly. "Guess I'm wired, too. Slater's old news. Bad news, but old."

"Boggs told me about the race in Lexington, when Sun Spot broke down."

"Hard. That was hard on her. Slater tried to stir up a hornet's nest there, but they stung the wrong person. Benny Morales was a good jockey. He was making a comeback that year. He'd been out for a while with a broken back. Cunningham put him up on his colt. I was never sure if Benny doctored that colt because he needed the money that bad, or if he just needed to beat the Chadwick colt."

It hardly mattered why, Moses thought now. The worst had happened.

"He'd been riding for Three Willows when he took a bad spill at a morning workout. It was a year and a half before he was back on his feet. Mr. Chadwick offered him a job, assistant trainer. But

Benny wanted to ride, wanted to prove himself. So Cunningham put him up."

"Was he capable?"

"I can't say. He ate a lot of painkillers. Worked himself to death to get back down to weight. There weren't a lot of takers, so Cunningham bought him cheap. It ended up costing a lot more than a cut of the purse. Well"—he stroked Pride again—"that's old news. We've got a new race here. *The* race. It's almost time to take our boy to the paddock."

A HORSE WOULD TAKE THIS walk from barn to paddock on the first Saturday in May only once. Less than three years before, he would have frolicked cheerfully alongside his mother in green pastures. One of the first steps in a dream. As a yearling he might have danced in meadows, raced his companions, or his own shadow. Training, growing as muscle and bone developed, learning the poetry and power of movement that was exclusive to the breed. He would come to the bridle eager, or fitful, feel the first weight of man on his back in a dawn-washed stall.

One day he would be walked to an iron gate and urged to accept the confinement. He would have trained on the longe, on the practice oval. He would learn the scent of his groom, feel heat in his legs and the crop on his back.

He would do what he had been born to do. He would run.

But he would take this walk, to this race, only once. There was no second chance.

At 5:06 they were in the paddock, Pride moving into his stall to be saddled. Tattoos were checked, as were the colors and markings of each of the seventeen entrants. No different from any other race, and different from any other.

There had been only one scratch. No one mentioned the colt from California who had broken down at the morning workout with an injured foot.

Bad luck.

Inside the jockeys' quarters, riders stepped on scales. One hundred and twenty-six pounds, no more, no less, including tack. Reno stepped up, watched the scale, and smiled. The hours in the steam room had been worth it. Moments later, the silks bright, riders made their way from the second floor of their quarters to the paddock.

The waiting was nearly over.

In the stands people grew restless, excited, jubilant. Celebrations continued in the infield, some of them heated from liquor smuggled inside hollowed loaves of bread or diaper bags.

The odds board flickered, and the betting windows were packed.

It was 5:15. The horses were saddled, their lead ponies outfitted brightly with braided tails and flowers. Despite the powder-puff clouds riding high overhead, the air was thick. Tension had weight.

"Don't worry about taking the lead," Moses told Reno. "Let the Kentucky colt set the pace through the first turn. Pride runs well in the pack."

"He'll thread like a needle," Reno agreed. Though his voice was cool, casual, he was sweating under his silks.

"And talk to him. Talk to him. He'll run his heart out if you ask him to."

Reno nodded, struggling to keep his cocky smile in place. There was so much riding on that quick two minutes.

"Riders up!"

At the paddock judge's announcement, Moses slapped a hand on Reno's shoulder, then vaulted him into the saddle. They would head back through the tunnel now, on the way to the track.

"Ready?" Naomi clasped a hand over Kelsey's.

"Yeah." She took a deep breath, then another. "Yeah."

"Me too." After two steps, Naomi shook her head. "Wait one minute." In her trim red suit and elegant pearls, she made a dash across the paddock. She was laughing when she caught up with Moses, threw her arms around him, and kissed him.

"Naomi." Blushing with a combination of pride and embarrassment, like a schoolboy caught pinching the head cheerleader, he wiggled away. "What's wrong with you? There's—"

"People watching," she finished, and kissed him again. "The hell with your reputation, Moses."

She was still laughing as she dashed back to Kelsey. "Well, that settles that."

Amused, and oddly touched, Kelsey fell into step with her. "Does it?"

"A running argument we've had for more years than I care to count. He hasn't wanted our relationship made public because it's unseemly for a woman in my position." She tossed back her hair. God, she felt young and free and incredibly happy. "Nothing but male pride, of course, which they all wear in their jockstraps."

Kelsey snorted out a laugh. "Why don't you just marry him?"

"He's never asked me. And I suppose I have too much female pride to ask him. Speaking of males." She saw Gabe walking toward them. "I'd like to say, before he can hear me, that there is one of the most gorgeous examples of the species that I've ever seen."

"There's something about the eyes," Kelsey murmured. "And the mouth. And the cheekbones." Her smile curved slyly. "And of course, there's that incredible butt."

"I've noticed." Naomi giggled. "Just because I'm nearly old enough to be his mother doesn't mean I've lost my eyesight."

"Ladies." Gabe cocked his head. When two women had gleams like that in their eyes, something was up. "Want to share the joke?"

They looked at each other, and shook their heads in unison. "Nope."

Each hooked an arm through one of his and strolled to their box to the strains of "My Old Kentucky Home."

*

248

DEEP IN THE STANDS, SURROUNDED by picture hats and silk jackets, Rich Slater swirled his third mint julep. The seats Bill Cunningham had arranged for him weren't choice, but he'd sprung for a new pocket-size set of binoculars. With them, he watched Gabe escort the women up to their glitzy box.

Quite a picture they made, he thought. Naomi in her flashy red suit, the daughter in her flashy blue, both blond heads gleaming. Like a couple of sexy bookends for the tall dark man between them.

He wondered if the boy had taken them both to bed yet. A blond sandwich with four milky legs and arms. He'd bet they could fuck like rabbits.

"Look, honey, aren't they the cutest things with the flowers in their hair?"

Cherri, who'd lasted out the week with him due to tireless sex and a high tolerance for sloe gin fizzes, tugged on his arm. Dutifully, Rich shifted his attention back to the game at hand.

"They sure are, baby. Cute as can be."

The entrants were ponied around the track, their flower-bedecked escorts carrying liveried riders. The Arkansas colt danced and tried to nip at the colt in front of him. The pony rider helped the jockey calm him.

The entrants cantered around the track to the cheers of the crowd.

"It's incredible," Kelsey said. "All of it. Just incredible." She shook her head at Gabe's offer of a drink. "I can't swallow. I can hardly breathe. Oh, God, they're loading them in the gate."

Everyone was in place, horses, jockeys, assistants, officials. In the stewards' stand, two judges stood outside, peering through binoculars, waiting for the start. A third remained in the stewards' room, with two television monitors. Others were stationed at poles and the finish line.

From the announcer's booth: "It is now post time."

Once they started the Derby with a whip. Now it was the press of a button, and the words everyone had waited for.

"And they're off!"

A plunge through the gate, the roar of the crowd, and the first feet of the race were eaten up by flashing hooves. Kelsey's heart leaped to her throat and stayed there.

So much color, so much sound, could be lost in the blur of dazzled eyes and speeding pulse. The pack swept past the grandstands for the first time, around the clubhouse turn. The first quarter whizzed by in a fraction more than twenty-two seconds with the Kentucky-bred favorite in the lead.

With her binoculars all but glued to her eyes, Kelsey searched the pack for Pride. His colors blazed as he began to surge forward, almost hoofbeat to hoofbeat with Gabe's colt. Cunningham's game Big Sheba thundered between them.

"He's moving up! He's moving up!" She was screaming but didn't know it. Her voice was lost in the wall of sound. Naomi's fingers were on her arm, digging in.

Pride nosed out Midnight Hour at the half-mile, in forty-five seconds flat, Reno curved over his back.

She could see the turf fly, the swing of silk as bats were whipped, the incredible power of long, slender legs bunching, reaching, lifting.

Midnight Hour dropped back to fourth, horse and rider battling for the rail.

At three-quarters, Pride inched ahead, a neck, a half-length, but the Longshot colt dug in and stole back the distance. A two-horse race, some would say, with the valiant filly behind by two lengths at the mile.

The Arkansas colt surged from the pack, making a bid for a come-from-behind that had the crowd frenzied.

Then that last sprint for the wire, all or nothing.

It happened fast, just before the sixteenth pole. Pride stumbled, those plunging forelegs folding like toothpicks. Reno, balanced in the irons, sailed over his head and rolled like a stone into the infield. As horses and riders fought and veered in the dust cloud to prevent a collision, the colt made one fitful attempt to rise, then crumpled on his ruined legs and stayed down.

Double or Nothing sailed under the wire in two minutes, three and three-quarter seconds as grooms scurried from everywhere onto the track to aid the injured champion.

# Chapter Sixteen

THERE WAS NO THRILL OF VICTORY FOR GABE IN THE winner's circle. A gold trophy, a blanket of roses the color of blood. Cameras whirled, capturing the Derby winner, the champion Virginia colt with his red-and-white silks stained with dirt and sweat. The jockey leaned forward over Double's glistening neck to accept his own dozen blooms, his face grim rather than triumphant as he stroked the colt.

"Mr. Slater," was all he could say when Gabe gripped his hand. "Ah, Christ, Mr. Slater."

Gabe only nodded. "You ran a good race, Joey. A Derby record."

Joey's eyes, circled by the grime where his goggles had shielded them, registered no pleasure at the news. "Reno? Pride?"

"I don't know yet. Take your moment, Joey. You and the colt earned it." Gabe's arms went around the colt's neck, ignoring the sweaty dirt. "We'll deal with the rest later." He turned to Jamison, trying to block the cameras aimed at him, the questions hurled. "You were closer, Jamie. Could you tell what happened?"

His face nearly translucent with shock, his eyes glazed with it, Jamison stared down at the roses in his arms. "He broke down, Gabe.

That sweet colt just broke." He looked up then, a flare of desperation burning through the shock. "Double would've taken him. He'd have nipped him at the wire." His voice was a plea. "I know it. I feel it."

"It doesn't matter now, does it?" But Gabe laid a hand on his shoulder in support. The taste of victory might have been bitter, but he couldn't refuse it.

The guards kept the press and the fans at bay. Kelsey could hear the tide of their voices from behind the privacy screen, see the shadows moving on it. There were cheers, there were questions, there were demands. But all that was another world behind the thin white wall between life and death. Here, there was only her mother's quiet weeping.

"Moses." He rocked Naomi, stroking her hair, holding on to her and her grief. "Oh, Moses, why?"

"I shouldn'ta bet." Boggs stood, tears streaming down his face, Pride's saddle clutched to his heaving chest. "I shouldn'ta."

Gently, Kelsey ran her hand over Pride's neck. So soft, she thought. So still. Dirt streaked his coat, a testament to the effort. He should be washed, she thought dimly. He should be washed and brushed and pampered with the apples he loved so much.

She lingered over one last caress, then forced herself to rise. Kelsey picked up the dirt-streaked blinders and laid them gently over the saddle. "Take his things back to the barn, Boggs."

"It ain't right, Miss Kelsey."

"No, it isn't." And her heart was aching with the horrible wrongness of it. "But you take care of his things, like always. We need to get my mother away from here."

"Somebody's got to stay—somebody's got to see to him."

"I'm going to stay."

Eyes blurred with tears, he stared at her, then nodded. "That's fittin'." Like a page bearing away his warrior's sword and shield, he turned and left them.

Holding on to her own control, Kelsey crouched. "Moses, she needs you. Will you take her back to the hotel?"

"There's a lot to handle here, Kelsey."

"I'll handle what I can. The rest will have to wait." She put a hand on Naomi's back and gently moved it up and down as if to smooth out the trembles. "Mom." Only Moses was aware it was the first time Kelsey had used the term. "Go with Moses now."

Ravaged by guilt and grief, Naomi rose limply when Moses lifted her to her feet. She looked back down at the colt. Virginia's Pride, she thought. Her pride. "He was only three," she murmured. "Maybe I can't hang on to anything longer than that."

"Don't." Though she had her own demons to fight, Kelsey gripped Naomi's hand. "There are a lot of people out there. You have to get through them."

"Yes." Her eyes went blind. "I have to get through them."

Kelsey walked her past the screen and winced at the sudden press of bodies and sound. She knew she would remember this all of her life—the thrill of the race, the shock of the fall. The cheers and screams of the crowd that had fallen into sudden, terrible silence. The way the grooms had raced toward the fatal spot, and all the confusion and movement of getting both horse and rider from the field.

How many times would she close her eyes and see the way Pride's legs had buckled at that crazy angle?

Or hear her mother's soft, breathy weeping.

"Kelsey." Gabe had rushed from the winner's circle to the stables, holding on to one thin thread of hope. It snapped the moment he saw her face. "Goddammit." He pulled her against him, held on. "They had to put him down?"

She allowed herself one moment, just one with her face pressed against his chest. "No. He was already gone. Boggs reached him first, but it was already over."

"I'm sorry. Christ, I'm sorry. Reno?"

She drew in a steadying breath. "They've taken him to the hospital. The paramedics don't think it's serious, but we're waiting for word." She straightened, then brushed the tears from her cheeks. "I have to deal with the rest of this now."

"Not alone."

She shook her head. If she let herself lean, she'd crumble. "I need to do it. For my mother. For the colt. I'll see you back at the hotel later."

"I'm not leaving you here."

"I have Boggs, the rest of the crew."

The heat died from his eyes. He stepped back, increasing the distance, nodded briskly. "I'll get out of your way. If it turns out you need anything, Jamie will be around."

"Thank you."

IT WAS A NIGHTMARE. WHEN Kelsey staggered back to the hotel near midnight her emotions were like a raw wound. She knew the officials had already spoken with Moses and her mother. They'd told her. They'd told her she hadn't just lost a prized colt. It hadn't simply been chance or fate, or Boggs's bad luck.

It had been murder.

Pride had been injected with a lethal dose of amphetamines. A drug that had overworked his heart, one that, as he'd galloped valiantly around turns, down the stretch, had fed off his own adrenaline and sped greedily through his nervous system until, at the sixteenth pole, that heart had stopped.

Now, Three Willows and everyone involved would face questions, speculation, investigation. Had they drugged their horse, misjudging the dose, gambling somehow that the drug wouldn't be found in Pride's saliva?

Or had someone else, a competitor, doctored the horse, and the odds? Someone who wanted to win so badly he would assassinate the colt and risk the life of the man on his back.

She hesitated in front of the door to her mother's suite. What else could be said there? Naomi had Moses to comfort her, to reassure her.

She turned to her own room but couldn't face it. Under the

fatigue was a ruthless energy that continued to whip at her mind. Riding it, she walked quickly down the hall and knocked on Gabe's door.

He wasn't sleeping. He hadn't expected her, not after she'd sent him away. Certainly not after he'd gotten the news about Pride. But she was there, her eyes shadowed, her face so delicately pale he thought he could pass his hand through it. He simply stepped back and let her in.

"You've heard?"

"Yes, I heard. Sit down, Kelsey, before you collapse."

"I can't. I'm afraid if I sit still I'll never get moving again. Someone killed him, Gabe. That's what it comes down to. Someone wanted Pride out of the running so badly, they murdered him."

He crossed the parlor to the wet bar and busied himself opening a bottle of mineral water. "My colt won."

"Yes, I'm sorry I haven't even congratulated you, but—" Then she saw his eyes, and stopped cold. "Do you think I came here to accuse you? Even to ask if you had something to do with it?"

While his blood raged, his hands were steady, casually pouring sparkling water over ice. "It's a logical step."

"The hell with that. And the hell with you if you think so little of me."

"I think so little of you?" His laugh was quick and harsh. "What I think of you, and about you, Kelsey, is hardly the point. The facts are your horse is dead, and mine raced me to somewhere in the neighborhood of a million dollars in just over two minutes. That's a pretty good motive for murder, and you won't be alone in thinking it."

"So." She shoved away the glass he offered to her, spilling water onto the carpet. "Facts and logic, then. You forgot an ingredient, Slater. Character."

"So I did." He set her glass aside and sipped leisurely from his own. "Well, mine's black enough."

256

"Let me tell you something about yourself, Gabriel Slater, high roller, tough guy. You're a marshmallow about those horses. You're as dazzled by and devoted to them as any twelve-year-old girl dreaming about Black Beauty." She tossed back her head, delighted to see those carefully controlled eyes widen in shock.

"Excuse me?"

"You love them. You fucking love them. Did you think it wouldn't get around that you tried to buy Cunningham's filly because you were worried she was being mishandled?"

The shield dropped down again, but she'd seen behind it and plowed on.

"You think your crew doesn't talk to ours about how you play with the foals like they were puppies, or sit up at night when you've got a sick horse? You're a sucker, Slater."

"I've got an investment."

"You've got a love affair. And another thing," she continued, poking a finger into his chest. "I don't appreciate you telling me what you think I should think when I *know*. You wanted to win that race as much as I did, and fixing a race isn't winning. For somebody who's spent his life playing the odds, you should know that. So if you're going to stand here feeling sorry for yourself when you should be feeling sorry for me, I'll just leave you to it."

"Hold on." He grabbed her arm before she could storm out. "You've got a fast trigger, darling." Setting his own glass aside, he rubbed his chest. "And a hell of an aim. You got me, okay? So can we sit down now?"

"You can sit. I still need to walk this off."

Not entirely sure if he was embarrassed or amused by her accuracy, he lowered himself to the arm of the sofa. "I'm sorry, Kelsey. I know that doesn't cover much, but I'm so goddamned sorry."

"I'm trying not to think about how bad I feel right now. I'm worried about Naomi."

"She'll fight back."

"I guess we all will." She paced by the table, picked up one of the glasses, and soothed her scratchy throat. "It was horrible when they told me about the drug. It was like losing him all over again. They're checking the sharps boxes. Every needle, but even if they find something, what difference will it make? Pride's dead."

"If the Racing Commission finds the needle that killed him, it might lead to who used it."

She shook her head. "No, I don't think so. I can't believe anyone would be careless enough to toss it into a sharps box, or if they did, to leave fingerprints or any other evidence." Restless, she stuffed her hands in her pockets, then pulled them out again. "When I find out who—and I will find out—I want them to suffer." She picked up her drink again, looked down into the glass, and watched the tiny bubbles rise. "He raced his heart out, literally raced it out." She shuddered once, then pulled back the grief. "Reno dislocated his shoulder, snapped a collarbone, but that's all. Thank God."

"Joey let me know. You'll have him up again in a few weeks, Kelsey."

"Maybe by the Preakness." Shift gears, she ordered herself. Think about tomorrow. "You know our colt High Water. He could make a decent showing."

"Atta girl," he murmured.

She smiled. "We'll have a lot of work to do. I watched them take Pride away today, and it hurt. I've never lost anyone I cared about. I didn't realize the first time I did it would be a horse. And I did care."

"I know."

"So did you." She walked over and laid a hand on Gabe's cheek. "I'm sorry if I was cold when you offered to stay with me. I'd have fallen apart if you had, but I knew I could get through it by myself."

"I figured you didn't want me around, reminding you I'd won."

"I'm glad you won. It's the only bright spot in the day. If I could have, I'd have watched you walk into the winner's circle. I'd love to have seen them hand you the trophy." On a quick laugh, she reached into her pocket. "God, I forgot. See?" She showed him two tickets, one on Pride, one on Double. "I hedged my bets."

He stared at the tickets, as touched by them as he would have been by a declaration of undying love. "Same money on each horse."

"I guess they both mattered the same amount to me."

He looked up. The color her earlier temper had brought to her cheeks had faded again, leaving her face as pale and delicate as fine glass. The hand in his had toughened with work, but was long and narrow and elegant. She still wore the trim blue silk and slim heels she'd donned for the race.

He lifted a hand and ran it over the hair that was escaping from the intricate French braid. It was the color of wheat struck by afternoon sunlight.

The touch and the sudden silence had her pulse jumping. She was tired, she reminded herself. Drained. She'd spent hours facing reporters, avoiding them. Answering questions, fighting off speculation in what promised to be only the first course of a media feeding frenzy. So why did she feel so energized?

"It's late. I should go." She hadn't meant to jerk back, but she found herself in retreat when he rose. "I should check on Naomi."

"She has Moses."

"Nonetheless."

Now he smiled, slowly, his eyes warming on hers. "Nonetheless," he repeated.

"It's been a long day."

"The longest. The kind that stirs up every emotion and wrings it out to dry. Do you know how arousing it is to watch everything you're feeling on your face?" He moved closer, but didn't touch her. "Nerves, needs, doubts . . . urges."

How could they not be on her face when they were storming through her like gale winds? "I'm no good at this, Gabe. You might as well know that up front."

"No good at what?"

259

"At—" She bumped into a chair, cursed, skirted around it. "At this seduction, surrender, satisfaction business. And the timing—"

"Sucks," he agreed. "The timing sucks." He could step back and let her go. He'd suffer, but he could do it. "You're going to have to tell me you don't want me. Right now. You're going to have to say yes or no, Kelsey. Right here."

"I'm trying to, if you'd just let me think." She jerked back again when he pressed his palms to the wall on either side of her head.

"You figure it's risky, and you haven't quite figured the odds." The old familiar recklessness was moving through him now, churning like an engine. Win or lose, he'd let it race. "The stakes are high, and it's always safer to fold. Is that what you want? To be safe?"

Hardly aware she was moving, she shook her head, slowly, from side to side. Because her eyes never left his, she saw the quick flare of triumph in them.

"The hell with the odds." He pulled her against him. "Let's gamble."

She tossed aside logic and caution. She didn't want them now. She wanted exactly what he was giving her, a hungry mouth, urgent hands. Whatever the risks, she'd already lost herself in the game.

Her breath caught in a gasp of shock when he shoved her back to the wall and dragged her jacket from her shoulders. She hadn't expected this hair-trigger urgency from him. From herself. But her own fingers were tearing at his shirt, rending cloth and buttons in a heedless race for that basic feel of skin.

Then he was under her hands, the taut muscles, the narrow planes. On a surge of greed she locked her mouth on his and fought for more.

She didn't want soft words, slow hands. Something was erupting inside her, and she wanted it to happen fast, to happen hot. Take me. That thought, only that, pounded in her brain, in her blood. She heard her own laugh, husky, breathless, and strange, when his mouth seared a line of fire down her throat, over the shoulder bared by her crumpled blouse.

It was the sound of it that snapped whatever thin hold he had on the civilized. With what was nearly a snarl, he grasped her hands and pulled them above her head. She was trembling, but her eyes were almost black with passion and challenge.

With her wrists trapped beneath his fingers, he tore her blouse down the center, sending tiny gold buttons flying. Her body quivered, like a string rudely plucked, but her gaze never faltered.

There was silk beneath the silk, a sheer little fancy that barely covered her breasts before skimming down to disappear beneath her skirt. He watched her face as he skimmed a hand up her leg and found the top of her stocking, the lace-edged hem of the silk. He watched her eyes unfocus as he cupped the fire he'd ignited. As he plunged recklessly into it.

She cried out, shocked, shattered, bucking frantically against his probing hand like a mustang with the first weight of man on her back. Sensations slapped at her, smothered her, staggered her with heat and light and a grinding, glorious need that clenched its sweaty fist in her stomach. Panicked, pleasured, she shook her head while her body exploded.

Her release was like a geyser, boiling from deep inside, thundering up, closer and closer to the surface. Unstoppable. When she was sure she was drained, when even the colors kaleidoscoping behind her eyes began to dim, he drove her up again.

His hands, ruthless and rough, tugged at her skirt. His mouth worked eagerly at the silk dipping over her breasts, then beneath until she was caught, hot inside it. The flavor of her flesh was exotic, spiced with sweat and soft as water. He could hear her quick thirsty pants, the dazed whimpers that caught time after time in her throat while her heart plunged desperately under his hand, his mouth.

There was the sheer animal pleasure of her nails scraping down his back, of her body straining, shuddering, pumping against his greedy hands.

Those hands tangled with hers in a frantic race to yank away his slacks.

The instant he was free, he drove himself into her, hard, deep, his fingers digging bruises into her hips. Twin moans trembled on the air when he mounted her, dragging her legs up to open her fully. Then his mouth was on hers again, swallowing gasps as they rode each other to the hot, sweaty finish.

Her head drooped onto his shoulder. Her body, so filled with frenzied energy, went limp as wet paper. If he hadn't been pressed against her with the wall solid at her back, she would have slid bonelessly to the floor.

"Who won?" she managed.

With what breath he had left, he laughed. "A dead heat. Good Christ, you're amazing."

She didn't have the energy to question that. As her mind began to clear it occurred to her that she'd just made violent, frantic love standing up, and what was left of her clothes, and his, were scattered ruined at their feet.

"This has never happened to me before. Nothing like this has ever happened to me."

"Good." Realizing they could spend the night leaning against the wall like drunks, he scooped her up.

"No, I mean . . ." She trailed off, noting hazily that she still wore one strappy high heel. Carelessly, she kicked it off. "I mean ever. When I was married, we just . . . I mean. Never mind."

"Don't stop there." He carried her into the bedroom. "I love comparisons. When they're in my favor."

"That's the only one I have. Other than Wade—there wasn't anyone other than Wade."

He stopped in the process of lowering her to the bed. His eyes focused. "There was no one before him?"

This was her problem in the bedroom. Kelsey thought grimly. She talked too much. "So?"

"So." Gabe straightened and kissed her again. Maybe it was a dated male fantasy to imagine yourself the only one. But he decided to eliminate Wade and enjoy it. He dropped her onto the bed from a high-enough perch to make her bounce twice before settling. "Your ex wasn't just a bastard. He was an idiot."

"Thanks, I guess." When he continued to look down at her she started to tug on the strap of her camisole—only to discover it was broken. "I think you're going to have to lend me a robe or something so I can get back to my room."

He was smiling when he climbed onto the bed and covered her.

"Really, Gabe, I can't walk down the hall wearing this." She felt the wrinkled ruin of silk bunch between them. "What's left of this," she corrected.

"It looks incredible on you." He skimmed his hand up until her breast was snuggled in his palm. "But this time I figure I'll get you all the way out of it."

"This time?" Her heart stuttered as he stroked his thumb lazily over her nipple. "I couldn't possibly. You couldn't possibly."

His brow arched as he lowered his grinning mouth to hers. "Wanna bet?"

SHE'D HAVE LOST. SEVERAL times. By the time dawn began to seep through the windows she was sprawled over him, her body still quivering from the last assault, her mind too numb to sleep.

"I have to go. I need to get to the track."

"You need to sleep, then you need to eat. Then we'll go to the track."

"Can we get coffee?" Her words were beginning to slur as fatigue sneaked through to overpower everything else.

"Sure. In a little while." He stroked her hair, her back, not to arouse now, but to lull. "Turn it off for now, darling."

"What time is it?"

He glanced at the clock and lied without compunction. "About four," he said although it was past six.

"Okay. Couple hours." She felt herself drift down a widening tunnel, light as a feather. "Just a quick nap."

263

He shifted her gently, brushing the hair away from her face, spreading the tangled sheet over her. Her face was still pale, the shadows under her eyes like flaws on marble. For a few minutes he watched her sleep. And watching her sleep, he fell in love.

Uneasy with the sensation, he backed away from it, and the bed. He reminded himself that great sex, no matter how much affection was involved, was a long way from love.

He'd wanted her. Now he had her. That didn't mean he had to know precisely what happened next. She needed a friend every bit as much as she needed a lover. Since he intended to be both, he'd better get started on being a friend.

Gabe took a shower, and when he came back to dress, she hadn't moved. Without a thought to her sensibilities, he walked into the parlor and picked up her purse. Her wallet, a palm-size pack of tissues, a leather appointment book, and, he discovered to his amusement, a hoof pick. Her key was tucked inside a little zippered pocket along with a lipstick, a small vial of perfume—which he indulged himself by sniffing—and a twenty-dollar bill. Items, he supposed, a woman like Kelsey wanted to keep handy.

He slipped her key into his own pocket and left her sleeping alone.

His initial stop was Naomi's room. Moses opened the door at the first knock. He looked strained and tired, but he offered Gabe a hand and a genuine smile. "I didn't get a chance to congratulate you. Your colt ran a beautiful race."

"He had top competition. It wasn't the way I wanted to win."

"No." Moses led him inside with a slap on the back. "It's a hard one, Gabe, for all of us. Now that we know something about how it happened, well, it's harder yet."

"There's no more news, I take it?"

"The investigation's rolling. And Three Willows will roll one of its own." In his seamed face, his eyes were hard as onyx. "All I know is somebody meant that horse to die. Goddamned waste."

"Whatever I can do—whatever anyone at Longshot can do—you have only to say the word. I want the answers every bit as much as you do." Gabe glanced toward the bedroom door as it opened.

Naomi stepped out. If she'd been a boxer, he might have said she was in fighting trim. None of the frailty that had haunted her the day before showed now. She wore a dark purple suit, as close to mourning as she had available, and a look of grim determination.

As Gabe had said, she'd fought back.

"I'm glad you're here." She crossed to him, put her arms around him, and rested her cheek against his. "This is hard on both of us." She drew back, keeping her hands on his shoulders. "A lot of the talk's going to circle around you, too. I want a united front."

"So do I."

"I hate what happened. I hate it for me, for you, and I hate it for racing. But we're going to deal with it. I've just scheduled a press conference. I'd like you to be there."

"Where and when?"

She smiled, then touched his cheek. "At noon, at the track. I think it's important that we do it there. We'll be taking Pride home immediately after the autopsy." She paused, took a long breath. "We should both be prepared for a lot of press in the coming weeks—and with the Preakness, even more speculation." Her eyes hardened. "You damn well better win that one, Gabe."

"I intend to."

Satisfied, she nodded. "I'm going to give Kelsey another hour or so before I call her room. She took on a lot yesterday. I hate to ask her for more."

"She's got more." The nerves that trickled down his back struck him as ridiculous. He slipped his hands into his pockets, fingered Kelsey's room key. "Kelsey stayed with me last night. She's sleeping now. I'm going to get some things for her out of her room, then make sure she eats."

The silence dragged on. Five seconds. Ten. Naomi broke it with a sigh. "I'm glad you were with her. I'm glad it's you."

"You might not be when I tell you it's going to stay me."

She arched a brow. "Are you talking about marriage, Gabe?" For the first time in hours, she laughed. "Ah, the face pales. Such a man thing." She patted his arm as he continued to stare at her. "You'd better get out of here, honey, before I start to ask you more embarrassing questions. If you could have Kelsey here by eleven, we could all go out to the track together. Oh, and get her the navy suit with the coral blouse."

Naomi nudged him out the door, closed it, then rested back against it. "Oh, Moses, what a horrendous twenty-four hours this has been. And now, for just a minute, I feel so good. Do you think she knows he's in love with her?"

ALL KELSEY KNEW WAS THAT she was furious with him. Not only had he let her oversleep, but he'd taken off—with her key. She was stuck, without a decent stitch of clothing, in his room.

She stepped out of a frigid shower, which had done little to cool her off, and wrapped herself in the hotel robe hanging on the back of the door. With her hair bundled in a towel, she paced from bedroom to parlor and back again.

She debated calling Naomi's suite, but shied away from the idea of explaining that she was essentially naked and marooned in Gabe's room.

When she heard the parlor door open, she marched in, fire on her tongue. "I'd like to know what the hell you think you're—oh."

She and the room service waiter stared at each other with equal parts of distress. "I'm sorry, miss. The gentleman said I should come right in and set up breakfast quietly because you were sleeping."

"Oh. Well. That's all right. I'm up." She folded her hands, and her dignity. "And where is the gentleman?"

"I can't say, miss. I only had my instructions. Would you prefer I come back later?"

"No." She wasn't letting that coffee out of the room. "No, this is fine. I'm sorry I startled you."

While he set up, she debated whether to gather up the scattered clothes or to pretend not to notice them. Opting for the latter, she accepted the check, added a tip she hoped would make Gabe bleed, and signed it with a flourish.

"Thank you, miss. Enjoy your breakfast."

She was pouring her first cup of coffee when Gabe strolled in. "So, you're awake."

"You pig." She gulped the coffee black and hot enough to blister her tongue. "Where's my key?"

"Right here." He drew it out of his pocket, then laid her suit over a chair. "I think I got everything. You're an organized hotel guest. Cosmetics, toothbrush. By the way, you've got great underwear. I figured this little navy thing went with the suit." He held up a teddy and grinned. "Want to put it on?"

She snatched it out of his hand. "You've been pawing through my things."

"I collected your things. Your mother suggested the suit."

"My—" Kelsey gritted her teeth and prayed for patience. "You've been to see her?"

"She's doing fine. More than ready to handle the backlash. She's set up a press conference at the track for noon. How's the coffee?" He poured some for himself. "We're to meet her at eleven in her room, and go out together. She suggested the suit, but not whatever baubles you wanted to go with it. So I picked what I liked."

"She told you what clothes to get for me?" Kelsey drew in air, then expelled it slowly. "Which means you told her I was here."

He sat, then lifted the silver dome from a plate to reveal ham and eggs. "I told her you were with me last night." His gaze flicked up. "Is that a problem?"

"No, but . . . No." Giving up, she pressed a hand to her temple. "My head's spinning."

"Sit down and eat, you'll feel better." When she did, he reached over and closed a hand firmly over hers. "We're in this together. Got that?"

She stared down at their joined hands. He hadn't meant the press conference, not just the press conference, and they both knew it. Another risk, Kelsey thought, but she lifted her eyes until they were level with his.

"Yeah, I got it."

# Chapter Seventeen

"YOU NEVER SAID YOU WERE GOING TO KILL THE HORSE."
Cunningham mopped his sweaty face. It seemed he spent all his
time sweating these days. In front of the cameras with a big sloppy
grin on his face. At celebration parties where people thumped him
on the back and bought him drinks. In bed, staring up at the dark
ceiling, reliving that final stretch of the Derby over and over.

He'd wanted to win, but had gratefully settled for second place.
Yet the cost had ballooned into more than he'd ever expected to
pay.

"You never said," he repeated, while sweat soaked his shirt and
pooled nastily at the base of his spine. "Disqualify him, you said,
so Sheba would have a chance to place."

"You wanted the details left up to me," Rich reminded him. He
was drinking top-grade Kentucky bourbon now and enjoying the
view of D.C. from a lofty hotel suite. He could afford it. He could
afford a great many things now. "And you got what you wanted.
Your filly placed at the Derby. Nobody's going to call you a sucker
now, are they? Nobody's going to snicker behind your back."

"You were just supposed to see the colt was disqualified."

"I did." Rich grinned. "Big time. The Chadwicks lose, suspicion points at them, at my cocky young son, and you, Billy boy, come out smelling like a rose." He chose a candied almond from a bowl. "Now, let's be honest here, Billy. You don't mind giving Gabe a backhanded slap, do you? After all, he cost you the family farm and a good dose of your dignity five years ago."

"No, I don't mind taking him down a peg. But—"

"Both of us know that filly of yours didn't have a chance in holy hell of winning that race," Rich continued. "Likely with Three Willows and Longshot in the running, she maybe takes third if she's beat all the way to the wire—more likely fourth or fifth. That wasn't good enough, was it?"

Not with the hole he'd dug himself, Cunningham thought. "No, but—"

"No." Rich crunched down on another almond, his face as earnest as any used-car salesman's. "You needed an edge, and I supplied it. Now, truth is, I didn't expect her to do better than show, but that girl ran with her heart. She'll breed champs," he said with a wink. "That's the bottom line, right? You'll syndicate her now and make yourself a pot of money as long as she'll lift her tail for a handsome stud."

It was true, all true, but Cunningham's glands were still in overdrive. "If it comes out, Rich, I'll be ruined."

"How's it going to come out? Am I going to tell somebody?" He grinned again. "You haven't been bragging to that pretty little piece in bed, have you? Some men can't keep their mouths shut once they've dipped their wick."

"No." Cunningham swiped a hand over his mouth. "I haven't told her anything." Not that he thought she'd notice. Marla was more interested in spending his money than how he came by it. "But people are asking questions. And the press is hounding me."

"Of course they are," Rich said heartily. "All you have to do is shake your head and look sad and reap some free publicity. You can always add a little flourish about how you know Naomi Chadwick and Gabriel Slater, and can't imagine either of them would stoop so low. You make sure you link Gabe's name in there. I'd appreciate that."

Cunningham licked his lips, inched forward. "How'd you do it, Rich?"

"Now, now, Billy boy, that's my little secret. And the less you know, the better. Right? You're just a lucky guy who picked up a horse at a claiming race and carried her through to the Derby."

"The Preakness is in two weeks."

Rich grinned, brows wiggling. "That's greedy, friend. And dangerous. You know how risky it is to race that horse again."

"She has another in her." He forgot his guilt, and his fears. He forgot the men who had died and the sight of the colt falling at the sixteenth pole. "I only need her to show."

"No can do." Chuckling, Rich wagged a finger in the air. "Even if you put her in, and she didn't break down, that leg of the Triple Crown has to run clean. Otherwise they might start looking at you, Billy boy. And who knows—if they look at you, they might start looking *for* me. That happens, and, well . . ." He rattled the ice in his glass. "We wouldn't be friends anymore."

"A lot of money's at stake."

"You want more money? Bet on the Longshot colt. I know my boy. He'll put everything he's got into winning. Vindicate himself." Rich's grin turned sour. He poured more bourbon into the melting ice. "Always had a tight ass about winning clean. Taught him every trick I know, every fucking one, but he figures he's better than me, see? Too good to salt the game." His eyes narrowed, went hard as he drank. "We'll see who comes out on top this time. We'll see."

There wasn't any use arguing, not when Rich started pouring with a free hand. "What am I supposed to do?"

"You scratch her from Pimlico, Billy. Say she pulled up lame in a workout and you don't want to risk her. Look disappointed and righteous, then put her out to pasture until it's time to choose her a lover."

271

"You're right." It hurt, but Cunningham put aside his greed. "Better not take the chance. I'm going to syndicate her, get the bitch pregnant next spring." He smiled a little. "I might even make a deal with your boy, Rich, to breed her with his Derby colt in a few years."

"Now you're talking." He leaned forward and slapped a hand on Cunningham's knee. "I've worked out a little bonus, Billy."

"Bonus?" Instantly wary, Cunningham drew back. "We had a deal, Rich. I kept my part."

"No argument there. Not a one. But look here, Billy, you raked in a bundle at that race, between the purse and the betting window. I've got to figure your take at three, maybe four hundred grand." His smile widened as Cunningham began to sweat again. "And with the syndication deal, the foals she's going to drop in oh, say, the next ten years, you'll be sitting real pretty. Couldn't've done it without me, could you?"

"I paid you—"

"You did indeed, but let's tally up the cost here. I had to pay Lipsky."

"That was your idea. I had nothing to do with it."

"I'm like a subcontractor, Billy," Rich explained patiently. "What I do all leads back to you. You don't want to forget that. Now, Lipsky took out that old groom, and I took out Lipsky. Now, we won't get into details about the others on my payroll, but they're necessary expenses, and I have to pass them on. We've got ourselves two dead men and a dead horse, and what's standing between them and you is me." He beamed, ticking off murder on his fingers. "So, keeping me happy's got to be pretty important to you. It ought to be worth another hundred thousand."

"A hundred— That's bullshit, Rich! Just plain bullshit. I've got all the expenses. Do you know what it costs to keep a Thoroughbred? Even just one fucking horse? Plus the entry fees."

"You don't want to nickel-and-dime me, Billy boy. You really don't." Rich's smile was as friendly as a death's-head. He kept his hand on Cunningham's knee, squeezing. As Rich intended to squeeze his wallet for some time to come. "A hundred thousand's a bargain. Take my word. I'll give you another week to figure out how to cook your books. You bring it on by here the day before the Preakness. In cash." He sat back, delighted with himself. "I've got a hankering to lay down a bet on my boy's colt. Family ties, you know."

He was laughing as he dumped more bourbon into his glass.


HER OWN FAMILY TIES HAD GIVEN Kelsey a splitting headache. She'd expected the trip to Potomac to be difficult, but it had been much more than that. Her father had been furious, as angry as Kelsey had ever seen him. It had hardly mattered that his temper hadn't been directed at her. As Candace had coolly pointed out, she was the cause of the problem.

Milicent had made good on her threat. She hadn't been able to break the terms of Kelsey's grandfather's will, but she had altered her own. In Victorian and melodramatic terms, Milicent no longer had a granddaughter.

With her car still idling in the drive at Three Willows, Kelsey rested her aching head on the steering wheel. It had been a horrible, horrible scene. Milicent's cold fury as she made the announcement, her father's shock, then his outrage. And Candace, already prepared, aiming little darts of blame toward Kelsey's heart.

On a quiet moan of pain, Kelsey straightened and turned off the ignition. She hadn't realized it would hurt so much. She and Milicent had been at odds for so long, it would have made more sense to be relieved.

But she wasn't relieved. She was wounded.

Wearily, she got out of the car, thinking aspirin at least would take care of her throbbing head.

She heard the music, the hard, driving beat of vintage Stones. Mick and the boys were grinding out their sympathy for the devil. Kelsey followed them around the side of the house.

There was a splattered drop cloth over the stones of the patio. A boom box belched out rock and roll from the glass-topped table. At an easel, her hair pulled back in a stubby ponytail, an oversize man's shirt hanging to her knees, Naomi fenced with a crimson-tipped brush.

She might have been wielding a sword, Kelsey thought. Dueling with the canvas that had already exploded with color and shape. Her face, turned in profile, was set in stone, her eyes spewing smoke.

It seemed a very intimate battle, and Kelsey started to back away. But Naomi's head whipped around, and those angry eyes pinned her.

"I'm sorry," Kelsey began, drowned out by the music. Naomi reached over and turned it down to a pulsing throb. "I didn't mean to disturb you."

"It's all right." The passion was fading quickly from her eyes, as if when not facing the canvas she was calm again. "I'm just having a private tantrum." She set down her brush, then picked up a cloth to wipe her hands. "I haven't painted in a while."

"It's wonderful." Kelsey stepped closer, studying the streaks of violent color, the still glistening brushstrokes. "So primal."

"Exactly. You're upset."

"Dammit." Kelsey shoved her hands into her pockets. "I'm beginning to think I have a sign on my forehead that broadcasts my feelings."

"You have an expressive face." So had she, Naomi remembered. Once. "I take it the family meeting didn't go well."

"It went down the toilet. I've caused a rift between my father and my grandmother. A big one. And, I think, a smaller but no less difficult one between him and Candace."

"By staying here."

"By being who I am." She picked up the neglected glass of iced tea Naomi had brought out with her, and drank. "Milicent has not only cut me out of her will, but out of her mind and heart. As far as she's concerned, I no longer exist."

"Oh, Kelsey." Naomi laid a hand on her arm. "I'm sure she doesn't mean it."

Glass clinked against glass as Kelsey set the tea down. "Are you?"

Sympathy and concern hardened into fury. "Of course she means it. It's just like her. I'm sorry I've caused you this kind of trouble."

"*I* caused," Kelsey exploded. "This is mine. It's time everyone started to understand that I can think and act and feel for myself. If I didn't want to be here, I wouldn't be. I'm not here to spite them or to placate you. I'm here for me."

Naomi took a deep breath. "You're right. Absolutely right."

"If I wanted to be somewhere else, I'd be somewhere else. But I won't be threatened or bribed or guilted into giving up something that's important to me. My family is important to me. Three Willows is important to me. And so are you."

"Well." Naomi reached for the glass herself, and her hand was unsteady. "Thank you."

Kelsey resisted, barely, the urge to kick a pot of geraniums. "It's hardly a matter for gratitude. You're my mother. I care about you. I admire what you've been able to do with your life. Maybe I'm not satisfied about all the years between, but I like who you are. I'm certainly not going to go scrambling back and pretend you don't exist because Milicent would prefer it."

To keep herself from buckling into a chair, Naomi braced a hand on the table. "You can't imagine, can't possibly imagine what it's like to hear from a grown daughter that she likes who you are. I love you so much, Kelsey."

Her anger skidded to a halt. "I know."

"I didn't know who you would be when I saw you again. All the love I had was for that little girl I'd lost. Then you came here, and you gave me a chance. I'm so dazzled by the woman you are. So proud of you. If you left tomorrow and never came back, you'd still have given me more than I ever thought I'd have again."

"I'm not going anywhere." Leading with her heart, Kelsey

stepped forward and opened her arms. "I'm exactly where I want to be."

With her eyes tightly closed, Naomi absorbed the feel, the scent of her daughter. "I want to say I'll make it up to you. That I'll find a way to soften her heart."

"Don't. It's not for you to worry about." Steadier, she eased back. "You can be mad with me. I'm so goddamned mad." Riding on the mood swings, she whirled away to pace. "And hurt. I can't believe how much it hurt. For her to think I cared about her money. For her to use it, and my feelings, against me. To try to control me with them."

"Control is essential to Milicent. It always has been."

"She couldn't break my grandfather's trust. I bet that burned her. Not having the power to change that. And Dad was so upset. He shouted at her. He's never raised his voice to her."

"Yes, he has." There was a grim satisfaction in Naomi's smile. "It's probably been some time. I'm glad he stood up for you."

"I wish I could say I was. It was horrible to see them fight that way. And to see the distance all this has put between him and Candace. To know, right or wrong, that I'm responsible. Grandmother's so unbending, so unwilling to see someone else's side." And hadn't the same been said about her? Kelsey remembered. And shuddered.

"Then she has two choices," Naomi put in. "She'll bend, or she'll die lonely."

"I have to believe they'll make up," Kelsey murmured. "I have to. I'm not sure Grandmother and I will ever come to terms again. Not after today. She actually used Pride against me. She said that you'd probably gotten one of your hoodlum friends—her exact words, by the way—to drug the horse. After all, if you'd killed a man . . ." Appalled, Kelsey trailed off.

"Why would I stop at the idea of killing a horse?" Naomi finished. "Why indeed?"

"I'm sorry." Disgusted with herself, she rubbed at her still aching temples. "I'm wound up."

"It doesn't matter. I'm sure she's not the only one who's had the thought. One of the reasons I'm out here, venting," she said, gesturing toward the canvas, "is that a rumor's circulating that I might have arranged for Pride's death to collect the insurance."

Kelsey dropped her hands, then balled them into fists. "That's hideous! No one who knows you would believe that."

"It's not an unheard-of practice, unfortunately. There's a lot of ugliness in this world, too, Kelsey. The rumor will pass." She picked up her brush again, contemplating. "Simple arithmetic will scotch it eventually. Even though he was heavily insured, Pride was worth a good deal more alive, at the track and at stud, than he is dead. But it stirs memories. Mine. Others."

Calmer, she began to paint again. "This was my therapy in prison. More, it was a way to survive, a way to channel emotions. You don't want to bring attention to yourself inside. With anger, grief, with fear. Especially not with fear."

"Can you tell me about it?" Kelsey asked quietly. "What it was like?"

For a moment Naomi continued to paint in silence. She'd wondered when Kelsey would ask. Not if. The need to know the answers, to find the solutions were as much a part of her daughter's makeup as the color of her eyes.

So she would paint another picture, with words rather than with her brush.

"They strip you." She said it quietly, reminding herself it was done, over. "Not just your clothes, though that's one of the first humiliations. They take everything away from you. Your clothes, your freedom, your rights, your hope. You have only what they give you. The tedious routine of it. You're told when to get up in the morning, when to eat, when to go to bed at night. It doesn't matter what you feel, or what you want."

Kelsey stepped up beside her. The birds were singing now, celebrating spring. The air was ripe with flowers and paint.

"You eat what they give you," Naomi continued, "and after a

while, you get used to it. You forget what it's like to go out to a restaurant, or just to wake up at night and go down to the kitchen." She let out a little sigh without realizing it. "It's easier if you forget. If you keep too much of the outside with you, it'll drive you crazy. Because you know it's not yours anymore. You can see the mountains, flowers, trees, the seasons changing. But they're all outside, and really have nothing to do with you. You can't be who you were anymore. And even if you ache for companionship, you don't get too close to anyone. Because people come and go."

She changed brushes and began to paint with the energy that was boiling up inside. "Some of the women kept calendars, but I didn't. I wasn't going to think about the days passing into weeks, the weeks into months, the months into years. How could I? Some had pictures of their family, their children, and liked to talk about them. Or what they would do when they got out. I didn't do that. I couldn't do that. It was simpler for me to focus on the routine."

"But you were lonely," Kelsey murmured. "You must have been so lonely."

"That's the deepest punishment. The loneliness, and the conflicting lack of privacy. It's not the bars. You think it's going to be the bars, closing you in. But it's not."

She took a deep breath, and made herself continue. "If you had free time, you read, or you watched TV. Fashion magazines were big, but I stopped looking at them after the first couple of years. It was too hard to watch the way things were changing, even something as frivolous as hemlines."

"Did you have visitors?"

"My father. Moses. Nothing I could say would stop either one of them from coming. God knows I wanted to see them, no matter how I suffered after they were gone. I watched my father grow old. I suppose that was the hardest part, watching the years pass on his face. That was my calendar. My father's face.

"The last year was the hardest. I was coming up for parole, and it looked as though I'd get it. Knowing freedom was almost within reach—and yet being afraid to be cut off from the world you'd lived in for so long, that was hard. How would you know what to do now, and when to do it? The days dragged, giving you too much time to think, to hope again, to sweat out those last months. Then they let you put on civilian clothes. My father brought me a new suit. Gray pinstripes, very lawyerish. My hands shook so badly I couldn't button the blouse. The sun hurt my eyes when I walked out. It wasn't as if they'd kept us in a hole. It was a decent prison, with decent people in charge, at least for the most part. But the sun was different that day, stronger, brighter. I couldn't see anything through it. And then I saw too much."

She exchanged brushes again, her eyes focused on her work. "Do you really want to hear the rest of this?"

"Go on," Kelsey murmured. "Finish."

"I saw my father, how frail and old he was. The new Cadillac, blindingly white, he drove me home in. I know he spoke to me, and I to him, but I can't remember any of it. Only that everything seemed to move too fast, and the roads were so crowded. And I was afraid, afraid they would take me back. Afraid they wouldn't. We stopped and ate at a restaurant. Linen napkins, wine, flowers on the table. He had to order for me, as if I were a child. I couldn't remember what I liked. And I started to cry. And he cried. So we sat and wept on the white linen cloth because I couldn't remember what it was like to sit in a restaurant and order a meal.

"I slept most of the rest of the drive, exhausted from freedom. Then I woke up and he was turning through the gates. I could see that the trees had grown. The dogwoods that had been saplings, the ones I'd planted myself, were adult trees that had bloomed year after year without me. New paint in the living room, a vase that hadn't been there before. Every little change terrified me.

"I didn't go down to the barn, not for days, until Moses came to the house and bullied me into it. There was a foal I'd helped birth. Now he was sixteen hands high and at stud. New equipment, new men. New everything. I stayed in the house for a week after that. Slept with the light on and my door open. At first I couldn't stand for a door to be closed. But after a while it got better. I had to learn to drive again. I was terrified, but I did it. The first time I went out alone, I drove to your school. I watched the baby I'd left behind as a young girl, learning to flirt with boys. I made myself accept that you'd learned to live without me. And I tried to start over."

Naomi set her brush down, and stepped back. "It's done."


KELSEY WASN'T CERTAIN OF THAT. The painting might have been finished, but not the emotion behind it. Nor, as far as she was concerned, was the story done. It wasn't a matter of clearing Naomi's name. A man had been killed, and a woman had paid the price. But she wanted to see that the pieces fit.

Still it was a shock to find Charles Rooney's name in the phone book. The private investigator whose evidence had weighed most heavily in Naomi's trial still had an office in Virginia. Alexandria, now. The discreet ad in the yellow pages declared Rooney Investigative Services handled criminal, domestic, and custody. Licensed and bonded and confidential. The first consultation was free.

Perhaps, she thought, she'd take advantage of that.

"Miss Kelsey." When Gertie hurried into the kitchen, Kelsey quickly slapped the phone book closed.

"You startled me."

"Sorry. That policeman's here again." Her homely face expressed simple and loyal annoyance. "Says he's got some more questions."

"I'll see him. Naomi's down at the barn. No need to bother her."

"You want me to make coffee?"

Kelsey hesitated only a moment. "No, Gertie. Let's get him in and out."

"Sooner the better," Gertie muttered under her breath.

Rossi stood when Kelsey entered the sitting room. He had to

280

admire the way she wore jeans, though he'd been equally impressed with the clip from the press conference, and the way she and her mother had looked, trim and blond in their silk suits.

"Ms. Byden, I appreciate the time."

"I don't have much of it, Lieutenant, but I'm willing to stretch it if you have news for us."

"I wish I did." He had nothing but frustration. No unaccounted-for prints in Lipsky's motel room, no witnesses, no trail. "I'd like to offer my sympathies for your loss at the Derby. I'm not much of a horse lover, but even cops watch that race. It was a terrible thing."

"Yes, it was. My mother's devastated."

"She looked sturdy enough at the press conference."

With a frigid nod, Kelsey sat, and gestured for Rossi to join her. "Did you expect her to fall apart, publicly?"

"Actually, no. But I did find it interesting that Slater sat in on it."

"We're neighbors, Lieutenant. And friends. Gabe is also an owner. And the fact that his colt won, under such tragic circumstances, made it difficult for all of us. We asked him there to show our support, and he accepted to show his."

"You'll excuse me, Ms. Byden, but from what I've seen in the press, you and Mr. Slater seem to be more than friends."

The Byden genes swam to the surface, adding a cool, arrogant tilt to her head. "Is that an official statement, Lieutenant?"

"Just an observation. It's natural enough; you're both attractive people with mutual interests." She didn't rise to the bait. But he hadn't expected her to. "I was hoping you could help me out with the details of what happened at Churchill Downs."

"I thought you weren't interested in horses, Lieutenant."

"Murder interests me, even in horses." He waited a beat. "Particularly if it ties in with a homicide case I want to close."

"You think what happened to Pride is tied in with Old Mick's murder? How? Lipsky's dead."

"Exactly. From what I'm told, it's not easy to get to a Derby entrant."

"No, it's not. The security is tight. We have guards." Her brow furrowed. "It was Gabe's colt Lipsky was after, not ours. And I was under the impression Lipsky's death was considered a suicide. You think it was murder?"

"There's debate on that," was all he would say. "I'd like to snip any loose ends. If you could tell me who had official access to the colt before the race?"

"I would, of course. My mother, Moses, Boggs, Reno." She blew out a breath. "The official who checks identification, the handlers at the gate. The outrider, the one who ponied him onto the track. That was Carl Tripper. The other members of the crew." She ticked off names.

"The guards?"

"Well, yes, I suppose."

"And unofficially?"

She shook her head, but her mind was working. "You'd have to be very slick to get through security on Derby day, Lieutenant. It may look like a free-for-all on television, but the horses are closely watched."

"The drug. It's hard to tell when it was given to the horse."

"That's part of the problem." She took a steadying breath. It was still hard to talk about it. "Pride had traces of digitalis and epinephrine in his bloodstream. It killed him, overworked his heart. He was edgy, but he usually is before a race. Moses keeps him that way."

"Now, why would that be?"

"Some horses run better when they're wired up. Others need to be soothed and calmed. Pride ran best wired."

"How do you know about that?"

"A lot of it comes from the horse. They know when they're going to race. They're not fed as much, they're prepped differently. There's atmosphere. And you might hold them back at the workout when they're itchy to have their head."

"No chemicals?"

Her face went very still. "No drugs, Lieutenant. We don't doctor our horses here with anything that isn't approved and necessary for their health. What someone gave Pride pumped up his heart rate, his adrenaline. The race, the strain of driving him hard for more than a mile, killed him."

Which was precisely what the colt's autopsy report had told him. "Shouldn't the jockey have known something was wrong?"

Her jaw tightened. She wouldn't permit anyone to blame Reno. Not after what he'd been through. She'd seen for herself the way he'd suffered. The way he'd continued to suffer.

"Pride ran because that's what he was born to do, what he'd been trained to do since he took his first steps. He didn't falter. He didn't fight Reno. You only have to look at the tape to see he was putting everything he had into winning that race. And killed himself trying. Reno was lucky he wasn't killed as well."

Rossi studied his notebook. He'd watched the tape of the race over and over, slowing the speed, freeze-framing. Finally, he nodded. "I've got to agree with that. If he'd have gone onto the track instead of the infield, I don't see how he'd have escaped being trampled. And the way he went down, I figured a broken neck."

"So did I. As it is, he won't be up for another month, at the earliest."

"That should do it for now. I'm going to want to talk to some of the names you gave me. Check out their perspective."

"I appreciate your interest, Lieutenant. I'd rather you didn't question my mother, unless it's vital."

"It was her horse, Ms. Byden."

"I think you understand what I'm saying." She rose, ready to defend. "You're perfectly aware of the background here, and how difficult it is for my mother to undergo police interrogation."

"A few questions—"

"Amounts to the same thing, for her. And whether you can

understand it or not, she's grieving. You can ask me anything you like, or you can go to the Racing Commission."

"I can't make any promises, but there's no need to disturb her at this time."

"Thank you." She started to walk him to the door. "Lieutenant, you weren't involved in my mother's case, were you?"

"No. I was still at the police academy back then. Green as iceberg lettuce."

"I was curious who was in charge."

"That would have been Captain Tipton. Jim Tipton, retired now. I served under him when he was a lieutenant, and after he made captain. A good cop."

"I'm sure he was. Thank you, Lieutenant."

"Thank you, Ms. Byden." Rossi walked back to the car, nibbling on the seed of an idea. Kelsey Byden had something on her mind, he mused. It wouldn't hurt to do a little digging back himself.

# Chapter Eighteen

"Why do I get the feeling the only place I'm going to get you in bed is in a hotel?"

"Mmmm." Kelsey twirled her bouquet of black-eyed Susans, part of the centerpiece Gabe had stolen for her from their last Preakness party. "I suppose things have been a little hectic. And you have been busy—giving interviews."

"I'm going to give more of them tomorrow."

"That's what I like. A confident man." They strolled across the lobby to the elevators. "And Double is being housed in stall forty. The base of Secretariat, Affirmed, Seattle Slew. Are you superstitious, Slater?"

"Damn right I am." He stepped into the elevator and tugged her in behind him. His mouth was hot on hers before the doors whispered shut.

"The button," she managed, crushing flowers as she pawed her way under his shirt. "You forgot to push the button."

He groped, swore, and managed to press the right floor. "I didn't think I was ever going to get you alone. Two weeks is two weeks too long, Kelsey."

"I know." She let out a breathless laugh when his teeth scraped her neck. "Naomi needed me. And there's hardly been time to think with the investigation, and trying to get the colt ready for tomorrow. I've wanted to be with you."

The doors opened, and she jerked back. Her cocktail dress was a great deal more than off the shoulder. She tugged it back into place, amazed that she'd lose control in an elevator, and grateful that the hall beyond was empty.

"You don't know whether to be pleased with yourself or embarrassed."

She fluffed her hair back into place. "Stop reading my mind," she ordered, and caught the doors before they shut again.

"Your room or mine?"

It was as simple as that, she realized. They'd both been waiting all evening for the chance to pick up where they'd left off in Kentucky.

"Mine," she decided. "This time you can wake up in the morning without any decent clothes to wear."

"Is that a promise to rip them off me?"

She swiped her key card through the slot and tried to come up with a suitable answer. Even as the light beeped from red to green, the phone began to ring. "Hold that thought," she told him, and dashed to answer.

"Hello?" She tossed the crushed flowers onto a coffee table, tugged off one earring, then passed the phone to the unadorned lobe. Her fingers went still as they closed over the second sapphire cluster. "Wade? How did you know I was here?" Very carefully, very deliberately, she removed her other earring and set it down on the table. "I see. I didn't realize you kept in touch with Candace . . . Of course. That's cozy, isn't it? . . . Yes, I'm being sarcastic."

Her eyes flashed to Gabe, then dropped. Without a word he crossed to the minibar, opened a bottle of Chardonnay, and poured her a glass.

"Wade. You didn't call at"—she checked her watch—"eleven-fifteen to make small talk, and I really have no intention of discussing my mother with you. So if that's all . . ."

Miserably, she accepted the glass from Gabe. Of course that wasn't all. It was never all with Wade.

"Do you want my blessing? . . . No, I'm not going to be gracious, and this is as civilized as it gets." She thought about swallowing her venom, but instead let it spew as his oh-so-reasonable voice nattered in her ear. "Does the lucky bride know that you have a habit of boff-ing your associates on business trips? . . . Yeah, I'm real good at holding a grudge. You bastard, you oily, self-centered jerk. How dare you call me up on your wedding eve to soothe your conscience! . . . How's this? . . . No, I don't forgive you. No, I refuse to share in the blame . . . That's right, Wade, I'm as rigid and unforgiving as ever, but I have stopped wishing you'd die a long, painful, and ugly death. Now I just want you to get hit by a truck while you're crossing the street. If you want absolution, find a priest."

She hung up, slamming the receiver hard enough to strike a whining ring.

"Well," Gabe murmured into the silence, "that's telling him." He toasted her with a can of Coke. "Does he make a habit of call-ing you?"

"Every couple of months." She kicked the table, then ripped her shoes off her aching toes and heaved them across the room. "To chat. If you can believe that. We can't be married, but why can't we be friends? I'll tell you why. Because nobody cheats on me. Nobody."

"I'll keep that in mind." Gabe watched her, wondering if he should let her cool down, or if he should just scoop her off to bed and help her expel some of that energy.

"He's getting married tomorrow. He thought I should hear it straight from him, so he called Candace. They still belong to the same club, you know." She gulped down wine, found she didn't have the taste for it. "She told him where I was. She told him, as

287

if he had some unbreakable right to know. As if I give a damn about him getting married."

"Do you?" Gabe reached out to keep the glass she'd slammed down from tipping over onto the rug.

"No." She needed something to throw, anything, and settled on the complimentary travel guide. "I care that he can call me out of the blue and make me feel, even for an instant, that it was my fault he was with another woman. I care that when he does, I think back and remember how perfect it was supposed to be. A nice young couple, from good families, having their splashy society wedding, the romantic two-week honeymoon in the Caribbean, the charming little row house in Georgetown. The right friends, the right clubs, the right parties. And I hate when I look back and I realize I never loved him."

Her voice broke and she fisted her hands at her temples. "I didn't even love him. How could I have married him, Gabe? How could I have when I didn't feel even a fraction for him what I feel for you?"

His eyes flashed, then the light narrowed down to a pinpoint of heat. "Be careful, Kelsey. I don't cheat, but that doesn't mean I play fair. I don't give a damn that you're upset. If you say too much, I'll hold you to it."

"I don't know what I'm saying." Unnerved, trembling, she dropped her hands. "I only know that when I listened to him just now, I realized I'd married him because everyone said he was right for me. And because it seemed like the next natural step. I wanted it to work. I tried to make it work. But how could it? He never once made me feel the way you do." Her voice dropped to a whisper. "No one's ever made me feel the way you do."

He set down his drink, suddenly aware that his fingers had pressed dents in the can. "Everyone will tell you I'm wrong for you."

"I don't care."

"I hate country clubs. I'm not going to take you to spring balls."

"I'm not asking you to."

"I could get the urge tomorrow and put everything I've got on one spin of the wheel."

Her hands relaxed at her sides. She could almost see him doing it. "I think the wheel's already spinning, Slater. Maybe you're not enough of a gambler to put it on the line."

"You don't know what you feel for me." Clawed by his own emotions, he grabbed her, nearly lifting her off the floor. "You're working on it. Christ, I can almost see the gears turning in that head of yours. But you don't know."

"I want you." Her heart was lodged in her throat, pounding. "I've never wanted anyone the way I want you."

"I'll make you give me more. And once I've got hold, Kelsey, you won't shake me loose. If you were smart, you'd take a good look at what you're getting into with me, and you'd run."

She started to shake her head, but he swept her up.

"Too late."

"For you, too," she murmured, and shifted just enough so that her lips could reach his throat. "I'm not running away, Gabe. I'm running after."

And she knew what to expect now, what to anticipate, what to yearn for. Heat and speed and frenzy. She wanted the ache, knowing he could soothe it away, then incite it again until every pulse throbbed like a wound. And she reveled in knowing it was the same for him, that breathless, burning need, the panic, the thrill that they brought to each other from the first greedy touch.

Tumbling over the bed, groping, gasping, they fought with buttons and snaps until clothes scattered like fallen leaves. The quest was for flesh, the taste of it, the feel and scent that was a prelude to that most basic of desires.

He traced his hands over her, the firm, silky-skinned breasts, the narrow rib cage and hips. In the dark he could see her with his fingertips, every inch, every curve and muscle. Like a blind man seeking texture and shape, he explored the body he already knew.

She was everything he'd ever wanted, ever fought for. Ever gambled for. And she was quivering beneath him, ready, eager. Amazingly his.

Her body surged up, agile, quick. When their positions were reversed, she straddled him. In one fluid move, she imprisoned him inside those hot wet walls, arching back to take him hard to the hilt. Her hands groped for, then grasped his, their fingers tightly interlacing as she rocked them both toward madness.

His last thought was that it was indeed too late. Much too late for both of them.

MORNING DAWNED DREARY. Heavy clouds thickened the sky and the air, muting all the color to a gunmetal gray. Occasionally rain pricked its way through the layers and fell in sharp darts that stung and chilled. Men and machines raked the track, turned it up anew, sleeked it with furrows. Pimlico drained well, and its groomsmen attended it as carefully, as tenderly, as a man might tend a much-loved horse.

Rain didn't deter the crowds, or the press. By post time for the first race the stands were full. Brightly colored umbrellas seemed to float like balloons on a gray sea. Inside the clubhouse, people stayed dry, feeding on crabs and beer while they watched the action on monitors.

The weather had Kelsey opting for jeans and boots rather than the linen dress she'd expected to wear. It gave her an excuse to linger at the barn and weave black-eyed Susans through Justice's blond mane, to decorate him for his regal task of ponying High Water to the track.

And, in her opinion, there was nothing like a rainy day to make you stop and think.

Six months earlier, she hadn't known Naomi existed. She'd taken no more than a passing glance at the world she was now a part of. She'd been drifting, haunted by a failed marriage, and what she had begun to see as her own failed sexuality. Her job had amused her, nearly satisfied her, yet she'd been thinking of moving on.

There was always another job, another course to take, another trip to plan. She liked to tell herself she'd made all those restless, lateral moves to stimulate her mind. But in reality she'd done so simply to fill holes. Holes she hadn't wanted to acknowledge. Holes she certainly hadn't understood.

She had considered, carefully, whether she was doing the same now, using Naomi, the farm, even Gabe to plug those cracks in her life. Would she, as her family seemed to think, become disenchanted, dissatisfied with the routine, and move on yet again?

Or could she trust the feelings that were blooming inside her? The growing attachment to her mother, a simple, almost quiet evolution from anger and suspicion to affection and respect. Why not just accept that she'd found, and perhaps begun to earn, a place on the farm?

And Gabe? Wasn't it possible to relax and enjoy what was happening between them? She'd had no doubts the night before when they'd tumbled into bed. No doubts when she'd turned lazily to him at dawn and made slow, languid love.

Perhaps it was that inflexible sense of values, her own unwavering perception of right and wrong. How could she allow Naomi to depend on her when she couldn't be certain how long she'd stay? How could she take a lover and glory in lovemaking when neither of them had so much as whispered a word about love?

Maybe she was too rigid. If she couldn't take pleasure in the moment without questioning every motive, what did that say about her own makeup? And was she sulking, just a little, because her ex-husband was being married, perhaps had already taken those vows a second time while she braided flowers into a gelding's mane?

It was time to push that aside once and for all, she warned herself. Time to look forward. She wasn't drifting now. She had a purpose—and questions that needed to be answered. She'd deal

291

with them logically, starting at a twenty-year-old root. First thing Monday morning, she promised herself, she would make that call to Charles Rooney.

The rain had stopped again when they walked to the paddock. Watery sunlight sneaked through breaks in the clouds and fell on dripping eaves. Gutters rang musically and turned the ground to mud.

Kelsey sneaked a look at Boggs. He seemed old, more frail than he had two weeks before. She knew he'd been assigned as High Water's groom as much for his skill as to help heal the wounds.

"The rain's a plus," she said, hoping to lift the shadows from his eyes. "High Water likes a wet track." And so, she remembered, did Double.

"He's a good colt." Absently, Boggs patted his neck. "Steady and kind. Might be he'll surprise us all today."

"Last word, he was five to one."

Boggs shrugged. He'd never paid much heed to the odds. "He ain't run much this year, so they haven't seen what he can do. Still, he's finished in the money more times than not. He'll move if he's asked."

But he's no Pride. Boggs didn't have to say it. Kelsey understood.

"Then I'll ask him." Kelsey went to the colt's head and held his bridle so that she could look in his eyes. They seemed so wise to her, and as Boggs had said, kind. "You'll run, won't you, boy? You'll run as hard and as fast as you can. And that's enough for anyone."

"You're not going to ask him to win?" Naomi laid a hand on Kelsey's shoulder, a small gesture that still touched both of them.

"No. Sometimes the winning isn't as important as the trying." She spotted Reno standing to the side, his arm in a sling, his face haunted and pale. "I'll meet you in the box in a minute."

Kelsey crossed to him and took his free hand. "I was hoping I'd see you."

"Couldn't stay away." He'd wanted to. The last thing he'd wanted was to stand on the sidelines and watch. "I figured to stay home, maybe catch the race on the tube. But I found myself in the car, driving out here."

"We'll have you up again soon, Reno."

A spasm crossed his face. He looked away from her, away from the horses, away from the track. "I don't know if I have the heart for it. That colt deserved better."

"So did you," she said quietly.

"I've spent most of my life dreaming about a Derby win. You can ride dozens of horses, cross dozens of wires, but the Derby's the one. That's gone now."

"There's another Derby next year," she reminded him. "There's always another Derby."

"I don't know if I want another chance." His face tightened when he saw a figure over her shoulder. "Good luck today," he said, and hurried away.

Rossi noted the jockey's quick retreat, and filed it. Despite the lack of welcome on Kelsey's face, he walked to her.

"Miserable day."

"It seemed to be clearing up, until a moment ago."

He smiled, acknowledged the thrust. "I was hoping for a few tips while I was wandering around."

"You're unlikely to get any, Lieutenant." She began walking, resigned to the fact that he fell into step beside her. "You look like what you are. A cop."

"An occupational hazard. I don't claim to know a lot about horses, Ms. Byden, but that one of yours seemed a little on the small side."

"He is. Just over fourteen hands. But I don't think you're here to talk horses."

"You're wrong. Horses are right at the center of this." He offered her his bag of peanuts, then cracked another for himself when she declined. "I've been doing some research. There are a lot of ways to kill a horse, Ms. Byden. Some of which are on the gruesome side."

"I'm aware of that." Much too aware now, she thought. It had been Matt who'd told her when she'd pressed for answers. Told her of electrocution. Putting a horse in standing water, then killing him with live battery cables. A cruel and clever murder, sometimes overlooked. Unless a vet spotted burn marks in the nostrils. Worse, she thought, was suffocating them with Ping-Pong balls, thrust up the nose. They were impossible for a horse to expel, causing a slow, hideous death.

"Your Derby colt," Rossi continued, "he wasn't just killed, he was killed in full view of millions of people. Risky. It's my belief that when someone takes a risk, a particularly unnecessary one, it's because he's anxious to make a point. Who'd want to slap down your mother in public, Ms. Byden?"

"I have no idea." But she stopped. The statement shifted the suspicion from Naomi and instead made her a victim. "Is that what you think this is about?"

"It's an avenue worth exploring. She had the colt insured, heavily. But there's no cash-flow problem at Three Willows, and in the long term, that colt could have generated a lot more. Your mother appears to be a sensible businesswoman. Now, there's Slater."

"He had nothing to do with it."

"That's an emotional response." And precisely what he'd expected. "Backing off that a minute, he reaped the reward. You always want to look at who benefits from murder, Ms. Byden. Any kind of murder. The problem with that is it puts a cloud over him, and his Derby win. So I ask myself, would it be worth it to him? He had a good chance of winning anyway, so would it be worth it to him to stack the deck in so obvious a way? He doesn't strike me as an obvious man."

"An emotional response, Lieutenant?"

"An observation, Ms. Byden. He's not the only one who benefited. There's his trainer, his jockey. They both got a piece of the pie. And there's anyone who bet."

She gave a short laugh, looking around at the crowds. "That certainly narrows the field."

"More than you think." He scanned the crowd as well, enjoying himself. "If it ties in with my two homicides, it narrows it a lot more than you think. Who did Lipsky trust enough—or who was he afraid enough of—to let get close enough to kill him? Someone he worked with, worked for? There were a lot more than two horses in that race, Ms. Byden, and a lot more riding on the Derby than a blanket of flowers."

She stopped, then turned to study his face. "Why are you telling me all of this?"

"You're new to the game. You might see a lot more than people think." He paused to crack open another nut. "And you're involved. Your relationship with your mother isn't making everyone happy."

So, he'd been prying into her personal life as well. She should have expected it. "That's family business, Lieutenant, and has nothing to do with murder."

"I could quote you statistics that would show you family business leads to murder more often than any other kind. I'm just asking you to keep your eyes open."

"They're open, Lieutenant." She stood her ground, unwilling to have him walk into view of the boxes. There was no point in upsetting Naomi moments before the race. "Now, if you'll excuse me, I have to join my mother."

"Good luck," he called out, and chose another nut. He had a feeling Kelsey Byden would be much harder to crack.

Kelsey stepped into the box just as the horses were being loaded into the gate.

"I was afraid you wouldn't make it."

"Ran into someone," Kelsey muttered, and glanced from her mother to Gabe. It was like him, she thought, to be here. To stand with them when this was so completely his moment. She took his hand and gave it a quick squeeze. "Side bet, Slater."

"You still owe me from the first one."

"Double or nothing, then. It's apropos." She studied the field through her binoculars. "Your horse by two lengths. The track's sloppy, but I'll say he runs it in a minute fifty-eight tops. Our colt takes third in two and twelve."

He lifted a brow. "That's a hard bet for a man to turn down. Since there's no way to lose."

The starting gun fired. From the first plunge, Double and his rider took the lead. It was as if, Kelsey thought, they both knew they had something to prove. This was a champion, bursting from the pack in a heartbeat with no need to feel the bat on his back to pour it on. By the first turn he was a half-length in the lead, with the Arkansas colt and the Kentucky roan fighting for second.

Again Kelsey lost herself in the grandeur of it. With her binoculars in place, she urged the horses on, not seeing, as she'd been afraid she would, an overlapping image of Pride going down. There was only the mud-splattered athletes, riders and ridden, thundering around the oval.

There was rain in the air, another misty, steady drizzle that blurred her vision and soaked her skin.

A full length now, and moving out, his red wrappings smeared brown, his rider balanced like a toy in the irons. She heard herself laughing at the glory of it.

Then, like an arrow from a bow, High Water shot up the outside. Kelsey's breath caught at the suddenness of the move. He was gaining, digging in, kicking up turf. Fighting, she thought, dazed, for honor.

Down the stretch, Double lengthened his lead. The crowd roared for him, a flood of sound that overwhelmed everything else. Then for High Water, the five-to-one shot that streaked into third and kept gaining during that heart-stopping final three-sixteenths.

"My God, look at him! My God, Mom, just look at him!"

"I am." Tears mixed with the rain running down Naomi's face. She wrapped her arm tight around Kelsey's waist as they finished

5–7–2. Double had the black-eyed Susans, but High Water had edged out Arkansas for second.

"He did it!" Kelsey let her binoculars drop. "The little guy did it!" She hugged Naomi first, laughing out the victory. "Nobody believed it. None of us believed it." She whirled and with a whoop launched herself into Gabe's arms. "Congratulations! What was the time? What was his time?"

Gabe held up the stopwatch, amused when Kelsey snatched it from him. A minute fifty-seven and a quarter.

She laughed again, rain dripping from her hair onto her face. "Gabriel Slater, you've just won the second jewel in the Triple Crown. What are you going to do now? And I know you're not going to Disney World."

"I'm going to Belmont." He lifted her high, spun her around once, then kissed her. "*We're* going to Belmont."

Inside the clubhouse, Rich Slater toasted the image of his son and Kelsey on the monitor, then downed the aged scotch. A handsome couple, he thought. A very handsome couple they made, much as he and Naomi would have done if she hadn't turned her icy nose up at him.

But there were other matters to contemplate. Other matters to celebrate.

He'd put ten of the hundred thousand he'd bled out of Cunningham on Double's nose. He was quite satisfied with the profits.

For now.

"I HOPE YOU DON'T MIND." Kelsey opened the champagne with a cheery *pop*. She'd already had several glasses in her mother's suite, but the night was young. "I'm going to finish this entire bottle. And I may get considerably drunk."

Gabe sat, crossing his feet at the ankles. He'd been fantasizing about a long, hot, very steamy shower for two. But he could wait.

It might be interesting to see how many more inhibitions Kelsey let fly after a bottle of Dom.

"Just because I don't drink doesn't mean I wouldn't enjoy watching you indulge yourself."

"I'm going to." She poured, then watched the bubbles froth recklessly over the lip of the flute. "You know, I've never really been drunk. I've been close, but I always pulled myself back." She took a long swallow, waved her hand. "Breeding. Don't want to get too loose at the club—people will talk. Don't want to get too loose at a party—other people will talk." This time she waved the bottle. "Bydens do not solicit gossip."

"What do they solicit?"

"Respect, admiration, and, above all, discretion." She closed one eye to narrow her vision and poured more wine. "The hell with that. Let 'em talk. We won. Isn't it incredible?"

"Yes, it is." He smiled at her. She was barefoot now, and her hair had dried in a glorious tangle of pale gold.

"Everyone was so down before. Trying not to be, but it was so hard. I saw Reno in the paddock, and it just broke my heart." She drank again, sighed, and decided she liked the way champagne made the room circle. Glass in hand, she executed two slow pirouettes to help it along.

"Do that again." He wanted the pleasure of watching the way her hair flowed out, settled, flowed out, settled.

With a giddy laugh, she obliged him. "See, those lessons were good for something. Taught me discipline, too, mental and physical. You know, you could break bricks on this body."

"I'm sure I can find more interesting things to do with it."

She laughed again, knowing he could. Would. "We were talking about the race. I hope it made Reno feel better. You could see how happy Naomi and Moses were. Even Boggs. Poor old Boggs, blaming himself 'cause he bet on Pride. It had nothing to do with it. People are always looking for ways to tie things together. Like Rossi."

298

"Rossi?"

"Mmmm." She poured another glass, then absently began to unbutton her shirt. It was getting warmer by the swallow. "He was there, at the race. I talked to him. Or he talked to me. He seems to be there every time you turn around, watching, working out his theories. Why should anyone want to hurt Naomi, or make people wonder?"

Gabe adjusted his focus. Her shirt was open to the first sweet curve of breast. But he wanted to concentrate on her words. "Is that what he thinks?"

"Who knows?" She gave a careless shrug. "I don't think he really tells you what he thinks. If you follow me," she said after a moment. "He just says things to sort of plant them in your mind and drive you crazy. But at least he doesn't seem to be looking at Naomi as some sort of horse assassin." She smiled winningly. "He's still got one eye on you, Slater."

"I never doubted it."

"But only one eye." She closed one of her own to demonstrate. "He doesn't think you're obvious."

"Quite a compliment, coming from that source." He decided he could concentrate on Kelsey's emerging flesh after all. "You've got a couple more buttons there, darling."

"I'm getting them. I've never stripped for a man before."

"Let me be the first."

She chuckled, and with her eyes half closed fumbled open the snap of her jeans. "It irritated me, seeing him there. Rossi, I mean. It started me thinking back over the Derby. All the things that happened. Watching the horses come back through the mist after morning workout. The smells, the sounds, the nerves. Boggs hanging up Pride's wrappings and talking about his last bet. How he thought he saw your father."

"What?" The blood Kelsey's careless striptease had been heating froze like a river of ice. "What did you say about my father?"

"Oh, Boggs thought he saw him at Churchill Downs. He

299

thought it was bad luck. But I don't suppose he was there, or he'd have let you know."

"Kelsey." Gabe rose, took her glass out of her hand and set it aside. "What did Boggs say about the old man?"

"Nothing much." She blew out a long breath. Her head was spinning, a lovely feeling, but Gabe's eyes were so intense they burned through the fog. "Just that he thought he'd seen him around the shedrow."

He had her arms now. "When?"

"Sometime that morning. But he wasn't sure. He said he only got a glimpse and his eyes aren't good anymore." She shook her head, trying fruitlessly to clear it. "What difference does it make?"

"None," Gabe said, gentling his hold. Or all. All the difference in the world. "I just wondered."

"The past has a way of squeezing the throat." She lifted a hand to his face. "We shouldn't let it. We have now."

"Yes, we do." It could wait, Gabe told himself. Odds were it was nothing, but whatever it was, he would deal with it when they returned home. "Let's see." He cupped her chin, studied her flushed face and blinking eyes. "Darling, you're going to have one hell of a headache come morning."

"Well, then." She hooked her arms around his neck. In one lithe leap she encircled his waist, legs locked. "Then we'd better make it worth it, right?"

"It's the least I can do. Let's go into the shower." He lowered his head and nipped at her bare shoulder. "I'll show you what I have in mind."

# Chapter Nineteen

SHE THOUGHT ABOUT TELLING GABE. CERTAINLY IT WASN'T a matter of dependence to tell a man you were so intimately involved with about your intentions. It wouldn't have been weak to ask him to come with her, to lend a little moral support when she faced her past.

But she hadn't told him. Because, intellect aside, it felt dependent. It felt weak. And it was, when you scraped away all of the excess, her problem.

In any case, he hardly had a minute he could call his own. It wasn't every year there was a viable contender for the Triple Crown who had two jewels already in place. His hands were full with the press, his mind full of tensions and possibilities, and his days full overseeing the interim three weeks of training before the Belmont Stakes.

She didn't want to distract him from the goal. A goal, she'd begun to realize, that meant a great deal more to him than money and prestige. To Gabe, the Triple Crown would be proof that he had taken something and not only made it his own, but made it extraordinary.

Underlying that, she didn't want him to toss her own advice back in her face. It wasn't wise to let the past strangle you.

But she couldn't break free of it, not completely. The longer she knew Naomi, the more she grew to care for her, the less Kelsey could believe that her mother had coldly killed a man. Or hotly, for that matter.

There was no disputing the fact that Naomi had pulled the trigger. That she had ended a life. Not only did Naomi admit it, not only had a jury convicted her, but there had been a witness.

Kelsey decided she couldn't lay the past to rest until she'd spoken with Charles Rooney.

She enjoyed the drive. It was difficult not to appreciate, no matter how crowded the highway, the green banks and bursting blooms of full spring. She had the top down and Chopin soaring. The better, she'd decided, to keep her mind off what she was about to do.

She hadn't lied, precisely, in giving Rooney's secretary the name "Kelsey Monroe" when she'd made the appointment. It was merely a precaution, a way to be certain Rooney didn't immediately connect her with Naomi.

A bending of those stiff codes of right and wrong, she thought. She'd always been amused by and disdainful of people who considered white lies acceptable. Or convenient. And here she was, using that same slippery rope to climb to her own ends.

Evaluate later, she told herself.

Nor had she been completely truthful when she'd made excuses to take the afternoon off. Errands and appointments had simply been evasions. She knew Naomi assumed she was going to meet the family. And she'd let Naomi think just that.

Whatever the outcome of the afternoon, Kelsey doubted she'd pass it along to her mother. For the first time since they'd lost Pride, Naomi seemed relaxed again. No one expected High Water to repeat his Preakness performance in the grueling mile and a half at Belmont.

The point had been made, the victory won. Now they could reap the rewards.

And she could steal a few hours and dig into the muck of the past.

She'd already mapped out her route in and through the city. Though she wasn't very familiar with Alexandria, she found the building easily enough, and slipped into an empty spot in the underground garage.

Nerves pressed on her, irritating her with damp hands and a skittish stomach. She took her time, deliberately setting the brake, locking the car, tucking her keys into the zippered compartment of her purse.

What could be worse? she asked herself. What could be worse than knowing your mother killed a man? Whatever Charles Rooney told her couldn't be much of a shock. It was only that she, somehow, wanted it to come together tidily in her mind. Then, once and for all, she would be able to accept the woman Naomi had become and stop dwelling on the woman she had been.

The elevator took her to the fifth floor, up from the echoing concrete of the garage to the hushed, carpeted hallways. Glass doors and windows etched with names flanked both sides. Inside them, people worked, with all appearance of industry, at word processors and telephones.

It made her shudder. How would it feel to be on display all through working hours to anyone who happened to wander down the hall? How would it feel to be trapped behind that glass with spring rioting outside?

Struck by her own thoughts, she shook her head. It hadn't been so very long ago that she'd been inside, and just as much on display as the exhibits she'd taken her little tour groups to see in the museum.

How completely a few short months had changed her outlook, and her desires.

Rooney Investigation Services took up the south corner of the building. It was not, as she had assumed, a small operation, nor did it convey that vaguely seamy atmosphere so often created in television and movie portrayals of detective agencies.

No rye in the file cabinets here, she decided, as she entered the glass doors into soft background music and the scent of gardenias.

The romantic fragrance wafted from the waxy blooms tumbling out of jardinieres on either side of a pastel sectional sofa. There were prints of Monet's floating water lilies on the walls and a reproduction Queen Anne coffee table fanned with glossy copies of *Southern Homes*.

The woman seated at the circular ebony workstation in the center of the room was as polished as the furnishings. She glanced up from her monitor and aimed a professional but surprisingly warm smile at Kelsey.

"May I help you?"

"I have an appointment with Mr. Rooney."

"Ms. Monroe? Yes, you're a few minutes early. If you'd just take a seat, I'll see if Mr. Rooney is ready to see you."

Kelsey sat next to the gardenias, picked up a magazine, and for the next ten minutes pretended to be absorbed in the fussy decor of an antebellum mansion outside of Raleigh. All the while her nerves and her conscience pricked at her.

She shouldn't have come. She certainly shouldn't have given a name she no longer used or wanted. She had no business poking fingers in Naomi's affairs. She should get up and tell the stunning and efficient receptionist that she'd made a mistake.

Surely she wouldn't be the first person to make a panicked dash from a detective's office. And even if she were, what did it matter?

She should be back at the barn, working with Honor, not sitting here smelling gardenias and staring at a picture of someone's overly decorated living room.

But she didn't get up, not until the receptionist called her name again and offered to show her in.

There were several doors on either side of the inner corridor. No glass here, Kelsey noted. Whatever went on inside those rooms was private. Discretion would be an integral part of the business.

And because it was, why did she expect Charles Rooney to tell her anything, even after twenty-three years?

Because she had the right, she told herself, and straightened her shoulders. Because she was Naomi Chadwick's daughter.

"Mr. Rooney, Ms. Monroe to see you." The receptionist opened one half of the double oak doors, scooted Kelsey inside, then retreated.

It was a simple room, furnished more like a den than an office, with glassy-eyed big game fish mounted on the walls, models of ships lining shelves. The man who rose from behind the desk might have been everyone's favorite uncle. Slightly paunchy, slightly bald, round-faced and narrow-shouldered. His tie was slightly askew, as if he'd recently tugged against the restriction.

He had a quiet, friendly voice meant to put the most nervous client at ease.

"I'm sorry I kept you waiting, Ms. Monroe. Would you like some coffee?" He gestured toward a Krups coffeemaker on the table behind him. "I keep a pot in here, to keep the juices flowing."

"No, thank you, nothing. But you go ahead." She made herself sit, using the time he gave her while pouring his own mug to study him and his milieu.

Such an ordinary man, she thought, in an ordinary place. How could he have had such a devastating influence on so many lives?

"Now, Ms. Monroe, you indicated you needed some help with a custody case." He seated himself, idly stirring his spoon around and around in the mug. Already a fresh legal pad was waiting for his notes. "You're divorced?"

"Yes."

"And the child? Who, at this time, has primary custody?"

She drew in a long breath. Now that she was in the door, it was time for the truth. "I am the child, Mr. Rooney." With her hands clutching her bag, she kept her eyes on his. "Monroe was my

305

married name. I don't use it anymore, as I've taken back my maiden name. It's Byden. I'm Kelsey Byden."

She knew the instant it clicked. His hand hesitated, his rhythmic stirring skipped a beat. His pupils widened, so that for a moment his eyes seemed black instead of green.

"I see. You'd expect me to remember that name, and that case. Of course I do. You look remarkably like your mother. I should have recognized you."

"I hadn't thought of that. You'd have seen her quite a lot back then. You had her under surveillance."

He didn't miss the faint distaste in her tone. "It's part of the job."

"This particular job took a sharp turn. My father hired you, Mr. Rooney?"

"Ms. Byden—Kelsey—it's difficult for me not to think of you as Kelsey," he said, measuring her and his own heart rate as he spoke. "Custody suits are never pleasant. You were, fortunately, young enough not to be involved in the more difficult aspects. I was hired, as I'm sure you know, to document your mother's . . . lifestyle in order to strengthen your father's case for full custody."

"And what did you discover about her lifestyle?"

"That isn't something I feel free to discuss."

"A great deal of it's public record, Mr. Rooney. I can't believe you're bound by client confidentiality after all this time." Hoping to influence him, she leaned forward, let some of the emotion she was feeling leak into her voice. "I need to know. I'm not a child who needs to be protected from those difficult aspects any longer. You must understand that I feel I have a right to know exactly what happened."

How, he wondered, had he looked at that face and not seen? Looked into those eyes and not known this was Naomi's child? "I sympathize, but there's very little I can tell you."

"You followed her. You took pictures, notes, you made reports. You knew her, Mr. Rooney. And you knew Alec Bradley."

"Knew them?" He inclined his head. "I never exchanged a word with Naomi Chadwick or Alec Bradley."

She wasn't about to be put off with so shallow a technicality. "You saw them together—at parties, at the track, at the club. You saw them together that night, when he came to the house. You were, technically, trespassing when you took the pictures that convicted her."

He hadn't forgotten it. He hadn't forgotten any of it. "I walked a thin line, agreed. And perhaps I crossed it in my zeal to do my job." He offered a small smile while his memories swarmed through his mind. "With today's technology, I could accomplish the same thing without the question of trespass." He paused, took a moment to lift his mug. "But the line still gets crossed, Kelsey. It's crossed every day."

"You formed an opinion of her. I imagine part of your job would be to remain objective, but it would be impossible not to form an opinion of someone when you're monitoring her life."

He began to stir his coffee again, even though the heaping spoonful of sugar he'd added had long since dissolved. "It was over twenty years ago."

"You remember her, Mr. Rooney. You wouldn't have forgotten her, or anything that happened."

"She was a beautiful woman," he said slowly. "A vibrant woman who got in over her head."

"With Alec Bradley."

Annoyed with himself, Rooney set the spoon aside, staining his blotter. "With him, yes. In the public record you spoke of, Naomi Chadwick was arrested for the murder of Alec Bradley, and convicted."

"And your photo of the shooting helped convict her."

"It did." He remembered, vividly, hoisting himself up into the tree, his camera bumping against his chest, his heart pounding. "You could say I was in the right place at the right time."

"She called it self-defense. She claimed that Alec Bradley threatened her, intended to rape her."

307

"I'm aware of her defense. The evidence didn't support it."

"But you were there! You must have seen if she was afraid, if he seemed threatening."

He folded his hands on the edge of the desk, like a man about to recite a well-rehearsed prayer. "I saw her let him into the house. They had a drink together. They argued. I can't now as I couldn't then testify to what was said between them. They went upstairs."

"She went up," Kelsey corrected. "He followed her."

"Yes, as far as I could tell. I took a chance and used the tree, thinking they would go to her bedroom."

"Because he'd been in there before?" Kelsey asked.

"No. Not that I had observed. But this was only the third night I had gone onto the property, and the first that I knew the rest of the household was absent."

He kept his hands linked, his eyes calm and level on hers. "Several minutes passed. I nearly climbed down again. But then they came into the bedroom. She entered first. It appeared that they were still arguing."

He remembered the look on Naomi's face, the way it had filled his viewfinder with beauty, with anger, with disdain. And yes, he remembered, with fear.

"Her back was to me for a short time." He cleared his throat. "Then she spun around. When she came back into view she had a gun. I could see them both, framed in the window. He put his hands up, backed away. And she fired."

The chill ran through Kelsey like a blade. "And then?"

"And then, Kelsey, I froze. I'm not proud of it, but I was young. I'd never seen . . . I froze," he repeated. "I watched her go to where he'd fallen and lean over. And I watched her go to the phone. I got out of there and sat in my car until I heard the sirens."

"You didn't call the police?"

"No, not immediately. It was foolish of me. It could have cost me my license. But I did go to them, took in the film, made my statement." He loosened his hands, abruptly aware that his fingers were aching from the pressure. "I did my job."

"And all you saw was a beautiful, vibrant woman who got in over her head and shot a man."

"I wish I could tell you different. Your mother served her time. It's over."

"Not for me." Kelsey rose. "What if I hired you, Mr. Rooney. Right now. Today. I want you to go back twenty-three years, take another look at the case. I want to know all there is to know about Alec Bradley."

Fear sprinted up his spine, stiffening it. "Let it rest, Kelsey. Nothing can be solved, and certainly nothing can be changed, by picking at old wounds. Do you think your mother will thank you for making her relive all of that?"

"Maybe not. But I intend to go back, step by step, until I understand. Will you help me?"

He studied her, but it was another woman he saw, a woman sitting pale and composed in a crowded courtroom. Composed, he remembered, except for the eyes. Those desperate eyes.

"No, I won't. I'm going to ask you to think this through, consider the consequences."

"I have thought it through, Mr. Rooney. And I keep coming back to one conclusion. My mother was telling the truth. I'm going to prove it, with or without your help. Thank you for your time."

He sat where he was long after the door closed behind her, long after he'd willed his hands to stop trembling. When he was steady, he picked up the phone and dialed.


HER NEXT STOP WAS THE university. The long wait in her father's cramped office calmed her considerably. It was always a balm to be surrounded by books, the scents and sounds of academia. That was why it always lured her back, she supposed. In this world learning was the primary goal. And every question had an answer.

309

Philip entered, chalk dust on his fingertips. "Kelsey. What a wonderful way to lift my day. I'd have been here sooner, but my seminar ran over a bit."

"I didn't mind waiting. I was hoping you'd have a few minutes free."

"I have the next hour." Which he'd been planning to use to prepare for his final lecture of the day. But that could wait. "If you can spare the rest of the afternoon, I'll treat you to an early dinner when I'm finished."

"Not tonight, thanks. I still have another stop to make. Dad, I need to talk to you."

"I don't want you to worry about your grandmother. I'll deal with that."

"No, I'm not worried about that. It's not important."

"Of course it is." He took her by the shoulders, his hands moving up and down her arms. "I won't tolerate this kind of a breach, nor her using your heritage against you." Furious all over again, he turned to pace the narrow confines of his office, as he would while contemplating a thesis. "Your grandmother is an admirable woman, Kelsey. And a formidable one. Her blind side is the family, and her tendency to confuse her own set of standards with love."

"You don't have to explain her to me, or excuse her. I know that, in her way, she loves me. It's just that her way hasn't always been easy." Had never been easy, Kelsey corrected. "I also know she isn't used to being crossed. This time, she'll either come to accept what I'm doing with my life, or she won't. I can't let it influence me."

He paused, picked up a smooth glass paperweight from his desk. "I don't want you to be at odds."

"Neither do I."

"If you and I went to see her, together . . ."

"No."

Sighing, he took off his glasses, polishing the lenses out of habit rather than need. "Kelsey, she's no longer young. She's your family."

Oh, she thought, the buttons loved ones push. "I'm sorry I can't

310

compromise on this. I know you've been shoved right into the middle of it, and I'm sorry for that, too. She can't have what she wants, Dad. And if we're honest, I've never been what she wanted."

"Kelsey—"

"I'm Naomi's daughter, and she's always resented it. I can only hope that in time she'll come to accept that I'm just as much your daughter."

Carefully, he folded his glasses and set them on his cluttered desk beside a timeworn copy of *King Lear*. "She loves you, Kelsey. It's the circumstances she's fighting."

"I am the circumstances," she said quietly. "I'm the motive, the reason, the child two people wanted long after they didn't want each other. There's no getting past that."

"It's ridiculous to blame yourself."

"Not blame. That's the wrong word. But do I feel a certain sense of responsibility? Yes, I do," she said when he shook his head. "To you, and to her. That's why I'm here. I need you to tell me what happened."

Suddenly weary, he sat, rubbing his fingers over his forehead. "We've done this, Kelsey."

"You gave me an outline, a sketch. You fell in love with some-one. Despite some family disapproval on your side, you married her. You had a child with her. Somewhere along the line things went wrong between you."

She moved over to his side, hating to hurt, needing the truth. "I'm not asking you to explain all of that. But you knew the woman you married, you had feelings for her. If you were willing to fight her for the child, to go to court, to hire lawyers and detectives, there had to be a reason. A strong one. I want to know what it was."

"I wanted you," he said simply. "I wanted you with me. Selfishly perhaps, not altogether reasonably. You were the best part of us. I didn't believe growing up in the atmosphere your mother thrived in was right for you. Was best for you."

Had he been wrong? he asked himself. Had he been wrong?

311

How many times had he asked himself that one question, even after everything that had happened had borne him out?

"Your grandmother and I discussed it at great length," Philip continued. "She was violently opposed to Naomi having primary custody of you. In the end, I agreed with her. It wasn't an easy decision, but it was one I believed in. Part of it was selfishness, yes, I can't deny it."

He looked up at her, at the woman, and remembered the child. "I didn't want to give you up, to become a weekend father who would eventually be replaced by the next man in Naomi's life. And the way she lived during those months after the separation seemed deliberately designed to challenge me. Her attorneys must have advised her to behave discreetly, so she did precisely the opposite. She courted the press, incited gossip. I detested the idea of hiring a detective, but the documentation was needed. I left that matter up to the attorneys."

"You didn't hire Rooney directly?"

"No, I—How do you know his name?"

"I've just come from his office."

"Kelsey." He reached out and gripped her hand. "What is the purpose of this? What do you hope to gain?"

"Answers. One answer in particular." She tightened her fingers on his. "I'll ask you. Do you believe Naomi murdered Alec Bradley?"

"There isn't any doubt—"

"That she killed him," Kelsey said tersely. "But murder. Did she murder him? Was the woman you knew, the woman you loved, capable of murder?"

He hesitated, feeling his daughter's fingers threaded through his. "I don't know," he said at last. "I wish with all my heart that I did."

KELSEY'S FINAL MEETING OF THE day was with her mother's lawyers. She'd gleaned little more there, coming up hard against the

312

unassailable wall of attorney-client privilege. She left the plush offices dissatisfied and determined.

There was always another avenue, she reminded herself. Every problem had a solution. All you needed were the factors, the formula, and the patience to see it through. A pity, she thought, that she'd always done so much better in philosophy and the arts than in math and science.

If she was discouraged, it was because she was tired. Too tired, she had to admit, to face Naomi with made-up tales of how she'd spent her afternoon.

She drove through the gates of Longshot instead.

If Gabe wasn't home, she'd go on to Three Willows and make some excuse—a headache, perhaps—and retreat to her room.

Another white lie, Kelsey? she asked herself grimly. If she kept it up much longer, she'd not only become good at it, she'd accept it as normal behavior.

She started toward the house, but instead of knocking, she simply sat down on the front steps and watched the evening bloom.

There would be sunlight for another hour or two, she mused. She wondered if the whippoorwill that sang outside the window of her room had a mate nearby. The call would come simultaneously with dusk—sweet, liquid longing.

The flowers were thriving here, bursting through their bed of mulch to color and scent the air. Dainty primroses, sassy pansies, a trellis that would soon be covered with the spicy perfume of sweet peas. Lilac bushes were heavy with blooms and fragrance, their petals littering the grass with deep purple.

Such a quiet spot, such a lovely spot, for a man of such energy and passion.

She heard the door open behind her, then his footsteps. In a move that was as natural as the flowers blooming beside the deck, she leaned against him when he sat and draped an arm around her.

"I saw your car."

"Who planted the flowers?"

"I did. It's my land."

"My father gardens. In Georgetown I had a lovely little court-yard in the back. So, naturally, I took a course in horticulture and landscape design. It was quite a showplace when I got done with it, but it never looked quite as lovely, quite as intimate as my father's. There are some things you can't get out of books."

"I plant what appeals to me."

"If I had it to do over, that's just how I'd approach it."

"I've been thinking about a rock garden, out there." He gestured toward the slope of the hill. "Why don't you do it with me?"

She smiled, turning her face into his throat where the skin was warm and welcoming. "I'd head straight for the library. I couldn't stop myself."

"So, we'd argue about logic and whim, then raid the nursery." He tipped a finger under her chin to lift her face to his. "What's troubling you, Kelsey?"

She could tell him, she realized. Of course she could. There was nothing she couldn't tell him. "I started something today, and I know I'm not going to stop. Everyone's told me I should let it alone, but I can't. I won't." She took a deep breath and eased back until they were no longer touching. "Do you believe my mother murdered Alec Bradley?"

"No."

She blinked, shook her head. "Just no? Without hesitation, without qualification?"

"You asked, I answered." He leaned over to snap off a spray of freesia and handed it to her. "Isn't it more important what you believe?"

She shook her head again, then dropped it into her hands. "You can say no, simply no, when you didn't even know her."

"Not really."

"Not really?" She lifted her head again. "What does that mean?"

"I knew of her. I'd seen her around." He angled his head and

314

toyed with the ends of her hair. "I've been a track rat a long time, Kelsey. I remember seeing her at Charles Town, Laurel, here and there."

"You'd have been a child."

"Not the way you mean. But it's true, I didn't know her, didn't form a solid impression. But I know her now."

"And?"

She needed specifics, he thought. She always would. He wasn't certain he could give them to her. "And I've made my living reading people. Faces, intonations, gestures, Gamblers, psychics, cops, shrinks. We all have that skill in common or we don't last long. Naomi pulled the trigger, but she didn't commit murder."

With her eyes closed, she leaned against his body again. The flower he'd given her wafted out a delicate scent. "I believe that, Gabe. Part of me is afraid I do simply because I don't want to accept that my mother could have done what she was convicted of. But that doesn't dilute the belief. I went to see the detective today. The one who testified against her."

His voice remained light. She wondered how she could have so often missed the steel beneath it. "It didn't occur to you to ask me to go with you?"

"It did. I wanted to do it alone." She shrugged. "It didn't accomplish much. He wouldn't tell me anything I didn't already know. And he wouldn't, when I tried to hire him, help me find out more about Alec Bradley."

"What do you want to know?"

"Anything. Everything. My mother's only part of this." She moved away. "What kind of a man was he? Where did he come from? What did he want? Naomi says he became abusive, tried to rape her. What triggered it?"

"Have you asked her?"

"I don't want to do that unless I have to. She'll close up, Gabe. She'd tell me what she knew, but it could bring whatever progress we've made to a dead stop. I don't want to risk that."

"She wasn't the only one who knew him."

Kelsey had already considered that, and rejected it. "I can't start asking questions around the track, pumping the other owners or crews. Whatever I'd learn wouldn't be worth the talk it would generate."

"What's your option?"

"I have the name of the officer who investigated my mother's case. He's retired now, lives in Reston."

"You've been doing your homework."

"I've always been a good student. I'm going to go see him."

Gabe took her hand and pulled her to her feet. "*We're* going to go see him."

She smiled. "Okay."

# Chapter Twenty

"BEEN A WHILE, ROSCOE." TIPTON SLAPPED HANDS WITH
Rossi. "How come you don't have my old job yet?"

"I'm working on it, Captain."

"Well, take a seat, and we'll work on these brews." Tipton eased
himself into the porch rocker. He had a small Igloo cooler beside
it, chilling a six-pack of Bud. "How's the wife?"

Rossi accepted the can Tipton offered, and popped it. "Which
one?"

"Oh yeah, forgot. You're a two-time loser." With a chuckle,
Tipton smacked his can against Rossi's and guzzled down.
"Divorce is almost part of the job, isn't it? I got lucky."

"How's Mrs. Tipton?"

"Sassy as ever." Very simple, very basic affection colored his grainy
voice. "Two weeks after I retire, she gets a job." Amused, Tipton
shook his head. "Tells me it's busywork, now that the kids are grown.
Hell, we both know it's to keep her from killing me with a blunt
instrument. So I got me my hobby shop in the back, and she's selling shoes down at the mall." He smiled, drank again. "I got lucky,
Roscoe. Not every woman can live with a cop, active or retired."

"Tell me about it." Two wives and two divorces in twelve years had taught Rossi that particular lesson too well. "You're looking good, Captain."

It was true. Tipton had put on a little weight in his three years off the force, but it agreed with him. The few pounds had filled out some of the lines the job had dug into his face. He looked relaxed and at peace in a work shirt and jeans. An Orioles cap covered what was left of wiry hair that was a mix of ginger and gray.

"A lot of people don't take to retirement," Tipton commented. "Makes them old. Me, I'm loving it. I got my workshop—built this chair, you know."

"Really?" Rossi tucked his tongue in his cheek as he examined the rickety rocker. The fact that Tipton had painted it a dazzling blue didn't disguise the way it listed to the left. "It must be rewarding."

"Oh, it is. I've got three grandchildren now, too. And time to enjoy them. The wife and I are talking about taking a cruise this fall. Up the St. Lawrence. Foliage."

"Sounds like you've got it all, Captain."

"Damn right." And if he had much more, Tipton was sure he'd run screaming into the night. "A long, peaceful retirement's a man's reward for a job well done."

"No one can argue about the job well done." Rossi sipped at the beer. He preferred imported but knew better than to say so. "I don't guess you pay much attention to what's going down now. But you might have read about a case I'm working on."

"Oh, I glance at the headlines now and again." Pored over them, greedy for any glimpse of murder and mayhem.

"The groom who was murdered at Charles Town, back in March."

"Stabbed. Trampled on top of it. You closed that," Tipton remembered. "Another groom, wasn't it? Lipsky. Suicide."

"That one's open." Rossi leaned back and watched a trio of

starlings fluttering around an obviously homemade bird feeder on the front lawn. An orange striped cat sat below, eyeing them patiently. On the porch, he thought, they were just two men, passing the time with shoptalk. "No note, no predisposition to suicide. And the method doesn't fit. Here's how it shakes down."

He explained, as precisely as a written report, the events, from Lipsky's firing to his death. "We've got a picture here of a man with a quick fuse, a violent one, who knows his way around horses. Not a man who makes friends or rises in his chosen profession. One who's had a few scrapes with the law. Battery. Assault. D and D."

"A picture of a man who'd run, not who'd pour himself a cocktail of gin and horse poison." Tipton chewed on that awhile. "But he could probably get his hands on it."

"He could, someone else could. He was after Slater's horse. Now, could be that was personal. He was pissed about being fired, so he goes for the payback. The old man catches him at it, he panics. Now he's got a dead man on his hands. Why didn't he run, Captain? Why does he hunker down in a motel not an hour from Charles Town?"

"Because he's waiting for somebody. Somebody to tell him what to do next."

"And somebody poured him one hell of a drink. There were no prints on the gin bottle. It was wiped clean."

That particular angle had Tipton smiling. Small mistakes, he thought. He had always been fond of small mistakes. He watched his old cat waiting for one of the starlings to make one, and understood precisely.

"And you've got an open case of homicide. Have you taken a good look at this Slater?"

"Oh, I've looked at him. An interesting man. Lots of currents. Did some time."

"For?"

"Illegal gambling. If it had been a couple of months earlier, he'd have ended up in juvie instead of a cell." Absently Rossi tapped his fingers on the arm of his chair. "He's been clean since, so far as the record shows. Grew up mostly on the streets. Mother died when he was a kid. The father slid his way out of trouble. Had some arrests—fraud, forgery, passing bad checks. Mostly con games. Pounded on a working girl in Taos a few years ago. But nothing sticks. Slater slipped out of the system at about fourteen, tripped up and served his time, then kept his nose clean. I can't say he wouldn't have done Lipsky, but he'd have been more direct about it."

"Who else have you got?"

"Nobody who clicks. Did you catch the Derby on TV, Captain?"

"Roscoe, there's only one sport. That's baseball." He tipped his cap. "I did hear something about a horse breaking its leg."

"The horse was drugged, Captain. Overdosed. And it was Slater's ride that won the race."

"Well." Tipton mused over the last swallow of beer. "Where are you circling to, Roscoe?"

"I'm not sure about that, but it's a big circle. It goes back twenty-three years. Naomi Chadwick, Captain. What can you tell me about her?"

"Funny." Tipton set the empty can under his shoe, then crushed it flat. "That's the second time I've heard that name today. The daughter called me this morning." He glanced at his watch. "She should be here soon."

"Kelsey Byden's coming here?"

"She wants to talk to me about her mother." Tipton leaned back in the rocker, enjoying the way it creaked. "That does take me back."


"YOU SHOULD HAVE STAYED on the farm," Kelsey muttered. "There's barely a week until Belmont."

320

"Jamie can handle things without me." Gabe smiled as he nego-
tiated a turn. "In fact, he prefers it."

"I don't feel right about taking you away from work now. I
could have done this alone."

"Kelsey." With patience, Gabe picked up her hand, kissed it.
"Shut up."

"I can't. I'm too nervous. This is the man who arrested my
mother, who questioned her, who put her in jail. Now I'm going
to ask him to help me prove he made a mistake. And I lied to
Naomi. Again. I told her we were going for a drive."

"We are driving."

"That's not the point," she snapped. "I'm deceiving her, and
Moses. Everyone. And for what? So I can satisfy this idiotic need
to assure myself I don't spring from a line of murderers?"

"Is that what this is about?"

"No." She rubbed a hand over her eyes. "I don't know. Some
of it. Heredity's a scary thing." As soon as she'd said it, she
winced. "I don't mean to imply that heredity's the only factor in
the makeup of character. Environment ..." She trailed off,
defeated.

"I lose on both counts," he murmured. "I wondered when you'd
add it up."

"That's not what I'm doing. That's not what I've done." She
hissed out a breath and cursed herself. "I don't know what I'm
doing. It has nothing to do with you, or the way I feel about
you."

"Let's backtrack a minute." It had been a gamble, a foolish one
to hope this moment would never come. If he was going to lose,
he intended to lose big. "You have doubts about yourself because
of your family history. Don't," he said when she started to interrupt. "Let's lay the cards down. You have doubts about me because
of mine."

He was driving fast now, laying on the curves on the back roads,
letting speed eat up some of the tension.

"That's not true, Gabe. I couldn't have slept with you if I'd had doubts."

"Yes, you could. It's easy to ignore logic and doubts in the heat of the moment. And we're good in bed. We're better than good in bed. But sooner or later, logic clicks in again. I've got bad blood, Kelsey, and there's no draining it out."

His eyes stayed on the road, though he was very aware that hers were on his face, studying, considering.

"Where you come from always stays with you. You can clean it up, dress it up, but it's always underneath. I've seen things and done things that would shake that moral code of yours right down to the foundation. I don't cheat and I don't lean on the bottle, but that's about all I can say I haven't done. The simple facts are I wanted what Cunningham had, and I found a way to get it. I wanted you in bed, and I would have done whatever it took to get you there."

"I see." Now she stared straight ahead. The speed didn't frighten her, but he did. "Is it just sex?"

He didn't answer for a moment. They both watched the road twist ahead. "No. I wish to Christ it was."

She closed her eyes on a quiet, shuddering sigh. "Pull over," she murmured. When he ignored her, she straightened in her seat. "Pull over, Slater," she said firmly, "and stop the damn car."

The tires screeched when he slapped a foot on the brakes and jerked the wheel to the shoulder where gravel spat. "If you think I'm letting you get out here, you're a goddamned idiot. I'll take you into Reston, or I'll take you back home."

"I've no intention of getting out here."

"Fine, that's fine. You'd better understand I have no intention of letting you go, not here. Not anywhere. I gave you your chance to run."

She'd never seen him so completely unnerved. "No, you didn't."

He snatched her lapels and jerked her around in her seat. "It's all the chance you're getting. Fuck your right and wrong, Kelsey, and your country club upbringing and anything else that's in my way. You're not walking out on me without a fight."

Her own temper began to rumble. "Fine. Since you're going to take that insulting, Neanderthal attitude, it hardly seems appropriate for me to tell you I'm in love with you."

His hands went limp. For an instant every muscle in his body went numb. Her eyes were on his, sulky, signaling fight in progress. But he was already down for the count.

"You don't know what you are."

She hit him. Both gasped in surprise when her fist jabbed just under his heart.

"I'm not tolerating that." She smacked his hands aside. "I'm not tolerating that attitude. I'm sick to death of people I care about assuming I don't know my own mind or heart. I know it very well. And though at this particular moment it galls me, I'm in love with you. Now start this damn car and let's get this over with."

He couldn't have driven a tricycle. "Give me a minute."

She huffed out a breath, crossed her legs, and folded her arms. "Fine. Take your time. It'll give me the opportunity to plan several ways to make you suffer."

"Come here."

She jabbed out, and connected with her elbow when he reached for her. "Hands off."

"Okay. I just imagined I'd be touching you when I told you I love you."

Not particularly mollified, but thoughtful, she turned her head a fraction. "Have you been imagining it for long?"

"A while. I thought it would pass. Like a virus." He held up both hands when she jerked around. "Are you going to hit me again?"

"I might." Damned if she was going to laugh, no matter how much his eyes tempted her. "A virus?"

"Yeah. Only there's this thing about viruses I'd forgotten. They don't go away. They just sneak into some corner of your system and kick back in when your defenses are down." He took her hand, fisted it in his, and brought it to his lips. "I've been trying to get used to this one."

"And how are you doing?"

"Better now." He lowered his brow to hers. "Christ, what timing. We should be home, alone."

"It doesn't matter." She tilted her head so that her lips brushed his. "We'll make up for it when we are." When he deepened the kiss, she sank into it. "How can everything be such a mess, and this be so right?"

"Luck of the draw." He eased back, and looked into her eyes. "We'll make sure it stays right."

"This is enough for now." Gently, she lifted a hand to his cheek. "This is better than enough."

THE FIRST THING TIPTON NOTICED when the couple climbed out of the fancy foreign car in his driveway was that they were lovers. The man did no more than lay a hand on the woman's shoulder. She did no more than glance up, smile. But Tipton pegged it.

The second thing he noticed was that the woman was almost a dead ringer for Naomi. Or the Naomi he had put behind bars.

Oh, there were subtle differences, and his trained eye nailed them as well. The daughter's mouth was softer, a tad more generous. The cheekbones were slightly less prominent, the walk more fluid. Naomi's gait had been an energetic, even a nervous scissoring of legs. One that had drawn the eye of every male within a mile of her.

But all in all, he was glad Kelsey Byden had called first. It would have been a shock to have glanced up and seen her strolling up his walk like the ghost of the woman he'd never forgotten.

"Captain Tipton." Her smile was fleeting as her gaze shifted. "Lieutenant Rossi. I wasn't expecting to see you here."

"Small world, isn't it?" Irritating her only amused him, and he helped himself to another beer. He wasn't on duty, after all. "Why don't I make the introductions. Kelsey Byden and Gabriel Slater, my former commanding officer, Captain James Tipton."

"Roscoe here was always one for procedure." Tipton grinned as Kelsey lifted a brow at the nickname. "Sit down, have a beer?"

"Mr. Slater doesn't drink," Rossi put in.

"Oh, well. I think the wife brewed up some iced tea. Why don't you go on in, Roscoe, and pour our company a couple of glasses?"

"That would be nice." Pleased to put Rossi in the position of serving, Kelsey made herself comfortable on the top step. "I appreciate your taking the time to see us, Captain."

"No problem. I got nothing but time. How's your mother getting on?"

"Very well. You remember her, then?"

"I'm not likely to forget." But he shifted tactics, preferring to get a lay of the land. "Roscoe tells me congratulations are in order, Mr. Slater. You've got a horse that might cop the Triple Crown. Not that I know a lot about it. Baseball's my game."

Gabe knew something about tactics as well. "My money's on the Birds this year. They've got a solid pitching rotation, and an infield so tight you can barely squeeze a mosquito through it."

"They do." Delighted, Tipton slapped his knee. "By sweet Jesus, they do. You see them tromp the Jays last night? Goddamned Canadians."

Gabe grinned, slipped out a cigar. "I caught the last couple of innings." He offered one to Tipton, lit it for him. "That last triple took fifty out of my assistant trainer's pocket and put it into mine."

Tipton puffed. "I'm not a betting man myself."

Gabe flicked on his lighter at the tip of his own cigar, watched

Tipton over the flame. "I am." He blew out smoke, nodded when Rossi came back with two tall glasses. "Thanks."

"Roscoe's a football fan. I never could educate him into the thinking-man's sport."

"I'm beginning to develop an interest in the sport of kings." Rossi took his seat again. "I'll have my eye on the Belmont, Mr. Slater."

"A lot of us will."

"Now, the lady didn't come out here to talk sports." Tipton offered Kelsey a friendly smile. "You're here about murder."

"What can you tell me about Alec Bradley, Captain?"

He pursed his lips. She'd surprised him. He'd been sure she would focus on her mother. Intrigued, he shifted gears and turned back the clock. "Alec Bradley, thirty-two, formerly of Palm Beach. He'd been married once to a woman, oh, fifteen years his senior. She paid him off with a nice settlement in the divorce. Apparently he'd worked his way through most of it by the time he met your mother."

"What did he do?"

"Charmed the ladies." Tipton shrugged. "Sponged off acquaintances. Played the horses when he could. He owned his own tuxedo." Tipton paused for a sip of beer. "He was killed in it."

"You didn't like him," Kelsey commented.

To amuse himself, and to help align his thoughts with his words, Tipton blew three smoke rings. "He was dead when I met him, but no. From what the investigation turned up on him, he wasn't the kind of man I'd ask home for dinner. He made dallying with married women—*rich* married women—a profession. They'd pay him off with money and presents, introductions to other restless married women. If they didn't pay him enough, he'd use blackmail. In my day we called them gigolos. I don't know what you call them now."

"Slime," Gabe said pleasantly, and earned an approving nod from the captain.

Slater had taste, he decided. In women and cigars. "That says it well enough. The man had a way about him. Fancy manners, fancy education, a family line that went back to some puffed-up English earl. And he had that way with women, married women who couldn't afford scandal."

"My mother was separated, Captain."

"And in the middle of a custody suit. She couldn't afford the carryings-on with Bradley to come out if she wanted to win it."

"But she saw him publicly."

"Socially," Tipton agreed. "It didn't seem to bother her that people assumed they were lovers. No one could prove it." He tapped cigar ashes into the crushed can of Bud. "There were rumors about Bradley sniffing expensive white powder up his nose. No one proved that either. Until he was dead."

"Drugs." Kelsey paled but continued. "My mother said nothing about drugs. I didn't read anything about them in the newspaper reports."

"No drugs at Three Willows." Tipton sighed. Her eyes, so much like her mother's, were taking him back. "The place was clean. Your mother was clean. Bradley had a mixture of alcohol and cocaine in his system when he died."

"If that's true, he could have been irrational, violent, just as my mother said."

"There weren't any signs of struggle. The lace of your mother's nightgown was torn." He touched a hand to his chest. "She had a couple of bruises. Nothing she couldn't have done herself."

"If she did that herself, why didn't she knock over a few tables, break some lamps?"

Smart girl, he thought. "I asked myself, and her, that same question."

"And what did she say?"

"The first time, we were sitting downstairs. They were still taking pictures in the bedroom. She'd put on a big robe over her nightgown." As if she'd been cold, Tipton remembered. As if she'd been shivering under that heavy quilted material. "When I asked her, she snapped right back, 'Maybe I didn't think of it.'"

He smiled, shook his head. "Pissed at me is what she was. Those were the kind of answers she gave until her lawyers shut her up. The second time I asked her was in the interrogation room. She was smoking, one cigarette after the other. Practically eating them whole. When I asked her again, she said she wished she had thought of it. She wished she had because then someone might believe her."

He set his beer aside and sighed deeply. "And you know, Ms. Byden, the thing was—just like I told Roscoe here before you drove up—I did believe her."

Kelsey unfolded legs she could no longer feel, and forced herself to stand. "You believed her? You believed she was telling the truth, but you sent her to prison."

"I believed her," Tipton repeated, and his eyes narrowed, focused. Cop's eyes. "But the evidence was against her. I spent a lot of sleepless nights looking for something to weigh on the other side. All I had was my gut. I did my job, Ms. Byden. I arrested her. I booked her. I presented the evidence at her trial. That's what I had to do."

"Is that how you live with it?" Kelsey held her fists at her sides. "You knew she was telling the truth."

"I believed," Tipton corrected. "That's a long way from knowing."


"WELL, ROSCOE, THAT TOOK me back a few." Tipton watched the Jaguar back out of the drive, then set his chair to creaking again. "How many times do you see real gray eyes? No green in them, no blue, just smoke. You don't forget eyes like that."

"Naomi Chadwick got to you, Captain. That doesn't mean she was telling the truth."

"Oh, she got to me. I was a happily married man, Roscoe, never once caught any action on the side. But I thought about Naomi Chadwick. Did I believe her because she played some elemental tune on my libido?" He sighed, shrugged, and crushed his second can of beer. "I don't know. I was never sure. The D.A. was pushing for an arrest. He wanted that trial. And the evidence was there, so I did my job."

Rossi studied his second Bud. "What did you think of Charles Rooney?"

"The P.I.? He was a hotdogger. There were plenty of fancy names on his client list back then. Mostly divorce cases. I leaned on him, and he stuck to his story. He had the film, he had his reports, and the Bydens' lawyers backed him up."

"He witnessed a murder and didn't report it."

"We pressed that button. Claimed he was shaken up. A guy thinks he's going to snap pictures of a bout of hot sex, gets murder instead. Allegedly he was still sitting in his car when the black-and-whites arrived. He logged the time down to the minute."

"Then waited three days to bring in the film."

Tipton wiggled his wiry eyebrows. "How deep are you digging here, Roscoe?"

"As deep as it takes." He set the half-full beer on the porch between his feet and leaned forward, hands on knees. "Twenty-three years ago, you've got a dead horse in a race, drugs, a suicide, and a murder. Now we've got a murder, a suspicious death with the earmarks of suicide, a dead horse in a race, and drugs. Does the pendulum swing like that, Captain? Or does it get a shove?"

"You're a good cop, Roscoe." Like a veteran firehorse, Tipton quivered at the sound of the bell. "How many of the players are around on this swing?"

"That's what we need to find out. Maybe you could take some time out from your workshop and give me a hand with the research."

Tipton's smile was slow, and settled comfortably on his round face. "I could probably work it into my schedule."

"That's what I'd hoped you'd say. The jockey who hanged himself? Benedict Morales. Benny. Maybe you could flesh him out for me."

KELSEY STRAIGHTENED IN HER seat when Gabe drove through the gates at Longshot. "Gabe, I should just go home. I'm not good company."

"No, you're not." He braked, turned off the ignition. "And I figure you might as well have your explosion here rather than at Three Willows where you'd have to explain it to Naomi."

"I'm just so angry." She bounded out of the car and slammed the door. "He believed her, but he sent her to prison."

"Cops don't send you to prison, darling, juries do. Believe me, I've been there."

"The point is she spent ten years behind bars. Isn't that the point?"

"The point," he said, taking her arm and steering her into the house, "is that that part's done. You can't change it. How much are you willing to risk to turn back the clock and prove it was a mistake?"

Stunned, she stared at him. "Risk? What's the matter with you? The risk doesn't count—it doesn't matter! What happened to her was wrong. It has to be put right."

"Black and white?"

There was a twist in her gut, one quick churn. "And if it is?"

"Then it is," he said simply. "But don't overlook the gray areas, Kelsey. Not everything you find out if you go on with this is going to fit neatly into one column or the other."

She stepped back from him, and the distance was much wider than the simple movement. "You want me to stop."

"I want you to be prepared."

"For?"

Deliberately he closed the distance, cupping her stiff shoulders in his hands. "Not everyone you care about is perfect. And not everyone who matters to you is going to thank you for sweeping away two decades' worth of dust."

She shrugged irritably in a fruitless attempt to dislodge his hands. "I'm aware that Naomi wasn't—isn't—a saint. I don't expect perfection, Slater, or look for it. But I want the truth."

"Fine. As long as you can handle it when you get it. No use trying to shake me off," he said, and smiled when she shoved at his hands. "The first truth you're going to have to swallow is that you're stuck with the cards you've been dealt. You and I are going to play out this hand."

"I'm not trying to shake you off. I just need to think about what to do next."

"I can help you with that." He urged her closer, those clever hands slipping down her back, cruising up again. "You're going to relax, take a swim."

"I don't have a suit with me."

"Darling, I'm counting on that." He was kissing her now in a way that always turned her mind to fluff. "After, I'm going to talk you into trying out some of those culinary skills you once bragged about."

Relaxing seemed like an excellent idea. With a little murmur of pleasure, she turned her head to ease his access to her neck. "You want me to cook for you?"

"I do. Then I want to take you upstairs and seduce you."

"What are you doing now?"

"This is just a preview. Tomorrow, when you're relaxed and your mind's clear, we'll start thinking again."

"It sounds sensible."

He nipped his way back up to her mouth. It wasn't particularly fair, he knew, to keep certain ideas to himself. But he wanted to clear the tension out of her face. And to celebrate the fact that they'd found each other. For one night, he wanted them both to concentrate on only that.

"Let's be sensible." He stepped back, sliding his hands down her arms until they were linked with hers. "I love you."

Her heart took one long, slow turn in her breast. "How can I argue with that?"

# Chapter Twenty-One

IN THE ROSY LIGHT OF DAWN, MOSES WATCHED THE MARES lead their babies to water. He knew the pecking order as well as they. Big Bess, with an arrogant swish of her tail, was first, always. Then Carmen, the hardheaded red, followed by Trueheart, and so on down the line until shy, self-effacing Sunny.

The foals scampered with them, frisky and secure. Unaware, Moses thought, that in a few short weeks they would be weaned and separated from Mama in the next step toward their destinies.

Some would be trained for the track, some would be sold at yearling auctions. One might show a different promise and be culled out as a jumper, or for the show ring. Moses wasn't much on show horses himself. It seemed as shallow to his mind as beauty pageants. Some would be gelded, others bred.

And one, maybe one, would show the mark of a true champion. There was always another Derby, he told himself. Always another chance for that win.

Maybe that one, the little chestnut with the blaze. The one with the cocky tilt to his head. Naomi had named him Tomorrow's

Arrogance because of it. He had the lines, the breeding, and time would tell if he had the heart.

In his own breast, Moses's heart was heavy. He'd put too much on the line at the Derby. He knew better. Both sides of his heritage warned against testing the gods. Yet he had tested them, putting all of his hopes, all of his heart, into one two-minute race.

And the cost had been staggering.

"They're beautiful, aren't they?" Kelsey murmured from behind him. "It's hard to believe that in another year they'll be ready for the saddle."

Moses tucked his hands into his front pockets and kept his eyes on the foals. "So, you decided to show up."

"I'm sorry. I'm a little late."

"A little late today. Half a day yesterday, and the day before that."

"There were some things I had to take care of."

"Things." He turned to her, knowing he was about to take out some of his frustration on her. Certain she deserved it. "Only one thing comes first for anybody who works here, and that's the horses."

He strode off toward the barn with Kelsey trotting guiltily after him. "I'm sorry, Moses, really. It was unavoidable—"

Her heels dug in when he stopped abruptly in front of her and swung about. "Listen, little girl, this isn't one of your playgrounds. You don't get to call time here and tie your shoe. What you do is you pull your weight, all day, every day. Because if you don't, some-one else has to pick up the slack. That's not the way I run things. Just what were you doing yesterday when you should have been with your horse, when you should have been taking your orders from the yearling manager?"

"I was . . ." Kelsey all but sawed at her tongue. "It was personal business."

"From now on you get your hair fluffed and your nails painted on your own time. I'm not wasting mine. You've got stalls to muck."

"But I—I need to work with Honor."

"She's already on the longe. You can cool her off when she's done. Now get a shovel."

He strode away, disappearing inside his office. Grooms and stable hands who'd stopped to listen immediately got back to work. Everyone enjoyed a public flogging, but no one liked to get caught watching one.

"Well, you've been accepted." Naomi stepped up to Kelsey and ran a comforting hand up and down her spine. "He wouldn't have spoken to you that way unless he considered you part of the team."

"He might have slapped me down privately," Kelsey muttered. "And goddammit, I wasn't getting my hair done. Look at these." Incensed, she fanned out her fingers, the nails short, clipped, unpolished. "Does it look like I've had a manicure recently? I'm not here to play. Just because I needed a few hours off—" She stopped, swore again. "It was important to me."

"Sometimes we can forget there's anything else going on in the world that doesn't happen right here. You're under no obligation to throw yourself into this. The fact is, most owners aren't nearly so involved with the day-to-day work. If you'd rather—"

"You don't think I can handle it." Color bloomed and rode high on Kelsey's cheeks. "You don't think I can see it through."

"I'm not saying that, Kelsey."

"Aren't you? Why should this be any different? I've always moved from job to job, interest to interest. Why should anyone believe that I can stick, that this means any more than writing ad copy, or explaining Impressionist art to tour groups? If I can give up on everything else, why shouldn't I give up on this?" She tossed back her hair. "Because it is different. Because everything's different."

Turning on her heel, she stalked to the barn.

Naomi only sighed. It was, she realized, a surefire way to forget your own troubles when two people you loved dumped their own at your feet. Gauging temperaments, she decided that Kelsey could use some time wielding a pitchfork to cool off. So she started with Moses.

He was at his desk, barking on the phone to Reno's agent. "No, I'm not putting him up at Belmont. He's not ready, and Corelli rode High Water to place in the Preakness. He knows the colt and he deserves the ride. Yeah, that's final."

He slammed the phone down, cutting off the voice yammering through the receiver.

"I'm not putting up a spooked jockey with a bum shoulder."

"I agree with you." Ready to placate, she sat on the corner of his desk. "And so does Reno. He knows he's not ready." In a gesture she hoped would serve as truce, she covered his hand with hers. "Weren't you a little rough on Kelsey out there?"

His face closed, and Moses drew his hand away. "Are you here as the owner, or as her mother?"

"I'm here, Moses," she said, and left it at that. "I know she's taken some time off recently. Just as I know that something's troubling her. Just," she continued quietly, "as I know something's troubling you."

"Let's stick with one issue, Naomi." He pushed back from the desk. "She's been slacking off. So maybe the bloom's faded."

Puzzled, she studied his face. Not just annoyed, she realized, but worried. "And maybe she just had some loose ends to tie up. We can't forget the fact that she's had to make a lot of adjustments in a very short time. I thought you were happy, even impressed with her work up until now."

"Up until now," he agreed. "I've been anything but happy and impressed the last few days. She needed a shot, and I gave her one. Maybe you've forgotten that's one of the things I do around here. If you want her treated differently—"

"I didn't say that." Annoyance snapped into her voice. "But I know you, Moses. You don't slap someone down like that in public for a couple of infractions So, who's decided to treat her differently?"

He turned so that they faced each other with the desk between them. "As far as I see it, that's a girl who's gotten pretty much everything she wants her whole life. She's spoiled, she's reckless, and she's used to coming and going as she pleases."

"Just like I was."

He acknowledged that with a nod. "Some. But you finished what you started, Naomi."

"Maybe this is the first time she's found something worth finishing."

"And maybe she's getting bored and is going to pack her bags. Do you think I don't know what it's going to do to you if she turns away now?"

The chill had Naomi hugging her arms. "You're the one who told me she wasn't going to do that."

"Maybe I was wrong. Maybe I was just so damn happy to see you smile all the way again. Everything seemed to be moving in the right direction. And then . . ." Disgusted, he dropped back down into the chair, scrubbed his hands over his face. "Goddammit. She got in my way at the wrong time."

"What is it, Moses?" She reached for him again. This time he gripped her hand.

"The gods laugh, Naomi. Especially when you forget that they can step in at any time and snatch away what you want most. I've had my heart broke before." He looked up at her again, smiled a little. "You did it first. But it's been a while. I'd forgotten how much it hurts."

"Pride," she murmured. "You let me do all the grieving over him."

Miserable, he looked down at the joined hands. "I missed something, Naomi. I had myself so revved up about winning that I had to be careless, even for a minute. It cost too much."

"You can grieve, Moses, but you can't take the blame."

"That was my horse, Naomi." His eyes cut back to hers. "Your name might be on the papers, but he was mine. And I lost him. I wasn't looking in the right place at the right time. I didn't sense what I should have sensed. Even now, I go back over that day. I go back and back and back, and I can't see it. It had to be under my nose." He rapped a fist against the desk. "Under my fucking nose."

There was, she knew, only one way to handle him in a mood like this. "Okay, Whitetree, it was all your fault. You were in charge. I pay you to train my horses, to know them, to understand them, and to guide them from birth to death. I also pay you to oversee the men, to hire and fire, and to decide which team works for which horse for which race. It looks as though I've also been paying you to foretell the future." She cocked her head. "Since that's the case, I don't know whether to fire you or give you a raise."

"I'm serious about this."

"So am I." She rose and skirted the desk to knead his knotted shoulders. "I want to know what happened, Moses. I want to know who did it, and I want them to pay. What I don't want, and can't afford, is to have you, someone I love and depend on, losing heart. We've got less than eleven months to the first Saturday in May."

"Yeah." He blew out a stream of breath. "I guess I should go apologize to that girl of yours."

"Leave it. She can take a lump."

He smiled again. "She wanted to give me a few. Christ, she's got your eyes. I don't have a lot of regrets about things I haven't done, Naomi. In fact, I can count the big ones on one hand. I've never made a pilgrimage to Israel, never walked in the footsteps of my ancestors on either side. And I never made a child with you."

Her hands stopped, and he reached back and gripped them hard. "I'm sorry."

"No." She lowered her head so that her cheek rested on his hair. "Don't be. Why are there so seldom second chances on the big ones, Moses?"

*

338

RICH WAS THINKING THE same thing. Second chances were as rare as hens' teeth. It was a lucky man who could snare one. Rich Slater was a lucky man.

He put two grand on the trifecta at Laurel and moseyed back to the bar. Mostly, trifectas were a sucker's game, but he was on a roll.

Sticking with the ponies, he thought. The hell with cards, fuck point spreads. The horses were his babies now.

He ordered another bourbon, his new, sentimental drink of choice, then drew out a five-dollar cigar.

The lighter that flared under it caused his brows to rise. Rich puffed the cigar into life, then swiveled to smile affably at his son. "Well now, just like old times. Bring my boy here one of the same," he ordered the bartender.

Gabe merely held up a finger. "Coffee, black."

"Shit." Rich drew the word out to three syllables. "Don't be such a pussy, boy. I'm buying."

"Coffee," Gabe repeated, then studied his father. He knew the signs: flushed cheeks, bright eyes, big toothy smile. Rich Slater was not only half drunk, but he had money in his pocket.

"I thought you had trouble coming out from Chicago."

"Got that all straightened out. Don't you worry about me, Gabe. Everybody knows old Rich Slater's good for his markers."

"Oh?" Gabe lifted a brow. "I thought the trouble had something to do with dealing from the bottom of the deck."

Was that what he'd told the boy? Rich wondered, and searched back through his soggy memory. Well, it didn't matter. "Just a difference of opinion, that's all. All tidied up now. This here's my race." He gestured toward the monitor. "Number three," he muttered. "Yeah, number three."

Gabe glanced up at the screen just as the gate sprang open. "I've heard you've been playing the track again."

"Come on, baby, hug that rail. Where'd you hear that?"

"Here and there. Somebody spotted you at Churchill Downs on Derby day."

339

Rich continued to watch the race, urging his horse on with little jerks of his body. His mind was working, though, picking carefully through the minefield Gabe was setting for him.

"He's got it. He's got it! Now, come on, wire. Ha! Son of a bitch, I can pick 'em." Pleased that the first horse on his ticket had come in a winner, he signaled for another drink. "I've got the touch, Gabe, I've always had the touch."

"What kind of touch did you have in Kentucky last month?"

"Kentucky." The broad, amiable grin only widened. "I haven't been down in Kentucky for oh, five, six years or more. Shoulda stuck with the horses, though, that's the truth."

"I saw you myself, the morning of the race."

Not by a flicker did Rich show reaction. His eyes stayed on his son's. "I don't think so, buddy boy. I've got me a nice set of rooms outside Baltimore. All the action I need is within an easy drive. Pimlico, Laurel, Charles Town. Now, maybe you're thinking of Pimlico, the Preakness. I was there. Sure was." He winked. "Had some money down on your colt, too. You didn't let me down. Maybe, seeing as I'm rolling hot, I'll take a trip up to Belmont. Think you can cop the whole Crown, do you, Gabe? You do, we'll have ourselves a real celebration."

"There was trouble at the Derby."

"I know about that. Shocked I was, too, sitting in my room watching it on TV. Crying shame to see a horse go down that way." He shook his head sadly over his drink. "Damn shame. But then, it didn't hurt you any, did it?"

"Somebody helped that horse go down."

Lips pursed around his cigar, Rich nodded. "Now, I heard about that, too. Nasty business. Christ knows it happens." He reached for the beer nuts, popped two in his mouth. Gabe noticed he was wearing a ring on his pinky, little diamonds shaped into a dollar sign.

"Oh, not as much as it used to," Rich went on. "Harder to get away with pumping a horse up with chemicals these days." He puffed out smoke, amusing himself by stringing Gabe along. "Now, back in the days when your granddaddy and me used to play the ponies, there were plenty of tricks. Didn't have so many tests then, so many fucking rules on the horses and the jocks. But that was forty years ago and more." He sighed reminiscently. "Too bad you never got to know your granddaddy, Gabe."

"Too bad he got a bullet in the brain over a . . . difference of opinion."

"That's the truth," Rich said, with no sarcasm. He was a man who'd loved his daddy. "It's like I always tried to teach you, son, sometimes cheating's just part of the game. It's a matter of skill and timing."

"And sometimes it's a matter of murder. A horse, a man. One's not so different from the other to some people."

"Some horses I've liked better than some men."

"I remember another race, in Lexington. I was just a kid." Gabe picked up his cooling coffee, watching his father over the rim. "But I remember you were nervous. It wasn't that hot. The Bluegrass Stakes is in the spring. But you were sweating a lot. You had me working the stands, looking for loose change, panhandling. A horse broke down that day, too."

"Happens." He turned back to the monitor. Despite the chill from the air-conditioning, the back of his neck was damp. "I've seen it happen plenty in my day."

"It was a Chadwick horse then, too."

"No shit? Well, that's bad luck. Hey, can't you see I'm dry here?" Rich slapped a hand on the bar.

"A jockey hanged himself over it. As I recall, we didn't stick around long after that race. A few days, that's all. That was funny, too, because our room was paid up."

"Itchy feet. I've always had them."

"You were flush after that. The money didn't last long. It never did, but you had a nice fat roll when we headed out."

"I must have bet some winners that day."

341

"You're on a roll now, too, aren't you? New suit, gold watch, diamond ring." He picked up Rich's hand. "Manicure."

"You got a point here, boy?"

Braced against the stench of bourbon, Gabe leaned closer. His voice was low, icily controlled. "You'd better hope I don't find out you were in Kentucky on the first Saturday in May."

"You don't want to threaten me, Gabe."

"Oh yes, I do."

With fear and rage circling through his system, Rich picked up his fresh drink. "You want to back off is what you want to do. You want to let things lie and get your mind on that horse you're running next week. Keep your mind on that and on that pretty blond filly you're banging."

In a flash, Gabe had a hand wrapped around the knot of his father's new silk tie. The bartender hustled over.

"We don't want any trouble here."

"No trouble." Rich grinned into Gabe's face. "No trouble at all. Just a family discussion. That's a prime piece you're putting it to, son. Blue blood. I bet a thoroughbred like that's got plenty of kick, and lots of endurance. Maybe it's time she met your dear old daddy."

Gabe's hand ached with the pressure of making a fist. The fist ached to connect. Yet no matter how repugnant, there was no escaping the fact that the man was his father. "Keep away from her," Gabe said quietly.

"Or?"

"I'll kill you."

"We both know you haven't got the guts for that. But we'll make a deal. You keep out of my business, I keep out of yours." Rich smoothed down his tie when Gabe allowed him to jerk free. "Otherwise I might just have me a nice long talk with your pretty lady. I'd bet we'd have lots to talk about."

"Keep away from what's mine." Gabe took out a bill and put it on the counter beside the coffee he'd barely tasted. "Keep far away from what's mine."

"Kids." Rich beamed a fresh smile at the nervous bartender when Gabe strode away. "They just never learn respect." He picked up his drink, tried to ignore the fact that his hand was unsteady. "Sometimes you just got to pound it into them," he muttered.

Nursing his drink, he turned back to the monitor and waited for his horse to come in.

IT WAS NEARLY DUSK WHEN KELSEY walked out of the barn for the last time. She'd put in a backbreaking twelve hours, hauling manure and straw, scrubbing down concrete, polishing tack. Now every muscle in her body was weeping. All she wanted was a blissfully hot bath and oblivion.

"Want a beer?" Moses sat on a barrel, two cold bottles dangling from his fingers. He'd been waiting for her.

"No." She gave him a nod as frosty as the brews. "Thanks."

"Kelsey." He held a bottle up. "I couldn't find my peace pipe."

Reluctant, she gave in and accepted one. She'd have preferred a gallon of water, but the beer washed away the taste of dirt and sweat just as well.

Moses narrowed his eyes at the purpling bruise on her upper arm. "What happened there? Pacer take a bite?"

"That's right. So?"

"You're not going to be able to stay pissed off at me for long. I'm too charming."

Kelsey drank again. "No, you're not."

"Works with your mother," he grumbled. "Listen, I think you screwed up, and I let you know it. Now I'm telling you you've done a good job. And not just today. For the most part."

"For the most part?"

"That's right. You learn fast, and you don't make the same mistake twice, but you still need somebody looking over your shoulder. You've got a temperament problem, but we're used to that around here, between the horses and your mother."

343

"My—" Her jaw dropped. "My mother."

"She can be a mule when it suits her. Not that she flies off the handle much now the way she did when she was younger. I'm sorry about that sometimes." He looked down at his boots. "Damn sorry about that. It's not that they broke her, but they changed her. Toughened her, I guess, so she learned how to pull in. I came down on you today more because of her than because of the job."

"I don't understand."

"If you turn away from her now, it'll kill her. She wouldn't want me to say it, but I'm saying it. There's nothing that means more to me in this world than Naomi. I don't want to see her hurt again."

"I'm not turning away. I'm not trying to hurt her. That may be a lot for you to take on faith, but I wish you would. I wish you could."

"You know, I figure anybody who can purge a horse and not run for cover's got to be trusted. See you in the morning."

"Sure." She started away, then looked over her shoulder. "It's a pretty evening."

"It is that."

"Women like to walk in the moonlight."

"I've heard that."

"There should be plenty of it in a couple of hours." Satisfied, Kelsey continued toward the house. She'd done her job, all around, she decided. Now she was going to let Gertie stuff her with anything available in the kitchen, then soak out all the aches in a marathon bath.


AN HOUR LATER, SHE WAS dozing amid a swirl of bubbles and scent. Her world had smoothed out again. She was in the middle of a lazy yawn when the door opened.

"Gabe." Flustered, she scooted up, spewing froth dangerously close to the rim of the tub. "What are you doing?"

"Gertie told me I'd find you up here." He hooked his thumbs

in his belt loops and simply enjoyed the view. "I was going to get you and bring you home with me. But it doesn't look like you're dressed for the ride."

"I often bathe naked. It's a habit of mine."

"How about I wash your back, and any other hard-to-reach places?"

"I can handle it." She pushed her hair out of her eyes and struggled not to give in to the urge to cross her arms over her bubble-bedecked breasts. "Listen, why don't you wait downstairs until I'm finished?"

He considered, then shook his head and began unbuttoning his shirt. "Nope. I'm coming in."

"You are not. We're in my mother's house, for God's sake."

"She's not here."

"That's not the point." Hurriedly, she scooped her bangs out of her eyes. "Keep that shirt on, Slater. Gertie's downstairs," she hissed.

"She'll have to stay there. There isn't room in that tub for the three of us." He tossed his shirt aside and sat down to pry off his boots.

"It's not a joke. It's just not appropriate."

"I need you, Kelsey."

Her protest turned into a sigh. She could see it now, the tension in the set of his shoulders. It was all but coming off him in waves. "Dammit," she murmured. "Lock the door."

"I already did."

His jeans joined hers on the floor, then he was easing himself into the steamy water behind her. His arms encircled her waist. He buried his face in her hair.

"God." He drew in her scent, wallowed in her texture while he fought off the fury that had roiled inside him since the confrontation with his father.

He needed it to go away, just for an hour. She could do that for him. She could do anything for him.

"Gabe, tell me what's wrong."

"Ssh." He slicked his hands up to the slippery curve of her breasts, skimmed wet fingertips over her nipples. "Just let me touch you. I only need to touch you."

He drowned her in tenderness. He'd never been so gentle before, so patient, so careful. With her leaning against him he did only what he'd said he'd needed. Only touched her. Fingers sliding along a long thigh, skimming down from knee to calf, flowing up again to dip inside her so that the heat melted her bones.

Shuddering, she tried to turn to face him, but he pressed her back. "Not yet." His mouth danced over her glistening shoulder, along the nape of her neck where falling tendrils curled damply.

So she surrendered, more completely than she had before, letting his hands take her where he chose. Water lapped, bubbles dissolved. Each time she climaxed, felt her body tighten, tremble, explode, she was sure it was the last. Yet he slowly, patiently, quietly, built a new fire.

She could float on the smoke of it, drift, deaf to her own throaty moans. When at last he shifted her, letting water spill carelessly over the rim, over the tiles, she sank back through the clouds of smoke, into the flames.

# Chapter Twenty-Two

THAT HORSE WAS NOT GOING TO WIN. RICH HELPED HIMSELF TO Cunningham's scotch. After all, a man shouldn't get himself hung up on one kind of liquor. Or one kind of woman. Or one kind of game.

The boy had never understood that, he thought as he downed a double and poured another. He'd never been able to teach that little son of a bitch anything.

Well, he was going to teach him now. Good and proper.

There would be no Triple Crown this year. No, indeed. He was going to see to that. He'd come to do a job, and if it turned out it had the benefit of a little personal revenge, so much the better.

He settled into Cunningham's easy chair, propped his shiny new Gucci loafers on the footstool. And smiled. This was the life for him, all right. Lord of the manor. A fine house in the country, a couple of spiffy cars in the garage, a hungry woman in bed.

He was going to have it too. Once he tied up this last loose end, he was taking his winnings out to Vegas. They knew him in Vegas. Yes, sir, they knew good old Richie Slater in that town. He'd be a high roller, penthouse suite at Caesars, a top-heavy babe hanging on his arm.

When he'd cleaned up there, he'd buy himself a house. Maybe right in Nevada, come to that. One of those fancy digs with cactus and palm trees and a pool in the backyard. Then when the urge struck him, or the level got low in his billfold, he'd just slip on into town and clean up again.

He sat there, dreaming a bit about a wheel that always spun to his tune and cards that fell like angels into his hand.

"What the hell are you doing?" Flushed and breathless, Cunningham stood in the doorway. Rather than the commanding tone he'd hoped for, his voice came out in a squeak.

"Hey there, Billy boy. All finished talking with your partners? Word is you're syndicating that filly for a million flat."

"That's my business." The deal was nearly set, and nothing, *nothing*, he promised himself, was going to interfere. There was a loan to pay off, and it was nearing deadline. "You got your money, Slater. You and I are done."

Lips puckered, Rich contemplated his last swallow of scotch. "Now, that's downright unfriendly, Billy."

"What are you doing in my house?"

"Can't an old pal drop by for a visit?" He grinned guilelessly. "That pretty little bed-warmer of yours was a lot more welcoming when she let me in. On her way out shopping, she said. Down to Neiman Marcus. Needless Markup, that is. Get it?" He chuckled at his own wit.

"Marla," Cunningham said with what dignity he could muster, "is my wife."

"No shit?" After slapping himself on the knee, Rich rose to pour another drink. "Got yourself a ball and chain with first-class tits, did you? Well, congratulations, Billy boy. You're a bigger fool than anybody could've guessed."

If he wasn't a fool now, Cunningham thought, he'd certainly been one when he'd slid back into a deal with Rich Slater. But now, and from now on, everything was legitimate. The syndication deal, which Cunningham had just shaken hands on down at his barn, was every bit as big as Rich had heard. So it was time, way past the time, to cut old ties. All of them.

"I'm going to ask you to leave, Rich. We're square, you and me, and it isn't smart for us to be seen together."

"Nobody here but you and me." Rich winked and settled back in the chair again. Oh, he knew what Cunningham was thinking. Yes, indeed, he did. Billy boy figured he didn't need good old Rich anymore. "Now, don't you worry. I'm not here to squeeze you for more money. You just rest easy on that."

It pacified him, a little. "What is it, then?"

"A favor, that's all. Just a favor between old friends and former business associates. There's a horse that needs to be taken care of, Bill." He lifted his glass, enjoying the way the sun burst through the window and struck the facets.

"I don't want any part of it."

"What you want and what you've got are two different things." He shifted his eyes from his glass to Cunningham. "I'm going to take out my son's colt, Billy. And you're going to help me."

"You're crazy." Shaken, Cunningham swiped at the sweat beading on his upper lip. "You're crazy, Rich, and I don't want anything to do with it."

"Let's talk about that," Rich said, and smiled.


KELSEY'S SUITCASES WERE NEATLY packed and lined up next to Gabe's by the bedroom door. They would leave for New York at seven A.M. sharp. Six hours from now, she thought as she gazed up through the skylight over the bed.

She sighed, shifted, and snuggled up against Gabe. It struck her, amazed her, as it always did, to find him there. Warm, solid. Hers. That body. She skimmed her fingers down his chest, up again. Long and hard and tireless. The face that could make her toes curl every time he looked at her.

And that was only the shell.

349

A terrific shell, she mused, tracing his jaw with her fingertip. But what was inside it was equally impressive. The strength, the kindness, the courage. He'd already beaten the odds, time and time again. Overcoming a birthright of misery and meanness to make it on his own.

Right now, sleeping in his place of honor in the barn was a horse who had the same kind of strength and courage. Together, they were going to make history.

"It's no use," she murmured, nuzzling her lips against his throat.

"Hmm?" Automatically he stroked a hand down her back. He'd been enjoying the lazy caress of her fingertips for some time.

"I can't sleep. I'm too revved."

"Well, then." Always willing to accommodate, he rolled her over so that she was stretched on top of him. "Enjoy yourself."

She chuckled, wiggling away. "That's not what I meant." Kneeling, she looked down at him, letting herself linger over the long silhouette. "Not that it isn't a tempting offer." Leaning down, she gave him a smacking kiss. "I'll take you up on it when I get back."

He made a grab, but she was already scrambling off the bed. "Get back from where?"

"I need to walk. I want to look in on Double."

She tugged jeans over naked legs and hips, made his mouth water. "Darling, it's one o'clock in the morning."

"I know." Her head popped out of the opening of a baggy T-shirt. "In a little over eight hours, we'll be at Belmont. So who can sleep?" Tossing back her hair, she pulled on boots.

He could have, but it seemed a moot point. "I'll come with you."

"You don't have to. I won't be long."

He sat up, raked a hand through his hair. "I'll come with you."

"Okay. Catch up with me." She dashed out the door and down the stairs.

It was a perfect June night. Warm, just a little breezy, star-shattered. She heard the long, double-toned hoot of an owl, smelled roses and night-blooming jasmine. Moonlight showered on the outbuildings, lending them a timeless, fairy-tale aura.

Perhaps this was her fairy tale, she thought. Her personal happily-ever-after. It was true that tragedy had brought her here, opened the door to her future. But fairy tales were rife with tragedy. Orphans and spellbound princes, betrayals and sacrifices, evil intent and lost loves.

But right always triumphed. Maybe that was why the analogy appealed to her. If this was her fairy tale, she would see that right triumphed. She wouldn't give up on finding the truth.

She would see Captain Tipton again, and Charles Rooney. She would talk to Gertie, to Moses, and yes, to Naomi. To anyone who had had even the smallest role in the events leading to Alec Bradley's death. She would convince Naomi to allow her lawyers to speak freely.

But for now, for the next week, there was only the Belmont. And she was a part of it. With a quiet laugh, Kelsey lifted her face toward the sky. She had a place in the grandeur and the grit, the sweat and the seduction of racing's finest hour.

In a week's time, she promised herself, she would watch Gabe and his spectacular colt accept the last jewel in the Crown.

A barn cat dashed across the path, his long sleek form a gray bullet that shot her heart to her throat. Chuckling at herself, she rubbed a hand there as if to ease it back into her chest again.

The stable door opened with a thin squeak. The smells came first, old friends rushing at her through the dark. Horse, leather, liniment, manure. Rather than turn on the lights and disturb those sleeping, she groped along the wall from memory and found a flashlight. Its beam cut a narrow swath. Her boot heels clicked after it.

From the second stall a pair of eyes gleamed goblinlike from the shadows. Her breath caught; the beam bobbled. Fairy tales, indeed, she thought, and was grateful Gabe wasn't with her to see how she jumped at a couple of barn cats.

She smiled when she saw the cot pulled in front of Double's box. The security system aside, a warrior like this merited a personal guard. Well, she wouldn't disturb the groom, she promised herself. Just one quick peek over the cot and into the box, and she'd leave them both sleeping.

But the cot, she saw with some surprise, was empty. Alarmed, she shone her light into the box. Double was there, fully awake, staring back at her.

"Sorry, fella. I guess I'm jumpy. Did your friend here go off for a smoke, or a call of nature? Are you all packed?" She laughed and reached for the box door.

It wasn't latched, was open fully three inches.

"Oh, God." A movement behind her had her swinging about, flashlight gripped like a weapon. The blood thundered in her ears as she zigzagged the beam and cursed the cats who hunted at night.

But a cat, however quick and clever, hadn't unlatched and opened the stall door. Her one clear thought was to protect, to defend. Kelsey shoved the door open and rushed to the colt's side. Even as she pivoted, to shine her light into the corners of the box, the blood in her ears exploded.

She was aware of one vivid flash of pain, the high, alarmed whinny from the colt. Then nothing.

While the figure dashed from the box, breath harsh and panicked, the colt danced, lethal hooves arching over Kelsey's unconscious form.

HALFWAY BETWEEN THE HOUSE and the barn, Gabe balanced two mugs of tea. It appeared to him that they were going to be up most of the night, but the herbal brew Kelsey preferred was a better idea than coffee at this hour. Particularly if he could coax her back into bed and channel her nervous energy into a more intimate arena.

They hadn't been wasting much time on sleep in any case, he thought. Not since the night he'd joined her in her tub. It had been tricky to convince her to move in with him for a few days. He'd shamelessly used the race as a reason for it—his need for some moral support.

It worked, he reminded himself, grinning as he sipped from his mug. He intended for it to continue working, stage by stage until it was a permanent condition. But he'd calculated that a woman still raw from a divorce needed to be eased into the idea of a second marriage.

The biggest surprise was that *he* hadn't needed to be eased into the idea at all. It had simply appeared, full-blown, in his mind. Or maybe in his heart. He'd never given a great deal of thought to the traditional boundaries of marriage, wife, family. With an upbringing like his, the idea of it was absurd, even destructive.

But not with Kelsey. With her he wanted the promise, the future. The chance.

Together they would share all of this. He skimmed his gaze over the outbuildings, the hills, the fences. Together they would make more.

And maybe, while they were doing it, they could help each other bury the past.

The shrill, frenzied cry of the colt split the quiet. Both mugs shattered on the gravel as Gabe lunged forward. With Kelsey's name bursting from his lips, he dragged at the barn door, slapped the lights. Ice-edged panic chased him between the boxes, sliced nastily into his spine.

She was sprawled on the straw, facedown, the colt backed into the rear of the box, eyes rolling as he pawed his bedding. The world upended, draining the blood from Gabe's head out through the soles of his feet.

He moved like lightning, shielding her with his own body as he gathered her up. He took a blow to the shoulder, unfelt as he lifted her. Her face was corpse white, her body limp as rags. Ignoring the flailings of the colt, he laid her on the cot. His fingers trembled as he pressed them to the pulse at her throat.

"Please, baby. Please."

It was there, that quick flutter of life. He kept his fingers pressed to it, as if by removing them that life beat would drain away, and buried his face in her hair.

There was only panic and relief, panic and relief, a bright and giddy pendulum swinging inside him. He stayed as he was, his fingers at her throat, his face in her hair, one arm cradling her.

"Gabe. Jesus Christ, Gabe."

The frightened voice of his trainer snapped him back. He lifted his head and watched the somehow dreamlike movements of Jamison stepping into the box to calm the colt.

"Easy, boy. Easy now." Jamison dragged the colt's head down, using his voice and his hands to soothe. "Settle down." But his eyes were anything but calm when they focused on Gabe. "What happened here? Where's Kip? He's supposed to be bunking outside the box."

"I don't know where the hell he is. But you're going to find him. Find him and the fucking night watchman." Forcing himself to move slowly, Gabe ran his hands over Kelsey, checking for broken bones. He located the knot at the back of her head. His fingers lingered there, gentle as a kiss, while his eyes sliced back to Jamison and burned. "Call a doctor, and the cops. Now."

"She's hurt." Jamison continued to stroke the quivering colt. "How bad?"

"I don't know. Call, goddammit!"

As if in answer, Kelsey stirred under his hand and moaned.

"Kelsey." He had to yank himself back from snatching her up. "Kelsey, take it slow."

"Gabe." Her eyes fluttered open, but her vision swam, touching off nausea. "God." She closed them again, struggling to breathe evenly.

"Don't try to move yet."

"I'm not. Believe me." She concentrated on moving air in and out of her lungs. When it seemed she had that down, she cautiously opened her eyes again. This time, she brought his face into focus. There was murder in his eyes, she thought dimly. Then remembered. "The colt. Someone was in with the colt."

"It's all right. He's all right." Gabe cursed viciously when she winced in pain. "I'm going to take you up to the house now. I'm going to take care of you."

"Somebody was in there. The groom was gone. The door was open. But I couldn't see who it was. Did they hurt him?"

"No." Gabe glanced at Jamison, who was sliding the box door closed. "Make the calls, Jamie. I want Lieutenant Rossi. I want Gunner, too. See that he gets out here and checks the colt over."

"He looks fine," Jamison began, but was already nodding. His eyes were bloodshot and strained. "I'll get him here, Gabe. Take her on up, do what you can for her. I'll sit up myself with the colt tonight."

"I want two men on him." Gabe lifted Kelsey as carefully as a man handling spun glass. "No less than two at any time. Is that understood?"

"It is."

"And find Kip. I want to talk to him."

"All right." With a heavy heart Jamison watched Gabe carry Kelsey outside. He turned to the colt, rubbed his weary eyes, then went to make the calls.

"I'm all right, really." But Kelsey kept her eyes closed on the trip from barn to house. "Just a headache."

"Be quiet," Gabe told her, fighting to keep his voice light. "Just rest."

His jaw tightened as his boots crunched over bits of the shattered mugs. If he hadn't stopped to make the goddamned tea. If he'd been with her . . .

"Are you sure Double's all right? I didn't have a chance to see."

"Will you stop worrying about the fucking horse?" It exploded out of him, and unlocked the gates. "Do you think I give a damn about that horse right now? I'd have killed him myself if he'd have hurt you."

"Gabe—"

"Shut up! Goddammit!" His face a mask of rage, he shoved the door open. She cringed, chiefly because his shouting caused her head to swim.

"There's no need to yell. You're entitled to be upset, but—"

"Upset?" He laid her down on the couch in the living room. The way his muscles were beginning to tremble, he wasn't certain he could carry her up the stairs. "Is that what you think I am, upset? A little out of sorts maybe because someone knocked you senseless? Yeah, that's right. I'm upset."

He fisted his hand and worked off a fraction of the emotions boiling inside him by ramming it into the wall.

The words she'd been about to speak slid soundlessly down Kelsey's throat. She stared from the dent in the wall to his battered knuckles.

"I guess I'm upset because I found you unconscious in a stall with a panicked horse who might have trampled you to death at any minute."

She hadn't thought of that, and the image it presented made her stomach lurch. She began to tremble. "Gabe. Don't."

"I was a little upset because I thought, for a minute, the longest minute of my life, that you were already dead."

The tears began to spill over. One, then two, then a stream. "I guess 'upset' was the wrong word."

"Christ." Abruptly hollowed out, he rubbed his hands over his face. But it didn't help. He went to her then, gathering her close, holding her when she curled into a ball on his lap. "Christ, Kelsey, I lost my mind." He kissed her, gently now, drying her cheeks with his lips. "I'm sorry. Let me get you some ice."

"No, don't go. Just don't go."

"Okay. Let me see if you're hurt anywhere else."

"It's just my head. He must have been behind me. It was stupid to rush in that way, but I wasn't thinking. I saw the cot was empty, then that the stall door was open. All I could think of was what had nearly happened to him before. What happened to Pride."

"Next time think what would happen to me." He tipped her face up. "I couldn't handle losing you."

She took his hand, pressed his torn knuckles to her lips. "I guess we could both use some ice."

"Yeah."

But they stayed where they were until Rossi knocked on the door.


AN HOUR LATER, GABE WALKED back from the barn again, this time with Rossi at his side. "You've got a hole in your security, Mr. Slater."

"I'm aware of that." A hole big enough, he thought, for someone to slip through when the night watchman made his hourly outside rounds.

"Somebody could have come in from the outside. Somebody who knows your setup here. You've got a lot of land, a lot of ways in and out."

Rossi scanned through the dark. He didn't envy Gabe that. He much preferred his tidy apartment, the claustrophobia and comfort of the city.

"I like taking the easy way," he continued, "and looking at the inside."

Gabe was looking at the inside as well, at every hand he'd inherited from Cunningham, at every man and woman who had been hired on, or fired, in the ensuing five years.

"You've already got a list of everyone who works for me. Do whatever you have to do with it."

"I intend to."

"I've arranged to have two men with the colt at all times. I'd be one of them myself, but I'm not willing to leave Kelsey any longer than necessary."

357

"I can't blame you for that." Rossi paused. It was a pretty night, what was left of it. He might as well enjoy the breeze. "She's toughing this out pretty well. I'd say she's taking her knock on the head better than your groom's taking his."

"Could be her head's harder." They'd found Kip groaning back to consciousness in the empty box adjoining Double's. "We didn't have any trouble shipping him off to the hospital."

"She'll be fine." Curious, Rossi brushed a shard of china with the toe of his shoe.

"I was carrying a couple of mugs when I heard the horse," Gabe explained. "Guess I dropped them."

"Mmm. Like I said, she'll be fine. You're favoring your right shoulder."

Instinctively, Gabe straightened it. "It's nothing. The colt caught me." If it hadn't been his shoulder, it might have been Kelsey. Her head, her face. The thought roiled in his stomach. "You've done a background check on me, haven't you, Rossi?"

"Standard procedure."

"Then you know a little something about my father."

"Enough to know he wouldn't win any Daddy of the Year awards."

"He's in town. Has been for several weeks." Gabe spoke without inflection. He might have been discussing the weather. "I'd say I was one of his first stops. I brushed him off with some money. Not nearly as much as he wanted. That tends to make him surly. He knows his way around the track, around the shedrow."

"You think your father would try to hit at you this way?"

"He hates my guts," Gabe said simply. "He'd hit at me any way he could, especially if he could make a profit at it. I thought I saw him at Churchill Downs during Derby week. So did one of the grooms at Three Willows. I tracked him down at Laurel a couple of days ago. He denied it." Gabe reached for a cigar he didn't have. "He's lying."

Understanding the gesture, Rossi took out a pack of cigarettes, offered one. "I'll check it out."

"You do that, Lieutenant." Gabe's eyes glowed steady in the flare of the match. "And keep this in mind while you do. The odds are he knew Lipsky. Rich Slater's a man who likes to cheat. Winning the game's more fun for him that way—and he's been winning. He's flashing money around."

"I'll see if I can find out where he came by it."

"There was another race, when I was a kid. A horse from this farm was running against a horse from Three Willows." Gabe drew smoke into his lungs, watched it drift away on the breeze when he exhaled. "The Three Willows colt stumbled, shattered his legs. They had to put him down. My father flashed some money after that race, too."

"That would have been in Lexington. Spring of '73."

Gabe eyed Rossi through a cloud of smoke. "That's right. That's exactly right."

"Funny you didn't mention this before."

"He didn't hurt Kelsey before."

"Excuse me." Matt Gunner strode up to them. His hair was still in sleep tufts. "The colt's fine, Gabe."

"Good. I appreciate your coming out."

"That's no problem." Matt glanced toward the house. "Kelsey?"

"She's resting. The doctor advised a trip to the hospital, but she won't budge."

"I'd like to look in on her, when she's up to it."

"Sure." He said his good nights, then turned back to Rossi. "You'd better find him before I do."

"You don't have any proof your father was involved in any of this."

Gabe tossed down the cigarette, crushed it out. "I don't need to prove anything."

*

KELSEY HEARD HIM COMING UP the steps and gingerly shifted to a sitting position. The pills the doctor had given her had smoothed the edges, but she wasn't taking any chances.

"Double?" she said the minute Gabe came into the room.

"Matt gave him a thumbs-up." And he had personally discarded the colt's night feed bag and replaced it.

She sighed, relaxed. "Thank God. I've been sitting here thinking of all the possibilities."

"You're supposed to be resting." He sat on the bed, careful not to shake the mattress. "You've got shadows under your eyes again." Gently, he traced them with his thumb. "Why do I always find that so sexy?"

"Machismo looking for vulnerability." She smiled. "Come to bed. Maybe we can both get a couple of hours' sleep before we have to leave."

"I want you to stay here, Kelsey. Not here," he corrected, "at Three Willows. You're not up to the trip, and it would be safer and smarter for you to stay with Gertie. Rossi can arrange for a couple of men."

"Gabe." She framed his face, touched her lips to his, then spoke softly. "No way in hell."

"Listen to me."

"I could," she agreed. "I could listen to you, and you could listen to me, and we could bat this ball back and forth until morning. I'd still go. So why don't we just pretend we've argued and discussed?"

"You're being selfish." He pushed himself off the bed and began to undress. "You don't want to miss the race, so it doesn't matter that I won't be able to concentrate or enjoy it myself."

Slowly, she ran her tongue over her teeth. "That was a good one. And guilt usually works with me, but not this time. You'll worry whether I'm there or not. And I'm going to be there for you, Gabe. All the way."

"Goddamned mule."

"That won't work either. Though name calling is an acceptable stage in a good fight. I could counter that by calling you an over-protective ass, but I'll refrain because I'm a lady. So—" Her breath caught on a hiss. "Oh, God, what did you do to your back?"

He twisted his head but could get only a marginal glimpse at the dark, spreading bruise on his shoulder. "Took a kick."

"When? It wasn't there before . . ." She trailed off, realizing just when and just how he'd come by it. "Now I will call you an ass. What kind of numb-headed heroics is this? The doctor was just here. He could have treated it."

"It wasn't heroics, numb-headed or otherwise. I was distracted." Cautiously he rotated his shoulder. The sting wasn't so bad, but the throb went deep and had teeth. "Just needs some liniment."

"Jerk."

He started to snap back, then sighed, defeated. "I love you too." Slipping into bed, he cradled her against him.

"What are you doing?"

"Getting some sleep. I'm supposed to check on you every couple of hours. We don't have much more than that anyway."

"The liniment."

"Later. I just want to hold you."

Content with that, she brushed his hair from his brow. "Gabe. I'm going with you."

"I know. Go to sleep."

# Chapter Twenty-Three

NO ONE WOULD LET HER WORK. FOR HER FIRST TWO DAYS in New York, Kelsey was all but barred from the track, outnumbered and outflanked by everyone from Gabe down to the scruffiest stableboy. It seemed the trip itself was to be her only victory.

With too much time on her hands, and too much of it spent alone, she decided she had two options. She could go quietly mad, or she could treat the enforced inactivity as a short vacation.

The vacation seemed healthier.

She made use of the hotel facilities, swimming each morning to keep the muscles she'd developed over the past few months in shape. She shopped, began a love-hate relationship with the Nautilus equipment in the health club, and generally fought off boredom.

It helped that Gabe had decided to give a pre-race party, using the hotel ballroom on the evening before the Belmont. It gave Kelsey the opportunity to plot out the details, talk strategy with the florist and the hotel caterer. Gabe, after one look at the yards of lists, took the coward's route, and left the entire matter in her hands.

Nothing could have pleased her more.

She spent hours with the hotel manager, the concierge, the chef, debating and dissecting what could and couldn't be done. As Gabe had put no ceiling on the budget, she had already decided there was nothing that couldn't be done, and set about convincing the staff.

"I'd have been smarter handing you a pitchfork and letting you clean out stalls all week." Gabe grabbed a quick cup of coffee and watched Kelsey pore over the final menu for the evening. "You'd have gotten more rest."

"Stop fussing. You're the one who started this."

"I thought a party would be a good idea." He moved over to stand behind her, rubbing her shoulders as she muttered over her papers. "A little food, some music, an open bar. I didn't realize I'd be backing a David O. Selznick production." He narrowed his eyes. "*How* much champagne is that?"

"Go away." But she rolled her shoulders under his hands. "You're not going to drink it anyway. You gave me carte blanche, Slater, and I'm using it. Just be in your tuxedo by eight."

"More like Captain Bligh than Selznick," he muttered.

"Now you sound like the caterer. Go meet your reporters."

"I'm sick of reporters."

"You're just jealous because they put Double on the cover of *Sports Illustrated* instead of you."

"I got the spread in *People*," he reminded her, and entertained himself by nibbling on her ear. "This is a great spot right here," he murmured, nipping his way up her left lobe. "I could be temperamental and miss the interview."

The quick, delicious shivers distracted her. Gabe took advantage and had the first two buttons of her blouse undone before she shook herself free.

"Stop that! I have an appointment in fifteen minutes."

"I'll work fast."

"I mean it." Breathless, she squirmed away, scrambled out of the chair. "I'm getting my hair done."

He grinned. Just now it was tumbling out of the bright, cloth-covered elastic. He'd done that. "I like your hair exactly the way it is."

"Keep your distance, Slater. The rest of my day is booked, minute by minute, and I didn't schedule any time for you to chase me around the desk."

"Adjust."

"This may be just a party for you." As ridiculous as it was, she scooted so that the desk was between them. "But putting it together has kept me sane all week. I have an emotional invest-ment."

"So do I." He put his palms down on the desk, leaned forward. "Come here."

"Absolutely not."

"I've got something for you."

"Oh, please." She'd have rolled her eyes if she'd dared take them off him. "That's very lame."

He straightened, cocked a brow. "A present." He took a small velvet box out of his pocket. "Now aren't you ashamed?"

"A present?" Despite the instant flare of pleasure, she eyed it warily. "Is this a trick?"

"Open it. I was going to give it to you after the race, but I thought it would be better luck for you to have it before."

It lured her. She came around the desk to take it from him, then lifted her mouth to his for a kiss. "Thank you."

"You haven't opened it yet."

"For the thought first."

Her breath sighed out when she snapped the top open. The horse glowed against the black velvet, caught forever in mid-gallop, airborne and magnificent. The pin was fashioned of ruby jade, carved so intricately, so delicately, that she almost expected to feel the bunch and flow of muscles as she ran a fingertip over it. The diamond eye glistened with triumph.

"It's beautiful. It's perfect." She looked up at him. "So are you."

"That was my line." He slipped his arms around her waist, bringing her closer. "You're welcome," he said as his mouth closed over hers.

OF COURSE, SHE WAS LATE. Kelsey dashed into the beauty salon babbling apologies. She was checking her watch anxiously by the time the manicurist was trying to do something elegant with her neglected nails.

"Honey, why don't we go for some tips?"

"No, I'll just break them off." Her hair was bundled in huge foam rollers, her face coated with a pale green cream she'd somehow allowed herself to be talked into, and time was ticking away. "Just shape up what's there and slap on some clear polish."

"Don't you want something a little snazzier?"

Kelsey stole a peek at the manicurist's lethally long, carmine-slicked nails. "No, I'll stick with subtlety."

With a shake of her head, the woman dunked Kelsey's right hand in warm water. "Whatever you say, honey."

"It's Kelsey, isn't it?" A woman at the next station smiled at her. "I'm Janet Gardner. Overlook Farms, Kentucky?"

"Oh, yes, Mrs. Gardner." Kelsey decided not to say she hadn't recognized the woman, not with the flame-colored hair coated with glistening blue cream and her face plastered with shocking pink. "It's nice to see you again."

"A face-lift without the scalpel, they tell me." Janet laughed as she tapped a finger to the drying pink mask. "We'll see about that. Yours?"

"Oh, something about relaxing. Apparently I looked harried."

"Who doesn't by the Belmont? My Hank and I are going to sleep for two weeks when we get back home. We promised ourselves."

Kelsey remembered Hank now—the stringy man she'd danced with the night before. He'd had sun-scored cheeks, a pencil-thin mustache, and a voice as rich as molasses. He'd wanted to teach her to tango.

"Give your husband my best. He's a terrific dancer."

"Oh, that's my Hank." Janet chuckled and preened. "All the ladies want a turn around the floor with him. He likes to tell people I married him for his feet."

Obliging the manicurist, Janet slipped off an emerald ring that could have doubled for a paperweight.

"I saw your mother today at the track. It's hard to believe we've been making the rounds together for ... Well, that would be telling."

"You've known Naomi a long time."

"Since I married into this horse race. Of course, she was born into it." Much more interested in gossiping than in the fashion magazine she'd been thumbing through with her free hand, Janet set it aside. Her eyes brightened with curiosity. "You were, too."

"Belatedly."

"Oh, I think it's more that you came back to it belatedly. I remember seeing you at the track when you were in diapers."

"Really?"

"Oh, goodness, yes. Naomi was prouder of you than of any wall full of blue ribbons. We used to call you Naomi's thoroughbred. But you wouldn't remember that."

Naomi's thoroughbred. The idea both pleased and saddened her. "No, I don't."

"I met your father once or twice. Poor dear, he always looked so lost. He was a librarian?"

"My father is the head of the English department at Georgetown University."

"Oh, yes," Janet bubbled on, oblivious of the stiffness in Kelsey's voice. Obligingly she dunked her fingers in the soaking bowl for her own manicure. "I knew it had something to do with books. Naomi doted on him. We all thought it was a shame things didn't work out. But then, it happens all the time, doesn't it?"

"According to the statistics."

"Hank and I are the lucky ones. Twenty-eight years this September."

"Congratulations." Since there was no escape, Kelsey tried a shift in topic. "You have children?"

"Three. Two boys and a girl. Our DeeDee's married now, and has two little girls of her own." If she'd had a hand free, Janet would have gone straight for the pictures in her wallet. "My boys tell me they're still looking. Of course, my youngest is barely twenty. He's studying structural engineering. Not that I know anything about that."

She went on about her children at some length until Kelsey relaxed into the rhythm.

"But there's something special between a mother and daughter," Janet said, cagily veering back. "Don't you think? I mean, even after all these years of separation, you and Naomi look so sweet together. To tell you the truth, it's been so long a lot of people forget she even had a daughter, if they knew in the first place."

Janet held up one hand, examined the first coat of mauve polish. "Yes, dear, that's very nice." When she shifted her attention back to Kelsey, her voice took on a confidential air. "I hope you won't be offended if I tell you that most of us who knew Naomi, and the situation, were rooting for her. I mean, the idea of taking a child from its mother just seems unnatural."

Well aware that both manicurists had their ears pricked, Kelsey kept her voice cool. "I'm sure Naomi appreciated it"

"Not that it did any good. I'm sorry to say she was her own worst enemy during that trying time. I've always thought it was anger at your father that made her behave so recklessly. And the social scene was a bit . . . wilder back then. Still, Alec Bradley." She clucked her tongue. "Naomi should have known better than to flirt in that direction. Oh." As if she'd just remembered the outcome of that flirtation, Janet blinked and squirmed. "Oh, dear, I'm sorry. That would be a sore point."

The idea of a shooting death and a decade in prison being termed a sore point might have amused Kelsey under different circumstances. But she backtracked to the one statement that had caught her attention. "Did you know Alec Bradley?"

"Oh, yes. Most of us back then at least knew of him. He was drop-dead gorgeous, as my DeeDee would say. Tall, dark, and handsome, with a smile that could melt a woman's heart. He knew it, too. Believe me, he knew it and he used it. He even fluttered around me a bit—but Hank put a stop to that." She giggled girlishly. "I admit I was a little flattered, even knowing his reputation."

"What reputation was that?"

"Well, dear"—eagerly she scooted forward in her chair—"his family would barely acknowledge him. They may have had some financial reversals, but the blood was still blue. And there was that scandal with his first wife." She hunkered still closer, assuming the gossip position. "He had a taste for older women, you know. Wealthy older women. Everyone knew his first wife settled on him generously in the divorce to save face. Not that it helped, really, because everyone knew he'd been, well, servicing the fillies, shall we say?"

"So, he was a womanizer."

"Oh, a champion. And the buzz was, he charged for the service."

"He—women paid him, for sex?"

Another giggle, slightly embarrassed. Janet preferred cagey euphemisms. "I don't know if it was quite that blunt, but it was common knowledge that he could be bought. As an escort. There are a lot of single women, even in racing. Unmarried, divorced, between husbands. Alec could be hired to fill the gap. A handsome arm to hold for a party, at the track. He was, as I said, quite charming. And he tended to bet heavily. And badly."

When she smiled, pink flakes cracked from her face and drifted onto her black-and-gold bib like colorful dandruff. "Now, no one thought it was a business deal between him and your mother, dear.

A woman like Naomi could have had any man she wanted. Still could. Alec seemed quite besotted with her. Though he did continue to indulge in the side flirtations. Naomi wasn't one to put up with that sort of nonsense. They argued heatedly about that, and she gave him the boot."

This time Janet's flustering was quite genuine. "That is—I mean—"

"You were there that night." Not interested in evasions or a sudden attack of conscience, Kelsey pressed. "The night he died?"

"Yes, I was." Janet moistened her lips, surprised and a bit unnerved by Kelsey's direct question. "Hank and I were in Virginia on business. A number of racing people were at the country club for a party. There now, looks like I'm done." She held up her hands. "And speaking of parties, I'm so looking forward to tonight. That handsome young man of yours has us all on the edge of our seats."

"They argued." Kelsey ignored the squawk of protest from her manicurist when she shot out a hand and gripped Janet's arm. "That night, they argued."

"Yes, dear." Sorry now that she'd let her yen for gossip sink her over her head, Janet spoke kindly. "Several of us were questioned about it after the ... difficulties. They argued quite audibly, and Naomi told him, in blunt terms, that their relationship was finished. They'd both been drinking perhaps a little more than was wise. Words flew. Naomi dashed a glass of champagne in his face, and walked out. It was the last I saw of her for a very long time."

In the bright clown mask, Janet's eyes softened. "I was fond of Naomi. I still am. The man wasn't worth it, dear. He simply wasn't worth one minute of her time. I think the real crime is she didn't realize it until it was too late."

For the rest of the afternoon, Kelsey struggled to put the conversation in the back of her mind. She wanted to take it out again, to examine each and every word separately. It made a difference, didn't it? Somehow it made a difference that Alec Bradley had been for hire.

But however it altered the puzzle she so badly wanted to piece together, there was too much interference to concentrate.

Whatever her mood, she had no intention of spoiling Gabe's moment, or her mother's contentment.

She dressed early, and left Gabe a note in the center of the bed for him to meet her in the ballroom at precisely eight.

Final details required her attention, whether the caterer, the florist, and the hotel staff agreed or not. It was to be perfect. And as she stood in the center of the huge, chandelier-lit room, it was.

The red-and-white colors of Longshot predominated. In table-cloths, candles, flowers. To honor the three jewels in the Triple Crown, banks of red roses, sunny black-eyed Susans, and white carnations spilled from tables, tumbled from baskets. Black-suited waiters were lined up for inspection while the catering staff put the finishing touches on three enormous buffet tables.

But her inspiration, her pièce de résistance, and her biggest headache had been the gambling.

Oversize play money was available for purchase, and all for charity, but the details had kept her racing for days with the bureaucracy. Naomi's thoroughbred had nipped all opposition at the wire.

Now she could stand and study the roulette wheels, the dice and blackjack tables, and know she was presenting Gabe with the party of the season. And one, she thought, that would suit him like a second skin.

While the orchestra tuned up she walked over and gave the wheel a reckless spin.

"I'll take red."

With a laugh, she turned around and smiled at Gabe. "You're on time."

"You're beautiful." He didn't cross to her, not yet. He just wanted to look. She wore glimmering white, a column that shimmered from the curve of her breasts to her ankles. His gift was pinned at her heart. Her hair was a tumble of curls, scooped back

370

with glittering clips, falling over bare shoulders. Diamond and ruby drops dripped from her ears. "Really incredibly beautiful."

"Your colors." She held out her hands to his. "What do you think?"

"I think you astonish me." Still holding her at arm's length, he scanned the room. "What have you done here?"

"Besides driving every merchant and city official within fifty miles insane? I've given you a casino for the night. Slater's."

"And the proceeds?"

"There's a shelter for abused women and children in D.C."

His eyes darkened, then lowered to their joined hands. "You humble me, Kelsey."

"I love you, Gabe."

Moved, he lifted her hands to his lips. "What spin of the wheel brought you to me?"

"The luckiest one of your life." She glanced down, smiled at the silver ball nestled in its slot. "Red," she murmured. "You win again. You know, Gabe, this isn't just for you."

"No?"

"No." She inched closer, slipping her arms around his neck. "I want to watch you work here tonight. I have a feeling I'm going to find it very arousing."


AND SHE DID. HOURS LATER when the room was crowded with people, the buffet tables decimated, the dance floor spinning with couples, she stood at Gabe's shoulder and studied his technique.

She'd thought she'd understood blackjack. A simple card game of luck and logic where you tried to get as close as possible to twenty-one. If you went over, you lost. But she couldn't for the life of her understand why Gabe held and won on a measly fifteen one hand and hit, and won, on sixteen the next.

"It's just numbers," he told her. "Nothing but numbers, darling."

That's exactly what she'd thought. Until she'd seen him play. "There's no way you can possibly remember all the numbers, the combinations."

He only smiled, tapped his cards, and added a four to his seventeen for twenty-one. "Here." He pushed a stack of red and white chips at her. "You play for a while."

"All right, I will." She took the seat he vacated, then glanced up when Naomi sat down beside her.

"I've just lost a bundle at craps. I'm giving this game ten minutes before I nag Moses into dancing with me." She tucked a sweep of golden hair behind her ear, then crossed her legs. After pushing out some chips, she scanned the room. "Quite a party."

"Your daughter's amazing."

"I know." Naomi's brow furrowed as she studied her cards. "Hit me," she instructed, then huffed out a breath. "Busted."

"It's all for a good cause. Losing should warm your heart." Nibbling her lip, Kelsey contemplated her eight and five. "Okay, I'll take one. An eight! Another eight! I won!" She was chuckling as she raked in her chips, until she caught Naomi's narrowed eye. "Well, winning warms the heart, too. Dance with my mother, Gabe, and I'll see how much of your money I can lose."

"How could I turn down an offer like that?" He held out a hand, curling his fingers around Naomi's. "You look wonderful tonight," he said when they matched steps on the dance floor.

"How would you know? You haven't looked at anyone but Kelsey."

He said nothing for a moment. "I don't seem to have a smooth answer to that."

Tilting her head back, she studied him carefully. "I'd be disappointed if you did. I like watching what she feels for you rush into her face. And I like knowing what you feel for her causes you to miss a step. In an odd way you've both been so structured. You trip each other up."

"But you're worried."

"Not about what's between the two of you. About everything else." She glanced back to where Kelsey sat laughing at the black-jack table, shoving more chips forward. "I know she tried to brush off what happened the other night. But it terrifies me."

His eyes went cool, deceptively so. "It should never have happened. I should have been with her."

"No, it should never have happened," Naomi agreed, but she was still looking at her daughter, not at Gabe. "I think she should stay at Three Willows—or better yet, go back to her father until this is settled."

He'd thought the same, but hearing it didn't make it easier. "Even if she agreed to that, we don't know how long it will take to settle any of it."

"Any of it?"

He cursed himself, another misstep. As far as Naomi knew, there was only the current trouble over the horses. "Who broke through my security, and what they intended to do. On the other hand, it might be over tomorrow, after the race is run."

"I'm going to count on that. I couldn't stand for anything to happen to her, Gabe. I hate the idea that she's been touched by any of the ugliness—just the kind of sordid business Milicent always claimed was part and parcel of racing." She shook her head back, her eyes flashing. "But it's not. It's not what it's about. Not what we're about. But when it happens, it's all people remember."

"Are you worried about Milicent Byden's opinion?"

"Hell, no." The old defiance came back. "But I won't let her be right. And I'll be damned if I let her smirk over another blot on my honor. So I want this over. For Kelsey, for you. And for myself."

THE ROOM WAS COOL AND DARK when Kelsey woke. She shifted lazily while images from the night before flowed through her mind. Color and light, voices, music. The dizzying spin of the

373

wheel, the lightning toss of dice. She'd lost half of Gabe's winnings at cards; he'd doubled them back at craps.

Most of all, she remembered how he'd looked, dark and dangerous in evening clothes, those mouthwatering and unreadable blue eyes following the spin of the wheel, the fall of the cards. Then the way they would suddenly lock on hers and stop her breath.

And when they'd been alone, when the evening and the noise and the crowds had been behind them, he'd lowered her to the bed. Those clever hands had played her then, teasing out moans, tempting out darker and darker needs.

He had done things to her, done things for her she'd never imagined allowing, much less demanding.

Now, waking, her body felt soft and tender, bruised and cherished. Eyes closed, she skimmed her hand over the sheet, wanting him. Groggy, she pushed herself up in bed and found herself alone.

He wasn't getting away that easily, she told herself. Still half dreaming, she crawled out of bed. She stumbled out into the parlor of the suite, belting her robe.

She grimaced as the light through the open drapes blinded her. Shielding her eyes, she braced a hand on the doorjamb.

"God. What time is it?"

"Just past ten." Naomi poured a cup of coffee from the pot on the room service tray. "Your timing's good, Kelsey. Breakfast just arrived."

"Breakfast? Ten?" She squinted through her splayed fingers. "Gabe?"

"Oh, at the track since dawn."

"But—" Fully awake now, she dropped her hand. "That jerk! He promised he wouldn't go without me this morning. Of all mornings."

"Mmm." Naomi poured a second cup for her daughter. "According to him, you were an ill-disposed lump who told him to go away when he suggested it was time to get up."

"I did not." She took a sip of coffee. "Did I? He's probably making it up."

"He probably wanted you to get a little rest."

"He's my lover, not my keeper." Then she flushed. However unusual the relationship, Naomi was still her mother. She cleared her throat and sat down. "What are you doing here? I thought you'd be at the track."

"It's not a big race for us. A mile and a half." She shrugged and spread blackberry jam on a triangle of toast. "We'd just like to see High Water hold his own. I guess we could get lucky since the Arkansas colt is scratched."

"Scratched? When? What happened?"

"Oh, he pulled up lame in yesterday's workout. A sprained fore-leg. I guess I forgot to tell you."

Pouting, Kelsey bit into a slice of bacon. "I feel like I'm outside the party, with my face pressed against the window while everyone else eats the cake."

"I'm sorry, honey. You'll just have to tolerate all of us being wor-ried about you. When I think of what could have happened—" She sighed, spread more jam. "All right, all right, we won't get into it. I know that butt-out look on your face. I've seen it in the mirror often enough."

"It didn't mean butt out," Kelsey said with a smile. "It meant don't worry."

"It goes with the territory, even for a come-from-behind mother. So, eat your breakfast. I have instructions to see that you do."

"Gabe again."

"I imagine you know he loves you."

"Yes, I do."

"Do you know he's besotted?"

This time the smile crept onto Kelsey's face. "Do you think so?"

Naomi only laughed. "Never mind, you already know it. It's thrilling, isn't it, and terrifying to have a man tangled up over you that way."

"Yes. And twice as thrilling and terrifying when you're just as tangled up over him. I know it might seem soon to be this involved with someone after the divorce, but—"

"Kelsey, not only am I not in a position to criticize, but I'm going to point out that you and your ex-husband were separated for two years."

"Still—" Kelsey shook her head. "I'm second-guessing myself because it doesn't seem right. It only feels right." She toyed with her breakfast, hoping she wasn't choosing the wrong moment. "When you separated from Dad, did you still love him? I'm sorry." She lifted her eyes. "Someone said something to me yesterday that made me wonder. If you'd rather not answer, I understand."

"I told you once that whatever you asked I'd try to answer." But this one was hard. It wrenched at an old wound in the heart, an almost forgotten one. "Yes, I still loved him. I loved him for a long, long time after it was foolish to do so. And because I did I was angry, with him, with myself, and determined to prove it didn't matter."

"Is that why you . . ."

"Threw myself into parties?" Naomi continued. "Enjoyed fanning gossip about myself and other men? Courted small scandals? Yes, at least partly. I wasn't about to admit I'd failed. I wanted Philip to suffer, to have sleepless nights thinking about me reveling in my freedom. And because I undoubtedly succeeded in that, I drove him further and further away until what I wanted most was impossible for me to have."

"You wanted him back."

"Desperately. I was vain enough to think I could have him on my terms, and my terms only."

"And Alec Bradley?" She saw Naomi flinch, and forced herself to finish. "Was he someone you used to make Dad suffer?"

Naomi switched from coffee to water. "He was a kind of final gauntlet flung. A man with as sterling and blooded a pedigree as Philip's, but with a faintly unsavory reputation."

Kelsey's stomach knotted. She had to know, and to know, she had to ask. "Did you hire him?"

The discomfort in Naomi's eyes vanished. "Hire him?" she repeated, blank.

"I've heard that he put certain skills on the market." She gulped at her coffee. "So to speak."

The last reaction Kelsey had expected was laughter. But it came now, rich and delighted across the table. "Christ, what a thought. What a thought! The very last thing I wanted from Alec was stud service." Her amusement fled. "The very last thing."

"I'm sorry, that was a stupid question. I didn't mean it precisely as it sounded. I was thinking more of public displays than private ones."

"No, I didn't hire him. Though I did lend him money a time or two. He was always in between deals, you see," she said dryly. "Always in the midst of a little cash-flow problem. It might be vanity again, coming back to color memory, but as I recall, he pursued me. Not that I evaded," she added, and chose a single raspberry from a bowl. "I wanted the attention. I needed it, and he was very charming. Even when you knew differently, he could make you believe you were the only woman in the room. I was certainly aware of his reputation, of the fact that he could be bought. That added to the appeal, I suppose. The fact that he was with me, charming me, hoping to conquer me, because he couldn't help himself, did wonders for my ego." And a great deal of it, she remembered, had been simple ego. "In the end, he refused to accept, or wasn't able to accept, that I didn't choose to be conquered. And that's what killed him."

"But rape isn't about sex."

"No." She'd once thought it was, or had wanted to believe it was, because sex was easier. "He wanted to hurt me. To humiliate me. I've never really understood why he seemed so desperate that night. There wasn't passion in his eyes. There wasn't lust. I think I could have fought them, have outmaneuvered them. It was the desperation in his eyes that made me reach for the gun."

Naomi shuddered once, then cleared out her clogged lungs with a long quiet breath. "I'd forgotten that."

"I'm sorry I made you remember." Though she promised herself she would think everything through later, Kelsey covered Naomi's hand with hers. "Let it go. We'll both let it go. This is a day to look forward, not back. Why don't you come check out the outfit I bought for the race? If I don't get into it soon, we'll miss the first post."

# Chapter Twenty-Four

RENO WORE A SLATE-GRAY SUIT AND MAROON TIE. HIS SOFT Italian boots shone like mirrors. The pencil-slim woman on his arm was a head taller than he, and kept her artfully painted face tilted toward the cameras.

He knew it was a pathetic cliché, the short man proving his masculinity by latching on to tall, stunning women. He didn't give a damn. Right now he needed something to prove his manhood, his worth. His *cojones*.

The sling on his arm precisely matched the silk of his tie. They were, he knew, the only silks he'd be wearing that day.

He smiled and preened for the cameras, as eager for the attention as the woman posed with him. Beneath the bravado, the quick, sassy answers about his next ride, his next season, he was a whirlwind of nerves and misery.

He watched the jockeys stride to the paddock, knew what each and every one of them was feeling, thinking. The concentration, the little mental games to keep the adrenaline up.

Only one would win, but others could prove their mettle with the ride. Some would come back, another race, another year.

Others would fade—gain weight, lose interest, take a fall. They might choose to headline in the sticks, preferring second-rate wins to first-rate losses. The great ones would stay on one circuit, getting rich, drawing their own following, avoiding or overcoming the broken bones and bad spills.

The middling ones would move from track to track, following trainers, harassing agents, disappearing perhaps to resurface as a groom or valet, or as an assistant trainer on some tiny farm in the boondocks.

But none of that showed now. Now they were warriors, soldiers, showmen, eyes tensed and narrowed behind the plastic goggles, bodies lean and tight and limber under the silks, their feet encased in supple, dainty boots. The helmets were in place beneath the cloth Eton caps, the post-position number a cardboard garter on the arm.

Some of them would have risen at dawn to work their partners themselves. Others would have slept late, their relationship with their horse purely business and unemotional. Fear of the scale would have kept most of them away from food, seduced them into another hour sweating in steam.

Now they were weighed and ready. Reno watched them with grinding envy and despair.

He should be the one listening, with the air of narrowed focus, to the trainer's final instructions. It should be him garnering the praise, admiration, and hopes of the owners.

It should have been him flying down the track with the whip between his teeth.

His worst fear was that it would never be him again.

He forced himself forward, that quick, cocky smile fastened to his face.

"Miss Naomi."

"Reno." Automatically Naomi reached out, clasping his good arm. "You look great."

"I'd rather be wearing your colors."

"You will, soon." She glanced toward the woman he'd left entertaining some reporters. "Pretty girl. She looks familiar."

"You might have caught her in a couple of commercials. Shampoo and toothpaste, mostly. She's trying to break into movies." He shrugged his date off, and looked at the colt. "He'll run for you, Miss Naomi."

"Yes, I know he will."

"Just the man I wanted to see." Kelsey stepped forward. "I was hoping you'd have some time in the next couple of weeks to look at my yearling again, Reno. Honor needs a rider who can coax the best out of her."

His stomach churned once, hard. "Sure. Sure, I'll do that. I got nothing but time. I'm going to go give Joey a send-off."

"Did I say the wrong thing?" Kelsey murmured when he hurried off.

"I don't know." Distracted, Naomi looked toward Moses. "He's probably just strung out like everyone else."

"I'm sure you're right. I'm going to go wish Gabe good luck. Meet you in the box."

"Make history for me, Joey." Gabe shook hands with his jockey.

Joey flexed his fingers, cracked his knuckles. "I'm going to do that, Mr. Slater."

"You hold him back, like I told you," Jamison added. "I don't want him to drive until the head of the stretch. We're not looking for a record here. We're looking for a win."

"Me and Double here, we could get you both." He grinned and saluted when Reno joined them. "Get yourself a front-row seat, pal. And have some of that fancy champagne you like waiting."

"I'm going to do that." Reno kept his smile in place as he nodded to Gabe. "Good luck today, Mr. Slater. You've got a horse in a million here." His hand grew sweaty in his pocket. "I'd like a chance to go up on him myself one of these days."

"We'll talk about that when you're back to a hundred percent."

"A man gets spoiled riding the kind of horse I've been riding the past year or two." His eyes locked on Jamison's. "That's the way it is, isn't it, Jamie? We get spoiled."

"You could say that, Reno." Jamison kept a hand around Double's bridle.

"I won the Belmont for you two years back, remember? Everybody called it an upset, an apprentice jockey and a long-shot colt. But the truth was, it was my day. My horse. My race." Inside his pocket, his damp fingers opened and closed, opened and closed. "People forget, though. They forget all the races, all the wins. It's the Derby they remember. It's the Derby that puts you on top."

His hand trembled when he took it out of his pocket, when he laid it flat-palmed on the colt's neck. "Well, you got yourself the Derby, and a lot more." He forced a laugh. "Win or lose, they won't forget this Belmont. So you win it. You win it big."

"Riders up!"

At the call, Reno stepped back. His face was white, sheened with sweat. Turning quickly, he strode away. Kelsey snatched at his arm as he passed her.

"Reno?"

"I'm sorry," was all he said before shaking her off and rushing away from the paddock.

"Jockeys." Jamison launched Joey into the saddle. "Temperamental."

"He looked ill," Kelsey murmured, but there was no time to worry, barely any time to think. After the race, she promised herself, she'd try to find him and see if she could help. But now it was Gabe's moment. She wasn't about to have it spoiled.

"Even though you went off without me this morning, I'm going to wish you luck."

"It would have taken a crowbar to get you out of bed at dawn." And he'd wanted the morning to himself, to search for signs of his father. But he'd found none. More relaxed, Gabe tilted his head to study her. Her hair was scooped up under a white straw hat, its wide brim tipped flirtatiously over one eye. Her short, snug red dress was topped by a waist-length white jacket. His pin galloped over her breast.

"Now that I see what a few hours' extra sleep did for you, I'm glad I didn't have a crowbar handy."

"A very clever way of sliding out of it, Slater."

"I thought so." He tucked her arm through his. "You're wearing my colors."

"Today they're the only colors worth wearing." She pressed a hand to her heart as they walked to his box. "Why aren't you nervous?"

"Nerves won't change anything."

"Tell that to my stomach," she muttered, and dug in her bag for her binoculars. "I'm beginning to think I want this more than you do."

"No, you don't."

He kept a hand on hers as the horses were led to the gate.

The odds were locked in, the betting windows closed. Overhead the sky was the clear dreamy blue of summer. The oval, the mile and a half of meticulously tended turf, was fast today. The crowd that massed in the grandstands was on its feet, setting up a steady drone punctuated by shouts and cheers.

It was easy to forget how huge it all was. For those who had seen the sport only on a television screen it would seem small, intimate, rather than the world that it was.

It had, through ambition, through luck, and through a steady inner drive, become Gabe's world. Now, all the work, the disappointments, the triumphs, and the hopes came down to this single race. This single horse.

He watched Double being loaded, and remembered the night he had been born. The way the laboring mare had wheezed, the way the wind had blown, keening against the walls of the foaling barn. The snow and sleet hurling down, the endless wait while the mare strained and labored.

Then the first sight, the terrifyingly fragile legs stabbing their way free in a gush of blood. And the mare's cry, eerily human, heralding that last pang of birth.

That small, wet life had lain on the soiled straw, taking the first breath that would lead Double or Nothing, out of Bold Courage, to the starting gate at Belmont Park, Long Island.

And now, three years later, Gabe remembered the thrill that had passed through him, arrow bright, when he had looked into the foal's eyes.

"I love that horse."

He didn't realize he'd spoken aloud until Kelsey's fingers tightened on his. "I know you do."

The gate opened with a scream of metal. Almost at once there was a gasp from the crowd as Double swerved to the right from his number six post position, nearly unseating his rider. Whatever had spooked him, the disastrous move had placed him behind a wall of horses with his jockey fighting for balance.

All of Jamison's careful instructions on how to run the race became useless in the space of a heartbeat. Joey's only goal now was to get Double or Nothing back into the Belmont.

There was a split-second decision, whether to fight through the field or go around it. Rider and horse made it together, swinging wide, in a move—depending on the outcome—that would be seen as either valiant or foolish. As if he knew what had to be done, the colt bore down.

He charged down the field, eating up the distance with wild speed. When they passed the wire the first time he was a length behind the leader, and gaining.

From his position in the box, Gabe kept his binoculars in place. He was focused on only one horse. The race itself was nearly forgotten, shadowed under the bright flash of admiration. There was more than beauty there. There was courage. Win or lose, he wouldn't forget it.

The half mile went in forty-six seconds flat, with Double and the leader pulling steadily away from the pack. The crowd roared, a frenzy of sound. But Gabe heard only Kelsey's voice beside him, quietly murmuring encouragement. It might have been only the two of them, standing hand in hand, watching a single horse.

At the far turn Double made his challenge, battling for advantage as they hit the top of the stretch. It was here, in its demanding, heartbreaking homestretch, that the Belmont tested valor. The Kentucky-bred colt was rallying from behind, shooting toward the leaders like a spear.

But it was too late. What had been born in the Longshot colt that windy night in late winter, what Gabe had seen in his eyes during those first wonderful moments of life, drove him faster than the whip laid across his back.

With heart, with honor, he thundered across the wire two lengths in the lead to take the Belmont Stakes, and the Triple Crown.

For a moment, Gabe could only stare. The emotions swirling inside him came too fast, too hard to sift out only the thrill of victory. That was his horse, cantering easily now, with its rider high in the irons. That was his dream, covered with sweat and dirt and glory. Whatever happened now, no one could ever take away from him, or the spectacular colt, this dazzling moment.

"That's a hell of a horse," Gabe murmured in a voice that felt rusty. Dazed, he looked down at Kelsey, saw her cheeks wet with tears. "That's one hell of a horse."

"Yes." Even as the tears rolled, a laugh bubbled up in her throat. She lifted her arms, circled Gabe's neck. "Congratulations, Slater. You've done it."

"Christ." No amount of control could hold back the foolish grin that spread over his face. "Jesus Christ, we did it!" He swung her up and around, oblivious of the cameras. She was still laughing when he covered her mouth with his.

*

IN HIS ROOM A FEW HUNDRED miles away, Rich stared at the television screen. He hadn't gone to New York. With what he'd expected to happen, it was smarter, safer, for him to stay behind.

He nodded as the cameras cut from the victorious colt to its owner. "Enjoy it while you can, boy," he muttered, and toasted himself with twelve-year-old scotch. A smirk twisted his lips over the celebrational kiss, the announcer's breathless voice identifying Gabriel Slater and Kelsey Byden as very friendly rivals.

Rich sat back and waited for the chaos. The colt would be led to the spit bucket, as he would be after any race. And then, Rich thought, and then Gabe wouldn't be smiling so big. Even better this way, he decided. Even better to snatch away the prize after it had been granted.

Things had worked out perfectly. Thanks to Naomi's pretty little girl. If she hadn't come out to the barn that night and interrupted what was planned for the colt, he'd never have raced.

But he had raced, and he'd won. Now, moments from now, the shocking announcement would be made that Double or Nothing had an illegal drug in his system.

Not only would Gabe lose, but he would face scandal, derision, and shame.

Preparing for his own victory, Rich topped off his drink. Liquor slopped, spilled by a jerk of his hand as the official announcement was made.

Nine. Five. Two.

His shocked brain didn't take in the nattering about purses and payoffs. He gaped as the screen filled with the horse and rider, each blanketed with white carnations. He saw Gabe, his arm possessively around Kelsey's shoulders, congratulating his rider, then lean in, as sentimental as a movie cowboy, to kiss the sweaty colt.

His glass struck the screen, and both shattered. The air reeked of liquor as he lunged out of the chair. For a minute he lost his mind, kicking and beating the television until his knuckles ran red, then he heaved it off the table. His only motive was to destroy it, to somehow destroy the machine that showed him such images.

When he finally stopped, gasping and drained, the air stank of smoke and scotch and his own violent sweat. His knuckles were bleeding, and his breath was coming in shuddering rasps. He tripped over a broken chair and righted the bottle of scotch. Most had pooled on the rug, but there was enough to clear the bile from his throat when he chugged from the bottle. Enough to clear his mind again.

Heads will roll, he promised himself. And since he apparently could trust no one to carry out a simple task, he'd have to take care of things himself.

IN THE WEEK THAT FOLLOWED Double's Triple Crown win, there was barely time to think. The routine at Three Willows had to continue, despite the celebrity of their neighbor. The racing season didn't stop at Belmont, nor did the daily care and training of horses allow for sitting on laurels.

And Kelsey had her own ambitions, not the least of which was to mold her own champion. She'd been given her opportunity with Honor, and she was determined to make the most of it.

She had not forgotten her goal of piecing together the puzzle of the past. Charles Rooney might have refused to take or return her calls, but she had every intention of running him to ground. He would talk to her again eventually. She would visit Captain Tipton again as well. And if necessary, she would go to her father and ask him to relive those months of his life day by day until a clear picture emerged.

For the one that was taking shape now was of a woman who had loved her husband. One who had certainly made mistakes, mistakes of pride and vanity and stubbornness in trying to force his hand. But no matter how coolly, how calmly she tried, Kelsey had yet to find the piece that turned a willful, even reckless young woman into a murderer.

"Hey, sis."

"Channing." Kelsey turned, sponge in hand, to kiss him. "I haven't had five minutes to tell you how glad I am you're here."

"Despite the ache in my back, I've only been here a couple of hours." His shirt was already streaked with sweat. "Moses put me to work so fast it feels as if I never left."

"I didn't think you were coming back." With careful strokes, Kelsey sponged off her yearling's face. "We're midway through June."

"It took me a while to work it out."

"Candace is still against your being here?"

"We can safely say she's not too happy with me. We had a hell of a battle."

"I'm sorry.

"No, it was good. A lot came out that had been festering. In me, anyway. She wanted me to carry on the family tradition. All my life that's been a given. I'd be a brilliant surgeon like my father, like his father, and so forth. She expected it. I let her expect it."

"It isn't what you want?"

"I'm going into veterinary medicine." His eyes held steady, as if he expected a protest, or worse, a quick, indulgent laugh. Instead, she stepped forward and kissed both cheeks.

"Good."

"That's it?"

"I could give you the routine about how impossible and how frustrating it is to try to live up to other people's expectations. Especially family. In the past few months I've had firsthand experience with that. But I figure you already know. She'll come around, Channing. She loves you, and under it all, she only wants what you want."

"Maybe." He shuffled straw under his foot. "I hated fighting with her. I guess I hate knowing I'd have backed down if the Prof hadn't stood up for me."

"Dad? Really?"

"It was like having the Seventh Cavalry charge in—without the bugles and blazing guns." He grinned. "He just talked, in that slow, patient way of his. I've never seen him go against her that way. I think it was the shock that he took my part instead of hers that turned the tide."

"He loves you too." Nibbling her lip, she went back to her work. "Are they having problems, Channing?"

"Things are a little strained between them. But with me here, they'll have the time and the privacy to work it out. Anyway, she blames you more than the Prof."

Kelsey made a face. "I guess I'd better patch things up there."

"Mom's not one to hold a grudge. Not for long, anyway. Her sense of order's been shaken, that's all. It's going to take her a while to get used to it."

"Excuse me." Reno stood at the opening of the box.

"Reno, hi." Kelsey shifted, her hands still busy brushing the yearling. "You remember Channing, my brother."

"Sure. How's it going?"

"Good. How's the shoulder?"

Instinctively, Reno rotated it. "It's coming along. I'll be ready to get up in a couple of weeks. I've got some offers to ride the European circuit this season."

"I heard Moses mention it," Kelsey said. "We're sending High Water over in a few weeks. I hope you take him up on it."

"Might. That's Honor, isn't it? Naomi's Honor."

"It sure is. What do you think of her?"

"I'll let you two talk horse," Channing cut in. "If Moses catches me loitering, he'll dock my pay. Good seeing you, Reno."

"Yeah. See you around." He stepped into the box and crouched. A Thoroughbred's legs always came first. He said nothing, circled the horse, ran his hands along the chest, the flanks, the withers before coming around to examine the eyes and teeth.

"She's a pretty one," Reno said at last. "Terrific form, lots of heart room. You've had her in the gate?"

"Yeah. She doesn't have any trouble there. She spooks some-times, but since we started using a shadow roll, she's settled." The colt nudged her arm, and obliging, Kelsey took a carrot out of her pocket. "She's gentle, but there's fire in there. Moses thinks we should try her out in a couple of races next year. Are you inter-ested?"

"She's a pretty one," Reno said again, and felt twin tremors of hope and despair. "Why do you want to put me up on her?"

"I've seen you ride, for one. And I like the fact that you don't just mount a horse for a race. You come to workouts, you come to the barn. You treat it like a partnership." She hesitated, nuzzling the horse. "I know you loved Pride, Reno. It showed, the way you felt about him, and how you thought about him. That's the kind of rider I want for Honor."

He looked away, fighting the urge to curl up in the straw and weep. Her words were like small, sharp knives slicing at him. "I did love that horse." He couldn't steady his voice, and gave up trying. "He'd have done anything for me. He broke his heart for me."

"Reno, you can't blame yourself for what happened."

"I wouldn't have hurt him. How were we supposed to know the race would kill him?" He stared blindly into Kelsey's face. "How were we supposed to know?"

"You couldn't," she said gently. "Sooner or later we'll find out who wanted to hurt him."

He let out a trembling breath. "Sooner or later." He took a step in retreat. "That's a fine horse."

"Will you ride her?"

Reno gave her a look of such crushing despair that she moved toward him. But as she reached out, he made one low, animal sound in his throat, and fled.

# Chapter Twenty-Five

"I TELL YOU, GABE, IT BROKE MY HEART."

Kelsey cupped her wineglass in both hands and tucked her legs up under her on his long, comfortable sofa. It was a lovely evening, the doors and windows wide open to welcome the flower-drenched breeze. But she could still see Reno's face, the utter hopelessness of it, washed in the striped sunlight of Honor's box.

"He needs to get up again."

Gabe was stretched out on the same sofa, puffing smoke at the ceiling, his feet in Kelsey's lap. It wasn't that he didn't sympathize with Reno's plight, but he was, quite simply, exhausted. Who could have known that the rapid-fire round of publicity, meetings, phone calls, and requests would be more tiring than a week's ditch digging?

At the moment he'd have preferred a shovel and a sweaty back to the mind-numbing figures and futures tallied by lawyers, accountants, and brokers.

Just that afternoon he'd had to turn down an offer for the rights to his life story, and Double's, for a TV movie-of-the-week.

"I don't know," Kelsey continued, while Gabe's thoughts

wandered. "I thought that, too, that he just needed to get up for another race, Until ..." She rested her head against a cushion. Gabe had put on Mozart, for her. She knew he preferred basic rock or the wail of blues to the classic melding of piano and orchestra. "It wasn't just an altruistic gesture, you know, my asking him to ride Honor. I want the best, but I did think it would help him. Instead, I made things worse."

"You can't know that."

"You didn't see his face. When I think it through, I know what losing Pride did to me. How much it hurt. And even though I loved that colt, I couldn't have been nearly as attached as Reno was. He's blaming himself, Gabe, because he was on the colt when they went down." She toyed with her wine. "I'm thinking of asking Naomi if she could persuade him to find some therapy. Do you think ..." She glanced toward Gabe. His eyes were closed. "Am I keeping you up?"

"Sorry." He opened one eye. "I was drifting."

"No, I'm sorry." She shifted, began to rub his feet. "You're worn out. I saw that when I walked in the door. I should be asking you how your meetings went today instead of trying out my Psych 101 theories on you."

"If you keep rubbing my feet, you can try out anything you want on me."

She chuckled, then set her glass aside so she could do a better job of it. "So, how did the meetings go? Should we be celebrating a new record for syndication?"

"No." It was fascinating, he thought, and rewarding, to discover just how many erogenous zones there were on the sole of a foot. "I'm not syndicating Double."

"You're not?" Her hands paused. "But, Gabe, the last set of figures you mentioned were astronomical."

"I don't want to share him." His eyes opened again, fastened on hers. "I listened to all the advice, the offers, the numbers, and I decided to do what I want. When something's mine, it's mine."

"That's a very impractical, emotional decision."

"What's your point?"

She shook her head. "Well, there goes my plan to scoop up some shares of a Triple Crown winner."

"That depends." He used all of his willpower to keep his muscles relaxed, to keep his voice light. "You can have half of him."

"Half?" Her brows rose as she pressed her fingers to Gabe's instep. "I think that's a bit more than I can afford."

"A lot of people will tell you you're right. You can't afford the terms."

That had her lips moving into a pout. "I think I'm a better judge of what I can or can't afford. Okay. What are the terms?"

"There's just one." His eyes flashed to hers. "All you have to do is marry me."


RENO WENT TO THE BARN FIRST. The barn that had once been Cunningham's. No one stopped him. The guards, the grooms all knew Reno. He had a meeting with Jamison, he told them, and they accepted it. They accepted him.

He had a need to see horses again, to smell them, to touch them. He did give some thought to going to Jamison, to pouring out body and soul. But what difference would it make? Nothing could be changed. Nothing could be fixed.

He'd spent a great deal of time during the last weeks blasting out scattershots of blame. But in the end, he understood that they all ricocheted back to him. He'd been the one who had taken the syringe. He'd been the one to plunge that poison into a beautiful, courageous athlete.

It didn't matter how the instrument had come into his hands. He understood that now. He accepted that now. He'd murdered something he'd loved, and in doing so, he'd destroyed himself.

Like father, like son. Reno leaned against a patient mare and wept. It came through the blood, he thought. It came through the breeding. The excuses he'd used were smoke and mirrors. Had he really believed he'd been trying to avenge the father he'd never known? That was the weapon used against him as surely as he'd used the needle on the horse.

Weak. He was weak as his father had been weak. And damned, as his father had been damned.

So, there was only one thing left to do.

He would end it as his father had ended it. Complete the cycle begun by a man he'd known only through photographs and grainy news clips. The man whose ghost he had honored above even his own dignity.

As if in a dream, Reno left the barn and the soothing scent of horses. He walked to the tack room. The tack room that had once been Cunningham's.


IT WAS A FULL TEN SECONDS before Kelsey could find her voice. It was, she supposed, a typical-enough proposal from a man like Gabe. Challenging, cool-blooded, and risky. Very deliberately she shifted his foot out of her lap and picked up her wine.

"If I marry you, I get a half share of Double."

"That's right." He'd been expecting, at least hoping for, a different kind of reaction. "A half share of Longshot, and all that goes with it."

She sipped, studying him. "And a half share of you, Slater?"

That irritated him. The amused patience in her voice, in her eyes. He swung his legs off the couch and stood. "I'm not Wade, Kelsey. We go into this, we take each other whole. This won't be a tidy, make-the-best-of-a-bad-hand deal with an option to fold."

"I see. Once I ante up, I'm stuck."

"That's it exactly. Since I'm naming the stakes, I'll show you the cards I'm playing with. I want you. That's my high card. It's going to take a lot for you to beat that. Maybe you figure the odds are tilted. You got stung once before, and you don't want it to happen

394

again. But this is a different game, with different players, and from where I'm standing, the stakes are a lot higher."

She kept her eyes on her wine. And he'd said she couldn't bluff, she thought with some pride. Still, she knew better than to let him get a good look at her face until she was ready to call.

"You think I'd back off from marriage, shy away from a full commitment because I lost once before? That's incredibly insulting. Nearly as insulting as this half-assed proposal you're stumbling through."

"You want flowers and candlelight, a ring in my pocket?" He'd meant to give them to her. The fact that he'd rushed his fences only infuriated him more. "I'm not giving you anything he gave you."

Her eyes lifted then, with just enough temper in them to mask her heart. "Oh, now who's hobbled by the past, Slater?" She slapped her glass on the table and rose. "Why don't you just drag me off to—to Vegas? That would be a perfect milieu, wouldn't it? We can say our I dos over a crap table."

He nodded stiffly. "Fine. If that's what you want."

"What I want is a simple, straightforward question to which I can give a simple, straightforward answer. So, you can either ask me, or you can go to hell."

Narrow-eyed, he studied her, but for once he couldn't read her face. How could he, he realized, when for the first time in his life someone else held all the cards?

"Will you marry me?"

"Yes," she said. "Absolutely."

Gauging her, he let out some of the breath he hadn't been aware he'd been holding. "That's it?"

"That's it," she agreed. "So, who gets to rake in the chips?"

His lips curved slowly. "This seems like a good time to start splitting the pot." He stepped toward her, combing his hands through her hair, taking a firm hold. "I love you, Kelsey."

"You must, or you'd never have flubbed that so badly."

"Flubbed, hell." He kissed her, hard. "I've got you, don't I?"

"Yeah." With a laugh, she threw her arms around him. "Yeah, you do."

He scooped her off her feet. "About that trip to Vegas."

"No."

"You're not considering the possibilities." With only one goal in mind now, he headed for the stairs. "It's quick, convenient, colorful. We could spend our wedding night in a big heart-shaped bed under a full-length mirror."

"As appealing as that sounds, I'm going to pass. Why don't we—"

The crash at the back of the house had Gabe dropping her to her feet. "Stay here," he ordered, and he shoved her toward the stairs. Before he could get halfway toward the sound, one of his grooms stumbled in, white-faced and wide-eyed.

"Mr. Slater. Jesus, Mr. Slater, you've got to come. It's Reno. Oh, my God, I think he's dead."

THERE WAS NO DOUBT OF THAT. Though someone had had the courage and compassion to cut him down from where he had swung from a rope tied to a beam, there was no mistaking the sight of death.

Kelsey couldn't take her eyes from it, the limp body decked out in riding silks, the horrible angle of the head with its livid bruises around the neck.

"Call the police," Gabe ordered. He turned Kelsey around roughly. "Get out of here. Go home."

"No. I'm staying. I'm all right. I'm staying with you."

He didn't have time to argue. "Wait outside, goddammit!" he exploded when she remained stubbornly beside him. "Wait outside!"

She only shook her head. She did look away from Reno and found her eyes locked on Jamison's. His were glazed, with devastation or shock, she couldn't be sure. But she walked to him, gently leading him to a chair.

"Sit down now, Jamie."

"I found him. Somebody told me he was around and looking for me. I don't know why I came in here, I don't know why, except I did. And I found him. Just like last time. I found him."

"Last time?"

"Benny. Just like Benny. Oh, God." He buried his face in his hands. "Oh, God, when will it stop?"

"There's a note, Mr. Slater." A young stableboy crept closer. He whispered, as though death had ears. "There's a note on the bench there. I didn't touch it," he added. "They always say you're not supposed to touch anything."

"That's right. Go wait outside for the police, will you?"

"Sure, Mr. Slater." He hesitated. "We cut him down," he blurted out. "Maybe we weren't supposed to, but we couldn't just leave him like that. We had to get him down."

"You did the right thing." Gabe put a hand on the boy's shoulder. "Wait outside now." Already dreading what he would find, Gabe walked over to the bench, to the single sheet of paper, handwritten.

I'm sorry. It's the coward's way, but the only way I know. I'll never ride a horse again. I killed the best horse I ever had under me. As God is my witness, I didn't know it was a lethal dose. It was supposed to disqualify him, that's all. And settle a score. I never believed my father was guilty. Until now. What he did, I did. What he did, I'll do. Bad blood. There's no fighting bad blood.

Gabe turned from the note and looked at his trainer. "Did you know, Jamie?"

Tears dripped onto Jamison's hands as he nodded. "I knew. I knew Reno was Benny Morales's son. God help him."

THE PIECES FIT PERFECTLY ONCE they were turned to the light. Benny Morales, disgraced, despairing, had hanged himself, leaving behind a young, pregnant widow. She'd fled Virginia and had settled in Kansas, secluding herself and the infant son she bore from the scandal.

When Reno was five, she married again. Reno took his stepfather's name, but he never stopped dreaming of his real father. From Benny he inherited his small stature, his quick hands, and his love of horses. So he followed in his father's footsteps, working his way up from hot-walker to exercise boy and to apprentice jockey.

Obsessed with his father's memory, he moved to Virginia. He trusted only Jamison, his father's closest friend, with his secret. And Jamison kept it.

"He had scrapbooks on his father." Two days after the suicide, Rossi shared some of the details with Gabe. "Almost a library of them. Several of them were dedicated to the accusations made against his father, the investigation, and the suicide. His mother and stepfather are coming out today from Kansas to claim the body. I can tell you from my talk with her that she supports the fact that he had an unhealthy obsession with his father. Reno saw him as a hero and a scapegoat, and he was determined to right the old wrong."

"By drugging the Chadwick colt," Gabe said softly. "Disqualifying it from the Derby."

"Morales was riding for the Chadwicks when he took the fall that kept him out of racing for more than a year." Rossi didn't need his notes, but he flipped through his book out of habit. "Then, when the horse, Sun Spot, had to be put down at Keeneland, Matthew Chadwick was one of the most outspoken against Benny Morales. He had, after all, lost a valuable investment due to the tampering."

"Bad blood." Gabe set his teeth. "There's still a matter of where Reno got the drug. I think we can figure he injected the horse sometime after weigh-in and before they were loaded in the gate. Most probably while they were in the tunnel. But how did he get it, and from whom?"

"It doesn't seem it would be that difficult for a man in his position, Mr. Slater. Reno'd been around tracks since he was a teenager. He'd have known the right people. And the wrong ones."

"If he'd gotten the drug himself, he wouldn't have mistaken the dose. He didn't intend to kill the horse, Lieutenant. That's clear to me."

"He made a mistake."

"Or he was duped. Have you looked up my father?"

"This is a real family affair, isn't it? No," he said when Gabe remained silent. "He's moved out of his rooms, no forwarding address. The only reason I have to pursue that particular thread is your instinct. I'm trusting that, Mr. Slater. If he shows up around the track, anywhere in the area, we'll bring him in for questioning."

"He'll show. He's too vain to know when to cut his losses."

HE HADN'T BELIEVED IN HIS father's guilt. Kelsey stood at her bedroom window, fresh from a late-afternoon shower, and stared out over the hills. Reno hadn't believed in his father's guilt and so had spent most of his life pursuing that ghost. Wanting to vindicate it, to avenge it. In the end, he had discovered something about the man whose blood ran through him, and about himself, that he had not been able to live with.

It was always a risk to pry open doors to the past. She was encouraging Gabe to shrug off his own yoke of inheritance and be who he was. Yet she couldn't.

Wasn't she risking everything she'd built with Naomi over the past months by probing, poking, prodding at that door? And when she opened it, when she found what was lurking in the dust behind it, would she be able to live with it?

Let it go, she ordered herself. Why pick at something everyone wants locked? She had her whole life ahead of her. A life with Gabe. Fresh new beginnings everywhere. All she had to do was turn away from the shadows and accept what was.

"Miss Kelsey?"

Kelsey answered without looking around. "Yes, Gertie?"

"Mr. Lingstrom's office is on the phone. He wanted to speak with Miss Naomi, but since she's out, he'll talk to you."

"All right, Gertie. I'll take it downstairs."

She took the call in her mother's office, on the business line. She listened, managed to make the appropriate comments. When the call was complete, Kelsey replaced the receiver carefully. She was still sitting at the desk when Naomi walked in.

"God save me from those foolish, time-wasting luncheons. I don't know what makes me think I'm obliged to go. The only bright spot was that I happened to go into this little boutique near the restaurant when it was over. There was the most incredible dress, absolutely perfect for a simple, garden wedding. They'll hold it for twenty-four hours if you . . ."

She trailed off, the impetus that had carried her straight through the house to her daughter fading. Kelsey was staring at her, her hands locked together tightly on the desk.

"What is it?" Naomi asked. "Is it about Reno? Is there something else?"

"No, it's not about Reno." She watched the relief flutter over Naomi's face. "Your lawyer just phoned."

"Oh?" Fresh nerves had Naomi lifting a hand to toy with the star-shaped pin at her lapel.

"He wanted you to know that the documents you requested he draft are ready for your signature." She paused. "The ones transferring half of Three Willows into my name."

"Well, then. That's fine."

"Why would you do something like that?"

"It's something your grandfather and I discussed before he died. It was always my intention, Kelsey, and his. I'm just making it legal."

"Without telling me."

"I didn't want it to have the tone of an obligation," Naomi said carefully. "On either my part or yours. There hasn't been a lot I've been able to give you. This is something I can. My father left the when and how up to me, but basically this comes down to you through him. I felt this was the right time, and the right way. This isn't a rope to tie you here, Kelsey. Or to tie you to me."

"You must know I'm already tied here, and to you. You gambled that I would be when you asked me to come."

"Yes, I did. I couldn't guess, or even hope that you'd feel any-thing for me. But I was sure you'd feel it for Three Willows."

"One's very much the same as the other."

A ghost of a smile moved over Naomi's lips. "So I've been told."

"It's very difficult to love and respect one without loving and respecting the other." She rose, holding out her hands across the desk. "I haven't been able to do that. I don't see why I should."

"Not everyone would have given me the chance." Naomi took Kelsey's hands, and gripped hard.

Not everyone had, Kelsey thought. But she would take the risk, and try to change that.

IT WAS NEARLY FIVE WHEN SHE pulled up in Tipton's driveway behind his dusty late-model pickup. The neighbor's dog sent up a din, racing back and forth along the chain-link fence that separated the lawns as if to warn her his ground was sacrosanct. A woman leaned out of an upstairs window and shouted the dog down before eyeing Kelsey.

"Looking for Jim?"

"Yes, I am. Is he home?"

"In the shop." She pointed, shook her head. "Can't you hear the racket?"

Indeed she could, now that the dog had quieted to low, throaty snarls. She followed the high-pitched whine of a power saw into the backyard. There was a small shed, one that could be put together from a kit bought at most lumberyards.

401

Kelsey knocked on a door that hung crookedly on its jamb. At the slight tap it swung wide and banged against the inner wall.

Tipton stood at a bench, safety glasses and ear protectors in place, his Orioles cap turned into the catcher's position. Sawdust flew as he sheared off a two-by-four. Kelsey decided it was safer for both of them if she waited for the blade to stop whirling.

"Gotcha, you son of a bitch," Tipton muttered as a chunk of wood hit the ground.

"Captain Tipton?"

He whirled around, looking very much like something out of a B horror movie, his eyes shaded by amber-toned plastic, his ear protectors bulging and gray, and red splotches dotting his shirt.

"Oh, God, you've cut yourself."

"Where? What?" Alarmed, Tipton checked to make sure all his fingers were in place as Kelsey dashed across the shed. "Oh, this." Grinning, he patted his chest. "Cranberry juice. The wife doesn't like me to work in good clothes."

Kelsey leaned weakly against the bench and swore.

"Scared you, huh?" Still chuckling, he pulled off his ear guards and pushed up his goggles. "Want to sit down?"

"No, I'm fine."

"I'm building some shelves." He picked up a wide, flat board, sighted down it for warping. "The wife and I have this little game. I build shelves and she fills them up with doodads. Keeps us both happy."

"That's nice. I wonder if you could spare a few minutes."

"I might be able to squeeze you in. Lemonade?" Without waiting for her assent, he hefted a big plastic jug and poured two paper cups. "You had some more trouble out your way, I hear."

"Yes. It's an odd coincidence, isn't it? That Reno should so completely mirror his father's life. And death."

"The world's full of odd coincidences, Ms. Byden." But he wasn't happy about this one. He'd completed his background check on Benny Morales, and had gathered all the details only hours before Reno's suicide. Another twenty-four hours, he thought, and events might have taken a different turn. "It solves one of your problems, though. You know who did your horse."

"Reno didn't mean to kill him. I'm certain of that." She sipped the lemonade, found it tart and swimming with pulp. His wife, she thought, must squeeze her own. "Someone used him, Captain. There's a lot of that in the world, too. People using people."

"Can't argue with you there."

"My mother was using Alec Bradley to make my father jealous, to prove her own independence, even to incite gossip. I wonder, though, how had Alec Bradley been using her?"

The girl had a nice, tidy mind, Tipton decided. He picked up a square of sandpaper and began to rub it over a curved slat of wood. "She's a beautiful woman."

"This isn't about sex, Captain. Rape isn't about sex."

He huffed out a breath. "Maybe not. We only ever had her word about the attempted rape."

"I believe her. So did you. Did you ever ask yourself why—if she was telling the truth—why Alec Bradley chose that particular night to attack her? They'd been seeing each other for weeks. She's not the kind of woman who could continue to see a man who abused her. Or who threatened to abuse her."

Tipton continued to sand the wood. It would be a rocking chair for his granddaughter on her birthday in September.

"If she was telling the truth, Ms. Byden. If. He'd been drinking. They'd had a public scene. She'd given him his walking papers and a faceful of French champagne. That kind of combination could push a certain kind of man in the wrong direction." He blew lightly at the wood dust. "But, like I said, there was no evidence to support it."

"Her nightgown was torn. She had bruises." Kelsey let out an impatient sound at his shrug. "All right, as easily self-inflicted as not. But if we say not, if we believe not, how do you prove it? You checked his background, certainly. If there was another woman, someone else he'd abused or attacked, that would weigh on Naomi's side, wouldn't it?"

"I never found one. A lot of rapes go unreported. Especially the kind you're talking about. The date-rape kind."

He didn't like that particular term. Date rape, acquaintance rape. It made the vicious act seem much too friendly.

"And back twenty years ago, people had a different attitude. Bradley had a reputation, but violence wasn't part of it. He had some heavy debts," Tipton continued, almost to himself. "About the time he started seeing your mother, he paid off some of them. About twenty thousand dollars' worth. But he needed at least that much again to pull himself out."

"So he needed money. My mother had money."

"He never asked her for more than a couple of grand." Tipton set the wood aside. "That's her own statement. He never asked her for big money. And that's one of the things I found odd. Because it was his pattern to sponge off women."

"He might have been biding his time. Or . . . he might have been expecting it from another source."

"That was a thought." Tipton pulled a Baby Ruth bar from his back pocket, snapped it in half, and offered a share to Kelsey. "I never tracked it down, though. I always wondered where he got that twenty grand. Could've won it at the track. But the word there was that he lost as much as he won, and most of it was penny-ante. He talked big," Tipton added with a mouthful of chocolate. "Let a lot of people know he had a deal in the works. Just talk, as far I could find."

"But if he did, if it had something to do with my mother." Kelsey began to pace the shop as she worked it out. "She was through with him, told him it was over. So he panicked, tried to force her. If she cut him loose, the deal was dead. He needed money. A lot of people knew he needed money. But who would have used him to get to my mother?"

As the answer swam into her mind, she stopped. The hand holding the paper cup tightened, crushing it into a damp blob.

"That's the trouble when you turn over rocks," Tipton said kindly. "You hardly ever like what you find under them. I never linked your father to Alec Bradley. And I tried. I subpoenaed your father's bank records, went over them with a fine-tooth comb looking for that twenty-thousand-dollar payment. He was clean. Phone records, too. No calls came from or to Alec Bradley's number from the house in Potomac or his office at the university."

"He would never have done such a thing." But Kelsey's lips were stiff and cold. "My father would never have done such a thing."

"The way it looks, you're right. Of course that puts the heat back on your mother."

"There's another answer." Kelsey whirled back. "I know there's another answer."

"You want another answer," Tipton said gently. "Maybe you'll find it. Maybe you won't like it." He sighed and reached out to take the squashed cup from her hand. "I only had one thing linking Philip Byden with what happened that night at Three Willows. That was Charles Rooney."

# Chapter Twenty-Six

IT WAS OBVIOUS SOMETHING WAS WRONG. SHE'D COME TO him after dark, saying only that she wanted to be with him. Gabe wanted to believe it was as simple as that. As true as that.

But her eyes were distant, her smile too bright, with strain at the edges. Her needs, always a delight to him, were frenzied. She'd torn into sex with a wild abandon that couldn't quite mask the desperation.

As if she'd been purging herself, he thought now that she lay quiet beside him. His body had responded, and in that most elemental link they had met, clashed, and joined. But, he thought now, as the silence stretched out between them, neither of them had been satisfied.

"Are you ready now?" he asked her.

She turned her head, looking for a cooler place to rest her cheek on the warm sheets. "Ready?"

"To tell me what's eating you."

"What should be eating me?" Her voice was dull, tired. "A man I knew and liked killed himself a few days ago."

"This isn't about Reno. It's about you."

She turned on her back, staring up at the dark skylight. No moon tonight, she thought. The clouds masked it like smoke. It really took very little to hide so much.

"He loved his father," she began. "He didn't even know him, but he loved him. Believed in him. Everything Reno did circled back to that love and belief. Blind, unquestioning love and belief." She sighed once. "And when he realized it had been misplaced, at least the belief had been misplaced, he couldn't live with it."

She shifted restlessly, the sound of her skin against the sheets a whisper in the darkness.

"It would have been better if he'd turned away from it, wouldn't it? Better for him, better for everyone, if he'd left what happened all those years ago alone. What's to be proved, Gabe, what's to be solved by insisting on looking back?"

"It depends on how badly you need to look. And what you find." He touched her hair, let it sift through his fingers. "This is about you, isn't it, Kelsey? About you and Naomi."

"She considers it over. Why can't I? There's no turning back the clock, giving her back those years we lost. That we both lost. She killed Alec Bradley. I should accept that. I shouldn't let it matter so much why."

Kelsey moved again, pushing herself up, drawing in her knees, circling them with her arms in a move of such poignant defense it tore at his heart.

"Then let it go."

"Let it go," she repeated. "It's the sensible thing. After all, whatever wrong she did, whatever mistakes she made, she's paid for. I didn't know her then, or don't remember knowing her. What makes me think I can go back and sort it out? Or that I should? She's happy. My father's happy. Neither of them would thank me for digging into it. I've no right to scrape open old wounds just to satisfy my own ridiculous need for truth, for justice."

Squeezing her eyes tight, she pressed her face to her knees. "They're not always the same, are they? Truth and justice?"

"They should be. One of the most admirable things about you is that you want them to be." He brushed a hand over her shoulder, felt the knots of tension, and began to massage them out. "What stirred this up, Kelsey?"

She took a long, steadying breath and told him about her visit to Tipton. He didn't interrupt, and tried to deal with his own knee-jerk anger that she had gone without him.

"And now you're worried that your father was somehow involved."

"He couldn't have been." Her head shot up. In the dark her eyes shone with defiance and a plea for understanding. "He couldn't have been, Gabe. You don't know him."

"No, I don't." Annoyed with himself, Gabe drew away and reached for a cigar on the night table. "We've skipped that little amenity."

She passed a weary hand through her hair. Somehow she'd managed to hurt him. "This has all happened so fast, everything between you and me has happened at double time. And the situation, my family situation, is on very rocky ground. It isn't that I've kept you from him."

"Forget it." He snapped on his lighter and scowled into the flame. "Forget it," he said again, more quietly. "It's hardly the point. And it's not what's annoying me. I would have gone with you today. I should have been with you."

"It was an impulse." That was the truth, she thought, but only half the truth. "Maybe I wanted to go alone. Maybe I needed to. I don't want to be protected, Gabe. All my life I've been protected without even knowing it. I can't live the rest of it that way."

"There's a difference between being protected and being supported. I need you to lean on me, Kelsey. Just like I need to know I can lean on you."

After a moment she took his hand. "Do you have to be right?"

"I prefer it that way." He lifted her fingers to his lips. "What do you want to do?"

"What I want is to forget it. To let it all alone and go from here. But I can't. I have to know. And when I do I have to live with whatever I find out." She measured her palm against his, then laced fingers. "I'm going to go see Rooney tomorrow afternoon. Will you come with me?"

MORE LIES, KELSEY THOUGHT. Of the little white variety.

"You're going to love the dress." Naomi held out the pale lavender business card. "The clerk's name's on the back. Ilsa. They do alterations right there."

"That's great."

"If it doesn't suit you, I'm sure you'll find something else. It's a wonderful shop. Oh, and I spoke to the caterer at the club. I know you want to keep the wedding simple, but you have to have food. He's going to work up a couple of menus for you to choose from. And . . ." She snatched up another list. "I know Gabe has a wonderful garden, and he's got an innate touch with flowers, but you'll want some patio plants and cut arrangements to fill things out. Once you decide on your colors, we can order what you like."

"That's fine."

"Listen to me." Laughing at herself, Naomi set the lists back on her desk. "I've fallen headfirst into the mother-of-the-bride trap. I'm annoying myself."

Kelsey forced her lips to curve, tried to make the smile reflect in her eyes. "No, I appreciate it, really. Even with a small, informal wedding at home, there are dozens of details."

"That you're perfectly capable of handling yourself," Naomi finished. "I know you've had the big splashy wedding, Kelsey, and that you want this to be different."

"I do, yes." Kelsey turned the business card over in her hand, then stuck it guiltily in her pocket. "Candace orchestrated that. I barely had to do more than show up." Hearing herself, she hissed out a breath. "That sounds ungrateful. I'm not. She was wonderful."

409

"But you'd like to handle this one yourself."

"Let's just say I'd like more of a hand in it. But I don't mind delegating."

"I never thought I'd have this chance. Planning my daughter's wedding." Determined, she pushed all her lists into a pile, topped them with a brass paperweight. "Just yank me back when I threaten to go overboard. And . . ." She eased a hip onto the corner of the desk. "About the dress. I promise I won't say a word if you don't love it. But you will. Now, you'd better go before I nag you into letting me go along with you instead of Gabe."

"We'll shop for your dress together," Kelsey said as guilt piled over guilt. "Maybe over the weekend."

"I'd like that." Breezily, Naomi linked her arm through Kelsey's as she walked Kelsey to the door. "It'll give me a chance to harass you about photographers. Now, go enjoy yourself."

Kelsey mumbled something and walked outside just as Gabe pulled up in the drive.

"We have to make a stop first," Kelsey told him, pulling out the business card after she'd settled into the passenger seat.

He lifted a brow. "Shopping?"

"Soothing my conscience."

IT DIDN'T WORK. EVEN WHEN it turned out that Naomi had been completely right about the dress. Or, perhaps, because of it.

Under any other circumstances the dress would have lifted her spirits. The pale rose color of the silk, the elegant tea length, the simple lines enhanced by raindrops of seed pearls. It was a wish of a dress that Ilsa assured her might have been made with Kelsey in mind. And didn't they have the sweetest hat to go with it? the clerk expounded. A little whimsy with a flirty fingertip veil so perfect for an intimate outdoor wedding.

Shoes, of course. Classic satin pumps that could be dyed to match. What flowers was she going to carry? She didn't know?

White roses would be lovely, she was assured. A bride was entitled to white. Now, did she want to take the dress and hat along with her, or have them sent?

She took them along, moving through the transaction as if in a dream. It was so strange. And so simple.

"You didn't model it for me," Gabe commented as he walked with her back to the car.

"Bad luck," she said absently. Then she stopped, pressing her hands to her flushed cheeks. "God, did I just buy a wedding dress?"

"Apparently." He took her shoulders, turned her to face him. "Second thoughts?"

"No. No, not about you, us. This. It's just moving so quickly. I just bought my wedding dress, and a hat. I actually bought a hat. I'm having shoes dyed. And I haven't even told my family."

"You can rectify that today. If it's what you want." He put the boxes in the trunk.

"Okay." She nodded, and reached for the door handle. Gabe closed his hand over hers, then drew it back.

"Let's try this on for luck, then." He slipped a ring on her finger, a single square-cut diamond centered in a gold band crusted with tiny rubies. "My colors. Our colors, now. That's official."

Tears pricked at her eyes. They may have been standing in a parking lot with the summer sun beating down, but to her, the moment was as romantic as a cruise down a moonlit stream. "It's beautiful, Gabe. I didn't need it."

"I did."


ACROSS THE LOT, RICH huddled in his car and watched the exchange, the embrace. He took a nip from his flask. And what a handsome couple they make, he thought bitterly. His son, and the slut's daughter.

It was Gabe's fault he was on the run again, that he was going to have to fold his tent and slink off. There would be no

411

triumphant drive to Vegas now. The cops were asking questions. Rich had dragged that much out of Cunningham when he'd squeezed the man for another two thousand.

Let them ask, he thought, switching on his ignition when the Jaguar's roared to life. He wouldn't be around to answer. No, sir, Rich Slater was taking the high road all the way to Mexico, just as soon as he took care of a little business.

He slipped out of the lot, keeping the Jaguar in sight.

"WE'RE GOING TO HAVE TO be obnoxious." Kelsey told Gabe as they wove their way through Alexandria's traffic. "Rooney refused to take any of my calls."

"So, we'll be obnoxious."

"You think I'm wasting my time."

"What's important is what you think. You want to talk to him, we'll talk to him."

She shifted in her seat, wishing they could hurry up, wishing they could take forever. "I suppose I want to know how involved my father was in Rooney's investigation. If Dad knew Alec Bradley or just of him. I need to clear it in my mind. I don't suppose it changes anything that happened that night, but I need to know."

"You could ask your father."

"I'll have to, sooner or later. For now I'd . . ." Her voice trailed off. Abruptly she straightened in her seat and leaned forward as Gabe turned into the parking garage beneath Rooney's building.

"What is it?"

"That car, the one that just pulled out."

Gabe flicked a glance at his rearview mirror in time to see the car turn left and join the flow of traffic. "The black Lincoln?"

"My grandmother." Kelsey rubbed at the chill on her arms. "That was my grandmother's car. It was her driver at the wheel. I recognized him."

"There are a lot of offices in this building, Kelsey."

"And life's full of odd coincidences. No." She shook her head, staring straight ahead when Gabe pulled the car into an empty space. "I don't believe it. She was here to see Rooney. I'm going to find out why."

As they crossed to the elevator, Gabe took her arm. She was all but vibrating with temper and nerves. "If you go in guns blazing, you'll just spook him."

"Whatever it takes." She stepped in, then jabbed the button for Rooney's floor.

She might have been packing six-guns, Gabe thought, the way she stalked the receptionist in Rooney's plush outer office.

"Kelsey Byden and Gabriel Slater, to see Mr. Rooney."

The woman's professional smile flashed. "Do you have an appointment?"

"No."

"I'm sorry, Ms. Byden, Mr. Slater—"

"Don't be," Kelsey interrupted, and leaned on the desk in a manner that had the professional smile dimming considerably. "Just tell him we're here. And we're not leaving until we see him. Oh, and you might mention that I just saw my grandmother leaving. Milicent Byden."

It turned the key. Within ten minutes they were being ushered into Rooney's office. He didn't rise from his desk this time, but greeted them both with a single terse nod.

"You've caught me at a bad time. I'm afraid I can't spare more than five minutes."

"We might have managed a more convenient time, Mr. Rooney, if you'd taken any of my calls."

"Ms. Byden." Trying to exude patience, Rooney folded his hands on the desk. He succeeded in looking like a man begging. "I've tried to save both of us time and trouble. I can't help you."

"Why were you there that night, Mr. Rooney? You see, that's a question I keep returning to. Maybe it's because it all happened so long ago and I see it from a different perspective from those who

413

were involved in the heat of the moment. But why that night? That particular night of all nights?"

"I was on routine surveillance. It's just as viable to ask yourself why your mother chose that particular night to shoot Alec Bradley."

"I know the answer to that," Kelsey returned steadily. "I'm wondering if you do. How much did you really see?"

"That's a matter of record." He rose, dismissing them. "I can't help you."

"How far did my father tell you to go? Did he approve your decision to sneak onto my mother's property and spy through her windows?"

"I'm paid to use my own judgment."

"You must have come to know my mother and Alec Bradley very well in those weeks that you followed them. Did you ever follow only him? See who he met, who he spoke with, who might have given him money?"

He could barely swallow, then realized it wasn't necessary. The saliva in his mouth had dried up. "I was hired to investigate your mother."

"But he was part of your investigation. How well did my father know him?"

Rooney's jaw tightened. "To my knowledge, they were not acquainted."

Outwardly cool, Kelsey merely lifted a brow. "He had no interest in the man his wife was allegedly having an affair with?"

"Estranged wife, and no, at that point in time Philip Byden was only interested in one thing. His child."

"But when you reported to him—"

"I reported to his lawyers. Whether or not he read the copies they sent him, I can't say. He didn't want to be involved." A small smile touched Rooney's mouth. "He felt the idea of hiring an investigator was undignified."

"But he did hire you?"

"Perhaps he felt the ends justified the means. I have another appointment. You'll have to excuse me."

"Why did my grandmother come here today?"

"That's confidential."

"She's a client?"

"I can't help you," he said, spacing his words. But his eyes flicked to Gabe, then away.


ALONE, ROONEY SAT BEHIND his desk, steadying his breathing. He reached into his pocket and thumbed out a Tums that would do little to ease the burning in his gut.

How could it come back like this? After all these years. He'd gone by the book. He'd followed the book to the letter for twenty-three years. How could one night so long ago spring back at him like a tiger?

He started at the sound of his buzzer, then cursed himself. He wouldn't help the situation if he let nerves rattle him. He answered the buzzer.

"Mr. Rooney. There's a gentleman to see you. He doesn't have an appointment, but he claims to be an old friend. I'm to tell you it's old Rich."

"I don't know any ..." His mouth went dry again, his palms damp. For one frantic moment, Rooney looked around his office for a route of escape. There was none, he realized. He was as terminally hooked as the glass-eyed swordfish on his wall.

"Send him in, and hold my calls, please."

"Yes, sir."

Rich was beaming when he stepped into Rooney's office. "Long time no see."

"What do you want?"

Rich sat, propped his feet on the desk. "You've put on a little weight, Charlie. Looks good on you, though. Used to look a little like a scarecrow. Why don't you buy an old pal a drink?"

"What do you want?" Rooney repeated.

"Well, you can start by telling me what my boy and that pretty lady of his wanted with you." Rich drew out a cigarette. "We'll work from there."

"I DON'T FEEL A WHOLE LOT BETTER," Kelsey said when they climbed back into the car. "Am I supposed to be glad that my father hired that man but kept himself distant so he wouldn't soil his dignity? Or should I be relieved that he had nothing to do with Rooney, or Alec Bradley?"

"Maybe you should spend some time wondering why Rooney was so nervous."

"Nervous? He seemed cold, remote, and annoyed, but not nervous."

"He had his hands locked together to keep them still." Gabe backed out of the parking space. "The air-conditioning was blasting in that office, but he was sweating. His jaw was locked so tight he had a tic at the corner of his mouth. He was bluffing his way through it." Gabe paid the attendant, then eased back into the street. "But little things kept giving him away. And his eyes. He had the look of a man who's holding trash but keeps bumping the pot."

Curious, and fascinated, Kelsey studied him. "You get all that from gambling?"

"It's a gift. Something's got him spooked."

"All we have to do is find out what." She sighed. "I need a phone booth, Gabe. I think it's time I rounded up the family."

MILICENT ACCEPTED THE SHERRY her son poured her and, feeling magnanimous, patted his hand. "She's finally come to her senses. Don't look so concerned, Philip. I'm quite willing to put these past few months behind us. She's a Byden, after all." She sat back, sighed, sipped. "Blood will tell."

"I certainly hope she's brought Channing with her." Candace paced to the window and flicked the lace curtain impatiently. "I see no reason why he should stay at that place if Kelsey's coming home."

"Channing's doing what's right for him." Philip put a gentle hand on Candace's shoulder. Part of her wanted to shrug it off, but another, deeper part couldn't bear the thought of any more harsh words between them.

"I want him to be happy, Philip. You know I do."

"Of course you do."

"The boy will come around," Milicent assured them. "It's just youthful defiance, that's all. And sentiment. A vet? Really, now. That will pass."

She flicked Channing's dream aside with one elegant hand. "Why, there was a time, if you can imagine it, when Philip was a boy—do you remember, dear?—and he wanted to be a baseball player. Of all things."

"I remember," he murmured. He'd been sixteen, eager, and despite his bookish appearance, he'd had an arm like a rocket. Of course, that dream had been aborted in its embryonic state. A Byden didn't play professional sports. A Byden *was* a professional.

"Channing will listen to reason, just as Philip did. Your mistake, Candace dear, was in not asserting your authority."

"Channing's over twenty-one," Candace said stiffly.

"A mother is always a mother." Milicent's smile settled comfortably when the doorbell chimed. "Ah, that will be the prodigal daughter now. Let her apologize first, Philip. She'll feel better for it. Then we'll have Cook kill the fatted calf."

But Kelsey didn't look apologetic when she entered the sitting room with Gabe at her side. She did smile at her father and go to him for a greeting kiss. Hoping to mend fences, she embraced Candace before turning to her grandmother.

"Thank you for seeing me." She leaned down and kissed Milicent's lightly powdered cheek. "Grandmother, Dad, Candace, this is Gabriel Slater. Gabe, Milicent, Candace, and Philip Byden."

"It's nice to meet you." Philip offered a hand.

"I don't mean to be rude"—Milicent's eyes were cold as they lingered on Gabe—"but I had the impression there was family business to be discussed."

"Yes, there is. Old and new. I suppose I should start with the new. Gabe and I are going to be married."

There was a moment of stunned silence before Philip recovered. "Well, that's . . . a surprise. A happy one."

"A bombshell," Candace corrected. "And just like you, Kelsey." But she softened at the idea of orange blossoms. "Now I suppose sherry won't do. We'll have to have champagne."

"I won't have it." Milicent spoke, her face bone-white beneath her rouge. "I won't have this insulting behavior in my home."

"Mother—" Philip began tentatively.

"My home," she said again, thumping a fist on the arm of her chair. "Is this a slap at me?" she demanded of Kelsey. "A subtle insult? You would bring this person into my home, threaten to bring him into this family?"

Even knowing Milicent, Kelsey was shocked at the reaction. "It's not a slap, an insult, or a threat. It's a fact. We're getting married in a few weeks, at Gabe's home in Virginia. I'd like it very much if all of you would be there."

"Of course we will." Eager to smooth over the rough edges, Candace stepped in. "We're all just a little flustered by the suddenness of the announcement, but we wouldn't miss it for the world. I hope you'll let me help you with some of the details."

"Enough!" Milicent slammed her sherry down with a force that snapped the fragile stem. The remaining drops of amber liquid dripped down to spot the rug. "There is most certainly not going to be a wedding. Apparently, Kelsey, you've allowed yourself to be swayed by an attractive face. That's foolish but not irrevocable."

With an effort, she steadied her breathing and maintained her self-control. "There's been no public announcement, so there will be nothing to tidy up. You"—she pointed at Gabe—"you can save yourself some embarrassment now by leaving."

"I don't think so," he said evenly. "Embarrass me."

"We'll both go." Trembling with rage, Kelsey took his hand. "This was a mistake. Whatever else I have to say to my grandmother I can say at another time. I shouldn't have brought you here and subjected you to this."

"Stop it." Gabe brought their joined hands to his lips, kissed hers just above the ring. "Let her finish."

"I'm going to ask you to let me apologize." Philip moved between his mother's chair and his daughter. "Certainly this has come as a surprise. It might be best if we talk about it later."

"Don't shield the girl." Milicent rose and walked to a glossy Chippendale desk. "You've done that long enough. It's time she learned to face facts."

"I have been," Kelsey murmured. "For some time now."

"Then deal with these." She drew out a file from the desk. "I've compiled quite a bit of information on you, Mr. Slater. Quite a bit. Professional gambler, ex-convict. The son of an itinerant drunkard with no visible means of support and a cleaning woman. A runaway who lived on the streets and spent time in jail for illegal gambling."

She kept the file clutched in her hand as she studied Gabe with cold, condemning eyes. "You may have developed a taste for the finer things, and amassed some of them, but it doesn't change who you are."

"No, it doesn't," Gabe agreed. "Just as being born with them doesn't change who you are."

She slapped the file back on the desk. "Get out of my house."

"Wait." Kelsey's hand closed convulsively around Gabe's arm. "How dare you do this! How dare you pry into Gabe's personal life! And mine!"

"I'll do whatever is necessary to protect the Byden name. And you, despite this sudden attachment you've developed for that woman, are a Byden."

"That woman is my mother. Did you put a dossier together on her as well?" she demanded. "Did you search for nasty little secrets to throw in my father's face to try to keep him from marrying her?"

"It was, to my regret, one of the few times in his life he didn't listen to me."

The scene had been all too similar to this, Milicent remembered. Philip had actually shouted at her, and given her the ultimatum of accepting that woman or losing her own son.

"No, he didn't listen," she repeated. "And the results were disastrous."

"I'm one of the results," Kelsey tossed back. "Is that what you were doing in Rooney's office this afternoon?"

Milicent used one arm to brace herself against the desk. "I don't know what you're talking about."

"I saw you. You hired him again, didn't you? To spy on Gabe, to pry into his past."

"It was just a necessary evil to compile information that would bring you to your senses," Milicent defended.

"Well, you wasted your money. It doesn't make any difference to me. I already know all of it."

"Then you're more your mother than I wanted to believe. You deserve what becomes of you."

"You're right." Kelsey turned to her father. "Did you fall out of love with her, Dad? Or did you allow yourself to be shoved out of it?"

"Kelsey," he said, his voice hoarse, because all at once he wasn't sure of the answer, "what happened then, happened. I apologize with all my heart for this." Rigid with shock and embarrassment, he looked at Gabe. "To both of you."

"Apologize?" Milicent spat out. "I've told you the kind of man he is, the kind of man she's using to humiliate this family, and you apologize."

"Yes." With sorrow in his eyes, Philip looked at his mother. "I apologize for you, for the fact that you've used the family name like a whip. A name that has always meant more to you than something as simple as happiness."

Pale as death, Milicent gripped the edge of the desk. "I will not be spoken to like that, by my son, in my own home." Her eyes flashed back to Kelsey. "She's at the root of this. Naomi is the root of this."

Kelsey nodded slowly. "Perhaps she is. I'm sorry. I won't be back. Let's go home, Gabe."

"Kelsey." Flushed pink, Candace dashed after them, stopping them at the door. "Please, don't blame your father."

"I'm trying not to."

"He would never have allowed this to happen if he'd known . . . surely you know what kind of man he is."

Kelsey looked into Candace's worried eyes. "Yes, I do. You know, I always thought how well you and Dad were suited. How you complemented each other, filled in the blanks." Leaning forward, she kissed Candace softly on the cheek. "I didn't realize until right now how much you love him. I should have. Tell him I'll call him later, all right?"

"Yes. Yes, I will. And, Kelsey?" Her smile was a little crooked, but it was there. "Best wishes, to both of you."

# Chapter Twenty-Seven

"Quite a family you've got there, darling."

"Okay, Gabe." Once he'd parked in the drive at Three Willows, Kelsey got out of the car and closed her door with deliberate care. "This isn't the time to get cute."

"No, I mean it. I let you rant half the way home, and stew the other half. That ought to finish it."

She wasn't nearly finished. "It wasn't just about me. It wasn't really about me at all. It was about you."

"Hell." In an easy motion, he swung an arm around her shoulder. "I've had a lot worse tossed at me. She didn't bring up the showgirl in Reno, or the business in El Paso."

"That's hardly the point." She stopped dead on the first step. "What showgirl?"

"Got your attention." He gave her an almost brotherly squeeze. "Anyway, I liked your father, and your stepmother. That's two for three."

Baffled, she could only stare up at him. "You're not even angry. You're not even angry over what she did. Gabe, she hired a detective to pry into your life, to put together a file on you as though you were some kind of criminal."

"And what did she accomplish, Kelsey? You already knew the worst of me, and you defended even that. It makes my laying my cards out on the table up front the best gamble I ever took."

"It doesn't excuse what she did."

"But it makes what she did meaningless. Look, maybe I understand, a little, because I never had a family name to defend."

Now she stopped in her tracks. "You're standing up for her?"

"No. But I figure she made the wrong move. And it ended up costing her a lot more than it cost me."

She blew at her bangs. "Maybe I need a little more time to be open-minded. Get my dress out of the car, will you? At least we can make one person happy today when I show it to Naomi."

"Why don't I take you both out to dinner?" He rubbed his thumb over the ring on her finger. He liked seeing it there. "Celebrate?"

"Why don't you? I'll go tell her."

She hurried into the house, giving herself one quick shake, a gesture to toss off the worst of the day. She was halfway up the stairs when Naomi called her.

"Oh, there you are." One hand trailing along the banister, Kelsey rushed down again. "You were absolutely right about the dress. Gabe's getting it out of the car, then he's going to take us out to dinner. Should we see if we can drag Moses away from the barn?"

Naomi stood in the foyer, her hands clasped. "We need to talk. It might be better if we sat down."

"What is it? Oh, God, not one of the horses. Justice was a little wheezy, but I dosed him the way Moses told me."

"It's not one of the horses, Kelsey. Please, come in and sit down."

The stranger was back. That cool, controlled woman who had first invited her to tea. Baffled, Kelsey followed her through the doorway. "You're angry with me about something."

"No, I don't think 'angry' is the appropriate word." She glanced over when Gabe came through the door. "It might be best if we discussed this privately."

"No, there's nothing you can't say to me in front of Gabe."

"All right, then." Naomi walked to the window, faced out. She needed all her control now, all the self-reliance she'd had to learn to survive in prison. "You had a call while you were out. Gertie took the message. She left it on the desk in your room. I went in there a few minutes ago, to take in a guest list I'd been putting together."

Her face expressionless, she turned around. "I'll apologize for reading it. It wasn't intentional. It was simply there, and my eye fell on it."

"Why don't you just tell me who called?"

"Charles Rooney. The message was marked urgent. He wants you to contact him as soon as possible."

"Then I'd better see what it's about."

"Please." Naomi held up a hand. "After more than twenty years, I can't believe it could be so urgent. You've been to see him."

"Yes, twice."

"For what purpose, Kelsey? Haven't I answered your questions?"

"Yes, you have. That's one of the reasons I went to see him. Because you've answered my questions."

"And you?" She turned to Gabe, a flash of temper sneaking through the cracks. "You encouraged her in this?"

"It wasn't a matter of encouragement. But I understand."

"How could you understand?" she demanded, bitter. "How could either of you possibly understand? You can't imagine what went through me when I saw his name on the desk. I've spent more than a decade of my life trying to forget. I made myself dredge it up again, relive it again. A payment, I thought—I hoped—to bring my daughter back. But it's not enough?"

"I didn't go to see him to hurt you. I'm sorry I have. I went because I wanted to help, because I hoped I would find something that would change things."

"They can't be changed."

"If he saw something that night he didn't tell the police. If he held something back."

Stunned, Naomi sank to the arm of the sofa. "Did you think, really think you could find something to clear my name? Is that what this is about, Kelsey? A belated bath for the dirty family linen?" With a weak laugh, Naomi rubbed her eyes. "God. What possible difference could it make now? You can't give me back one second of the time I lost. You can't take away one whisper, one sneer, one sidelong look. It's done," she said, dropping her hands. "It's as dead and buried as Alec Bradley."

"Not to me. I did what I thought was right. And if Rooney called me, there's a reason. He didn't want to talk to me today. He was nervous, maybe even afraid."

"Just leave it alone."

"I can't do that." She stepped forward, gripping Naomi's cold hands in hers. "There's more. What happened to Pride, and Reno. It's so much like what happened all those years ago. Your horse, Benny Morales. It's like this terrible echo that's taken this long to catch up. And it hasn't stopped yet. Even the police wonder if there's a connection."

"The police." What color remained in Naomi's cheeks washed away. "You've spoken with the police?"

Kelsey released her mother's hands and stepped back. "I've been to see Captain Tipton."

"Tipton." The shudder came before she could stop it. "Oh, God."

"He believed you." Kelsey watched Naomi lift her head. "He told me he believed you."

"That's bull." Trembling, she sprang up. "You weren't there, in that horible room with the questions pounding at you, over and over and over. No one believed me, certainly not Tipton. If he had, why did I go to prison?"

"He couldn't prove it. The photographs—"

425

"Back to Rooney," Naomi interrupted. "Do you really think you can turn this around? Discover some long-overlooked clue that proves I was defending my honor?" The hurt throbbed in her heart, in her voice. "Well, you can't. And even if you want to help, you won't be able to. Because I can't survive going through it again. I just can't."

She walked from the room and hurried up the stairs. Moments later they heard the sound of a door slamming.

"What a mess." Kelsey dropped into a chair, closed her eyes. "What a mess I've made of things."

"No, you haven't. You've stirred things up. Maybe they needed to be stirred up."

"We'd come a long way. She and I had come such a long way, Gabe. I've ruined that."

"Do you really believe that?"

"I don't know." She lifted her hands, then let them fall. "I started off telling myself I was asking questions for me. Because I had a right to know. Somewhere along the line I twisted that, convinced myself I was doing it for her. But I think I was right in the first place. I wanted to tidy it all up. Make it clean. If I believe her, everyone should believe her."

"That doesn't make you a villain, Kelsey." He crossed over and sat on the arm of her chair. "Tell me what you want to do."

She drew in a deep breath, expelled it. "I'm going to call Charles Rooney. I have to finish it."

THEY MET HIM AT A BAR. Not a seedy, gin-soaked dive that might have added atmosphere to a clandestine meeting, but a plant-filled lounge that catered to white-collar professionals. Rooney had used every skill, every trick along his route to make certain he hadn't been followed.

When he saw them come in, he finished off his first gin and tonic. He was done, and knew it. He'd spent the hours since Rich

Slater had left his office making plans to disappear. He had the knowledge, the contacts, and now, he had the motive.

"Mr. Rooney."

"Sit down. I can recommend the house wine."

"Fine," Kelsey said, and nodded to the hovering waitress.

"Coffee," Gabe ordered. "Black. You said urgent," he reminded Rooney.

"So I did." He tapped his glass to indicate another. One more for the road, he thought. By morning, he planned to be sipping a mimosa in Rio. "I'm afraid I was a little rattled when I made that call. It was a day for unexpected visitors at my office. The last one was unpleasant. I've been an investigator for over twenty-five years. A long time. I've had a lot of interesting cases. I've never once discharged a weapon." He gave the table two brisk knocks. "I enjoy my work, always have. It's difficult to build up the right clientele. A certain class of people, the right class of people, generally don't care to have an overt association with someone in my line of work. They hire us with the same kind of dismay and disgust that they hire someone to exterminate their roaches. They want the results, of course, but they rarely want to discuss the execution. There are some who prefer a more hands-on approach."

He paused as their drinks were served.

"This is fascinating, Rooney," Gabe commented, "but hardly urgent."

"Milicent Byden," he said, and watched Kelsey's mouth tighten. "She's a woman accustomed to directing servants, giving orders, making certain they're carried out to her specifications."

"We know she hired you to investigate Gabe," Kelsey washed the bad taste out of her mouth with wine. "I hope you got a hefty retainer, Mr. Rooney. Believe me, she's far from satisfied with the results."

"Tossed them back in her face, did you?" He found that amusing and chuckled into his drink. "Maybe there's some justice in the

427

world. She was satisfied with the results the first time she hired me. More than satisfied."

"The first time?"

"It was your grandmother who hired me for the custody suit."

"My information is that you were hired by my father's lawyers."

"*Her* lawyers, Ms. Byden. You should remember they were her lawyers, too. And that's the way she wanted it to shake down."

He took the lime wedge from his drink and squeezed the juice into the glass.

"I'd done a job for an acquaintance of hers. Divorce. She must have figured I'd done a good one, a discreet one. And I fit the bill. Ambitious, still young enough to be impressed by who she was— who her husband was—and the size of her check."

He shrugged that out and dipped into the bowl filled with pretzels shaped like Chinese characters.

"I don't see that it makes a large difference where your retainer came from," Kelsey commented.

"Oh, but it did. I never even met your father. I saw him at the trial, but we never had a one-on-one. That's the way your grandmother wanted it. And she was good at getting things done her way. She wanted your mother out, all the way out of his life, and yours. And she'd worked out a very simple plan to accomplish it. My job was to follow Naomi, take pictures, make reports. That's all Milicent Byden told me. But I'm a good investigator, Ms. Byden. Even then I was good, and I found out more."

"More?" Kelsey felt that door creak open a little wider, and was afraid, very much afraid, of what she would see beyond it.

"It's easy enough to rub some elbows at the track. One of my sources had the goods on Bradley. Knew he'd played deep and was in debt to the wrong people. Bradley wasn't good at keeping secrets, and he'd talked. Talked about the big deal he was working on. All he had to do was make time with a beautiful woman, and he'd be set. Bradley and my source got chummy. They didn't run in the same circles, but they were cut pretty much from the same cloth. Bradley talked too much, my source put the arm on him for more, then passed the information on to me, for a fee."

"You're taking a long time to circle around to the wire, Rooney," Gabe said.

"Then let me make it simple." He loosened his constricting tie. "The custody suit was leaning toward Naomi. Courts don't like to take a kid from its mother. Maybe she liked to party, maybe she liked men, but she didn't fool with either when the kid was around. She had the money, and the means, and there were plenty of people willing to testify that she was a good mother, a devoted one. So, the Bydens needed something to tip the scales in their favor. Milicent found it in Alec Bradley."

"My . . ." Kelsey took a moment to steady her voice. "My grand-mother knew Alec Bradley."

"Yes, she knew him, knew his parents. Knew his character. She hired Bradley to seduce your mother. To lure her into a compro-mising situation, the kind of situation that would make her appear anything but moral and maternal."

Beneath the table, Kelsey gripped Gabe's hand. "You're saying that my grandmother paid Alec Bradley. Paid him to—why should I believe you?"

"You believe what you want." Rooney didn't give a damn. He was just clearing his desk, so to speak, before he retired. "You came after the answers, Ms. Byden. Don't blame me if they don't suit you. She gave him twenty thousand dollars, up front."

Kelsey made a small sound as the figure clicked.

"The trouble was, Naomi wasn't playing the game. Not the way Bradley and your grandmother wanted. She was keeping him on a leash. The way the custody suit was heating up, your grand-mother needed action. So she found another element to stir into the mix. There was some trouble at the track. A dead horse, a dead jockey. The publicity on that boomeranged in the Chadwicks' favor."

Gabe held up a hand. "Are you saying that's connected?"

429

"It's all connected. Bradley needed cash, but Milicent was keeping her wallet slammed shut until he produced results. So Bradley and his pal at the track worked out a little deal. When the horse went down, Bradley picked up some loose change, but he didn't get the bonus he'd hoped for when the sympathy went with Naomi. Milicent gave him a deadline."

Rooney studied what was left of his drink, debated indulging in another. With less than two hours until his flight, he opted to keep a clear head.

"She told me to have my camera and plenty of film. To be outside the house. I went to the club first, and watched Bradley stage the jealousy scene."

"Stage?" Kelsey repeated.

"It's easier to see through an act when you're not involved. Plus my source had alerted me. This was going to be the night. Bradley wanted to rile her. I don't think he expected her to cut him loose. He thought too much of himself when it came to the ladies. When your mother left, I was right behind her. There was nobody else in the house. Not until Bradley got there. My instructions were to take pictures, but only pictures that weighed in on the side of the Bydens."

"Your instructions," Kelsey said dully, "from my grandmother."

"That's right. It looked promising at first, her opening the door in that nightgown, letting him in. They had another drink, and he was pouring on the charm. I got a good shot through the window of them kissing. I didn't bother to take one of her shoving him away. That wasn't my job. They started to argue. I could hear snatches through the window when she shouted loud enough. She was telling him to get out. That they were through. He grabbed her, pawed at her."

Rooney lifted his eyes to Kelsey's. "There was a minute there when I thought about going in, breaking it up. She was in trouble. There was no way to mistake what kind of trouble. But I didn't go in. I had my job to do. In any case, she fought him off. She was

430

pissed, still more pissed than scared. She shouted at him, made a move for the phone, but he came after her again. I don't think she had any doubt about what was going to happen. She ran."

Rooney paused, wiped a hand over his mouth. "He knew I was there. The son of a bitch knew I was there. He looked right out the window and he pointed, like this." Rooney jerked a finger at the ceiling. "Upstairs, he was telling me. I'm going to take care of it upstairs. So I did what I'd been hired to do. I went up the tree. I couldn't hear anything, not the way my heart was pounding. I didn't let myself think. I had a job, a big one, one that was going to lead to a lot of others. And she'd asked for it, hadn't she? That's what I told myself. She'd asked for it, the way she'd been stringing him along."

"You knew he would rape her," Kelsey managed. "You knew. And you did nothing."

"That's right." Rooney downed the rest of his drink. "She came into the bedroom, came running in. She was scared then, but she was mad, too. That filmy robe she'd been wearing was falling off her shoulder where it was torn. He came in after her, and he smiled. He looked friendly, even apologetic. The way they were framed in the window, facing each other, so completely focused on each other, with her clothes falling off, and the shirt of his tux undone. It looked provocative. Even sexy. I don't know what he was saying to her, but she was shaking her head and backing up. He reached down, like he was going to unhook his pants. She slapped him." Rooney moistened his lips. "I got that on film. He slapped her back. I didn't take that shot."

He had to stop again. He hadn't realized how going through that night step by step would affect him. Then he'd felt small, and scared. Now he simply felt small.

"She made a dive. She was out of my view for a minute. He put his hands up. He was still smiling, but it didn't look so friendly now. Then I could see her again, and I saw the gun.

"I started taking pictures fast then. I was scared. I kept taking them after she shot him, even when there was nothing to see."

431

"It was self-defense." Kelsey's fingers dug into Gabe's. "Just as she said all along."

"Yeah, it was. Maybe, maybe she could have held him off once she had the gun. But she was scared. She was trapped. If all the facts had come out, I don't think they'd have charged her with so much as manslaughter. They sure as hell wouldn't have convicted her."

"But the facts didn't come out."

"No, I took them straight to Milicent Byden. I wasn't thinking, going to her house in the middle of the night, getting her out of bed. She poured me a brandy herself, told me to sit down. Then she listened to what I had to tell her. From beginning to end. She said it had worked out for the best. She instructed me to wait a day or two before going to the police."

"She knew," Kelsey whispered. "So, she knew everything."

"She orchestrated it. If Naomi hadn't been arrested by then, I was to take the film to the cops and give my statement. I was to tell them what I saw, only what I saw, not what I assumed, not what I interpreted. Then she told me what I'd seen. A woman, provocatively dressed, welcoming her lover into an empty house. They shared a drink, an embrace. Then they quarreled. The woman was jealous. That was obvious after the scene at the club. She went upstairs, her lover following to make apologies, amends, perhaps a seduction. And in a jealous rage, the woman took out a gun and killed him. She gave me another five thousand cash that night, and the promise of several references."

White-faced, Kelsey slid from the booth. With one hand pressed to her heaving stomach, she dashed toward the rest rooms.

Gabe watched her go. He found that his fists were balled under the table. "You're a revolting specimen, Rooney. A few thousand dollars and some fancy names on a client list. For that, you watched an attempted rape, then helped see that the victim was locked away."

"There's more," Rooney said. "We'll wait for Kelsey."

"Tell me this. Why did you decide to come out with all of this now? A few hours ago you had nothing to say."

"It's getting complicated. I don't like being squeezed from two sides." Rooney shrugged. "When this comes out, and I've decided it will, my reputation's shot. It looks to me like I'm about to retire a few years early. I might as well do it with a clean slate."

"I'm wondering," Gabe began, and his voice was cool, deceptively detached, "if I should take you outside and beat you to a pulp. Or if I should just let you live with this."

Rooney picked up his glass and sipped the melted ice cubes slowly. "We all make our choices, Slater. You're a gambler. When you know the house has stacked the deck, are you going to bet against it?"

"Some games you just don't play." He rose as Kelsey walked back to the booth.

"I'm all right. I'm sorry." She was still white around the lips, but her hand was steady when it gripped Gabe's.

"You hang on for a minute." He gave his attention back to Rooney. "Let's have the rest."

"You're not going to like it. Milicent Byden didn't hire me just to compile your dossier, Mr. Slater. That came later. She put me on retainer months ago, right after Kelsey contacted Naomi Chadwick."

Kelsey pressed her lips together, praying for her stomach to settle. "I don't understand." But she thought she did, she was terrified that she did.

"Flat out," Rooney continued, "she didn't want you there. Didn't want to take any chances that you and Naomi would click."

"How did she intend to prevent it?"

"Well, since there wasn't anything to smear Naomi with since she'd been released from prison, Milicent made use of the past. After Alec Bradley was shot, I took her my files. All of my files. There was a lot of detail in them. Not just about Naomi. I'm thorough, you see. I had documentation on Bradley and his associate.

433

The race fix, my suspicions on Cunningham's involvement. When she gave you a yank, Kelsey, and you didn't come to heel, she put that information to use."

"How?" Kelsey braced herself. "You'd better tell me how."

"She had me look up Bradley's old friend and lure him back to the area with the promise of a job. She didn't tell me what that job would be, but it didn't take long to figure it out. Not with history repeating itself. A fixed race, a dead colt. Gossip and suspicion circled around Naomi, and you." He jabbed a finger at Gabe. "Milicent didn't want you anywhere near her blood kin. Kelsey was supposed to see just how unsavory racing was, how ruthless. And she was supposed to run back home."

"But I didn't." Kelsey could feel tears burning at her eyes, but she wouldn't free them. Not now. Not yet. "You're telling me that she was behind it? Behind Pride's death? And, God, Mick's?"

"Even a woman like Milicent can't control a man with no ethics. You could say that her hireling momentarily got away from her. She was steamed after the groom's murder. Read me the riot act as if I'd stabbed the poor bastard myself." He shook his head, remembering. "The horse, now, that's what she wanted. A re-creation of crimes, a scandal to teach her granddaughter a lesson."

"Because of me," Kelsey murmured. Her hand lay limply under Gabe's. "All of it because of me."

"You're the last of the Byden line," Rooney pointed out. "She sets store by that. And she hates Naomi with a kind of cold-blooded passion that doesn't dilute with time. If she could ruin her again, and keep control over you, it would all be worth it. She lent Cunningham enough money to buy that horse, Big Sheba. More than enough to keep him under her thumb and persuade him to work with her button man. Not that she liked it," Rooney added. "Associating, even from a distance, with that type. But the ends justify."

"I don't think I know the woman you're talking about," Kelsey said slowly. "I don't think I recognize her. How could she ruin so many lives?"

434

"Control them," Rooney corrected. "She never considered any of it more than necessary control. And I went along with it." He rubbed a hand between his eyes. "The first time I was young, eager, impressionable. This time I felt trapped. And, hell, it was just a job. My last visitor of the day changed things." He studied Gabe's face for a long moment. "Maybe I'm getting old. Christ knows I'm tired. So when he showed up, trying to make a new deal, I cut my losses. And, maybe, I like to think that I figured it was time for a little atonement."

Rooney's eyes sharpened. "Do you want to know how Benny Morales's son did the Chadwick colt? How somebody nearly did one of yours, Slater? Look to your own organization, and look to your old man. That's right," he said, smiling a little. "Rich Slater wormed plenty of secrets out of Alec Bradley. And he was more than happy to use them, and repeat the sequence when Milicent Byden sent for him. Revenge and control, revenge and money. Her motives, and his. Makes a hell of a combination."

＄

# Chapter Twenty-Eight

"Pull over, will you?"

A half mile from Longshot, Gabe swung to the shoulder of the road. "Are you feeling sick again?"

"No." She was, but not in the way he meant. "I just need to walk for a minute. Can we walk?" Without waiting for his answer, she pushed out of the car.

The perfect night, she thought. The classic midsummer night in the country with a diamond-bright dome of sky, stars, and moon. Not even a wisp of a cloud to spoil it. The air smelled of the honey-suckle that was patiently burying the fence along the rolling field to the right. The high grass that grew beyond it was alive with the chirp of crickets. As she walked, the soft shoulder gave under Kelsey's feet.

"It's too much," she murmured. "It's just too much to take in. How can I tell her, Gabe?" She spun around, her hands reaching for his, for a solution. "How can I tell my mother that it was all planned? That everything that happened was all part of some scheme to keep her away from me?"

"First"—he reached up to tuck her hair behind her ear—"you stop blaming yourself."

"I'm not." She stopped, turning to lean on the fence, to look out over the shadowy hills. "But I'm angry that I was used, like a pawn. She wasn't even thinking of me as a child. I can see that. Not as a child, certainly not as a person. Progeny," Kelsey said bitterly. "That's all I was. All I am to her. Just the next Byden."

He started to speak, to offer some sort of comfort, then stopped. Sometimes it was kinder simply to listen.

"I think," Kelsey continued, "I really think she wanted to love me, that she tried, even succeeded for stretches of time. But the way she felt about my mother, and maybe—God, I hope—the guilt she lived with over what she'd done made it almost impossible. She wanted me to be a credit to the family name. Educated at the best schools, knowledgeable about the arts, competent in music and other acceptable pastimes. My friends had to be from the right families. Maybe that's why I never made any who were really close to me. And every small rebellion, every flash of my own personality or needs was seen as a mirror of the woman she'd ruined."

Kelsey plucked some honeysuckle from the vine and began slowly, systematically, to shred the fragile white blossoms.

"When I turned twelve, she wanted me to go to boarding school in England. My father refused. It was one of the few times I'd ever seen them quarrel. I needed discipline, I needed guidance. My father said I needed childhood."

With a sigh, she rubbed the tattered petals between her fingers, stinging the air with scent. "Did she realize that she was using him, too? Another pawn. How responsible is she, Gabe, for destroying their marriage, whatever chance they had of making it work? That's the least of it, though," she murmured, and let the blossoms fall. "Now I have to find a way to tell my mother why, and how, and who. And my father. I'll have to tell him too, won't I? He has a right to know everything she did then. Everything she's done now."

She turned to him then, pressing her face to his chest, grateful that his arms were there to wrap around her. "So much waste. So many lives lost or ruined. And it all trickles down to some horribly misplaced family pride."

"And a few more of the deadly sins," he said quietly, thinking of his own father. "Envy, greed, lust. I've always believed more in luck than fate. But it's more than luck that brought this full circle." He drew her back so he could see her face. "You and me, Kelsey. We've both been a part of it right from the beginning."

"And maybe we wouldn't be so close to ending it if we hadn't found each other. You'll want to find him now, won't you? Your father?"

"I'll have to find him."

"You could leave it to Rossi." Her grip tightened suddenly, urgently. "Gabe. He wants to hurt you. If he went to Rooney's office so soon after we did, he was probably following us. He's looking for a way to get to you."

"So, I'll find him first. That's my circle, Kelsey. I need to close it."

"But if we went to the police—"

"Why haven't we already called them?"

She looked away. He saw her heart, her needs too clearly. "All right. I need to talk to Naomi first, and you need to find your father. Then we'll end it. I guess you'd better take me home."

When they pulled up at Three Willows, she declined his offer to come in with her. She would do this alone. He waited until she went inside, until the front porch light went dark.

Gabe had his own demons to face. And the first wasn't his father.

Inside, Kelsey glanced up the stairs. It was late. Undoubtedly Naomi was in bed. Wait until morning, she thought. It's waited so long already, surely it could wait one more night. But that was cowardice. With a sigh, she headed toward the kitchen. She would brew a pot of tea first. That would give her a chance to sort out exactly how she would begin.

"Gertie?" Kelsey was surprised to find the housekeeper up, loading the dishwasher.

"Oh, Miss Kelsey, you gave me such a start." The woman pressed a hand to the bodice of her pink chenille robe.

"It's after midnight. You shouldn't be working so late."

"Oh, I was just putting my dishes in. There was a Bette Davis movie on the TV tonight, *Now, Voyager.* I had me some lemon cake and a good cry." She sighed happily over the thought of it. "They just don't make movies like that these days, Miss Kelsey."

"No, they don't." Struggling to hold a conversation, Kelsey moved to the range, her movements mechanical as she picked up the kettle and walked to the sink to fill it. "Is everyone else in bed?"

"You want some tea? Let me do that." Territorial, Gertie brushed her aside and set the kettle on to boil. "Channing's out with Matt Gunner. That Tennessee Walker of the Williamses got a case of the strangles. They don't know if he'll make it until morning."

"Oh, I'm sorry."

"Well, it's a shame, that's the truth." Gertie busied herself warming a china pot while waiting for the kettle to boil. "But I have to say Channing was mighty excited at the idea of sitting up half the night in a barn. I told him I'd leave the kitchen door unlatched for him, and there's a nice cold plate of chicken in the fridge."

"Then undoubtedly he'll be in heaven."

"It's a pleasure having him around here."

"For me, too. I need two cups, Gertie. I want to take a cup up to my mother."

"Oh, she's sleeping, honey." Gertie chose the chamomile and measured the leaves out by sight. "Fact is, she looked so tired out and upset about something, that I had her take a sleeping pill just an hour ago."

"A sleeping pill?"

"She said I was fussing, but she didn't look well to me. All drawn out and pale. A good night's sleep is what she needed, and I told her so. I was going to check on her before I went to bed."

"I'll do it." Kelsey looked at the teapot with a mixture of resignation and relief. "Just one cup then, Gertie, thanks. I'll talk to her in the morning."

"She'll be fine then. Just overtired, I expect." Gertie put the pot on a tray, arranged the cup and saucer. "She's looked better, happier these past few months than she has in a long, long time. That's your doing. It don't matter what else goes on, a mother pines for her child."

"I'm here now."

"I know it, honey. Don't you stay up too late."

"I won't. Good night, Gertie."

Kelsey carried the tray upstairs, setting it in her room before going to look in on her mother. In the slant of moonlight through the window, she could see Naomi sleeping, deeply.

So it would be in the morning after all, she thought, and slipped into her own room to wait for the dawn.


GABE DIDN'T BOTHER TO STOP in at the house, but drove straight to the barn. He saw the light above the tack room and grimly circled around and climbed the stairs. He didn't knock.

Jamison sat at his desk, paperwork in neat, organized piles, a single glass of brandy at his elbow. He looked up, blinking owlishly.

"Gabe. What brings you up here so late?"

"I could ask you the same."

"Oh, well." With a tired smile, Jamison gestured at the stacks of papers. "There's always something needs dealing with. It's easier to concentrate at night, when things are quiet. There's a jar of instant coffee over there," he added. "You can heat up the pot on the hot plate."

"No." Gabe studied his trainer, his friend, in the yellow light of the desk lamp. The past months of strain and worry had taken their toll. The shadows under his eyes were like bruises, the lines bracketing his mouth so sharp and deep they might have been carved by a knife.

440

Not the face of a man who had recently trained a horse to the Triple Crown.

"I used to hang around the barn a lot when I worked here, didn't I, Jamie? Tagged after you or Mick."

"That you did." Jamison relaxed the shoulders that had gone tense under Gabe's scrutiny. "Or you'd hustle us into a poker game and hose us out of a week's pay."

"Cunningham never gave you much peace, as I remember. If you had one winner, he wanted two. Always a bigger race, a bigger purse. I remember he was always saying Moses over at Three Willows knew how to turn out champions. And if you didn't, he'd find someone who could."

"He was a hard man to work for. I trained good horses for him, won a lot of races. Had Horse of the Year back in the eighties with Try Again. But I never satisfied him."

"He wanted a Derby winner. You never pulled that off. Even after the Chadwicks lost that colt at Keeneland back in—what was it? Seventy-three—and Cunningham's was the favorite, you didn't pull it off."

Gabe's voice was quiet, cool. "That colt came in third, as I remember. A disappointing third. That must have been hard to take after all you'd gone through to see him under the wire first."

The memory had Jamison's mouth twitching. "A show at the Derby's no shame. The colt didn't run his best that day, lost it in the last furlong. And things were hard around here, mighty hard." He lifted his brandy, drank. "After Benny hung himself."

"You and Benny were tight."

"We were good friends."

"Yeah. Good friends." Gabe turned a chair around, straddled it. "How much did you have to do with it, Jamie? Then and now?"

"What are you getting at?"

"You and Benny were close. Did you talk him into fixing the race, or did you just go along with it? I'll tell you what I think," Gabe continued, without waiting for an answer. "I think you asked him to help you out. Give the colt a little edge. Cunningham was pushing you for that edge. Maybe he offered you a bigger cut of the purse. Maybe he just kept the pressure on you until you broke. And when you broke, you took Benny Morales along with you."

His eyes never left Jamison's face. "A Derby win, Jamie. Something you've always wanted, and up until now, never quite pulled off."

"That's foolish talk, Gabe. You've known me too long."

"I have, Jamie. I've known you too long not to know that nothing goes on in that barn that you don't have a hand in. I didn't put you together with what happened to the Three Willows colt this time, or what nearly happened to mine. My mistake," he said, watching Jamison's eyes drop. "Never figured you'd kill a horse just to win a race. Any race."

Gabe took out a cigar, studying it from tip to tip while Jamison remained silent. "That's what blinded me, Jamie, until Reno. He didn't know it was a lethal dose. Neither did you. You were just giving my colt the edge, weren't you, by seeing that Pride was eliminated? Is that how my father put it to you, Jamie? Give yourself the edge."

"I wanted my own place," Jamison whispered. "A man deserves his own after so many years of tending someone else's. Any other year that colt would've won the Derby laughing. Why was it Moses should have one that could match him? Why was it?"

"Bad luck." Gabe lit his cigar. He'd stopped feeling sorrow. He'd stopped feeling grief.

"You wanted that win, Gabe. Don't tell me you didn't."

"Yeah, I wanted it. I won't tell you I didn't."

"Are you going to tell me you wouldn't have looked the other way if you'd known?"

Gabe's eyes flashed up. No, it wasn't sorrow in them. And it was a long way from grief. "If you thought that, why did you hide it from me?"

"You were a wild card. That's how Rich put it. You were a wild card, and you couldn't be trusted. Look how that colt ran, Gabe," he said, desperate. "Think about that. He took the three jewels and nothing could stop him."

"At what cost? It's not just a dead horse, Jamie. It's Mick, and it's Reno."

Jamison's eyes filled, swam with tears. "That wasn't my doing. Jesus God, Gabe, you can't believe that was my doing. Lipsky went off on his own. I didn't even know about it until after. Then it was too late."

His voice broke. For a moment there was only the sound of his labored breathing. With an effort, he pulled himself back. "Rich wanted to give you something to think about, but he didn't tell me until after. I didn't know he was going to go after Double, Gabe. God is my witness. It was to be the Three Willows colt. A scandal, a disqualification."

He shuddered, waiting for Gabe to speak, veering closer to the edge when there was only silence. "You've got to figure that Rich and Cunningham worked it out, Gabe. You've got to figure it."

"That's right. I've got to figure it."

"The disqualification wasn't enough for Rich. The money he got for fixing it wasn't enough. He's greedy, you know that. He used us to kill that colt. I suffered when that horse went down. When I knew what he'd had us do. And Reno." He buried his face in his hands. "I cared about that boy. Afterward, I told him it wasn't his fault, but he wouldn't listen. It's Rich who's responsible. For all of it. Then he comes around here, and he changes the rules."

"How?"

Jamison dropped his hands, wiped the back of one over his mouth. He picked up the brandy again, drank it like medicine.

"He didn't want you to win the Triple Crown, Gabe. It was eating him inside out to think you could. He told me it was a job, just a little side bet he had going. But it was money he wanted. He had me, don't you see? He had me and Reno both. But I wasn't going to hurt Double, you have to believe that. I got the drug myself this time. It was only going to be enough to eliminate him."

Gabe's eyes narrowed down into points of flame. "The night Kelsey came into the barn. It was you, wasn't it? You're the one who hurt her."

"I didn't do her any real harm. I just had to get out before she saw me. I got Kip out of the way. Didn't do more than give him a headache. Then, when she came in, I couldn't finish. I just—"

"I could break you in half for that alone, Jamie." Quick as a snake, Gabe's hand shot out, closed around Jamison's throat. "For that alone," he murmured, squeezing.

"I panicked, Gabe." Terrified, Jamison clawed at Gabe's iron grip. "Jesus, I was half out of my mind. Can't you see?"

"I see a lot of things." Disgusted, Gabe released him.

The ugly mottled red began to fade from Jamison's face as he gulped in air. "He had me trapped. Don't you see? I told Rich I wouldn't do it, but he said if it wasn't done, we were going to pay. So I tried, even though it was breaking my heart, I tried. But it didn't work. Reno was supposed to do it the day of the Belmont, but he couldn't. Jesus, Gabe, he hung himself. A horse isn't worth dying for."

"But it's worth killing for?"

"I told you, I didn't—"

"Tell yourself," Gabe spat out. "Tell yourself you were a victim, Jamie. That you were used. That what happened to Benny Morales, and Mick, and Reno, and even to Lipsky was just the luck of the draw. Then see if you can live with it." He rose, kicking the chair aside.

"I did what I had to do. And I stood up to him. Just tonight I stood up to him."

Gabe's head jerked up. "What are you talking about?"

"Rich was here. Not an hour ago. Drunk, mean. He was talking wild. About killing the horses, burning the barn. Christ knows what he'd have done if I hadn't held him off."

Gabe whirled and was bounding down the steps with Jamie shouting after him. He hit the lights in the barn, choking back fear as he systematically checked every box.

"I told you I didn't let him in here," Jamison said. "I told him to get out, to go sleep it off. That we were finished. I wasn't doing his dirty work anymore. Not after Reno. No matter what."

Gabe stood outside Double's box. The colt sidled forward, nuzzled lazily at his hand. "You're finished, Jamie. Pack up and get out tonight."

"A man's entitled to a place of his own. You should know that."

"Yeah, I know that. But yours isn't here, not anymore."

Within twenty minutes, Gabe had roused three grooms and posted them in the barn. Until he ran his father to ground, there would be a twenty-four-hour watch. He'd be back, Gabe thought, as he strode toward the house. The combination of greed and hate would draw him back.

Nothing would satisfy Rich Slater except his son's total misery. What was most important, most cherished, had to be destroyed.

But this time it would be different. This time ... The blood drained out of Gabe's face as his own thoughts circled back in his head. What was most important. Most cherished.

Kelsey.

GERTIE TRIED OUT A NEW NIGHT cream she'd ordered from one of the shop-at-home channels, a guilty pleasure she sometimes indulged in on the kitchen television. The young and perky saleswoman on the screen had touted the cream as something akin to a rebirth.

Gertie didn't expect miracles, only a temporary reprieve from the lines that seemed to bloom on her face with increasing regularity.

Vanity, she clucked at her mirrored reflection. Foolish vanity for a woman who had lived on this earth for more than half a century. But when she looked closely, she thought maybe, just maybe she could spot a slight softening around the eyes where the crow had dug his feet in the deepest.

Satisfied with the new nightly ritual, she stood to remove her robe, then smiled when she heard the sound of the kitchen door creaking open.

That boy would raid the refrigerator for sure, she thought, and likely leave a mess. Boys Channing's age never chased down crumbs. She'd just go along and fix him a plate herself, see that he washed it down with milk instead of that soda pop he was always guzzling.

"I hear you out there," she said as she swung into the kitchen from her adjoining room. "No use sneaking around. You just sit yourself down, and I'll . . ." She stopped, frowning. In the glow of the range light she'd left on for Channing, the kitchen was quiet, spotless, and empty. "Ears playing tricks on me," she muttered. "Maybe they'll start selling something for that on the TV."

She started to turn, then pain burst in her head. She managed one tiny, birdlike cry as she crumpled to the tile.

Rich stood over her, grinning. Coshed the skinny old bitch with her own rolling pin, he thought, and tapped the smooth heavy marble against his palm. He toed at her side, lightly, catching himself when the one-footed stance had him weaving.

Need a little balance, he decided, and reached into his back pocket for his flask. When no more than a few miserly drops hit his tongue, he swore. Stuffing the empty flask back into his pocket, he stepped over the unconscious Gertie. They were bound to have some liquor around here, he thought. Prime stuff, too. Once he'd fueled himself up, he'd hunt up Gabe's pretty little pigeon.

UPSTAIRS, KELSEY DRANK another cup of tea while she paced her room. She wished Channing would get home. At least then she'd be able to talk to someone. And who would understand better than he this horrible conflict of family loyalties? Even

Gabe, for all his support, didn't share the same memories, the same affections and frustrations. Channing, when the trouble was real, was a rock.

In the morning, in a few short hours, she would tell Naomi everything she'd learned. Once the story was told, Kelsey knew she would be freeing one woman she loved, and condemning another.

For under all the bitterness, the anger, and the painful disappointment, she still loved her grandmother.

The Magnificent Milicent, she thought, shutting her eyes. How would she survive the scandal, let alone the legal consequences? And there were bound to be consequences.

And how, Kelsey asked herself, would she be able to live with the fact that what she'd done, and what she would do, could send her own grandmother to prison?

A tinkling crash of glass from downstairs had her biting back a gasp. Channing, she thought, setting down her cup. She hadn't heard him drive up, but he was obviously down there, fumbling through the dark in a very poor attempt not to wake the rest of the house.

Relieved, Kelsey hurried out of her room and down the stairs to find him.

"Channing, you idiot. What did you break? If that was one of Naomi's crystal horses, there will be hell to pay."

At the base of the stairs she stopped, listening. The house was quiet now. Quiet enough to run a chill up her arms. Stop it, she ordered herself, and rubbed them warm. "Come on, Channing, I'm not in the mood to play games. I really need to talk to you."

She snapped on the light in the foyer.

"Look, I know you're down here. Your catlike grace always gives you away. It's important, Channing."

Annoyed now, she marched into the sitting room. In the glow of moonlight she saw the glint of shattered glass on the rug.

"Dammit! It was one of the horses. Nice going, ace." She hurried over, kneeling down to pick up shards.

447

"All the queen's horses," Rich said, and switched on the lights. "All the queen's men." He grinned down at Kelsey. "But can the queen's lovely daughter put any of them back together again?"

He threw back his head and laughed at the sheer poetry of it.

# Chapter Twenty-Nine

KELSEY GASPED IN SURPRISE AND PAIN AS HER HAND CONTRACTED around a sliver of glass. Blood welled on her palm.

"Careful there, honey pie." Rich sauntered over. "You could slice yourself to ribbons." He tut-tutted over the cut on her hand, then gallantly offered her a handkerchief. "Didn't mean to give you such a start, but I thought it was time we had ourselves a chat. Seeing as you're warming my boy's bed most nights."

"You're Gabe's father." Kelsey scrambled to her feet, but not quickly enough. Rich's hand shot out, locked around her arm.

"There's a family resemblance, isn't there? The ladies always said we made a handsome pair, me and my boy." His eyes, bright with liquor and anticipation, skimmed over her face. "Why, you're even prettier close up, doll face. It isn't hard to see why my boy's been sniffing around you. No indeedy. It isn't hard at all. Here now." He stuffed the handkerchief into her bleeding hand. "You wrap that up."

She obeyed automatically. "If you're looking for Gabe—" She broke off, reevaluated quickly. "He's—upstairs," she said. "I'll go up and tell him you're here."

"The one thing I never tolerated from a woman was a lie." With one flick, he shoved her into a chair hard enough to snap her head back. "You'd better get that straight right now." He leaned over the chair, trapping her between his arms. "Gabe's not upstairs, now, is he? I saw him drop you off out of his fancy car just a little while ago. Don't know why he'd go home to a cold bed when he has something like you. But I always had a hard time teaching the boy anything."

He patted her cheek, pleased with the swell of power when she cringed back. "But this works out real cozy. Just you and me, getting acquainted. Whoops. What's this here?" Chuckling, he pinched his fingers at her wrist, forced her hand up. "That's a whopper now, isn't it?" he said, eyeing her ring. "Is that what I think it is?" He wagged his finger in front of her face. "Is my boy going to make an honest woman out of you, honey pie? Well, you're a real step up from most of the sluts he's snuggled with before. No offense."

"No," she said, hoping to play the game out. "No offense taken. Gabe and I are going to be married in August. I hope you'll be there."

She cried out in shock when the back of his hand swiped across her face. His genial expression never altered. "Now, what did I tell you about lying? What you and that boy of mine would like is for me to drop dead on the spot. Wouldn't you?"

She blinked to clear her vision. "I don't know you," she said carefully. But she knew enough to be afraid, and her trembling gave her away.

"You know me. I'll give you odds my loving son's told you all about me. Your mama, too." The thought of Naomi soured his grin. "She'd have something to say about good old Rich Slater."

Kelsey anchored her chin to keep it from trembling. "I'm sorry. She's never mentioned you."

His smile thinned. "Bitch. Always was a bitch. You take right after her."

"In some ways. You're hurting me, Mr. Slater."

"Rich, honey. Or better yet, you call me Daddy. Since we're going to be family." The idea of it had him hooting with laughter until tears filled his eyes. "One big happy family. I bet that old icicle's fuming over that. Did I mention I know your grandma? I know her real well. She must be foaming at the mouth at the idea of her hoity-toity granddaughter playing house with a son of mine. She hated your mama, you know. Hated her right down to the ground."

"I know."

"You know what I think?" He reached up, pinched Kelsey's throbbing cheek hard enough to make her gasp. "I think you should fix us both a nice drink. Then we'll get to know each other."

"All right." When he stepped back, Kelsey eased out of the chair. Her eyes darted to the patio doors, to the doorway that led to the foyer. If she could get out of the room, she was sure she could outrun him.

"You don't want to try that, honey." He pinched her arm again, his fingers digging down to the bone. "You don't want to."

"There's brandy in the cabinet there. Napoleon."

"Well, that's just fine and dandy." He kept his hand on her arm and dragged her to it. "Pour us both a couple of healthy swallows."

He was already drunk, she thought frantically. If she poured with a generous-enough hand, she might slip past his guard. "Gabe said you've done a lot of traveling."

"I've been here and there."

"I like new places." She smiled and handed him a snifter. "Cheers." She tapped her glass to his.

"You're a cool one." Rich tossed back the brandy, then let out a long, pleased sigh. "That's one of the things that appealed to me most about your mother. She was one long, cool drink of water, that Naomi. She never would give me a sip, though. Let plenty of others drink great big gulps, but she never let good old Rich have

451

one little sip. Maybe she will now. I bet I can make her change her mind. Is she upstairs?"

"She's not home." Before the words were out, Kelsey was reeling back. The blow had stars bursting in front of her eyes as she fell.

"Lying bitch." With a thin smile, Rich drank more brandy. "Cold-eyed lying bitch, just like your ma. Maybe you'd rather I had a taste of you instead." He laughed until his sides ached at the expression of animal terror on her face. "No, no, that wouldn't be proper, poking in where my boy's already been. Besides, I prefer a more . . . mature woman. And Naomi, she's been around the track a time or two, now, hasn't she? Now, maybe if your grandma had hired me instead of the coke-snorting Bradley, things would be different. Why don't we go ask Naomi if she'd like to give Rich a try now?"

"Stay away from her." Her head spun sickeningly as she lurched to her feet. Her vision was blurred where the blow had struck her eye. "I'll kill you if you touch her."

"Yeah, just like your ma. Kill a man for doing what comes natural."

"We know all about you." Dizzy, she leaned against the cabinet. She just needed a minute, she told herself. To clear the pain from her head, to get some feeling back in her watery legs. "Gabe's not here because he went for the police. They'll be here any minute."

She teetered back, nearly falling when he lifted his hand again.

"You want to tell the truth to me, honey pie. Or I'm going to spoil that pretty face of yours."

"It is the truth. We met Charles Rooney tonight. He called after you came to his office. He told us everything." Praying for time, she began to list the details. He believed her now; she could see it in his face. And what she saw there told her he could do worse, a great deal worse than slap her again.

"They'll find you here if you stay," she continued. "They'll find you and they'll put you in prison. The way they put my mother in prison. You could probably still get away. They might not catch you if you ran."

"They've got nothing on me. Nothing." He took her untouched brandy and drank it down. "It's all air. And you're forgetting Grandma."

"No, I'm not. They put my mother away with lies. It'll be easy to put you away with the truth."

"He'd turn me in." Enraged, Rich tossed the snifter, shattering the glass on the hearth in a parody of celebration. "My own flesh and blood would turn me in. We'll have to make him sorry for that. Real sorry."

He lunged. Panic and youth had Kelsey spinning to the side so that he caught nothing more than the sleeve of her blouse. As the seam ripped, she tore away, making a dash for the doorway.

He caught her, bringing her down in a lumbering tackle that radiated pain down to the bone. Panting out sobs, she kicked out blindly, landing a glancing blow off his shoulder, another off his chest as she clawed her way inch by desperate inch over the rug.

He was going to kill her now, she was sure of it. Beat her or choke her with those big bruising hands. And when he was done, he'd go after Naomi.

She screamed once when he yanked her head back by the hair. Light flashed in front of her eyes, wheeled like comets fired by the hideous pain. If she had found her voice she might have begged then, pleaded and begged. But the air was searing in and out of her throat.

"Gotcha, don't I? Gotcha. Thought you were such a smart little bitch."

Her fingers dug into the carpet, reached, then closed over an inch-long shard of crystal. Mindless with terror and pain, she swung out.

Then it was he who screamed, rearing back, the blood spurting out of his cheek where the delicate foreleg of the glass Thoroughbred had pierced his flesh.

Whimpering, she dragged herself up and raced from the room in a panicked, limping run while his curses chased after her.

She fell on the stairs, fighting for breath, struggling to clear enough of the fear from her mind so that she could think. When she called out, trying to warn her mother, only little mewling sounds escaped. With blood and fear stinging her mouth, she clawed her way up, gaining her feet and the top of the stairs just as she heard Rich charging up behind her.

"No!" She snatched a vase of lilies and hurled it down at him. The crash and a grunt of pain bought her a few precious seconds, wasted as she fumbled with bloody hands at the knob of her mother's bedroom door. "Mom! Oh God, Mom!" With one blind burst of strength, she shoved through the door and slammed it behind her. "Mom! Get up!" She was weeping as she fought the lock with fingers gone numb with terror. "For God's sake, get up!"

In a lunge she was at the bed, dragging Naomi up by the shoulders, shaking, pleading.

"Wha—?" Groggy from the sleeping pill, Naomi pushed her daughter's hand away, annoyed. "What is it?"

"He's coming. Wake up! We have to get out. Do you understand me?"

"Who's coming?" Naomi blinked open heavy eyes. "Kelsey? What is it?"

"He'll kill us! Get out of bed, goddammit!" She screamed again when Rich hurled his weight against the door. "Get out of bed!" Breath coming in hot gasps, she turned terrified eyes to the door. "It's not going to hold. Sweet Jesus, it won't hold. The gun. Do you still have the gun?"

She babbled out little prayers as she clawed open the nightstand drawer. It was there, the chrome glinting in the moonlight.

"What are you doing?" Sleepy and dazed, Naomi managed to fight her way through the mists to kneel in bed. "Good God, Kelsey, what are you doing? Who's at the door?"

But as the wood splintered, Kelsey stared straight ahead. She held the gun in both hands, struggling to keep it from slipping out of her shaking fingers.

He burst in, blood glistening on his cheek. And saw only Naomi, kneeling in the bed with the thin silk gown sliding from her shoulders. His teeth flashed as he leaped forward. Kelsey felt the gun buck like a live thing, sending vibrations singing up to her shoulders.

She never heard the shot.

"Alec?" The wooziness floated over Naomi's mind, sliding images of past and present.

"It's not Alec." Kelsey heard her own voice, small with distance. "It's Gabe's father. I've killed Gabe's father."

"Slater?" Half dreaming, Naomi crawled out of bed and, as she had done so many years ago, bent over a dead man. Mechanically she checked his pulse before straightening again. "Rich Slater?" Confused, she rubbed her hands over her eyes. "What in God's name is happening here?"

"I killed him." Kelsey dropped her arm, the gun dangling from her fingers.

Naomi looked up into her daughter's face. She recognized the shock, the disbelief, and the fear. She forced her trembling legs to move forward.

"Sit down, Kelsey. That's right, sit down." She eased her gently onto the side of the bed. Nothing mattered now, nothing but Kelsey.

"Let me have the gun. Okay." Naomi set it aside for the moment. It would take no time at all to deal with it. "Put your head between your legs now and breathe."

"I can't. I can't breathe."

"Yes, you can. Slow and deep. That's it, honey." As Kelsey tried to obey, Naomi outlined her plan. "Now, I'm going to tell you what we're going to do, and I want you to listen very carefully and do exactly, just exactly what I tell you. Understand?"

"He was going to kill me, and you. He would have killed us both. But I killed him. I don't remember pulling the trigger, but I must have." Her teeth began to chatter. "Because I shot him."

"No, *I* shot him. Look at me. Kelsey." Gently, Naomi lifted Kelsey's ravaged face. "Oh, God." She shuddered, dug her nails into her palms until the pain cleared some of the shock. "Listen to me, baby. He broke in, and he . . ." She brushed at a cut on Kelsey's cheek. "And he hurt you. So I got the gun, and I shot him."

"No, that's wrong. I couldn't wake you up."

"No, no, honey. I woke up when you came in. You came in here to get away from him. Then he broke down the door and I shot him. I'm going to call the police now, and that's exactly what we're going to tell them."

"I don't"—Kelsey lifted a hand to her spinning head—"I don't—" She jerked around and screamed at the sound of feet pounding up the stairs.

"Jesus God." Gabe took one look at his father, then stared at the two women huddled on the bed. "Kelsey!" In one leap he was crouched in front of her, holding her wounded hands. "He hurt you. Look at your face." He jumped up, his eyes hard, deadly. "I'll kill him myself."

"I already have," Naomi said calmly. "Gabe, get her out of here. Take her to her room. I'll call the police."

"I'm all right," Kelsey insisted, but the room faded out as she pushed herself to her feet.

"You just need to lie down." Gabe picked her up. "I'll take care of you." He looked back at Naomi. "I'll take care of her."

"Make her stay in there until I've finished this." Naomi lifted the bedside phone.

"He was just there," Kelsey murmured, shivering as Gabe carried her to her room and laid her on the bed. "He was just there. He broke the horse."

"Just lie still." He wanted to hold her. He wanted to crush

456

something, someone into dust. Instead he whipped the bedspread over her. She was shaking badly, her pupils contracted to pinpoints with shock. And her face . . . Gabe's hands balled helplessly at his sides. Her face was bruised and bleeding. He couldn't think; just then he couldn't allow himself to think that his own father had done that to her.

He went quickly into the bathroom, dampened a washcloth, and filled a cup with water.

"Here, baby." Gently, he curved an arm under her and brought the cup to her lips. "Drink some of this."

"He was downstairs." Her fingers fretted at the bedspread. "It wasn't Channing. The little horse was shattered, and he was just there. He kept smiling. He kept hitting me and smiling."

The hand on the wet cloth clenched until the knuckles went white. "He won't hurt you anymore." With fingers no more steady than hers, he washed away the blood. "Hold on to me, Kelsey. No one's going to hurt you anymore."

"I couldn't bluff." Shivering, she curled against him. She was cold, so cold, and he held the heat. "I tried, but I was so scared, and so angry. And he knew, and he'd hit me again." She turned her battered face into Gabe's throat. "He has such big hands."

And preferred to use them, Gabe thought grimly, on women. "I'd have killed him for this," he murmured. "Killed him with my own hands for touching you."

"It wasn't me." Suddenly she was so tired, so horribly, horribly tired. "It was you. He wanted to hurt you."

"I know." He turned his head just enough to brush his lips over her brow, then he eased her back on the pillows. "It's over now."

She let her eyes close for a moment. As the worst of the shock ebbed, the pain crept back. Her body felt trampled. "You came." Blindly she groped for his hand, found it.

"Yeah." He looked down at their joined hands. "A hunch. The trouble was I moved on it too late."

Her eyes opened again, fresh panic flashing. "Naomi."

"She's fine. If you'd been alone ..." The thought of that had talons of fear clawing through his gut. "Kelsey, I'm going to give you an out. Right now."

"An out?" Though she wasn't sure she would like what she found, she lifted a hand to probe at her throbbing face.

"If I were fair, I'd do the walking."

"Walking?" The heavy fog was lifting. She could see him clearly now. The strain that tightened his face, the swirl of emotion in his eyes. "Gabe." She touched a hand to his cheek as if to brush some color and calm into it. "Don't. I'm all right now."

"He battered your face. He tore your clothes. He terrified you." Deliberately he pried her clutching hand from his and rose. "He was my father. It doesn't matter that I've worked all my life to rid myself of any part of him. It's blood, and it'll always be there. I've got no place in your life, Kelsey. The biggest favor I could do for you is to walk out of it."

With some effort, she pushed herself up. Pain was singing in every bone now. "Did I ask you for a damn favor?" she snapped out. She winced as the scream of sirens sliced through the night and into her throbbing head. "If you want to do me one, then get me a bottle of aspirin, and keep your ridiculous grand gestures to yourself."

He nearly smiled. "I'm trying to be noble."

"Well, you're no good at it. And I don't like noble. I like you." She brushed her hair back, eyed him narrowly. "Do you think you can sneak out of this when I'm down? We had a deal, Slater, and you're not going to welsh."

"I never welsh." He sat on the edge of the bed again, and placed his hands lightly on her shoulders. "And that's my last shot at nobility. A hell of a hero I make anyway. It should have been me who killed him, Kelsey."

She crossed a hand over her body to clasp his. "Don't. You couldn't know that he would be here, that he would do this. And still you came." Her brow furrowed. "Why did you come?"

458

"It doesn't matter now. But it should have been me. It should have been me and not Naomi who killed him."

Kelsey drew back, her face paling again. "It wasn't you," she said slowly. "And it wasn't Naomi. I killed your father, Gabe."

NAOMI SIPPED THE BRANDY SLOWLY. She was sitting in the kitchen. The lights were very bright, and hurt her eyes. Her hands were trembling.

But she could deal with it. Would deal with it.

All she could think was that her daughter was upstairs, hurt, terrorized. And Gertie, sweet Gertie was in an ambulance on her way to the hospital.

"He must have come in this way," she said. "Hit Gertie. She'll be all right, won't she?" Control slipped a notch, and her lips trembled. "She's so small and she's so harmless."

"The paramedics said she was lucid, Ms. Chadwick." Rossi kept his voice low. The woman looked as though she would shatter into bits at any moment. "We'll check on her once they've had time to get her to the hospital."

"Moses should have gone with her. I should have made him go."

"He's not going to leave you. We're having a hard-enough time keeping him outside. Just tell me what happened."

Naomi drew in a deep breath and began. "He got in the house. I don't know how. I was upstairs in bed, sleeping. A noise woke me. Before I could get up, Kelsey ran into my room. She was terrified, hysterical. Her face . . . I could see where he'd hit her."

She pressed a hand to her mouth. She'd slept through that. Slept while he'd beaten her child.

"Then there was banging at the bedroom door. As if someone were throwing himself against it. I got the gun out of the drawer beside the bed. When he broke in, I shot him."

Rossi watched her as she lifted her glass, cupping her other hand over it to try to keep it steady as she drank.

459

"You were in bed when you shot him, Ms. Chadwick?"

"Yes. No." She set the glass down. She had to be careful. She had to be very careful. "I was in front of the window. I'd gotten up. It happened very fast."

"You say a noise woke you, but your daughter ran in before you could get up and see what it was?"

"Yes." Why did they always repeat what she said? They'd done that before, she remembered. It didn't matter what she said. It never mattered.

"Have you been into the sitting room, Ms. Chadwick, since you notified the police?"

"No." She pressed her lips together. If it was a trick, she couldn't see it. "I didn't come down. I stayed upstairs until you came."

"You've got a hell of a mess in there. Blood, broken furniture. I'd say that much damage took some time to accomplish. Time enough for anyone to get out of bed and check things out."

"I—I was frightened." Should she tell him she'd taken a sleeping pill? Yes. No. "I stayed in my room because I was frightened."

"With a phone right beside you, and a gun in the drawer?"

She looked up, met his eyes. "He broke into my bedroom," she said evenly. "And I shot him."

"No, she didn't." Kelsey stepped into the kitchen. Though she was grateful for the support of Gabe's arm, she made herself move away from it. "She didn't kill anyone."

"You shouldn't be down here." Panicked, Naomi pushed away from the table. "Take her back upstairs, Gabe. You can see she's hurt." She clamped a desperate hand on Rossi's arm. "You can see she's hurt. Look what that bastard did to her. Look what he did to my child. She's in shock. She doesn't know what happened."

"Stop it." Kelsey stepped up to the table. In the strong light her cuts and bruises stood out in stark relief against her pale skin. "I'm not going to let you do this. It isn't necessary. And it isn't right."

"Why don't you sit down, Ms. Byden?" Rossi invited. "And tell me what happened."

"No!" In a lunge Naomi rounded the table and gripped Kelsey's arms. "Listen to me, Kelsey. You're hurt, you're confused. Gabe will take you to the hospital, and I'll handle this."

"No." She shook her head, moving in to draw Naomi close. "Mom, no."

"I'm not going to let you go through this. I won't!" Trembling now, she hugged Kelsey tight. "You don't know what it's like. It won't matter what you say. It won't matter what happened. They'll take you away, Kelsey. Please, please, listen to me!"

"It does matter," Kelsey murmured. "It's not like before."

But it was, Naomi thought. Of course it was. "My fingerprints are on the gun." Stone-faced, Naomi turned back to Rossi. "The gun was in my room. He was killed in my room. That should be enough for you."

"Naomi," Gabe said gently, "sit down."

"You said you'd take care of her." She turned to him. "You said you would. Now make her go upstairs."

"Ms. Chadwick." Rossi studied her eyes. "There's a very simple test that will prove whether it was you or your daughter who discharged the weapon."

"I don't give a damn about your tests. You're not putting my daughter in a cell."

"I think we can agree on that. Sit down. Please," Rossi added.

"Come on." Kelsey draped an arm over Naomi's shoulders. "There's nothing for you to worry about. I promise."

"Would you like some brandy, Ms. Byden?" Rossi asked when she was settled at the table.

Kelsey looked down at the snifter and shuddered. "No. I've lost my taste for it." She drew a deep breath. "I heard glass breaking downstairs," she began.

# Chapter Thirty

THERE WAS DEW SPARKLING ON THE GRASS. FROM HER CHAIR on the patio, Kelsey watched it gleam, knowing the sun would soon be strong enough to burn it away.

Down at the barn, horses were being worked, stalls cleaned, troughs filled. Her body still ached enough to prevent her from resenting the fact that she'd been banned from the routine for a week.

She glanced around as the door opened behind her, and she smiled at her mother. "Gertie?"

"She's feeling better. She's fussing." With a sigh, Naomi sat, stretched out her legs. She thought about pouring coffee from the pot Kelsey had on the table, but she felt entirely too lazy. "I'm using guilt to keep her in bed for another day or two. If she gets up, I'll worry."

"Sneaky."

"Whatever works. Right now she's buying out the shopping channels. How are you feeling?"

"I'm fine, until I look in the mirror." She grimaced. Over the last two days some of the bruises had faded, but others had blossomed. "Until I do, it all seems almost like a dream. I don't know if it's just a stage I'm stuck in. I know I killed a man, but I can't seem to feel the horror of it."

"Don't try. You did what you had to do to protect yourself. And me." Naomi lifted her face to the sun. "I don't even remember him, Kelsey. Not really. I suppose I saw him around the track now and then. Maybe even spoke to him. But I don't really remember. I keep thinking I should, that it all should be vivid in my mind. How can I not remember a man who had so much to do with the way my life turned out?"

"He never mattered to you. And he knew it. That was part of the anger that built up in him. He found a way to make you pay, and to make a profit." She pushed the plate of croissants toward Naomi.

"Sun Spot," Naomi murmured. "God, I loved that horse. Yes, he certainly made me pay."

"She—Grandmother—used Alec Bradley for that, for a lot of things. And Cunningham."

"Bill." On a long breath, Naomi shook her head. "He's so much more of a fool than I guessed. And what good did it do him, Kelsey, then or now?"

"He didn't pay before. But he'll pay now. The police, the Racing Commission, they'll see that Cunningham pays for what he did to Pride, and to Sun Spot."

"All those years ago. No one ever put it together."

"It might have ended there, with the lies and the misery, if Gabe hadn't come back. If he hadn't drawn an inside straight." She smiled as Naomi tore off a corner of a roll. "If he hadn't made himself into the man he is."

"And if you hadn't fallen in love with him. That's something that smooths away the worst of it, Kelsey. When I think of what could have happened—"

"It didn't. Rich Slater paid the price for his part in it. And the case is closed. Self-defense."

"I suppose it was foolish of me to lie to the police." She tossed the bite of roll aside. "He didn't believe me. It's ironic, isn't it? Once I told the truth, once I lied. Neither worked."

"You were trying to protect me." It was time to say it, Kelsey told herself, and she hoped the full meaning would be understood. "You tried to protect me before, when I was a child. You were wrong both times. And you were right both times."

"No easy answers."

"It's taken me a long time to realize there isn't always only one." She pressed her lips together before continuing. "I'm grateful for what you're doing for Milicent. No, please don't stiffen up on me. I'm grateful, even though I can't resolve it in my heart, even though it's a lie. I'm grateful."

"What difference would it make now, Kelsey? To have the whole story come out and destroy what's left of her life?" The birds were singing, and the sound was comforting. "It wouldn't give me back those years. It wouldn't change what happened to Mick, to Pride, to Reno."

"She's responsible for that, for all of it." Shame and bitterness warred inside Kelsey. "No matter that she couldn't have meant anyone to die, she's responsible. Hiring other people to do what she considered necessary to protect the family name? What name does she have now?" Kelsey demanded. "What honor?"

"And that's what she has to live with. I don't do this for her."

"I know."

Naomi lifted a brow. "It's not entirely unselfish, either. I don't want to go through it, to live through the press, the police. And I have the gift of knowing you believed me. You believed in me enough to stick."

"I wasn't the only one who believed you. And everyone would know what happened with Alec Bradley, what happened with Pride and all the rest if the story came out."

"I don't care about everyone." Naomi decided she'd pour coffee after all. "I talked it over with Moses last night, and we're agreed." She smiled, adding cream to her coffee. "When a woman has a man who'll stand by her through the worst, the rest is easy."

Naomi glanced over at the sound of a car pulling into the drive. "That's probably Gabe."

"It better be. We were supposed to go over these menus for the reception over breakfast."

"Then I'd better leave you two alone to do it."

"No, why don't you stay? That way you can agree with what I've already decided and give me the edge."

Kelsey leaned forward, took her mother's hand. "I love you."

Emotions swirled up, then settled beautifully. "I know."

Kelsey rose and started across the patio to greet him. Her eyes widened as they shifted from Gabe's to her father's, then back again. "Dad?"

"Oh, Kelsey." Instinctively Philip framed her face with his hands. Nothing Gabe had told him had prepared him. "Oh, sweetheart."

"I'm all right, really. It looks much worse than it is. I was going to come see you in a couple of days." When she looked more presentable, she thought, and shot Gabe a telling look.

"Your young man was right to tell me the whole story. The whole story," he repeated, staring into her eyes. "You left out a great many details when you phoned me, Kelsey."

Another kind of lie, she thought. The sin of omission. "I thought it best. I only wanted you to know I was all right before the papers reported it. And I am all right."

"So I'm told." He looked back at Gabe, then his gaze shifted, locked over Kelsey's shoulder. She moved aside and stood between her parents.

"Dad wanted to see that I was all right," she began.

"Of course he did." Naomi nodded, and kept her hands at her sides. "Hello, Philip."

"Naomi. You look well."

"So do you."

"Ah ..." Kelsey groped for some way to ease past the awkwardness. "Channing's down at the barn. Why don't you walk down with me, Dad? You'll get a kick out of seeing him work, and he can show off for you." She looked helplessly at Gabe.

"I'm sure you'd like to talk with Kelsey," Naomi said. "I was just on my way down to the barn myself. I'll tell Channing you're here."

"No, I—" Philip began, then composed himself. "Actually, I'd like to speak with you. If you have the time."

"All right."

"Let's take a walk," Gabe murmured, and grasped Kelsey's hand.

"I don't know where to begin, Naomi. Gabe told me everything. Everything," Philip repeated, heartsick. "He was kind enough to wait for me when I went to see her. I had to see her," he added, "before I came here."

"I understand."

"Understand?" Unbearably weary, he slipped his fingers under his glasses and pressed them to his eyes. "I can't. I can't understand. All that she did, all the pain she caused. And when I confronted her, she was unbending. Unshakable," he said, and dropped his hands. "She sees nothing that she did as anything but necessary. Men died, but she feels no responsibility. Not to them, not to you."

"And that surprises you?"

He winced. "She remains my mother, Naomi. Even knowing all I know. I've thought of hundreds of ways to try to apologize, and none of them begins to cover it. What she did. What I did." He took off his glasses, rubbed his eyes again, then replaced them. "And the simple fact is, I don't know what to say to you."

"It's over, Philip."

"I let you down. All those years ago, I let you down."

"No. There was a time I thought that. It helped, but it wasn't really true. I wasn't what you wanted me to be. Whatever she's done, Milicent wasn't responsible for that. Only for making sure you realized it."

"She could have prevented you from going to prison."

"Yes."

"And what she did now, to you—to Kelsey." His breath caught as the image of his daughter's bruised face swam into his mind. "My God, Naomi. She might have been killed."

"She protected herself. And me." She studied him, the pain in his eyes, the baffled disbelief behind it. "I can't tell you not to feel what you're feeling now. Kelsey was hurt, was forced to defend herself by taking a life. And you and I will never forget it. We'll never forget who started the chain of events. Maybe," she said slowly, "that's enough punishment for Milicent."

"There's nothing I can do"—Philip's voice faltered, broke—"nothing I can do to make up for it."

"There's nothing you have to do. Despite everything, Kelsey has what she wants. And so do I." Her lips curved softly. "I have everything I want. The farm, a man who loves me. My daughter. You did a wonderful job with her, Philip. I always knew you would."

"She's so like you." He studied the woman who had been his wife. So much had changed, and so little. "Good God, Naomi, if I could go back, do something. Anything."

"You can't." He'd always been so fair, she thought. So honorable. Now he suffered because no amount of fairness, no amount of honor could wipe away the pain. "We wanted things from each other that neither of us could give. And we made mistakes, mistakes we used against each other, and that other people used against us. We were both victims of someone else's needs, Philip."

"You paid dearly for it."

"I've gained, too. She loves me. It's just that simple. Just that marvelous. So let's leave the rest where it belongs. Closed." She drew a breath. "You know, I always wondered how I'd feel if I saw you again."

"I wondered, too. How do you feel, Naomi?"

"I'm glad to see you, Philip."


"Do you think we should leave them alone for so long?"

"Yes, I do." To prove it, Gabe gave her a helpful nudge. "They have old business to settle."

"But—" Kelsey looked back over her shoulder. They were still standing, yards apart. "He looked so sad."

"His world's been shaken, badly. It'll settle again. Maybe not quite in the same way, but it'll settle."

"Candace won't let him brood for long." Still, she dragged her feet. "Gabe, what made you bring him here?"

"We're closing the circle," he said, "before we start our own."

"I like the sound of that." She tipped her head toward his shoulder. "You're awfully smart, Slater. And sneaky, too, going behind my back to bring him here."

"Going to see him was my idea. Coming here was his. He needs to make his peace with Naomi."

"He will." She smiled to herself. It was, after all, her personal fairy tale. "I love it here," she murmured. "I love everything about here. Think of the champions we'll make, Gabe."

"Are we talking horses?"

She shook her head and laughed up at him. "Not only horses. Is that okay with you?"

"That's just fine with me."

He walked with her away from the barn, from the crews, toward the rising hills where mares grazed with their foals, and horses raced their shadows.

"Next spring, a foal will be born. His dam from Three Willows, his sire from Longshot." He turned her into his arms. "I'll remember the day he was conceived, how I looked at you and wanted you to belong to me."

"And I do." She linked her arms around his neck. "So, what's next?"

"We've got a fresh deck." He tapped his pocket. "Anything can happen."

"Anything? Well . . ." She drew his mouth down to hers. "Deal them."

piatkus

If you have enjoyed this book you can find out
more about Nora Roberts and her J.D. Robb books
on her websites

**www.nora-roberts.co.uk**
**www.jd-robb.co.uk**

To buy any Nora Roberts and J.D. Robb books
and to find out more about all other Little, Brown
Book Group titles, visit our website

**www.littlebrown.co.uk**

To order any Piatkus titles p & p free in the UK, please
contact our mail order supplier on:

**+ 44 (0)1832 737525**

Customers not based in the UK should contact
the same number for appropriate postage
and packing costs.